PRAISE FOR *HIRED MAN*

"The narrative has a distinct sense of menace, courtesy of the bad guys that crop up, as well as occasional moments of humor. A rock-solid premise produces an enthralling plot and characters."

—*Kirkus Reviews*

"The dialogue of Beyer's low life characters crackles with the same kind of poetic realism that Elmore Leonard is famous for. Once you get on this literary rollercoaster, hang on as the twists and turns come quickly and keep you guessing. Highly recommended."

—Dennis D. Wilson, author of *The Grand*

"A page turner. You will not be able to put this book down. [Hired Man] makes you think 'what would I do?' Beyer can tell a story, and he does it with perfect description of scene and character."

—Joe Calderwood, author of *Stained Fortune*

HIRED MAN

MARK BEYER

CEDAR
FORGE

Cedar Forge Press
7300 West Joy Road
Dexter, Michigan 48130

Published 2018 by Cedar Forge Press
Printed in the United States of America

Cover images by Elti Meshau, Doug Zuba
Cover design by Matt Schubbe

ISBN: 978-1-943290-34-5 (Paperback)
ISBN: 978-1-943290-35-2 (eBook)

Library of Congress Control Number: 2017953198

All of the characters, institutions, events and locations in this story are entirely the work of the author's imagination or, in the case of actual locations, are used fictionally.

1

Bobby Darin sang of true love somewhere beyond the sea as Terry Holbrook watched the car ahead of him leave the road. The road curved, but the car ahead didn't. It was night. Black ice. The music vanished from his ears with a *thup* as Terry saw twin red taillights go airborne, askew. They launched upward, rocketing off the inclined pavement and over the icy shoulder toward a knot of old apple trees. For a moment, the flying car stopped time.

Bobby's voice came bopping back and trumpets screamed as Terry watched the soaring car tilt clockwise an instant before it crashed. Even over the big band's blaring crescendo, he heard the shatter of glass and the gut-wrenching buckle of sheet metal.

Then his own car began to skid. It was the dip and rise before the curve left, just south of the railroad tracks. His rear tires lost grip, swinging out from under him. Terry instinctively stomped on the brakes before he remembered not to. Pulled his foot off the pedal too late. A ton and a half of Sebring spun out of control. The headlights swung madly left, the road disappearing, and Terry saw only bare, roadside branches reaching for his eyes, a blurry winter treescape ribboning past.

A violent bump smacked Terry's skull against the interior roof and sent his stomach to the floor as the Sebring slid jaggedly off the road. Tires scraped sideways across crusted ice. The car lurched to a rough stop against a snowplowed ridge, the passenger side rocking up high, and back to earth hard.

Then nothing. Only silent, shocked mental vibrations.

Terry didn't move. Muscles and brain on lockdown. Bobby crooned on from the playlist, sounding as sweet as a summer Sunday.

The vehicle had spun twice and a half and was now aimed in the direction from which it had come. It sat on the outside edge of the road's shoulder. By the orchard. Near the wreck.

Terry's heart was pounding. The dashboard clock said 10:37. A moonless Tuesday in February. He'd worked late. He remembered to breathe.

Both feet were suspended off the pedals. He lowered them gently. Fumbled the music off. The Sebring's headlights aimed back at the empty road. Its taillights washed the snow behind him in red. Far to his left, he saw the glowing taillights of the wreck tangled in dark trees. He turned off his headlights. Turned on his emergency lights. Shut off the engine.

The other car, jammed deep in the trees, was cockeyed. One taillight way higher on the left. One headlight dead. The remaining yellow beam choked by brambles, its stunted forward glow silhouetting a black hulk of crumpled automobile. The back of the wreck was thirty feet off the road, the big car swallowed by wild, overgrown trees. The vehicle had taken out a length of old barbed-wire fence and two wooden fence posts as it crashed, dragging the tangle of wood and rusty wire with it.

When Terry got out, his smooth-soled docksiders slid instantly in the snow, lacking any traction. Gaining his footing, he tried to listen. There was no wind at all. Cemetery quiet. All he heard was the ticking of the Sebring's emergency lights. He slipped wildly on his first step and grabbed the open Sebring door to keep from falling. Normally, home to work and back was snow-free treading. This wasn't normal.

The wreck was silent. It looked to Terry like a Chrysler 300 or maybe a Lincoln. Black or midnight blue. Terry zipped up his big leather coat. He didn't have gloves. His heaving, fast, shocked breaths puffed and vanished in the night air. No other traffic. No moon. No stars. No light anywhere except the Sebring's blinkers and the crippled glow from the wreck.

He fell twice scrambling toward it. Coarse pebbles of crusted snow slid freezing up his sleeves. As he pushed past the ravaged fence posts, claws of barbed wire tore his jeans, bit into his ankles, and snagged his coat. He grunted forward, scrabbling hand and foot.

It was a Lincoln MK-something. All four tires off the ground. The car held aloft by gnarled stumps, the choking tangle of a long-abandoned orchard. Whitish, wet wood freshly splintered. The whole front end of the car caved in.

Up close, Terry saw the Lincoln was a newer model. And clean. In Michigan, it takes a lot of work to keep a car clean in February.

Terry pulled out his phone. Dropped it in the snow. Swore. Found it. Called 911 with cold, wet hands.

"911." A woman.

"Hi, I want to report a car accident."

"Are you injured?"

"No, I wasn't driving. I mean it's not my car. I'm a … I was following. In another car. This one went off the road."

"What's your location?"

"Um. I'm on North Territorial just south of the railroad tracks. West of Ann Arbor. Almost to Dexter. Like two miles from Dexter." Terry lived in Dexter.

"And you're not injured?"

"No. But I saw it. It's really bad." From the Lincoln came a moan. Dry like torn cardboard. "I gotta go," said Terry into the phone. "Hurry! My car's got its blinkers on." Terry ended the call and waded through knee-high snow toward the driver's side. The car's door had ruptured outward from the nose-first impact, its glossy dark paint split like a burst blister.

The whole front end was test-dummy-crushed. Crimson taillights bled an eerie glow onto spidery branches that clawed the trunk like witches' fingers. The solitary headlight flickered once and then winked out. Darkness amplified the quiet. The only sound was the distant *tick tick tick* of the Sebring's blinking lights.

Then a cough. Wet. Muffled by glass.

Terry pushed through the snow, the last few steps to the driver's door. The windshield was shattered. Tree limbs pressed through the gaping hole. Terry, a big man, grabbed the door handle to pull himself closer. He smelled gasoline.

The driver's side window was tinted. The hole where the windshield had been now rimmed with broken glass. Terry ground his docksiders into the snow and yanked at the door. It didn't budge.

He tried again. Wedged his fingers under the handle and pulled with all his strength. The buckled door screeched open and the stump supporting the driver's side collapsed. The Lincoln lurched toward Terry and down a foot. Terry fell backward, his head crunching in the snow. Something sharp dug into his back. A rock or stump. Ignoring the pain, he scrambled to his feet and looked in the open door. The dome light had lit.

An airbag had deployed, then deflated. It now lay collapsed under the murky dome light. Red everywhere. Wet. Shiny. Dripping. The gray airbag shrouded most of the motionless driver. A man in a bloody suit. Alone. A mangled branch filled the passenger side. The dome light began to sputter and dim.

Terry clawed the bag off the man. Nuggets of shattered windshield bounced off his knuckles. He tried to pull the airbag out, but it snagged on something. So instead he shoved it up and through the empty windshield frame. Broken glass cut his palm. He ignored it when he saw the driver's face. An older man. Eyes closed. Maybe dead. The skin on his face looked as gray and lifeless as the spent airbag. Not much blood on his cheeks or in his silvery, disheveled hair, but his shirt, tie, and suit coat were soaked. His nose bloody and bleeding from a deep gash. Blood ran down over his pale lips. The man didn't move.

"Sir? Sir?! Are you alright?" Terry winced at the ludicrous sound of his question.

Nothing. No sound. No movement.

Then the driver's head lolled. Ever so slightly. A faint, visible breath in the cold night air. A puff of life, still hanging on.

"Sir?" Terry put a hand on the man's shoulder. The rich, dark overcoat was soaking wet and cold. It chilled Terry's skin beyond temperature alone. He shook the man's shoulder gently. Then firmly. The dome light pulsed in an uneasy flicker.

"Sir? Please wake up! You're going to be okay. You're alive.

You're..." The driver's head turned, or more accurately, released. It swung toward Terry. With effort, pale blue eyes dimly opened. A sliver of life. Glassy slits beneath coarse, steel-wool brows.

"You're big," said the driver through bloody lips.

Terry was six-two, 230 pounds with longish hair and a salt-and-pepper goatee. As a video editor, he worked from a chair all day. And liked snacks.

"Sir, you're going to be all right. I called 911."

"What's your name?" The words rough and raspy. Terry watched in horror as a rubbery bubble of blood swelled balloon-like from the driver's left nostril, burst, and dribbled down over the injured man's lips. Terry tried not to look at all the blood. It was everywhere. Instead, he thought of TV shows where they tried to keep the victim talking.

"Sir, my name is Terry Holbrook. I live around here." Another wince. *What difference does that make?* "Sir, are you...do you feel...?"

"I'm dying," the man interrupted. "I'm dying now."

"No, sir, you're not! You're not dying! 911 is coming!"

"No, son." The driver's head swung down. His gaze fogged. His eyes settled. Then Terry saw it.

The red splatters weren't all blood. Terry suddenly smelled it. Not just the gasoline. Something sweeter. Tannic. Red wine. It made him think of The Olive Garden. In the flicker of the dome light, he saw the smooth, wide shaft of dark glass. A wine bottle. Half of one anyway. Its base cracked off clean. Its fat, jagged maw pointing at the steering wheel. The rest of the bottle buried in the driver's chest, neck first. Driven in six or seven inches. Half the label inside him. The man's necktie pushed in with it. It took Terry a few moments to figure it out.

The airbag.

A gurgle snapped Terry's eyes to the man's face. Not a gurgle. A chuckle. A fluttery smile trembled across the older man's cracked lips. "Don't get the wrong idea." The driver snorted blood out his nose, red mucus splattering the glass shaft of the wine bottle. "It wasn't open. I wasn't..." He swallowed with difficulty. "...I wasn't drinking. I just..." He mimed holding the bottle in his right hand. Terry saw a gleam of cufflink. "I just didn't want it to break. In the crash." He coughed another gout of blood. "And the airbag." He breathed with difficulty. "The angle." He stopped talking. Stopped moving.

Terry had to focus to keep from freaking out. The bottle was freaky. *Keep talking. Keep the guy talking.* "Sir, 911 is going to be here any minute." Terry's phone buzzed in his coat pocket. He ignored it. "Sir? Sir, open your eyes! Stay awake! Try to stay awake."

"What's your name?" the driver asked again, stirring.

"Terry, sir. Terry Holbrook."

"Terry," the man murmured. The man's blue eyes were open now, furrowed in folds of septuagenarian skin. And aimed at Terry. "Are you a Christian?" The eyes calm, but glassy with black, dilated pupils. The old man waited, breath coming slow. Terry had no quick answer. He thought instantly, absurdly, of Christmas cookies.

"Yeah. Sure. I'm a...Presbyterian." His wife's church.

"Will you pray for me?" said the man. "Will you pray for me, Terry? Because..." The man abruptly coughed up a steaming stew of blood that Terry swore had chunks in it. "Because this isn't working out." Terry felt a sudden painful cold in his feet. Freezing in loafers in two feet of snow.

Then the man stopped breathing.

Terry thought fast. He was not a pray-er. Got images of droning ministers and robed choirs. Dry voices. Organ music. High ceilings. Thin communion wafers that tasted like nothing. "Sure, sure, mister. But 911 is coming, so let's..."

The punctured chest moved again. "Terry." The driver eyed him, wrinkled lids heavy with fatigue. "Now, please."

Terry nodded.

"Okay, but 911 is coming." Terry paused. He knew very little about praying. Or dying. "So, uh, what's your name? Sir? What's your name?"

The man looked asleep. But a breath came. The wine bottle rising and falling in his chest, its dark glass glinting in the faint dome light. "I'm Michael DeGraaf. Michael Robert DeGraaf." A fleeting smile below the lacerated nose. "Mike," he said, "To my friends."

"Okay, Mr. DeGraaf..."

"Pray for me now, Terry. Please. Please tell God I'm coming. Tell Jesus. Tell them...I'm coming."

"No, you're not. 911..." Terry looked back at the road. No vehicles had driven by. It was a lonely stretch of road by day. Even more so by night.

"Please, Terry." The man's eyes remained shut as he raised his left hand. Weakly groping. An invitation. Uneasily, Terry grasped the man's hand. It was cold and sticky.

"Okay," said Terry.

"So I can hear you, please."

Terry had not prayed since Christmas Eve in church. Even then he just said what everybody else said. Reciting what was printed on the handout.

"Our Father," he began, "Who art in Heaven. Hallowed be Thy name. Thy Kingdom come..."

"No, no!" Michael DeGraaf interrupted, pulling his hand from Terry's grip. "Not so general. Be specific. Terry, you have to pray for *me* now. Please. Please, tell my Father . . . " He pulled in a hard, shuddering breath. Turned damp, drifting eyes toward Terry.

" . . . that I can't wait to see Him."

DeGraaf sunk in the leather seat. Shrunk in his expensive clothes.

"Okay, Mr. DeGraaf."

"Mike," the driver rasped. The dome light began to flicker. More off than on.

"Okay, Mike," said Terry. The man's sticky, bloody hand had fallen to his lap. Terry looked at it, reached for it, raised it, and held it. Behind them, a small pickup truck rattled past without stopping. Its tires *zzzz*-ing on the ice.

"God," Terry began, watching his wispy breath fade in the night air. His voice sounding so meager it embarrassed him. "God, Mr. DeGraaf . . . Mike . . . is badly hurt, badly injured. But he's going to be *okay*. Right, Mike? Right?" Terry gently squeezed the cold, sticky hand. "You're going to be okay. Look at me. Mike! Open your eyes. Mike? Mike, look at me. Open your eyes!" DeGraaf managed a nod but did not open his eyes.

Terry held Mike's hand with both of his and closed his own eyes. "So. God. He needs Your help. Mike needs Your help to stay alive. Please. Please help him. Please help him right now, God. Right this second." He tried to feel it.

"Get me to heaven, Terry," said DeGraaf.

"Okay," said Terry, looking at the injured man. "So, God," he continued, "When it's time—" The man's hand was ice. "—and this is *not* the time, not right now . . . but when it *is* time . . . God, please accept Michael. Your, uh, Your child. Your, uh . . . "

"Servant," said DeGraaf.

"Your servant, right," said Terry, "To heaven. To Your, uh, Kingdom. With Jesus and…everybody else. Jesus and the angels. And Mary. And all the, uh, heavenly hosts up there." Terry stopped. He didn't know what else to say. He didn't know how to do this.

The clicking of the Sebring's emergency lights suddenly seemed very far away. An oozy drip fell from the jagged edge of the wine bottle protruding from DeGraaf's chest.. *Tick…tick…tick* went the distant blinking lights.

"Amen," said DeGraaf suddenly, after an exceedingly long pause.

"Amen!" blurted Terry, startled.

Then quiet again. Stillness.

The dome light in the Lincoln abruptly ceased its uneven flickering. For a few seconds, it flared into stark, white brightness with a pungent electrical smell, and for a moment, everything looked different. Terry fully saw the horrendous wound. Raw, torn flesh and splintered yellow bone awash in streaming blood. He felt suddenly faint, his knees briefly giving out. Then the brightness faded back to a dim, soft glow. But even the dimness looked different now. It felt different. Something had flip-flopped. Something had changed.

So this is how life ends, thought Terry, looking at the motionless body.

This is how *we* end.

Then DeGraaf's hand tugged itself free. Forcefully. Strangely.

"I need you to do something for me."

The man Terry thought was dead suddenly wasn't. DeGraaf shifted position. Sat up straight. The wine bottle in his chest bobbed like a harpoon in a disinterested whale. "Terry? Terry, was it?"

DeGraaf locked his suddenly piercing blue eyes onto Terry's. The injured man's voice now bold and commanding. More like a CEO than a bled-out, frail old man.

"Yes, sir." Terry stood straighter. DeGraaf's voice carried authority.

With his right hand, DeGraaf reached over the top of the protruding wine bottle to his left breast pocket and withdrew a slender pen and leather-bound checkbook. The gold pen gleamed in the faint dome light. He flipped open the checkbook with one bloody thumb and rotated the sleek barrel of the pen with the other.

"Holbrook? H-O-L-B-R-double O-K?" DeGraaf touched the tip of the ballpoint to his tongue and held Terry's eyes, awaiting confirmation.

"Yes," was all Terry could manage.

"Good," said DeGraaf. Silently, he began writing. Terry glanced back at the empty road.

Hurry, dammit, he told 911.

After a few seconds, DeGraaf said, "Okay." He cleared his throat, coughed a ragged clot of blood onto himself and then opened his eyes wide, blinking several times. He turned to face Terry, who now saw blood swimming in the whites of the old man's eyes. "Will you do something for me, Terry?" said the grisly visage, employing the brisk, paternal cadence of a C-suite executive. No nonsense. Accustomed to giving orders.

"Yes, sir. Whatever you want," said Terry, nodding like a bobble-head, shocked at DeGraaf's sudden recovery. "And 911's almost here, so sure, whatever you want. Just . . . you know. Whatever you want."

"I didn't get it done."

"Sure, but..."

"My fault," DeGraaf interrupted. An exasperated head shake. "I failed." He spat out a gout of reddish slime. "Now...this." Blood drooled thickly from his mouth.

"Okay, but..." Terry began.

"I need you to save my daughter."

Terry didn't know what that meant. But he also didn't care, because now it seemed like the guy was going to make it. The spark of life was back. Terry just had to keep it flickering.

"Okay, sure," said Terry, making a big show with his hands, spreading them wide. "No problem. You got it."

"It's going to be expensive. I'm writing you a check."

"Thanks, Mr. DeGraaf, but..."

"Call me Mike."

"Sure, Mike. But 911's going to be here any second, I swear, and..."

"A million ought to do it," said DeGraaf, writing, then shook his head in disgust, slinging shiny blood from his nose and chin. "It's a mess. A million five." The catastrophically injured man wrote in his checkbook as calmly as if he were buying a pair of shoes. It occurred to Terry that Mike DeGraaf should already be dead. A wine bottle impaled his heart.

A perforated paper rip. "Here."

The eyes of the two men met. Terry's astonished brown ones held by DeGraaf's icy blue ones. The pale, yellow check extended out the open door, clipped by bloody fingers.

DeGraaf jiggled the check up and down, the yellow paper moving in the dark, cold, winter air. "Take it," he said. His blood-and-snot grimed mouth was set and grim.

"Come on now," said DeGraaf, impatiently.

Just then Terry heard a haunting amplified *galoop* pierce the night, followed by the chattering staccato of an approaching electric siren. He turned and saw EMS coming over the icy hill as fast as conditions would allow. It was followed moments later by a lit-up police cruiser.

DeGraaf's eyes, strangely lifeless, did not waver from Terry's. "Hurry," he said. He jiggled the check again.

Terry pulled the check from the man's fingers. He tried to read it, but couldn't in the abandoned orchard's winter gloom. He heard the rescue vehicles brake on the icy shoulder, skidding to a stop. Car doors thrown open. Urgent voices. Terry shifted position, trying to read. He heard running feet. The crunch of boots on hard snow.

An amount inked in. Made out to Terry Holbrook. Dated today. Signed.

Terry looked at Michael DeGraaf. Mike to his friends. The old man's blue eyes drifting. Dulling. Sinking softly away, like sapphires in quiet water.

"Two million?" asked Terry.

"Taxes," rasped DeGraaf, barely above a whisper.

Then every muscle in the driver's body released at once. Every cell let go its light. Every memory swallowed by darkness. The head fell forward. The mouth closed. The eyes didn't. And 911 arrived.

2

"I called you in sick and took a personal day for me."

Christina didn't take her eyes off him. She wasn't wearing her usual purple or blue dental hygienist scrubs. Instead, she was in faded jeans, fuzzy slippers, and a forest green Eastern Michigan University hoodie. Her small, pale hands cupped a steaming mug of coffee. She watched him from the breakfast bar that separated their small kitchen from their small living room, sitting straight-backed in one of the honey pine swivel stools they'd found together at an estate sale. The mug was her favorite. It had a cardinal on it. From the set Hannah had given them for their anniversary, featuring Michigan songbirds. She'd poured a mug for Terry, too, when she heard him coming. The cedar waxwing with a splash of milk.

He approached slowly from the bedroom. Coming out of a fog. Sweats. Socks. Stubble. He rubbed his eyes and a cold morning shiver jittered through him. "Hannah get to school okay?" Murky words in the dark, narrow hallway.

"She took the bus," said Christina, watching her bearlike husband's slow advance. Hannah usually didn't take the bus to school.

Christina usually dropped her off on her way to work. The bus stop was a bit of a hike and it was the coldest month of the year.

"Did you really say I was sick?" Terry asked, drawn to the coffee.

Christina dropped her eyes solemnly. Too solemnly, it seemed to Terry. Always more solemn than he wished.

"No. I just said you were out all night with the accident and the police and everything." The plastic wall clock showed almost ten.

"You talk to Jeff?"

"No, Belinda. She'll tell Jeff."

"You tell her what happened?" The crash. The dead man.

"Yes." She looked up at Terry, her eyes sweet and sad. "She said to give you a hug."

"So give me a hug."

Christina slipped off the stool, padded over to him, and wrapped her small arms around as much of him as she could. She laid her soft cheek and mop of fine, cinnamon hair gently against his broad chest. He held her close and long. On her tiptoes they kissed. Then sat for coffee.

He sipped. Coffee was a miracle. "Thanks for taking the day off."

She looked up at him, resting her hand on top of his. "No problem," she said. He turned his hand palm up to gently enfold her fingers.

Christina could still pass for a coed in her loveworn EMU hoodie. She mustered a half smile for her weary husband, and when she did, her freckles danced for a moment. She had the softest hair he'd ever touched. A pixie's charm and fairy's grace. But this morning her eyes were tense and worried. The smile all too brief.

"I'm okay, sweetie." Terry thumped his chest twice with both hands. Flexed both arms. "In one piece." She sipped coffee, watching him.

"Seriously, I'm okay," said Terry, "Long night, but...you know." After a swallow of coffee, he set his mug down and slid his hand back to hers with a Formican squeak. Squeezed her fingers gently until he squeezed another smile out of her. A small one, but at least her eyes joined in this time.

"Thanks for calling the office."

"You're welcome," said Christina. She exhaled deeply, and most of the tension left the room. "I just thank God it wasn't you."

"Me, too," said Terry. "Did you tell Hannah?" Hannah was ten.

"I told her that her daddy helped a man in a car crash. She didn't hear the phone last night. Or hear you come in."

"When did I go to bed?"

"Two. A little after."

Terry nodded. He hoisted the cedar waxwing for another sip but stopped when he saw his wife's anxious eyes.

"Did you tell her...?"

"That the man died? No."

"Good." He drank coffee. "No need to." He looked out the window that hung over the kitchen sink. Low clouds over a scattering of subdivision rooftops. Another gray day.

"I'm going to take a shower," said Terry, rising.

"Don't forget your Metamucil."

"I'm going to have my Metamucil and take a shower."

"Then you'll tell me the whole story?" When she blinked, her long, delicate lashes softened a pensive face. She swept a gingery strand off her cheek.

"Yep," said Terry, sliding off the creaking stool and heading around the breakfast bar for the Metamucil. She watched him intently. The cardinal on her mug wore a similar expression.

"You want breakfast? Eggs? Toast? We have bacon."

He stopped in his tracks at the mention of bacon. Considering.

"Naw," he said. "Thanks." Bacon sounded great. "Not in the mood."

The hot water pelted down on him, rushing in his ears. Euphoric and normalizing. Coffee, Christina, and hot water. The urgent-voiced medics and officers and fluorescent lights and police station questions began to sluice away in the clouds of steam. Memory began to sort itself. DeGraaf dying and now dead. Blue eyes open and exposed yellow bone. The wine bottle. Jagged broken glass. The clumsy prayer. A snot bubble of blood.

I need you to save my daughter.

Water rushed hot at him. He put his face into it, feeling the sweet, deafening heat.

The check.

He'd told no one about that.

Inside forty minutes they were at Dolly's for an early lunch. Dolly's was Dexter's tried-and-true, no-frills diner, a 1920's storefront in the center of town, quaint and small and lovingly worn at the edges. Standard equipment in a tiny, old Michigan farm town like Dexter.

Dexter still had farms but was now primarily a bedroom community for families whose breadwinners worked in Ann Arbor or Ypsilanti. Downtown Dexter squired a modest sprawl of newer, less interesting establishments than Dolly's. A Dairy Queen. NAPA auto parts. A modest used car lot. And out by the interstate, the town's newest addition, an Applebee's.

Bonnie the blond waitress set their plates down at quarter to noon, her wrinkled face smiling. The lavender sweatshirt she wore had a photo of a cat on it. Terry had a club sandwich with fries. Christina, a tuna wrap. Coke for him. Water for her. Other customers, a few retirees and farmers and farmer's wives, began to trickle in.

After Bonnie left, Terry picked up and ate a crinkle-cut fry. Added salt. Put a blob of ketchup on the edge of his plate. He looked across the table at the best thing that ever happened to him. The beautiful girlfriend who actually married him. If she was wearing makeup, he didn't see it. He bit the corner of the sandwich where the most bacon stuck out.

"You look great," he said, chewing.

"You look better," she said. "Like you feel better, I mean." She managed a smile.

Last night he'd said little. Just wanted to sleep.

He started at the beginning.

How he'd had to work late, which she already knew. He'd called her earlier like always. It didn't happen often at Image Zoo, the small video production company where Terry worked, but it happened often enough. Terry was in TV-spot hell with Thurgood, their biggest client. One name, four dealerships: Thurgood Chevrolet, Thurgood Honda, Thurgood GMC, Thurgood Subaru. Lots of different prices and models in two dozen versions of four different 30-second TV spots. All that plus the Jameson Controls video. Loads of headaches but lots of revenue. Terry's editing skills with the Avid Media Composer were valued by Image Zoo and its clients. He liked his job and he liked to work. He kept his occasionally simmering temper professionally in check, which wasn't always easy in the work world, but he did it. The work didn't pay great, but it paid okay. Jeff, his boss for eight years and friend for twenty, was a good guy. Terry never let Jeff down. With Christina's salary, they managed okay.

Last night, he'd left work at quarter past ten, tired but alert enough for the twenty-five-minute drive home. Downtown Ann Arbor to Dexter was no sweat. He'd done it a million times. He knew where the bad spots were in winter. That curve before the railroad tracks was the worst.

Between bites and Coca-Cola, he told Christina what he told the police. How he'd seen the car ahead snake through the blackness, taillights swaying through the gentler curves. On country roads at night, it was helpful to have a car ahead of you. You saw what was coming in the other car's headlights. The driver ahead seemed under control. No sign of drunk driving.

"But going too fast," said Christina.

Terry nodded, chewing. "Didn't seem to be, but yeah." He didn't tell her about his own heart-stopping, car-spinning-out-of-control moment. It would just worry her.

He told her how the other car flew off the road while Bobby Darin sang *Somewhere Across the Sea*. How it tilted in the air before crashing into the apple orchard. How he pulled off the road (as he told it) and turned on his emergency blinkers and called 911. He told her about the barbed wire snagging his coat and scratching his ankle.

"Have you had a tetanus shot?" she asked quickly. "Let me look at it." She was squatting by his ankle in seconds, examining.

"I think so," said Terry. He had no idea.

"It's not bad. I'll call Kim," she said, retaking her seat. Kim was the receptionist at their doctor's office. As a health care professional mothering a fearless 10-year-old, Christina was on first-name basis with the entire staff there. "She'll know. She can look it up."

"Thanks."

He told her it was a Lincoln MKS. All smashed up. Windshield shattered.

How hard it was to open the door, and what he saw when he opened it.

The blood. He told her about the wine bottle stuck in DeGraaf's chest. Christina's eyes widened, her small mouth agog in horror. Terry pressed the capped neck of the ketchup bottle against his own chest to illustrate.

"The airbag did it," said Terry. He thumped the ketchup bottle cap against his heart. "Whammo. A freak accident."

"He shouldn't have tried to save the wine," said Christina.

"No," said Terry, "He should not have." He returned the bottle to the table and ate more sandwich and more fries. Sipped more Coke. "I can't believe he was alive."

"He was *alive?*"

Terry nodded, swallowing.

He told her about DeGraaf asking for a prayer. A believer, Christina listened intently. He told her how he started saying The Lord's Prayer and how DeGraff stopped him. Asked him to pray for DeGraaf to go to heaven.

"He said, 'Be specific,'" said Terry and ate a fry.

"So what did you do?"

Terry shrugged. "I tried to be specific. I asked God to welcome him. I told Him he was coming." He didn't mention the handholding.

"And then he died?"

She waited for his answer.

That was when he thought he was going to tell her about the check.

But something inside him stopped him. Something dark, deep in his gut. Inky black. Like a feeling but more like an urging. Like a voice but not a voice. A twisting, roiling thing darker than blackness. A lying thing.

It hadn't bothered him in years. He thought he'd outgrown it.

He usually told his wife everything. Or almost everything.

But this was different.

This was so much money.

Two million dollars.

He had to think it through.

The dark roil inside him shrieked with needling glee.

He knew he should tell her. He loved his wife.

But two million dollars. It was too bizarre.

It would upset her. Spoil this nice lunch..

He made a decision.

He'd tell her later.

"Then he died," said Terry, without missing a beat. He hoisted a thick wedge of sandwich to his mouth and bit into it, pushing the searing flare of shame from his mind. Then took a long sip of Coke from the red pebbled plastic glass. When he glanced from his food back to his wife, she was looking at him. Motionless as a painting. Unreadable. Neither spoke.

"That was it?" she finally asked.

Terry nodded, trying to look somber.

I need you to save my daughter.

"Yep, that was it." And one lie became two.

He felt something twist darkly inside him. A foul, grinning infestation.

Terry looked at his food, but nothing appealed to him. He wiped ketchup off his fingers.

"Then the police came. And EMS. At the same exact time. They got there like ten seconds after he died."

"How did you know he was dead?"

Terry glanced up. "His eyes. They stayed open." With one hand, he indicated his eyes, while with the other he dipped a sandwich corner in ketchup. He took a bite. "He didn't blink," he said, chewing. He tried to enjoy his sandwich, but the toast had cooled and the turkey, he noticed, was a bit slimy.

After a moment, she took a small bite of her tuna wrap. Chewed quickly, sipped water, swallowed. "He didn't say anything else?"

"Nope. He was…you know. That was it."

"I mean before."

Terry ate a fry, eyes on his food.

Thinking about the enormous check. Made out to him.

"Well," he said, "He rambled a little bit, earlier on. He was hurt so bad, you know."

He'd tell her about the check tonight. He just had to think it through.

"What did he say?"

"Well, he, uh," Terry smiled briefly at Christina. "He called me big. He said, 'Hey, you're big.'"

"Well, you are." She grinned.

"Yeah," said Terry. He took a deep breath. "Then we got into the prayer thing, you know."

"Well," said Christina after a moment, her eyes shining and moist. "I think it's great that you prayed for him." Terry nodded meaningfully. Did his best Gentle Giant. Christina was the churchgoer in the family. Terry watched the tiny gold cross she wore around her neck dangle on its slender chain.

"Yeah, it was kinda weird, but..." He sat up straighter. "I did what I could." He took his eyes off the cross.

His wife smiled at him with calm, strong eyes. Her Christian eyes. "I'm sure God heard you."

Terry nodded gratefully. He let her gentle voice wash over him. Her good words.

He chose to let himself feel good about himself. To forgot the roiling blackness. The darkness inside him.

After all, he'd prayed for the man.

He'd done that.

At the register ten minutes later, Terry pulled out his wallet and glanced over his shoulder. Christina was still at their table, putting on her coat. Keeping his wallet close to his chest, he thumbed past a few tattered ones, a twenty, a couple of Post-it notes, a jumble of receipts, and then stopped when he saw the yellow check. It had dried blood on it. He paid with the twenty.

3

Bad Axe sits high in the Michigan Thumb, a farm town just north of the topmost knuckle, dead center in a fertile land mass. It's eighteen miles west of Lake Huron and eighteen miles east of Saginaw Bay. The Thumb is flatland, almost all farms and farmers. In winter, it's a remoteness unto itself. No cities, just small towns. No malls. No stadiums. No reason to be there unless you live there.

The vast majority of the Thumb's overwhelmingly white population are decent, hardworking citizens. Farming is a seven-day work week. Hunting season is whenever there's something within range worth shooting and eating. There are a lot of guns in the Thumb.

The bomb that detonated in front of the Alfred P. Murrah Federal Building in Oklahoma City on April 19, 1995, and murdered 168 people while injuring 683 more was conceived in the Thumb. Timothy McVeigh and Terry Nichols thought up the plan in Nichols' farmhouse in the town of Decker, twenty-four miles south of Bad Axe. McVeigh and Nichols attended anti-government meetings together in the Thumb. Following the bombing, Nichols was sentenced to 161 life terms without parole, as a conspirator. McVeigh was convicted and executed for assembling, delivering and detonating the explosive device that killed so many, including 19 children.

Camo is worn year 'round in the Thumb. Survivalists, Bible misinterpreters, and persistent rumors of a shadowy Michigan Militia coexist with corn fed Rotarians, 4H boosters, and the PTA. Under more than a few homes are bomb shelters.

At 9 p.m., a mud-spattered Dodge Ram passed through Bad Axe, population 3,055, and turned west on County Road 142 toward Elkton, a much smaller town. The day's snowfall had ceased, leaving three fresh inches blanketing thousands of acres of hibernating soybean, corn, and sugar beet fields stretching in all directions. A mile before Elkton, the Ram turned right on an unlit dirt road with no signpost. The tire tracks the Ram made were the only tracks on it.

A half mile in, cultivated fields waned into dark thickets of scrub trees and deep, wild-growth woods. The driver, a compact man, eventually saw an isolated patch of light to the left. He slowed but did not stop. The singlewide sat eighty yards back from the road. The steel gate was open. He didn't cut the lights. They heard him coming, expected him.

He turned in. The two-track drive had been plowed. Dingy vinyl siding on the low-slung trailer was darker than the snow but lighter than the black, bare-limbed trees dense on both sides and behind the residence. In front of the singlewide was a rust-streaked propane tank, rounded on both ends. Next to it, a snow-covered GMC truck with a heavy snow blade was backed in alongside a beat-up Ford F-150. On a detached trailer near the trucks were two snowmobiles under a tarp. Smoke rose from a tin chimney. A lone bulb on a weathered pole cast sour yellow light.

He parked the Ram under the light. The snow was powdery and muffled his footfalls as he walked to the door. Out back a generator ran. He went up metal steps and knocked. No doorbell.

Movement inside without voices. The scuffed, dirty door opened, disclosing a very large man with a Stonewall Jackson beard. Low, shaded table lamps within silhouetted him. "Hey," said the big man. Beyond him cigarettes glowed.

The bearded giant pivoted to one side. Hands the size of baseball mitts.

The smaller man nodded and stepped in. The door was shut behind him.

The newcomer faced three burly men with beards, boots, and grimy ball caps. All wore soiled farmwear dirty from outdoor work. Stonewall's cap had a Ruger logo on it. On one end of a sagging couch sat the oldest man. His cap said DeWalt. At the opposite end, a younger man's cap said Cabela's. Both couch-sitters had cigarettes going and similar postures. Father and son. The older man stood and pulled brown Carharrts up under a solid, overhanging belly.

"Hands up," he said.

The visitor, blond with sharply razored sideburns and a precise Nordic moustache, stretched both arms to either side and spread his legs. "We're still doing this?" he asked.

"You bet your ass," said the older man. Cued by a nod, the sentry with the Stonewall beard patted down the visitor thoroughly. Arms, legs, chest, back, butt crack, groin. Then checked the gloves. No weapons, no wire.

"Boots?" asked the blond visitor.

"Why not?" rasped the older man, drawing a last hit from

his Marlboro. A crinkly smile flickered through nicotine whiskers. A glimpse of yellow teeth.

The visitor took a seat in a cheap dinette chair and removed his boots. Stonewall squatted, checked both boots, then returned them to the visitor.

"You're smart," said the visitor, easily the smallest man present.

"Didn't live this long bein' stupid," said the older man, sitting back on the couch. He lit another cigarette. The cheap plastic lighter had a Confederate flag on it.

"See anybody?" said the thickset son on the couch. Meaning cops. He had a pig nose, small eyes under the grimy cap visor, and a tangle of black beard wrapped around a wet, rubbery, lower lip. A big-framed man with jumpy hands.

"Nope," said the visitor. "Town was empty." In front of the couch was a pine coffee table scorched with cigarette burns and cluttered with overflowing ashtrays, a scatter of gun magazines, two Bud long necks, half a fifth of Maker's Mark, a hefty stainless-steel revolver, and an open laptop.

Beneath an end table glared the red eye of a cable router. The dish was on the roof.

At another nod from the older man, Stonewall returned to his post, taking a seat near the small wood-burning stove they'd rigged by the kitchen.

The older man exhaled a gray plume of tobacco smoke, unblinking.

"You got something for us?"

The visitor grinned, his straw-blond mustache widening. "Maybe I should frisk you?" Father and son cracked similar sneers.

"You could try."

The visitor's grin vanished. "I mean it," he said. "Show me you're not wearing a wire." He shot a glance at the man by the stove. "You, too. All of you show me." He waited.

This was new. The son swore loudly, rose and reached for the big pistol, but the old man stayed him with a hand. Tonight was different. Higher stakes. Eyes on the visitor, the father slowly stood and unbuttoned a shirt button. At his signal, the younger men followed suit, peeling off fleece and pulling off their shirts. They bared their pasty, hairy chests and flabby backs, and the old man did the same.

"Don't sit down," said the visitor. "Step away from the couch." The son's fists clenched, narrowed eyes like hot steel pellets.

"Just shut up and do it, P.J.," said the father. The son didn't speak but nipped the big pistol off the table cobra-quick, baring teeth through the beard. The blond visitor ignored him, stepping quickly to the couch. He pulled out the cushions, checked behind the couch, checked the lamps and shades, then underneath everything, including the end tables and coffee table.

"You think there was anything to find, you'd even be ambulatory at this point?" rasped the rough old farmer, buttoning his shirt. "Or alive?" The younger men followed suit.

Blond John grinned. He knew that's what they called him behind his back. He identified himself only as John. But he had other names. "I haven't stayed alive this long by being stupid, either," said Blond John. Everyone sat back where they'd been. The handgun went back onto the coffee table. Loudly.

"Drink?" said the leader, Bob Peet. He was on more than a few law enforcement watch lists. Locally. In Lansing. In D.C.

"Sure," said John.

"Dougie, get him a glass, wouldja?" Dougie of The-South-Will-Rise-Again beard rose and stepped to the kitchenette, its desiccated green linoleum crackling underfoot. He got a smudgy glass from the sink and gave it to the visitor without a word. The glass had a decal of a hunting dog on it.

"Thanks," said the visitor. Peet Senior unscrewed the Maker's Mark. John stepped close. Peet poured two fingers. He sat back down and raised his own glass. "To victory," he said.

"To victory," the others chimed in. Glasses clinked. The men drank.

Then Bob Peet said, "Well?"

"Where's the money?" said the blond man.

"Where's the data?" said Peet.

The visitor pulled a tiny black thumb drive from his truck key ring. Held it up.

Bob Peet looked at the man across from him, his foxy mind working.

They'd met a year and a half ago at a gun and knife show in Saginaw. Both had stood at the same display table admiring a Nazi field knife, and both at the same moment had declared it a fake, or rather, a reproduction. Still, they agreed the elegant weapon was magnificent, truly a work of art. Together, they examined a few more Third Reich items. The younger man said his name was John but grinned too long when he said it. Peet never asked his real name and didn't offer his.

At the gun show they soon separated, but just before Peet left, the younger man appeared out of nowhere. "I bought this for you," said the blond young man when Peet was just steps away from the exit. He showed Peet a large hardcover book, *Luger: An Illustrated History of the Handguns of Hugo Borchardt and Georg Luger* by John Walter.

"I already got it," said Peet, turning away. *Faggot* was the word he locked onto.

"Not this edition," the younger man said with a straight face and put the book in Peet's hands before stepping away, disappearing swiftly into the virtually all-white crowd. Outdoor men and boys who all looked different and all looked alike.

In his parked truck, Peet thumbed through the book. A paper scrap fell out, torn from the flyer for the show he'd just attended. On it was a handwritten phone number. Peet called it immediately. He knew how this went. He'd know in a second if this guy was for real or just another silky-skinned cocksucker. True believers vanished like smoke. They had to.

"Yes," the phone answered on the first ring.

"John?"

"Yes."

"Thanks for the book."

"You're welcome."

Peet ended the call. Checked **Recent Calls**. No number showed. Not even an <Unknown>. Scrubbed instantly. He'd never seen that before. Some trick.

Peet pulled out and drove east on State Road 81 and didn't see the black Ram three cars back until just outside Caro. Peet put some distance between them. Three minutes later, in tiny Caro, Peet ducked his GMC behind the grain silos at the train depot. He had a smoke and waited. The Ram didn't show.

Ten miles further on, Peet pulled into the first roadside bar he saw. There are plenty to be found dotting the farmlands. He found a stool and a beer. Rascal Flatts on the juke and deer hunting on TV. He lit a cigarette ignoring the *No Smoking* sign. He wasn't the only smoker in the bar. City laws meant little here.

A few minutes later, blond John walked past and slid into the booth farthest from the bar. Peet watched idly in the mirror. When the waitress approached, John ordered something and thumbed through a *Boat & RV Trader*, minding his own business.

After his drink came, John didn't look up when a hot whisper rank with garlic and tobacco brushed his ear.

"Leave, asshole. I see you again, nobody ever sees you again, y' hear me?"

John continued his reading. "Parker Ames," was all he said.

That's how it started.

Parker Ames was a liberal Detroit councilman. Black, flamboyant, wholly corrupt, as vile as Cain. Yet, every election cycle, Ames enflamed his constituency with vitriolic anti-white rants and outrageous promises expertly timed to ensure his reelection. Four more years of lining his pockets with graft, bribes, and a steady stream of cash from the government moneybox. Ames was a foul legacy of Motown's toxic political past, his flagrant racketeering protected and even celebrated by shady web of sycophants still embedded in city government. Everyone knew Ames was a crook, but nobody did anything about it. He coddled the media brilliantly and never met a camera he didn't like.

"What about him?" said Peet.

"I'm a businessman," said John. "Let's do business."

A very careful dance began that day. Bits of intel as ephemeral as confetti began to be passed to Peet. Facts that Peet and his people could use. Over time, an edgy trust grew between the two men, as fragile as stacking china teacups in a pitch-black room.

Like any good drug dealer, the first hit was free, or almost. John gave Parker Ames to Peet for a mere 500 dollars with a money-back guarantee. Hidden camera videos, recorded phone calls, photos, documents, and tax records were supplied to Peet. Peet's people then delivered them anonymously to the press. That done, Ames was crucified. Photographs showed Ames with prostitutes, male and female. Recordings and texts tied him to drug possession, extortion, fraud, receipt of stolen property, perjury, and tax evasion. After two months of fighting off the once-wooed microphones and news cameras, Ames fled not only the state but the country. Mexico, they said. Peet and his associates from as far south as Texas and as far west as California celebrated.

Bigger game followed. The old farmer and the young Aryan knew America had been whored out, the Founding Fathers shit-canned. The wrong people controlled Washington, Hollywood, and Wall Street. It was up to patriots like themselves to set things straight. Deep six the bastards.

John kept his distance, and Peet was fine with that. Peet had associates that John didn't need to know about. Cash changed hands, and John's intel helped Peet string up by the balls a number of state politicians and judges, whether they'd been born with a pair or not. Most resigned to spend more time with their families. They were all dirty. John delivered the dirt. The bigger the target, the higher the price.

Tonight was the Super Bowl.

"Your turn," said John, dangling the shiny black thumb drive from his fingertips. In the dim, smoke-filled singlewide, Bob Peet looked at the blond man across from him.

Peet licked his lips. Looked at his son. Gave him a nod. P.J. was bigger and dumber than he was, but still damned smart. And damned mean.

"Pay him," said Peet. P.J. stood and glowered at Blond John, picked up the pistol and went to the kitchen.

"We know where you live," said Peet to their guest.

"The paint store," muttered P.J. He was kneeling under the sink.

John nodded. Under another name, John owned and lived above a small paint supply store in Flint. He'd never mentioned it. "Understood," said John.

P.J. came back with a worn, mud-spattered camo backpack. His dark, hairy face was grim.

"Count it," said Peet.

John did. Standing at the dinette, he went through the stacks. Mostly hundreds, some fifties, a bunch of twenties. Thirty thousand. "Great," said John. He zipped the backpack and flipped the thumb drive to Peet, who caught it fast with a snaky smile. *I'm not as old as you think, you little fucker.*

"Better be worth it."

"Plug it in," said John. Peet gave the thumb drive to P.J., who pushed it into a port in the laptop.

"Can I see?" said Dougie by the stove.

"Sure," said Peet waving him over. John sipped his Maker's.

The laptop glowed as P.J. tapped keys. Dougie sauntered over to look. With a whir and churr, rows of tiny folder icons began to populate the screen. Sixteen folders. "Open one," ordered Peet. P.J. did. It was a folder on Michigan's lieutenant governor, Pia Moreno. To the Peets she was always The Wetback Slut. When the folder opened, her tax records appeared. Then her husband's tax records, their son's tax records, the husband's parents' tax records. And presto: a D.U.I. for Miz Moreno. And her mug shot. From last summer. All buried. Until now.

"Holy shit!" exclaimed P.J., his eyes dancing. He thumped the big pistol on the table, almost knocking over the whisky.

"They all this good?" said Peet with a cackle.

"Who're you looking at?" said John, sitting across from them.

"The governor's bitch. Moreno. The wetback slut."

John smiled knowingly. "That's a good one. They're not all that good, but a few are better." John rattled off state senators, county executives, judges, and religious leaders: Jews, Muslims, blacks, homosexuals. The cherry on top was the Democrat senior Michigan U.S. senator, a woman who had been in Peet's crosshairs for decades. In every folder was an enemy.

The three bearded anarchists were smiling and laughing when John stood up with his backpack. "I'm leaving."

"Sit down," said P.J. "You're not going anywhere. Not 'til we look through all of these."

"It'll take you all night. I'm going."

"I said, 'Sit down'!" said P.J. rising to his full height, six-three and change. He spun the pistol's cylinder noisily. Straight from a B-western.

"I'm leaving," said John to Peet Senior. He put on his coat. Slung the knapsack over his shoulder.

P.J. advanced. "Look, you little shit." Dougie advanced, too. Monkey see, monkey do.

"Bob?" said John.

"Shut the fuck up, P.J.," said Bob Peet. "Show a little class." He leaned back and lit a cigarette. "We know where he lives." Exhaled a plume of smoke.

John stepped forward and extended his hand to Bob Peet. Peet stood, hiked up his Carhartts, and shook it.

"It's a pleasure doing business with you," said John.

"Likewise," said Peet.

John shook hands with the other two men.

"Thanks," said Dougie.

"Thank you," said John.

P.J. said nothing. Just stared him down.

John turned and picked up his gloves.

After a long beat and a longer pull on his whisky, Peet said to John, "You don't give a goddamn about this country, do you?"

"About this country?" said John pulling on his gloves. "No." He looked Bob Peet in the eye. "About the next one? Yes. I care a great deal." He adjusted the camo backpack on his shoulder and let himself out the door.

As he walked to the Ram, he heard a fresh round of rebel yells. They'd opened another folder.

After driving eight minutes through dark farmland, the man the other men called Blond John shut off the headlights and pulled the black Ram behind a feed store closed for the night. He turned off the engine and retrieved a smartphone from under the dash. A cell tower stood nearby. Its close proximity provided added security to a unique, proprietary technology.

With a series of taps, Pearce Butler passed through four encrypted portals and entered a digital domain exclusively his own and expensively protected. Once there he worked for just under two minutes. Then he turned off the phone and resumed driving.

As he drove south, the data he'd just unleashed began to worm its way through the cloud. The black thumb drive that he'd left at the singlewide wasn't from Best Buy. Peet's white supremacist cell was already crumbling. It would be a week before the group realized that most of the folders were faked. By then the virus they'd unwittingly unleashed in their laptop would have sent all their data and years of emails to twenty-three different law enforcement officials at the state and federal level. The law would never know by whose hand it was sent, but the information contained therein would snowball fast, incriminating the Peets and dozens more in their network for mail fraud, extortion, armed robbery, possession of stolen property, assault, hate crimes, and murder by lynching.

Blond John would vanish. The paint store in Flint was already abandoned. Cleaned out. No paper trail. Not a fingerprint to lift. The Peets would no doubt trash it, maybe burn it to the ground. Any DNA or fingerprints found would be theirs.

The man in the guise of an Aryan hate criminal played no music as he drove. Instead, he thumped the steering wheel to a private beat in his head. As the dark miles passed, he gradually let the hard, sinewy knots of euphoric, intoxicating tension soften and loosen and flow away from his from neck and shoulders and down the lengths of his arms to his dexterous fingers and fingertips.

Energy transferred. Recalibrated. Reset.

He'd liked this truck. He'd miss it.

As he headed toward Detroit, Butler scrutinized the blond dye job in the rearview mirror one last time. Eighteen months ago, he'd wondered whether it would be too much. Too over-the-top. Then he looked at the camo bag of cash next to him. Evidently not.

4

After paying for lunch and dropping Christina off at home, Terry drove to work. She didn't want him to go, but he insisted. He avoided last night's route completely. Took Bobby Darin off his playlist. Shifted musical gears. As he got closer to Ann Arbor and headed up State Street toward downtown, he basked in a drummy Cuban salsa. Bloodstained checks and death and guilt were pushed away from his mind by happy rhythms and festive imaginings of sunny native smiles, spicy outdoor food, and sparkling azure waters tickling warm, sandy beaches. His spirits rose as he watched the bland office buildings and strip malls near I-94 morph into the picturesque shire of Ann Arbor, its rabskabble student housing fringing the majestic University of Michigan. The University was a veritable barony of teeming learning halls, bustling walkways, packed dorms, vast athletic fields, futuristic research laboratories and, at the center of it all, the colossal and ever-growing U of M Medical Center.

As the Gothic stone archways of the regal, Oxford-inspired law school hove into view, Terry aimed the Sebring away from campus and into downtown proper. While Terry hadn't attended U of M, he liked Ann Arbor, appreciated its bohemian *bonhomie,* and was energized by the antics of the student population.

Two blocks off Main Street was Image Zoo. Terry's boss and friend, Jeff Martell, son of a cop, had scratched his way up from wedding videographer to owner of Image Zoo, a full-service video production and post-production facility occupying 2,400 square feet of a converted 19th-century flour mill. Image Zoo occupied the entire second floor. Gazing east from one of the mill's rehabbed, vintage glass windows, you could just make out the nearest Starbucks.

Terry and Jeff went way back. They'd met playing pool in a Ypsilanti bar, randomly paired against the table's reigning duo when Terry's quarters on the rail happened to be laid right behind Jeff's. Terry was forty pounds lighter then. Jeff had a ridiculous mullet. Fueled by Budweiser and bravado, they vanquished the foe, held the table for most of the night, and became an instant buddy movie. "You got my back?" emerged as pet lingo that night. "Got it, Chief," the ready reply. They still said it and still meant it.

Terry had one stop to make before work. He drove past Image Zoo to a building he saw every weekday but had never set foot in. The Ann Arbor Third Bank on Main Street. Five Bauhaus stories rising above its shorter neighbors.

The bank on the check.

The check was no good.

It couldn't be. Alone in his car driving in to work after dropping off Christina, he'd had time to face reality. It was obvious. A dying man's fantasy. This was simply closure.

He looked for a place to park.

Inside, Terry paused to get his bearings. The building was not all bank. There were other offices, too. A big glass wall rose on his right. On the other side of the glass, he saw teller stations, and behind them a curved white wall on which videos played. Words appeared onscreen describing how great the bank was. Happy people of all ages and races represented incredibly satisfied customers. Behind the video wall, Terry saw discreet office cubes.

Terry entered and stood behind the only other customer in line, a bearded young man with John Lennon glasses, curly brown hair, a backpack, and an Under Armor fleece with the logo that looked like an "H."

Kids never dress warm, thought Terry in his big leather coat before reminding himself that this man was no kid. The bearded young man didn't look up from his phone, tapping his way through life and shuffling forward only when the lone teller spoke.

Terry pulled out his wallet. The disintegrating brown leather was years overdue for replacement. He carefully withdrew the check.

Two million dollars. Made out to him.

Ludicrous. Especially held alongside the pathetic wallet.

Save my daughter. The dead driver's plaintive plea rang in his head unbidden.

Terry handled the check carefully. EMS and the deputies last night never saw it.

He couldn't get the image of the wine bottle out of his head. He thought about DeGraaf's open eyes at the end. Mike's open eyes.

"Next," said the teller, a friendly-looking, young African-American woman in stylish horn-rimmed glasses. He stepped forward.

He set the check in front of her. It had dried blood on it.

"Hi," said Terry. "I think I'm probably going to have to talk to a manager about this." The teller whose name tag read *Jade* picked up the check with long, slender fingers. When she saw the amount, her perfect eyebrows jumped as though tugged by invisible strings.

"And you are…?"

"Terry Holbrook," he said. Indicated himself. Nodded at the check. He'd play this out.

"Do you have an account here, Mr. Holbrook?"

"No," he said. "Not yet." He pointed at the check. "But if by some miracle that's good, I sure will open one. I know banks don't like to, you know… see money like that walk out the door."

"Do you have some identification?"

"I do," said Terry and slid her his driver's license. She looked at it carefully. Looked at him carefully.

"I'm going to have to get a manager," said Jade, reaching for a sleek desk phone.

"I figured," said Terry. He glanced behind him. A sixtyish woman with long, frizzy gray hair waited next in line. She looked back at him and blinked several times with no expression. She wore fingerless ragg wool gloves and a long, puffy red coat and toted a worn, purple backpack.

Jade set down the phone after a brief exchange and stepped away with the check and her professional smile. *She must think I'm nuts*, thought Terry. She disappeared behind the video wall in her tight black dress.

A young male teller appeared at the next counter over. His name tag said *Eli*. He smiled at Terry and then at the frizzy-haired woman behind Terry. Frizzy went to Eli. Then Jade came back with another woman in tow. The new woman was older and thick-necked and wore red lipstick. Her shiny black hair was pulled back tight.

"Mr. Holbrook?" the new woman asked. She wore a black skirted suit with a white blouse buttoned to the neck with square black buttons. At her throat was a rectangular silver brooch. Darkened eyebrows. A long silver pin with a large garnet impaled a lapel.

"Yes?" said Terry.

She came around the teller counter, hand extended. "How do you do? I'm Ann Baker, the manager." They shook. In her left hand, she held the check pinched shut end to end. Her nail polish matched her lips. "Would you care to join me in my office?"

"Absolutely," said Terry.

Ann Baker led Terry off dark tile onto quiet carpet. Rows of tasteful wood cubicles topped with frosted glass panels stretched before them like horse stalls. Ann Baker ushered him into a small corner office with a privacy door, which she shut. "Won't you sit down?" Terry sat in one of two small, fabric-covered armchairs. Ann Baker sat at a large desk with nothing on it but a computer.

She sat very straight as she unpinched the check and laid it on the desk in front of her. She appraised it the way a parent looks at a bad report card. Then she appraised him, her mouth slightly open, her facial expression shifting to friendly, professional and expectant.

When it became clear that Ann Baker wasn't going to speak first, Terry cleared his throat. Then waited. Then said, "So, um." Then cleared his throat again.

"Would you like some coffee? Or water?"

"No, thank you." He couldn't get comfortable in the small chair. "So, I guess my first question is, is the check good?" He didn't have a second question. The bank manager closed her smiling lips but kept her eyes on his.

"Did you know Mr. DeGraaf?" she asked.

"No," Terry replied. Shook his head. "I didn't. I never met him before...last night. I was with him. When he died. In the car crash. You probably heard."

"I did hear." Baker nodded, hands clasped on her desk. "Horrible."

"I was right behind him." She said nothing. Terry filled the silence. "Just south of the tracks. When he crashed I pulled over, and I called 911." Terry shrugged. His heavy leather coat made heavy leather coat noise. "But."

Ann Baker's fake smile was long gone. Terry didn't miss it.

"It's terrible," she said.

Terry nodded. "Yeah."

"Mr. DeGraaf was very close to the bank."

Terry nodded. Now he wished he had a coffee or a Coke. She pointed at a brown smudge on the check with the enameled tip of a fingernail. "Is this blood?" she asked, sitting straight and still.

Terry leaned and looked. "I think so." He didn't mention the wine bottle.

"And Mr. DeGraff wrote this check? To you?"

"Yes, he did."

The bank manager looked down. Skootched her lips to one side in a strawberry pucker. With her fingernails, she slid the check close to her. Then bent over to further examine it.

"So?" said Terry, fighting the urge to squirm. "Is it good?"

Ann Baker said nothing, and Terry grew impatient with the manufactured silence. He felt himself sweating.

"Because if it isn't, just say so, and I'll get out of here. To be honest, I don't think too many people have two million dollars in their checking account. Even millionaires." He was rambling and knew it but couldn't seem to stop. "I think he was just being nice." Dumb remark. "Anyway, he wrote it, he gave it to me, I'm here, I just want to know if it's good. Or if it isn't good." He cleared his throat. "And, uh, you know, he wanted to thank me, I guess, so he wrote me that check." Terry pointed at the check. By way of emphasis.

He got nothing from Baker. No wonder she was a manager.

"Thank you for what?" she asked.

"What?" said Terry.

"You said you thought he wanted to thank you. Thank you for what?"

I need you to save my daughter. The prayer.

It seemed private.

He shifted in the chair. It squeaked. He couldn't believe how small this chair was.

"I'd rather not say."

Talk about dead air.

Baker didn't blink. Didn't move.

"Look," said Terry, "I just want to know if the check is good or not. Would you check that for me, please?" He made a show of looking at his watch and then back at Ms. Baker with hooded eyes. Did his best badass.

After two beats, she swiveled toward her computer. "Let's take a look." Her screen was positioned out of visitors' view. Terry watched her red nails clutch the mouse and slide and click. Slide, click. Slide, click. Click, slide, click. It dawned on Terry this was all for show. She already knew.

"Well, Mr. Holbrook." Swiveling back with a mannequin smile. "It appears the check is good."

Terry blinked first. "It's good."

"Yes."

"For two million," he said. "Dollars?"

"Yes."

In his mind Terry saw the check in DeGraaf's bloody fingers. Waving up and down in the cold night air. Cold blue eyes still and unblinking under steel-wool eyebrows.

"Made out to me."

"Yes," said Ms. Baker.

Terry clutched the skinny chair arms, feeling a sudden brain fever. His head dropped. He looked at his crotch and his face felt hot in this tiny office in a toy chair with a heavy coat on. His vision got swimmy.

Two million dollars.

He squeezed shut his eyes. Felt a little faint. Blew out a lungful of air. Sucked in more air. It tasted hoary and used.

When he looked up, Ann Baker wasn't smiling. She said, "If you'll excuse me, I have to make a phone call." And she reached for the phone.

"Wait a sec," said Terry, raising a hand. It was shaking. So was his voice. "Wait a sec. Just..." He motioned for her to put the handset down. She did so, a puzzled look on her face.

"Uh," said Terry. "Uh."

She faced him straight and silent. Crossed her arms. Leaned back with a frown. Her turn to glance at her watch.

"Can I open an account?"

After he left, she again picked up the phone and made several calls.

5

Outside, Terry failed to notice that pockets of light blue had appeared in the ashen sky. That a welcome shimmer of afternoon sun had finally broken through the oppressive, gray clouds.

Because in his brain, a tornado howled.

He walked toward his car in something akin to an agitated stupor, his eyes low, outdoor sounds fragmented, scarcely registering the busy sidewalk or the many people on it.

They'd kept the check, of course. He'd endorsed it, handed it over. They might be shredding it now. Burning it. He should have gone to a different bank. He hadn't made a copy.

He'd never see a nickel.

A block from the bank, a meter cop was ticketing the red Prius just in front of Terry's beige Sebring. Terry's meter had also expired. But the cop hadn't gotten to the Sebring yet. Another sixty seconds would've cost the Holbrook family forty bucks. The meter cop gave Terry a cheery This-is-your-lucky-day smile as Terry's key fob unlocked the door. Terry may have smiled back. He wasn't sure. His mouth moved, but he couldn't have said what shape it made, not with his head full of screaming, rollercoaster thoughts. He got in, avoided eye contact with the municipal officer, and pulled away.

He had to let this go. He felt guilty, but he hadn't done anything wrong. He knew the check would be stopped. *Of course, it would be stopped.* He'd told himself he wasn't going to fight it.

But it was good. She said it was good. So if it was good, he wanted the money.

His money. He flipped down the car's visor to shut out the sun.

In cold afternoon sunlight, he drove the maze of Ann Arbor's one-way streets back toward Image Zoo. Bundled-up pedestrians walked fast, hunkered down. A peal of feminine laughter at a red light cut through his roiling thoughts. Crossing in front of him was a vivacious coed in fake fur, her long, curly hair flying, clutching the arm of her smiling Asian male companion. She wore boots to her knees and a long green scarf. *The older I get, the younger they look,* thought Terry.

It was just before two when he rolled the Sebring past the renovated old mill's small parking lot that Image Zoo shared with three other small businesses. The mill's lot was full, so Terry parked in the parking structure a block away and walked. He had a magnetic pass for the structure. The short walk gave him time to decompress. To sort his thoughts.

Image Zoo was on the second floor. Video editing offered zero exercise, so Terry always took the stairs. The old oak boards strained pleasantly under his steps. When he opened the big, modern glass door to the office, he was instantly ambushed by fabric, feathers, and jangling jewelry. Belinda practically flew from behind the receptionist's desk.

"Terry! Oh, sweetie, sweetie! Oh, my God!" Belinda emoted, butterfly hands fluttering over him in a noisy tangle of bracelets, bangles, necklaces, and hair adornment. Long-limbed, parlor-tanned and brightly made-up, she hugged him close, pressing her cheek and flyaway blond locks hard against his chest. Her perfume comforted him. He had to chuckle before returning a brief embrace. Clutching his wide shoulders, she leaned back to look up at him. "Oh, my God!" was all she said, her mouth a rictus of agony. "Oh, my God!"

Hearing the ruckus, Jeff sauntered in. He was followed by Skip, the second cameraman. The entire staff. Belinda also did the bookkeeping. Image Zoo was small at the moment. Sometimes the team was bigger. Occasionally smaller.

"What's up, dude?" asked Jeff, grinning. Lanky, lean, and always in jeans, Jeff brought stability and friendliness into any room he entered. But at a cost. Running a small business and making payroll for fifteen years had stolen a few watts of sparkle from Jeff's kind eyes, and his face bore some premature lines. Now, however, his only concern was for his friend.

"You can't have him!" Belinda fiercely pulled Terry's bulk into her jewelry-festooned bosom. "He needs me!" Gently, Terry extricated himself from Belinda's muscular embrace.

"Alright, alright everybody," said Terry. He shot a look at Jeff. Jeff read the glance and shook his head.

"No clients on premises," said Jeff.

"So. Bad crash?" said Skip, bluff and direct as usual. A heavy nod from Terry.

Belinda shivered. "Eesh." She made a face, stuck out her tongue. "I don't want to hear about it." She skittered back to her desk as the phone conveniently rang. A quick look at Terry. "Tell me later," she said before professionally answering the phone.

Jeff looked at Terry. "Ready Room?" he asked.

"Sure," said Terry following.

"I think I gotta do something," said Skip to no one in particular, then headed back toward the studio. Protocol was understood at Image Zoo. Jeff and Terry were the team. Belinda did the phones and paperwork. Skip had his own life. Truthfully, no one knew much about it.

The Ready Room was Jeff's office. Spartan in the extreme, it was one of only two offices at Image Zoo. The other was Terry's editing suite, crammed with computers and monitors. The rest of the high-ceilinged workspace was mostly studio space with corners allotted for different activities. A corner for the kitchenette with table and chairs. Skip's camera gear corner with a desk for him. Another corner for tabletop shooting with lights, light stands, paper backdrops, and a green screen. And a large, comfortable corner that doubled as a conference room/client lounge. Notable was an eye-popping chartreuse sofa in the lounge that was comfy enough for late-night snoozing and long enough to fit Terry stem to stern. When digital files had to be compiled at the end of a long day, it often took an hour or more for the computers to do their thing. The couch got used.

Jeff stepped into his office and held the door as Terry came in. "Open or closed?"

"Naw, you can leave it open," said Terry. He exhaled loudly and lowered himself into one of Jeff's roomy guest chairs. Dropped his heavy coat in the other. Jeff was a stickler for comfortable chairs.

Terry shut his eyes and kneaded the bridge of his nose. He hadn't slept well. The bank had freaked him out.

Jeff sat down behind his desk. The only personal things in the office were two framed photos. One of Jeff's wife, Carla, and the other of their two middle-school sons, Clint and Steve, smiling in their hockey uniforms.

"You know, you didn't have to come in today," said Jeff. "The file you sent out late yesterday…last night…they're going to spend all day looking at it. We won't hear anything until tomorrow. It looks great."

"Thanks," said Terry. "Is the audio okay? I was pretty fried by the end of the night."

Besides the Thurgood TV spots, the hot project Jeff was referring to was an industrial video for Jameson Controls in Plymouth, just down the road. It promoted an innovative automotive seating foam product. To illustrate the technology, Terry had crafted a sophisticated animated sequence. He was continually impressed by the technical brilliance of automotive engineers. The time and effort that went into every modern auto part, finish and texture was amazing. Every car and truck on the road was a miracle of engineering that most people took for granted. Only the car guys cared. And these days, many of the "car guys" were women.

"Sounded fine to me. Good music choice. Anyway, they'll let us know. Dave's cool." Dave at Jameson was their best client. A great audience who paid his bills. "So," Jeff continued. "Are you alright?"

"Yeah," said Terry. "It was just, you know." He pressed his mouth closed, thumping the armrests. "A really bad accident. A really, really bad accident."

Jeff listened.

"I mean, the guy died," Terry went on. "He was hurt bad." He knitted his thick fingers together. "There was blood everywhere." He looked up at Jeff. "He had a wine bottle shoved through his chest."

"What?" said Jeff.

"No shit," said Terry. "He was holding a wine bottle when he crashed." Terry mimed the position, "And when the airbag went off when he hit a tree, blammo. Drove the bottle into his chest. Neck first, you know?" Terry pantomimed the bottle going into his own chest. "Right into his heart. I tell you, man. It was freaky."

"Was he drinking?"

"He said he wasn't drinking."

"He *talked?*" Jeff was incredulous.

"Oh, yeah," said Terry. "He said he wasn't drinking, just holding the wine bottle so it wouldn't break in the crash. He talked for maybe a minute. I'd already called 911. I called before I even saw him. He was in front of me on Territorial. Car just flew off the road. Hit some trees. Snapped the trunks." Terry kneaded his fingers and hands, remembering. "Old apple trees."

"What kind of car?"

"A Lincoln MKS. Pretty new."

"Wow." Jeff shook his head, trying to picture it.

Both men went silent.

"He was a nice guy," said Terry. *I need you to save my daughter.*

"He was a rich guy," said Jeff.

Terry eyed his friend. "How would you know that?"

"Michael DeGraaf," said Jeff. "That's who it was, right? It was on the radio driving in." Jeff listened to local news for business leads. "I've heard of him. He's a big shot." Terry's phone buzzed in the pocket of his coat on the chair next to him. He pulled it out, looked at it, raised a wait-a-second forefinger.

It was a text from Christina. **Check this out. lm** And a link. **lm** was their shorthand. *Love, me.*

"Just a sec," said Terry to Jeff.

He texted back **Thanks. Im** and opened the link. It was a story from Crain's Detroit Business from this morning. Crain's was Michigan's daily business news feed. Ann Arbor Investment Banker Killed in Car Crash.

"This is the story. Christina found it." Terry tapped his phone screen. "I just sent it to you."

"Thanks. Are you in it?"

"I don't know." Both men read in silence.

> Michael R. DeGraaf, 71, investment banker and CEO of Ann Arbor-based Pinnacle Equity, died Tuesday night in an automobile crash on North Territorial Road near Dexter, Michigan. Mr. DeGraaf was alone and no other vehicles were involved. DeGraaf was reportedly driving to his horse farm in Dexter when the accident occurred shortly after 10:30 p.m. Icy road conditions are believed to have contributed to the accident. He is survived by his wife, Millicent, three daughters, and two grandchildren.

Next to the story was a studio portrait of DeGraaf, smiling at the camera. He wore a suit, white shirt, and conservative necktie. The photo looked five or ten years old to Terry. More and darker hair. Confident smile. The face tan and healthy. Not pale and bloody.

"You knew this guy?" asked Terry.

"I know *of* him. But I never met him." Jeff was a great networker. He'd go to business events in Ann Arbor, Detroit, Lansing, and even Grand Rapids on the other side of the state to make contacts and schmooze. He enjoyed meeting business people and was always ready to plunge into any conversation and talk up Image

Zoo. He was great at it. Which was good, because Terry hated that part of the business.

"Horse farm," said Terry, rereading his phone.

"Is his place that big place out by you? With like miles of split rail fence all around it?"

Terry knew which property Jeff referred to. "I don't know," said Terry. Horses and riders were a common sight around Dexter in the milder months. The place Jeff was talking about was the only big new place around. He pictured the luxurious, sprawling ranch-style house with a wide porch all the way around. Riding pens in front, rolling hills out back. Big white barn near the road. Terry couldn't recall actually seeing any horses there. Maybe they were on the back forty.

"Well," said Jeff. "You did the right thing. You did everything you could."

Terry shrugged. "Hey, I'm just glad I didn't crash. The road was sheer ice. Like slick glass." He remembered his own frightening spinout. Trees swirling past.

Jeff nodded.

Terry thought for a moment.

"Hey," he said. Low voice.

Jeff caught the tone. Leaned forward, all ears. Terry stretched out a leg, put his toe against the door and pushed gently. It shut with a quiet snap.

"That'll piss her off," said Jeff with a smile. They both pictured Belinda standing quietly nearby, sipping coffee. Terry shrugged it off. Privacy was privacy.

"So last night I'm with this guy, and he's dying, right?" Almost whispering.

"Yeah?" said Jeff, also low.

"And he's covered in blood. Blood and red wine. All over his face. Everywhere."

"Yeah?"

"And he asks me to pray for him."

"Really?" says Jeff. Jeff was Catholic. Quite devout.

"Yeah," says Terry. "And he kind of guides me through it. 'Cause, you know, I'm not…you know."

"Right." Jeff knew Terry was not a big churchgoer.

"So I do what I can. I do the best I can. I prayed for him."

"Out loud?"

"Oh yeah, out loud. And…I can't even really remember what I said, you know?"

"Sure," said Jeff. "But you did it. You did the best you could."

"I tried to."

Jeff nodded sympathetically. "I'm sure you did fine."

"Well, you know. Whatever. So, I, you know, finish. And he says 'Amen.' And I say, 'Amen.' And then…" Terry stopped. Long pause. "I thought that was it. I thought he…died. Right then. I thought he was dead." Longer pause.

"But?" asked Jeff.

"But then he starts talking again. Says…" Terry leaned forward, level with Jeff's eyes. "…'I need you to save my daughter.'"

"Fuck no!"

"Fuck yeah!" The profanity toothless between old friends.

"And then," Terry whispered now, still leaning close. "He writes me a check."

"*What?*"

"He's got a wine bottle sticking out of his heart, right? I thought he was dead. He *should* be dead. But then he sits up like he's perfectly fine and pulls out a checkbook and a pen. Asks me how I spell my name. Says he needs me to save his daughter."

"You're shitting me!"

"I'm not! I swear to God. It was like ... he was perfectly okay."

"Except for the wine bottle."

"Except for that. And he writes me a check."

"So you said you'd do it?"

"What?"

"Save his daughter," said Jeff.

Terry paused.

"Well. Yeah. What was I going to say?"

"What's wrong with the daughter?"

"I have no idea," said Terry."

Jeff nodded slowly. Then asked, "How much?"

Terry's lips began to form the word *two*, but then he stopped. Closed his mouth. Jeff saw it.

"What?" said Jeff.

Terry considered saying two thousand dollars. But looking into Jeff's eyes, Terry saw the danger of lying. A chill forming and ready to emerge. Friendship is about trust. It's a delicate thing.

Terry kept his mouth shut and motioned for Jeff to hand him a pen and some Post-its. He wrote on the pad and slid it over to Jeff.

Jeff's eyebrows shot up. His mouth opened in a massive, toothy grin.

"Two million dollars!" Jeff mouthed the amount almost silently. Terry held his friend's eye and nodded slowly. Held up two fingers. Like a peace sign.

"To save the daughter?" said Jeff. He held up his phone with Crain's story on it. "There's three daughters."

"Yep."

"Who's the daughter?"

"No idea."

After three seconds Jeff said, "She must be in some deep…"

"Yeah," Terry cut in, finishing the thought. She must be.

Jeff pulled off the Post-it note, tore it up, and threw it into the wastebasket. Terry thought of something.

"Why don'tcha tear off a couple more?" said Terry. He held up the pen. "Ballpoint. Like in the movies."

Jeff laughed, pulling off and tearing up several more Post-its. He then held the pad at eye level scrutinizing for impressions.

"I think you're safe," said Jeff.

"I won't get it." Meaning the money.

"Probably not," said Jeff quickly. Which depressed Terry.

"I went to the bank. The bank on the check. They said it was good."

"You went today?"

"Yeah. Just now."

Jeff thought a moment, but then made a face. "Yeah. But come on."

"I won't get it," said Terry.

Jeff nodded knowingly. "Lawyers," he said, frowning.

"Exactly." On the drive in from Dexter, Terry had thought the same thing. Talking to Jeff helped. He felt the dream coming to an end. He stopped thinking about what he'd been thinking about. About bass boats and new cars and electric guitars.

"What did Christina say?"

"I didn't tell her. Not about the check. I told her about everything else."

"About the 'Save my daughter'?"

"No, I didn't tell her about that, either."

"Better tell her. Tell her about both."

Terry nodded. "I just wanted to, you know, check on the check first."

Jeff stood up behind his desk. "Call her," he said. "Tell her."

When Terry stood, they both heard high heels clack away. Terry shook his head.

"Aw, don't worry about it." Jeff waved it away. "This isn't gonna last. Go home. Tell Christina. Take a nap." Jeff put a strong hand on his friend's shoulder and squeezed.

Terry took his coat off the chair and stepped out of Jeff's office. He went down the short hallway to his own domain, the editing suite. On and under his desk were racks of video recorders, players, and hard drives. A waist-high, glossy black AVID mainframe filled a corner. Its blinking red and green LEDs made it look like Darth Vader's dorm room refrigerator. On the desk were two twenty-four-inch monitors. A forty-two-inch screen hung on the wall for clients to view. He and Jeff had picked out all the equipment and furniture and put the whole place together over one long weekend five years ago.

His desk looked just as he'd left it sixteen hours ago. Yet so much had happened. He sat down and checked his email. Nothing important. He rubbed his eyes. Skip appeared at the door, toying with a roll of duct tape. Video production guys always seemed to tote around duct tape.

"So," deadpanned Skip to Terry's back, "I was wondering if I could borrow a couple hundred thousand. There's a cabin for sale on the Au Sable I've had my eye on." Skip was a fly fisherman. The Au Sable River was Michigan's premier trout stream. Terry swiveled around slowly, offering Skip his most lethal Blue Meanie smile.

"Bite me," said Terry. He was going to kill Belinda.

6

Belinda remained alive. Terry tried to work but couldn't focus. All he really wanted was a nap. After an unproductive hour spent fiddling with footage, he said some quick goodbyes and left. The fleeting midday sun long gone, the weather back to cold and gloomy, he pulled into his garage at home at 3:30. Inside, he hung up his coat and was about to tell Christina about the check and the bank and everything when Hannah got home from school. All attention instantly diverted to their kinetic daughter. Christina always tried to be home before Hannah's school bus arrived on their street. They adored their only child. They adored The Product.

The nickname originated on a family vacation when Terry, photographing their daughter at a petting zoo, referred to her jokingly as The Product Shot, an advertising term. The name stuck. Rather than resent it, Hannah loved being The Product. "Because," she explained, "I'm the product of a happy home."

Christina and Terry were hearing about a video Hannah saw that day about Ancient Rome when Terry's phone rang. When not on vibrate, it played "Eleanor Rigby."

The Washtenaw County Sheriff's Department. They wanted to talk to him. Could he come in.

He didn't get his nap.

The Washtenaw County Sheriff's Department was south of Ann Arbor and west of Ypsilanti. It was a new building on a large campus of half a dozen older, smaller county buildings. Last night's 911 responders had been from Dexter and, after the ambulance left, Terry had somberly followed a squad car to this building. They'd wanted to get his statement. It took a while. It was past 1 a.m. when he finally headed home. They'd offered to drive him, but he declined. Now, late in the afternoon of the following day, he saw three flags on poles in front of the contemporary municipal building. The U.S. flag, the state flag, and a Washtenaw County Sheriff's Department flag. He didn't remember seeing any flags last night.

There was ample parking. Terry found a spot marked *1 Hour Limit*. He figured that was enough. He zipped up his coat and walked up the long walkway to the glass double doors. He watched his step. There was ice.

A polite but businesslike female officer in a brown uniform behind bulletproof glass took his name and invited him to take a seat. There was a sheriff's star embroidered in gold above her left breast pocket. He signed in like last night.

He chose the nearest seat, a cushioned, built-in bench. It was a spacious lobby painted in calming blue hues with a big window wall. High ceiling. No loose furniture or lamps. Everything built in. Bolted down. Probably a safety measure. Light came from the window wall and ceiling fluorescents only. He wished he had a breath mint.

A uniformed African-American female officer strode by with

a clipboard, her black pistol high on her right hip. She smiled at him. He nodded back. The only other person in sight was a young Hispanic-looking man across the lobby in a study carrel, filling out paperwork. It looked like he was applying for a job.

"Mr. Holbrook?" the desk officer spoke through thick glass. She pointed to her right. "If you go to the double doors, I'll buzz you in." Terry did as he was told, just like last night. Walked between two gray stanchions he assumed were metal detectors. Stopped at the two glass doors. The buzzer buzzed.

Terry pulled the door handle and was startled to see a smiling female officer on the other side waiting for him. She'd appeared like magic. She was maybe thirty, cheerful, dusky-complexioned with glossy black hair that seemed long, he thought, for a law officer.

"Terry?" Familiar.

"Yes."

"I'm Deputy Fayouz." She put her small hand out, and Terry shook it. She beamed. Great teeth. "Please follow me." Deputy Fayouz led him down the same hallway of offices he'd seen last night, but unlike last night, now most of the doors were open. Lots of activity. His tax dollars at work. The deputy stopped at the open door of a small, windowless office identical to all the rest.

"Mr. Holbrook." A man's voice. Terry looked in at an officer he'd met last night who had crinkly hair the color of a circulated nickel. Deputy Weston. The officer stood and came around his desk. He looked daisy fresh. They were the same height, both big men. The deputy had maybe ten years on Terry. Terry had maybe thirty pounds on the deputy. Terry shook the officer's outstretched hand. Deputy Fayouz disappeared after another megawatt smile.

"Thanks for coming in." Like it was a choice.

"Happy to," said Terry. He wasn't.

"Doug Weston."

"I remember," said Terry. The deputy shut the door and gestured to a chair in front of the desk.

"Please," said Weston.

As Terry sat he saw the bloody check he'd left with Ms. Baker at the bank on Deputy Weston's desk. In a clear plastic bag. An evidence bag.

"Would you like to hang up your coat?"

"No, I'm good, thanks." Terry stared at the check. Weston sat down.

"You get any sleep?" The deputy gave him concerned eyebrows.

"Yeah. Some." Terry broke his look from the check and looked at Weston. Once again, his insides twisted darkly. The roiling, inky blackness, biting at his insides. Screeching in his brain. Not guilt, not shame, but this time, fear. Helpless fear. His spit suddenly tasted sour.

"First off, Mr. Holbrook, I see your face, and you don't have to be worried," said Deputy Weston. "We don't think you've committed a crime."

"Good," said Terry.

Weston smiled, pushing large white teeth toward Terry. "You didn't commit a crime, did you?" Cop eyes like cold marbles.

"No, sir," said Terry. "Not that I know of. Sir."

Weston opened a drawer and withdrew a pair of drugstore half-glasses, which he put on. He slid a sheet of yellow lined paper from a manila folder and placed it next to the evidence bag. "Mr. Holbrook, were you at the Ann Arbor Third Bank this morning?" He peered at Terry over the half-glasses.

"Yes," said Terry.

The law officer pointed to the evidence bag without touching it. "With this check?" he asked.

"I didn't think it was going to be any good."

"With this check? Yes or no?"

"Yes."

"Well, Terry —" Off came the glasses. "May I call you Terry?" Deputy Weston smiled.

Good Cop.

"Sure."

"Terry, as you can probably imagine, with this situation being so …unusual…the bank's standard procedure in an event like this is to file a Suspicious Activity Report."

Terry nodded.

"At 11:50 last night, you were in this building and you gave a statement. A signed statement." He paused and then ran the tip of his tongue sideways between his lips before continuing. "You didn't mention this check."

Terry looked at his own hands.

"Why not?"

Terry pursed his lips.

"We asked you to tell us everything that happened at the scene. Everything you could remember. Everything." Weston held up the bag for Terry. "You didn't tell us about this."

"I didn't lie."

"You withheld truth. You signed a document. That's the same as lying. That's perjury."

Terry blinked first.

"This is a helluva big check, don'tcha think?"

Terry didn't say anything.

"Two million dollars." Weston leaned forward, fingers interlaced, his chin on his fisted hands, his crisp, uniformed elbows bracketing the bagged check on the desk. "And you said you never met the man before. You swore to that fact. Now, why would a total stranger write you a check like that?"

"I'm not going to get it," said Terry.

"That's not my point," said Weston. "Why did he do it? Why would he give it to you? And why did you lie about it?"

"I didn't…"

Weston silenced him with a hand. "Don't say you didn't lie. You lied. We're moving on. Why would Michael DeGraaf write a check like this to you?"

Terry didn't look away.

I need you to save my daughter.

It seemed like a private request. Between him and Mike.

Terry shrugged. "I don't know. I prayed for him." Then added, "I held his hand."

"That was it?"

Something held Terry's tongue again. But, this time, it wasn't darkness or guilt or greed. He didn't know what it was. But it was powerful.

"That was it," managed Terry.

"That wasn't it," said Weston. He spread his palms flat on the wide span of desktop, shaking his head. "I don't believe you, Terry."

Terry didn't blink this time. Because he felt something. Something near him or in him. Something he didn't understand. Like it was DeGraaf.

"People don't write checks to other people for two million dollars for a prayer," said Deputy Weston.

"How do you know?" said Terry. Emphasizing the *you*.

Weston spent a moment with the remark. Terry wondered if he went to church.

After a moment, the deputy leaned back, appraising Terry with hooded eyes beneath stiff-haired brows.

He picked up the sheet of yellow paper. "We looked into your past a bit." Weston held the paper aloft but didn't look at it. He looked at Terry.

"DUI, August 11," said Weston. "Sixteen years ago."

Fuck. Terry shook his head in disgust. He'd never get over that.

"Anything else?" asked Weston.

"What?" asked Terry, still battling the memory of that stupid, drunken Kalamazoo night, forever etched into his brain like a lurid, shameful tattoo.

The deputy set down the paper. "Anything else we don't know about? That you want to tell us about?" Weston inquired with his eyebrows. "Anything to help us...trust you a little more?"

Terry felt a trickle of armpit perspiration slide wetly down his side.

Either they knew or they didn't.

If they knew and he said nothing, they'd think he was a criminal. If they didn't know and he told them, they'd also think he was a criminal. This was a no-win. He looked up at the deputy.

"When I was sixteen, I was arrested for shoplifting."

The law officer listened.

"It was...a fluke," said Terry. "A dare." But it wasn't a fluke and it wasn't a dare. It was larceny.

"What did you steal?" asked Weston.

"A Hummel figure," said Terry. He held up a thumb and forefinger four inches apart. The size of the china figurine. Even Weston smiled at this.

"The little porcelain things? The little figures?"

"Yeah." Terry nodded. It had been a hand-painted figurine of a little boy catching a fish. Rosy-cheeked. Little alpine hat. A friend told him he could steal them and return them for cash. To buy pot. Ricky Barnett. Some friend.

"Why?" said Weston. He seemed genuinely curious.

"I don't know." Terry shook his head. "To see if I could get away with it. Just a dumb, stupid, kid thing."

"That's it?"

Terry nodded.

He could not read Weston's expression. The deputy knew more than he was saying. What that was, Terry couldn't guess. "Well," said Weston, "You were a juvenile. It's not on your record." Weston slipped the sheet of yellow paper back into the binder.

For a long moment, he sat and looked at Terry. His desk chair swiveled ever so slightly. Back and forth. Several times. Then Weston pushed back his chair and stood up crisply.

"Thank you, Mr. Holbrook, for coming in." Back to Mr. Holbrook. Weston came around the desk and extended his hand. Terry stood up and shook it. But something seemed off. Different. Shifted.

"You're welcome. Thank you, Officer."

"Deputy."

"Deputy." Terry looked at Weston carefully. Glanced at the desk. The walls. The floor. Something had changed in here. An altering. Like when a slightly different lens slides in front of your eye during an eye exam. A soft click, and everything looks almost the same, but not quite.

Terry paused a moment, then pointed to the check. "Do I get that back?"

"Actually, it goes back to the bank." Weston said no more.

"Okay," said Terry.

"I'll walk you out." Weston opened the door. The fit, muscular deputy offered a half smile that Terry couldn't interpret.

Weston walked close behind Terry down the busy hallway toward the lobby. They came to the thick glass double doors, surely bulletproof, between the inner offices and the lobby. They shook hands again, said goodbye, and Weston turned and walked back toward his office.

Terry wasn't sure what had just happened. He wasn't sure what he saw, or felt, or thought he saw and felt, a moment ago in Weston's office. The altering. The lens thing. But his editor's eye didn't miss much.

Weston could have grilled him more. But didn't. *Why?*

He'd been sweating more than he thought. He swiped his hair and his fingers came away wet. He didn't like leaving without the check. When he stepped outside, the cold air hit his damp skin with a harsh, unpleasant chill. It was only 5 p.m. but was already nighttime dark.

Driving home, he was not happy. Many unhappy things pushed into his mind. Dried blood. Lying to the police. That ass-wipe Ricky Barnett. Drunk in handcuffs in Kalamazoo many years ago. Prayers and promises to a dead man.

Mike to his friends.

He didn't know if he was more hungry, or more tired. He decided he was more hungry. He couldn't think.

He replayed walking out of Weston's office and Weston not closing the office door. The check on his desk in plain view in that busy hallway with all those people walking by. You heard about things like that. Evidence disappearing. Never to be seen again.

The temperature had dropped twelve degrees in half an hour. The road home was dark and icy.

I need you to save my daughter.

7

Grosse Pointe Farms is generally regarded as the second wealthiest of the five insular Pointes, the storied social cluster several miles northeast of and a world away from downtown Detroit. Of slightly lower status are Grosse Pointe Park, Grosse Pointe Woods, and the City of Grosse Pointe. Above them all is regal Grosse Pointe Shores, its mansions rising Gatsby-like along the manicured waterfront of sparkling Lake St. Clair. A handful of legendary Michigan families still employ professional butlers. All but two serve in The Shores.

The woman of the house hadn't been home two minutes. The four-bedroom Tudor was built in 1936 on a tree-lined street in The Farms, four blocks from the lake. Updated three times since D-Day.

She was done crying for the day. The midnight call from her mother. The whole day spent with the police, the medical examiner, at the police station, and at the morgue. Her father's body a shattered, empty shell. Her mother's insistence on remaining in her home; her stubborn refusal to come stay with them. A home nurse hired quickly to stay with her at the horse farm over Millie's sputtering objections.

Fran was spent.

Tall, dark-haired and effusively praised for her sublime, statuesque beauty since the age of thirteen, she was unloading grocery bags onto granite countertops, the final chore of this dreadful day, when a faint urge tugged at her. It drew her out of the kitchen, past the curving staircase to the front hall. It was after four, and the mail had come. Bryce was at work. He'd offered to be with her after her mother called, but she'd insisted he go to his job. She'd handle it. Truth was, she didn't like company when she couldn't predict her moods.

The mail was delivered through a brass slot in the door, and today's pile lay scattered on the big oriental rug. Bills. Statements. Direct mail ads. A couple of catalogs featuring sunny spring wear on willowy, smiling models.

But she immediately sensed it. Then saw it. A bright white envelope in the puddle of paper. Padded. Addressed to her. The familiar label. Computer-printed. Avery 8163 white. She'd matched the brand at an office supply store.

She froze in her tracks, listening hard. Nothing. No sound but the slow, sonorous ticking of the grandfather clock. She looked past the clock into the dining room. Drapes drawn. Mahogany table and chairs in place. She glanced toward the living room. Also quiet. The big lamp lit by its timer. A security measure.

The swirling thoughts of her father and mother vanished instantly. She peeked through the peephole in the door. Saw no one. Just stale February snow. Their shoveled walk. The cleared sidewalk fronting the street. Their yard covered with white.

No movement of any kind.

She made sure the door was bolted, with its heavy brass chain in place. In the dining room, she looked through the gap in the curtains, careful not to stand too close. She saw nothing strange. No one hiding behind the majestic trees that lined their street.

After a quick circuit to make sure all the doors were bolted, all windows were locked, and the garage door was down, she went upstairs to her bedroom and came down with tweezers and her small needlepoint scissors shaped like a golden stork. She had put on disposable latex gloves. Some months ago, she'd bought a whole box. The house was dead quiet except for the *tock* of the grandfather clock and the intermittent roar of the furnace.

She squatted in the front hall, using the tweezers to grip a corner of the white envelope. The other mail she ignored.

Pinching the tweezers tightly, she carried the envelope into the formal dining room and laid it on the table. She sat and examined the label. *Ms. Francine Siehling.* Their home address.

The clock in the hall struck 4:15, its single deep chime fading after long seconds. Gingerly, Fran Siehling used the tweezers to flip the envelope over. She looked for any anomalies, any clues. Anything different.

She found nothing. The address label and two *Forever* flag stamps were all there was to see. The stamps ruler-straight as always.

She exhaled without realizing she'd been holding her breath. The sigh turned to a soft groan. She knew or thought she knew what was inside. Holding the envelope's left corner with the tweezers, she used the gold stork scissors to snip off the right-side edge of the envelope. She didn't scissor it completely off, but left it barely attached at a corner. Holding the envelope tightly with the tweezers and using the stork's beak to bend away the scissored flap, she turned the envelope mouth down and shook it firmly. Once. Twice.

A pink plastic thumb drive fell out and skittered across the glossy, dark wood dining table.

Another shake. There was something else in there.

On the fourth shake, a red-backed Bicycle playing card slid facedown onto the table. Stuck to the back of it was a white sticker. Avery 8163. With instructions.

There were no other contents. Same as last time. She relaxed her grip on the tweezers and let the envelope fall to the table. She eyed the pink thumb drive.

Using only the tweezers and the sharp tip of the stork scissors and mindful of the mahogany, she levered an edge of the playing card and flipped it over.

The Five of Diamonds.

"Oh shit," she muttered.

Five.

She dropped the tweezers and stork scissors as if they burned her flesh. Tore off the latex gloves. After a long moment, she began running her slender, manicured fingers through her long, dark hair. Over and over. Over and over.

Over and over.

Staring at the five diamonds on the card. The five blood red diamonds. Closing her eyes, then opening them. Closing them again.

Five now.

Fifty thousand dollars.

And it hadn't even been three weeks.

At least Dad was spared this.

A few moments later, she wasn't done crying for the day.

Fran sat for a long time. Only when the dining room had become dark, swallowed by deep afternoon shadows, was she jarred back to her senses. With a start, she remembered the lemon sorbet, frozen peas, and lettuce she'd left in the bag on the granite counter top. The sorbet had melted, and the other food in the bag was wet.

8

Herbert Pearce Butler was his great-grandfather's name. Herbert the First was a gifted Detroit metalworker and machinist who corresponded with Edison and lost two fingers securing twenty-one patents over a forty-year career. In 1911, while still in his teens, his inventive talent was discovered, hired, and put to work by the rough-and-tumble Dodge brothers, Horace and John. John Dodge in particular liked whisky, women, and bare-knuckle brawling. He made a private game of perpetually tempting the young inventor with lurid invitations to partake of the automobile capital's second and third fastest-growing industries: barrooms and brothels. Herbert always demurred, preferring to spend his nights in the machine shop, tinkering under the gaslights.

The first name skipped two generations while H. P. Butler's portfolio of patents, always held close, soared in value.

Pearce Butler was technically Herbert Pearce Butler the Second, but his mother had permitted the name to appear on the birth certificate only on the condition that her son never be called Herbert. For which young Pearce was eternally grateful.

A century after his great-grandfather's heyday, Pearce Butler prepped for the night's work. He dressed in black, silent gear. No buttons, buckles, or zippers to catch light or make sound. Pulling a black turtleneck from what had been the Blond John locker, he glanced briefly at the narrow, wheat-colored mustache, matching sideburns, and pale blond temple tufts now stored in a clear plastic box for future use. He thought about the Peets.

In an adjacent locker were black pants, socks, jacket, silent boots, dark wig, and thick, dark mustache. Pancake makeup gave his skin a deep, Mediterranean hue. Gloves and tools were already in the Neon. Fifty-four metal steps down, he unlocked the small car with a silent remote. Butler walked quietly past a selection of other vehicles, past the speedboat held aloft in its sling, and past the empty space where the black Ram had been. Very little sound rose from his footfalls up into the massive framework of aging girders overhead. He smiled as he approached the rust-scabbed Dodge Neon. A sorrier-looking automobile could scarcely be imagined.

But when he turned the key, he relished its secret rumble and purr. Modifications never guessed by anyone who happened to glance his way. He put it in gear. Drove up the ramp. Through the gate. Off to work.

Four miles away Keno Reese had one more stop to make. Actually, make that two. One for the money, two for the show. He smiled to himself as he walked in the cold, his gloved hands slapping the deep, full pockets in his long leather coat. Leather to cut the wind. Rabbit lining to cut the chill. The cashmere scarf around his throat he considered a due spoil of living well. He rubbed his palms together.

Was a good night. Everybody paying but Boots, who could not, at present, be found. But Boots'd be good. He'd get it together.

As Keno walked between darkened buildings a few blocks north of the Motor City Casino, the dim roar of I-75 faded. He strode comfortably into a dark, forlorn patch of abandoned Detroit, where most streetlights remained broken and unlit. Long-dead factories loomed on all sides. Be he feared no evil. He was a known man. A needed man. He carried but never used, and seldom had to show. He never shot a man.

Didn't want to. Didn't need to.

He had other gifts. Better gifts. He smiled again, inhaling the cold, crisp air deeply. Exhaling twin plumes from his nostrils.

Ahead of him on the dark street between two shuttered tool and die shops, he saw a cigarette lighter flicker briefly inside a parked Escalade. Keno slipped off one glove, stopped walking, pulled a lighter from his coat and flicked his own Bic. After a moment, he put the lighter away and his glove back on and resumed his stride toward the Escalade.

"What? You got no heat in here?" said Keno, taking a seat, shutting the passenger door, and rubbing his hands briskly on his thighs. Actually, it wasn't that cold. The windows were steamy. The man next to him was big enough to throw off his own heat.

"I start up when it gets too cold," said the giant.

"Well, let's do this, 'cause it ain't getting any warmer." Without another word, Keno withdrew from a cavernous inside pocket a bulky Ziploc freezer bag stuffed with pills, tinfoil packets, and smaller bags of powder. Always show the product first. It built trust. And long-term customers.

Without a word, the big man at the wheel reached under his ass and pulled out a thick stack of money. He handed it to Keno in return for the Ziploc, which he tucked inside his ornately tooled

blue leather varsity jacket. Keno laughed, tossing the stack of rub-
ber-banded bills from one hand to the other. "Oh my! Still warm!
Thank you, brother."

"Mm," was all the driver said.

Keno slid the money into the pocket from which the Ziploc had
emerged. He didn't count it. He was in the Trust business, and this
last delivery wrapped up business for the night. He popped the
latch of the door to let himself out. "Later, brother. As always." The
driver grunted. Not much of a talker. Keno's proffered fist bump
got a halfhearted response.

Outside the vehicle, Keno shut the door as quietly as he could.
But there was no one around to hear. He walked back the way he
came. After half a minute, time enough to paw through the Ziploc,
Keno heard the Escalade start up and pull away, dark. No headlights swept the shuttered factories.

Keno kept walking toward the dazzling lights and candyland
luminescence of the Motor City Casino and hotel, its colorful, illuminated electric stripes dancing fitfully across the whole building,
brightening the sky from three blocks away. Grinning, he slapped
his fat pockets, repressing an urge to whistle. *Not tonight, Motor
City,* he thought. *No craps or cards for Keno. I got the money. I
want the show.*

The show was a pole dancer he met an hour later, a chesty white
girl named Sassy. She laughed in his arms as he carried her
squealing across the condo threshold. He almost dropped her.
Too much Chivas.

"Oh, my!" chirped Sassy, "Aren't you the gent? You must be
serious."

"Oh, I'm serious," giggled Keno, a raptor's glint in his eye. "Your coat, madame?" He helped her slide out of her silver fox without either of them wobbling too much. His own long coat stayed on as he led her by the hand into the townhouse proper. Brand new. In Midtown, birthplace of the sparkling new and awesome downtown Detroit. *"Entre vous."* He extended one languid arm toward the great room as recessed lights came up via handheld remote. A tasteful, Cathedral-ceilinged love pad warmed into view. Hardwood floors. Gas fireplace. A sumptuous red leather sectional; the biggest she'd ever seen. He laughed at her open-mouthed reaction.

In moments he had music on, a new slice from Childish Gambino, loud. He laid his long coat over a chair and fished out the fat stack from the Escalade. Not the biggest take of the night, but big enough to impress. He held it up for her to see.

"Look what Daddy got." Sassy squealed high, wordless girl sounds.

He led her to the glass dining room table and sat her down, gently brushing the stack of the bills up her bare back and over her creamy shoulder before setting them down in front of her. She stared at it, all kinds of pretty things in her eyes. But her smile faded when he pulled his nickel-plated Colt Commander .45 from the small of his back and scraped it across the glass to lay down by the money. He did it just to see her eyes pop.

When she looked up at him with scared kitten eyes, he winked at her. "Anyone come in, you shoot 'em. Be right back." He left and went to the bedroom for his special stash. *She be nekkid in no time.*

As anticipated, the music masked the faint hiss from eight brass tubes installed at floor level and hidden behind drapes and furniture. The odorless influx began shortly after the lights came on. The tubes pumped in Xenon, an easily synthesized, colorless, heavy gas that built up steadily from floor level. As its volume increased it pushed lightweight oxygen up toward the ceiling like foil rising on a pan of Jiffy Pop. The brass tubes, connected this evening to lengthy sections of rubber hose outside, had been installed before Christmas. Keno's lease began in January. The Xenon was in the Neon.

Sixteen minutes later Keno and Sassy were asleep. Their heads rested on the glass dining table. Sassy's champagne had spilled. Keno's hair and face were dusted with cocaine from the mound on the mirror in front of him. Fortunately, his falling head had missed the razor blade. The brass tubes had stopped hissing and had been removed, replaced by nondescript vinyl plugs. The black rubber hoses had been coiled and returned to the Neon.

With a turn of a key, the back door opened and a swarthy-appearing man clad in black and wearing a gas mask and tight black rubber gloves stepped into the townhouse. The quiet of his rubber soles was unnecessary with Childish Gambino loud in the high-ceilinged great room. Butler moved swiftly and confidently. Fingers on carotids found steady pulses. The money and gun on the table went into a black nylon sack. So did the C-note snort tube. From Keno's long coat, Butler pulled four more stacks of cash which went into the bag. He found two handguns in the bedroom and an ankle derringer under the red leather sectional. All the guns went into the sack.

He flushed the cocaine down the toilet and returned from the bathroom with a bottle of Excedrin. He set it on the table between their motionless heads. They'd need it in about eighteen minutes.

The gas dissipated fast. He paused, wondering if he could do anything for the woman. He was sorry she was present. This wasn't her fault.

He took a lipstick from her purse and wrote on the glass table. *It's not her, Keno. She's innocent.* He then drew a red lipstick arrow on the glass that pointed to the unconscious woman. *If you harm her, I'll hurt Lucille and Wanda.*

Keno's auntie and sister, whom Keno loved.

And hurt you, too, Keno. concluded the lipstick.

Butler wrote down the unconscious woman's name and address from her driver's license. She was Bridget Gunderson. He got her phone number. He already had all of Keno's contacts and information. He righted her champagne flute and cleaned up the spill with a dish towel from the kitchen. He blotted champagne from the plush carpet. *Good luck, Bridget,* he silently wished. He pulled off his gas mask, and gently kissed the top of her head. Laid a gloved hand briefly on Keno's head, as well.

Before he left, Pearce Butler shut off the music and helped himself to a wrapped Ghiradelli chocolate from a cut, crystal bowl. A shared sweet tooth with Mr. Reese. Then he turned off all the lights except one small lamp. To save electricity.

After all, he owned the place.

9

He let go the throttle when he saw colors in the night. The big snowmobile rumbled slowly to a halt. A ways ahead, wide arms of skimming blue, red, and white light cycled over snow and bare branches, rotating from a source out of sight. The lights were at the singlewide.

Ambulance? P.J. considered it, astride the purring Polaris. The old man was a heart attack waiting to happen. *Police? Fire?* He hadn't been gone that long. Fire trucks wouldn't get there that soon. Medics either.

He killed the halogen headlights. In darkness, P.J. throttled slowly off the road down a shallow ditch and up onto a flat, snow-blanketed soybean field. He approached the colored lights diagonally across the wide dormant field, going slow to keep the machine quiet. In seconds, he was deep in the field, where no roadway headlights could spot him. At that hour, none were evident.

P.J. shoved the Bud Light twelve-pack tight into his crotch. He loved these midnight beer runs in the middle of the week when he and the big Polaris had the run of the roads and fields. Tonight he'd ripped five miles east to Pigeon like an ass-fucked razorback for more beer before the bar closed and didn't see a single set of headlights. Now it looked like U.F.O.'s were in his front yard.

The scene ahead appeared quiet beyond the thrum of the snow-mobile. The Polaris Switchback was a mighty machine but not built for stealth. P.J. approached slowly to minimize engine noise, angling across the open field toward their road. A scrappy patch of wild birch at the northwest corner gave him cover. Unseen and unseeable, he watched colored police lights pulse through naked branches. Beyond the lights was the singlewide.

P.J. pushed his goggles up and narrowed his small eyes. He saw no movement other than the pulsing lights. He goosed the sled a few more yards and made out three vehicles. Two lit-up cruisers out front and a black SUV parked close to the front door. On their land. Peet land. The gate was open. They'd cut the chain.

P.J. shut off the engine, pulled back his parka hood and listened. Farmland silence. Maybe Big Bob and Dougie had already done the job.

He hadn't heard gunshots. But wouldn't have on a sled at full bore. No neighbors to hear. He pressed the starter and approached his home at a low 800cc rumble.

The road to their property was hardpacked dirt, snow-topped through March, and the iced ridges in the soybean field forced P.J. to ride half standing, legs flexing over each furrow. Beyond the rotating colors, the singlewide sat eighty yards back but the moving lights made it look closer. At the beanfield corner masked by trees, P.J. paused to reconnoiter.

The cruisers blocking their open gate were Michigan State Police. Trespassing on their land was a black SUV. A Suburban. On its roof a detachable light spinner spraying red and white light.

No ambulance. No fire trucks.

In the beanfield, P.J. could get no closer and stay hidden. He thought of approaching on foot but decided to stay with the sled.

He pocketed his goggles and studied the black SUV. It was clean. ATF, maybe FBI. He pulled off a glove, tore a gash in the twelve-pack, pulled out a can and cracked it quietly. Regloved, he took a long pull. The beer tasted crisp and good. He watched. He waited.

After a minute of nothing happening, he slid the empty back into the box.

He throttled up slow, aiming the Switchback toward the road. The closer he got, the slower he went. With a languid lurch that squeaked the suspension, he went down then up the ditch to the road. Fully exposed, he eased toward the flashing cruisers. He saw no one as he crossed the road diagonally.

Hugging the roadside closest to the singlewide, scrub trees gave him cover. The sled crept forward. Branch tips inches from his face reduced sight lines to a minimum. He stopped when the trees did and the view opened up. Still hidden, he could see half the singlewide. He shut off the engine. The sudden quiet pressed in his ears. All of P.J.'s senses sharpened.

Radios crackled from the unmanned cruisers, the only sound in cold night air. No wind. He inhaled through his nose for scent of cordite and burnt gunpowder. Smelled neither. Both Staties had parked across the gateway to block escape. The lead car's headlights illuminated straight country road for a hundred yards ahead before inky darkness took over.

P.J. pulled his right glove off with his teeth, unzipped his right coat pocket and pulled out The Runt. A Kel-Tec P3AT .38 caliber automatic. He stuffed the glove in the pocket.

The pistol was almost too small for his big hands and ugly as a dead skunk, but it had power. He'd had a gunsmith in Grindstone City switch out the trigger guard for a bigger hole and replace the factory grips with fat, non-slip Pachmayrs that made the small weapon uglier still.

A round was always chambered. He flicked off the safety but kept the hammer down. He squeezed the handgun gently, relishing its contours, balance, and weight. It empowered him.

Sound came from the front door. Voices. Animal fast, P.J. started the snowmobile under cover of door noise, footsteps, and talk. The Polaris thrummed awake low, like a panther on the hunt. Left hand pistol, right hand throttle. While not as accurate as his right, P.J. could still pepper bullseyes at 75 feet left-handed.

His brain got hot fast. Thoughts of the Waco massacre and Ruby Ridge washed over him as they often did. A dire prophecy from the Founding Fathers. A flaming beacon of truth. Freedom has to bleed.

He rumbled forward dark.

P.J. saw silhouettes emerge, backlit by the singlewide's open door. As they stepped toward him, the bare yellow light on the tall pole showed a state police trooper in body armor, sidearm holstered, leading Bob Peet down the steps. Bearded, grizzled, fat and drunk, with his hands cuffed behind him, his father looked weak and pale, his brown Carhartt coat draped over his shoulders. Behind them, another Statie led Dougie, also cuffed, downcast, drunk, and quiet. They were followed by a third trooper holding a 12-gauge alley sweeper on a combat sling, and last out was a thin and almost bald, narrow-faced man in a suit and dark overcoat. Other than the 12-gauge, P.J. saw no unholstered weapons. A second pump gun was strapped to the lead trooper's back.

P.J. knew the bright lightbulb on the pole combined with the lit-up cruisers would blind the lawmen for three or four seconds, starting now. He pressed the throttle as gently as petting a mouse. The Polaris crawled thirty feet toward the lit-up cruisers. If he could reach the far side, he'd have cover.

With ten feet to go, the big engine gave him away.

"Hey, that's P.J.!" yelled a trooper.

"Get him!" barked the suit, leaping off the steps. By the time the narrow-faced man hit the snow, his weapon was out. P.J. took one last look at his squinting, bleary-eyed father before squeezing the throttle.

The snowmobile jumped as the first trooper broke and ran toward the parked cruisers. The suit yanked open the SUV door. "P.J.! Stop!" yelled the trooper. It sounded like Karl Berndt, the stick-up-his-ass P.J. had played football with in middle school.

P.J. slowed on the far side of the cruisers and put two bullets in the rear cruiser and three more in the front cruiser as he roared ahead. A second trooper ran to the cars while the third, shotgun out, stayed with the prisoners. The SUV whipped around fast, but was denied exit by the cruisers blocking the gate. Instead, it spun on the fly and barreled toward the rusty link fence separating Peet property from the road. The fence might hold, it might not.

Before P.J.'s last gunshot faded, the SUV's siren pierced the air. P.J. had aimed at the electricals, hoping to disable both vehicles. His rounds were titanium-tipped cop-killers, personally hand-loaded. They'd penetrate deep.

The big snowmobile sped north on the straight road, passing the surging and rocking SUV on the other side of the chainlink. As P.J. accelerated, he heard the SUV crash into the fence behind him.

Either it got through or it didn't. He had one round left. The Runt
only held six. He lowered the hammer one-handed as the Polaris
hit top speed.

The Pro-Ride Switchback could do ninety m.p.h. all day long. At
104 a shimmy started that could shake the sled apart if you didn't
let up. When P.J. heard approaching sirens over the Switchback's
screaming engine, the dash readout said 103 on a flat, snowpacked
road with no headlights. He dared a backward glance. Lights were
coming, but he had a good jump.

Daddy and Dougie were gone. Probably never see them again.
Mama either, not that he cared. Dipshit woman. All his guns—gone.
His Heckler & Koch MP5. Four Uzis. Three AK's. The grenades. All
his knives. Took years to assemble that gear. And nothing left but
The Runt.

That bastard John. That fucking bastard. Or whatever that
blond faggot's real name was.

P.J. smelled stink on him from day one. That blond bastard was
a narc, a setup from the start. He'd warned Big Bob. He told him,
"Fuck this guy!" But Big Bob Peet knew fucking everything. Who to
trust. Who not to. And now Bob Peet was fucked. Probably for the
rest of his life. Because of that fucking faggot. P.J. squeezed the
throttle harder. The glowing readout jumped to 105. No shimmy
yet. But the headlights were closer, and the sirens, louder.

One more mile. He could make it. If he didn't hit an ice chunk
and disintegrate in a fireball.

The shimmy started.

Even in the dark, P.J. knew this road. His night vision honed
from countless hours of training. He knew the dips, rises, and wash-
boards and where they were and how the snow drifted. But how this

ride would end, he did not know. In less than a minute, it would come down to a chain. A chain that was supposed to be there.

The lights behind were gaining now, but he could tell it was only one siren. One cruiser. P.J. knew the sound. The Runt had disabled the other, and the SUV was M.I.A. But the cruiser was closing. P.J. sensed white and red bubblegum lights at the edge of his peripheral vision. The cruiser was topping 106. He wondered if his former schoolmate was driving.

Straight ahead darkness rose. Trees.

The end of the road.

Tall pines swept up in a towering black wall less than a quarter mile ahead. In the dark, they stood like somber giants, shoulder to shoulder. There the road stopped. Beyond that, nothing but tree trunks.

Reflected in his instrument panel, P.J. saw lights from the gaining cruiser. He flicked on the snowmobile's headlights. The twin beams lit up an unbroken wall of densely-packed, thick-trunked, fast-approaching trees.

But he saw what he was looking for. The sign: **Seasonal Road Only**.

Engine-deaf with tears freezing in his slitted eyes, P.J. looked past the small metal sign for a clue. Open only in dry months, the rough two-track ramped steeply off flat road into thick woods. It was unpassable on four wheels the rest of the year and chained for that reason.

As he sped forward, P.J. looked for the chain. He looked for the posts it was strung between. The posts were up the rise, set back in the woods.

The road ended in ten seconds, the speeding cruiser up his ass.

A loudspeaker ordered him to stop. A spotlight beam raked his back. P.J. slowed a little.

In the sweep of the cruiser's spotlight, P.J. glimpsed two posts in the woods a hundred feet away. He'd slowed to eighty.

He couldn't yet see the chain.

A voice on loudspeaker.

"Stop P.J.! Give up!"

P.J. didn't stop or give up. He gunned it as the road ended. With a lurch that lifted him high off the saddle, P.J. launched up the icy two-track at horrifying speed. Airborne. Trees swallowed him. What he saw next would kill him or not.

Two steel posts.

With the chain down.

God bless the snowmobilers.

With a fierce rebel yell, P.J. roared between the metal posts, boots on runners and ass off seat, his legs working suspension as he steered through dips and over humps, leaving the road and the law behind him. He sensed lights and skidding tires braking hard behind him. The siren silenced like a shamed dog. They knew where they couldn't go. He outran the searchlight in seconds.

P.J. was on home turf now. He knew this trail. He knew where it led. He slowed to twenty miles per hour. The trail was lumpy and drifted but other riders had been on it. No need to hurry. After two minutes P.J. began to breathe normal. After another minute, he let the Polaris stop. Zipped the Runt, safety on, back into his pocket. Put on his gloves.

He turned off the engine. Listened. Silence except for the hard sound of his own breathing, clouds panting from his mouth like a dray horse. His face freezing, his cheeks burnt, his beard iced.

They'd send cars to where the seasonal road emerged but P.J. wouldn't be there. He knew these woods. On a sled, there were many ways in, many ways out.

He looked down at his crotch. Still had the beer. The Bud Light twelve-pack still jammed between his thighs. He pulled out a cold can and cracked it.

In one long, satisfied swallow, he nearly drained it.

"Ahh," he said, beer breath condensing in the cold night air. He let his bull-thick shoulders and neck muscles loosen and relax. He finished the beer and had another in the silence of the dark winter woods.

Leered and spat.

A country boy can survive.

10

Terry hated neckties. A twenty-inch neck didn't help. He'd never gotten the hang of tying them. In the bathroom mirror, his face looked like a hairy balloon about to burst. The corduroy sport coat didn't help. It was too tight and made noise when he moved. He owned two ties, no suits, one coat. The ties were gifts. One from Christina, one from Hannah. The necktie Hannah gave him had Marvin the Martian on it. He wore the other one. It was Saturday.

Christina thought it was sweet that he wanted to go to the visitation. He let her think that. He still hadn't told her about the check. After the unsettling conversation with Deputy Weston and the sight of the check in an evidence bag, Terry didn't want to derail the weekend any further by initiating that particular conversation. He knew she'd get agitated, and the whole weekend would be shot. So when she asked what happened at the sheriff's department, he left most of it out. He just told her they wanted to clear up some facts.

The visitation was scheduled from 10:30 a.m. to 4 p.m. Terry had originally planned to arrive at 11:00. But he stalled. Lingered over breakfast. Put off showering. Watched ESPN.

When he finally emerged from the bedroom, dressed in his coat and tie, both Christina and Hannah said he looked very handsome. They liked it when he dressed up, which was rare. Even church, the few times the whole family went together each year, had become a no-tie affair, which was easier on everybody. Still, Christina always wore a dress or skirt to church, and Hannah did, too.

Christina had offered to accompany Terry to the funeral home. In fact, she'd wanted to go. But then on Friday after school at indoor soccer practice The Product rolled her ankle. It was swollen, but Hannah had not complained much, initially. She'd been bravely stoic all Friday night. But today she was ten again and a bit needy. Christina made a noon appointment at the clinic.

Clayton-Burroughs Funeral Home was one of the older, more established funeral homes in Ann Arbor. Terry had never been there before. He could count the funeral homes he'd been to on one hand. This one was only three blocks from the Big House, Michigan Stadium, home of the Wolverines. It was tucked away on a quiet side street that was mostly residential. As Terry pulled into the crowded parking lot, a considerable number of students cheerfully walked the sidewalks *en route* to happier destinations than a funeral home. The bright sun shining in a blue sky seemed celebratory, a coming attraction for spring.

There was no place to park. The funeral home's large lot was filled. Terry saw a valet and winced. He dug his worn and weary wallet out. He had a five. No ones. He pulled the Sebring up to a white-shirted, black-vested young man in a short, dark jacket, who opened the driver's door when the car stopped. Terry left the lone key in the ignition, taking his other keys with him. He got out and accepted the ticket the young man offered to him.

"Thanks," said Terry. He extended the five.

"No, sir," said the young man politely. "Complimentary."

"Well, this is for you." But the man raised both palms and backed up a step.

"No, sir. Thank you, but we can't accept. It's the family's wish. We're being taken care of."

"Oh," said Terry. "Okay. Well, thank you." Terry put the bill back into his wallet. He stepped under a long awning as the young man climbed into the Sebring. Under the awning, the air was heated by two hissing propane heaters. There was a metal railing. As Terry took his time walking up the carpeted walk, an older couple, older than DeGraaf, stepped out of the building and descended the steps. The funeral home was white brick with fluted columns and black shutters. Large brass coach lanterns were mounted on either side of double doors. The woman in the couple approaching wore an expensive-looking coat with a dark fur collar and matching hat. She was crying softly and dabbing her eyes with a lace-edged handkerchief. She wore beige gloves. The man looked older than she, bent and stooped, solemn and bereft. His lips were thin and bloodless. He held his wife's elbow gently as they ambled slowly toward Terry on the no-slip runner. Under different circumstances, they'd probably look ten years younger. But not today.

Terry made what he hoped was the right face and offered a small nod. He got small nods back. Very small. As if death's close proximity restrained movement in the living.

Inside the funeral home, Terry was greeted with a stock-photo smile from a meticulously-groomed man of late middle age in a pristine gray suit. "Mr. DeGraaf?" asked Terry. Smiling neither too little nor too much, the man silently retreated on thick carpet and gestured down a long, wide hall with the eerie politeness unique to undertakers.

"Good morning," said the man. "Down and to the left."

"Thanks," said Terry. He checked his watch. Almost noon. Later than he wanted.

He didn't hurry. The funeral home was fancier than the others he'd been to. More upscale. Elegant. Pricey couches and chairs that looked like they'd never been sat in. Ornate woodwork. Stairways that went up to he couldn't guess where. Flowers everywhere. Big chandeliers. There wasn't anything wrong with it, but you wanted to get out as fast as possible.

At the end of the hall, French doors opened into a murmuring, crowded room. It was packed. There were half a dozen people in the hallway, waiting to get in. Another door let people out.

Terry got in line and tried to see inside. Being six-two had its advantages. The crowd seemed mostly older couples. But there were some younger couples, too. Closer to Terry's generation. He also spotted a few teens, chattier and cheerier and more casually dressed than their parents or grandparents. Less affected by the presence of death. Maybe neighbors or friends of the family. Maybe grandkids.

Terry waited behind an Indian- or Pakistani-looking couple of about sixty, he guessed. The man in a dark blue suit, white shirt and dark tie. She wore a tangerine-colored sari type of thing. Terry didn't know the fashion rules with saris, but it looked to him like pretty thin material for February. She had the dark red circle on her forehead that was not unusual to see in Ann Arbor. Terry didn't know what the mark was called or what it meant. Ann Arbor was home to many highly educated Indian, Pakistani, Asian,

African, European, and Canadian scientists, doctors, researchers, academics, and entrepreneurs.

The line crept slowly into the big room. Terry signed the guest book. He caught a flowery whiff of grandma perfume as two older ladies passed by him on their way out. Over the heads of the bereaved throng, he saw the casket on the far side of the large room. The top half was open. From where he stood, he could just make out the tip of Michael DeGraaf's nose. The only person in the room he knew.

Terry headed toward the casket. There had to be a hundred people in the room, all of them talking. They could've used a bigger room. He stepped around small chatting clusters, some standing, some sitting on couches or folding chairs set in rows facing the casket. He wound his way toward the deceased.

The casket was a golden-hued wood like honey pine with brushed bronze handles. The satin inside the color of French vanilla ice cream. Dozens of extravagant flower arrangements were displayed throughout the room and filled the floor near the casket. He'd never seen so many large and beautiful flower arrangements in his life.

Standing before the casket, Terry looked down at the drawn cheeks and sunken, shut eyes of a dead man with whom he'd spent maybe three minutes. The last minutes of an obviously very full life. Minutes that rightly should have been spent with someone else. With loved ones. Family and friends. Not with a total stranger.

Bathed, combed, heavily made-up and lifeless, he didn't look to Terry much like the same man. The man he'd prayed for. Made a promise to. Took a check from.

Terry was alone at the casket. No one else close by. DeGraff's crisp white shirt and violet necktie looked fresh and hopeful. The suit looked expensive. He couldn't see the shoes but imagined them polished. He looked for some sort of indentation or divot in DeGraaf's chest but saw nothing odd. *That wouldn't be too hard to smooth out,* thought Terry.

There was a kneeler of maroon needlepoint between him and the casket. Low voices approaching from behind startled him. Without thinking and to escape awkward conversation, Terry stepped forward and kneeled on the kneeler. He interlaced his fingers and bowed his head, closing his eyes and wondering what the heck he was doing. The voices behind him quieted respectfully. He felt foolish. He was faking. Had nothing to say. So he didn't speak and tried not to think. But found himself thinking of DeGraaf's soul. He didn't mean to, but he did. He wanted Mr. DeGraaf…Mike—to have a soul. On the kneeler with his hands clasped, Terry's thoughts ran in fragments, incomplete sentences. He thought about God. About heaven and *I hope you're with God, and I hope everything's okay.* But all jumbled and confused.

Amen.

Terry opened his eyes and rose and looked one last time at the body in the casket. The people behind him waited. The remains of Mike DeGraaf looked shockingly old. Even covered with blood and wine and his hair wild and wet and his breath coming in jagged gasps, he hadn't looked this old. In the casket, he looked like all the air had gone out of him. Terry wondered if he still wore his wedding ring. Or if they took that off. He twisted his own gold band. He'd just as soon his family keep his ring. He should tell Christina that.

Terry turned from the casket, noting an older man and two

older women waiting patiently behind him. Three white-haired heads with sweet, sad smiles. Terry nodded and felt very out of place. Working his way to the exit, he hid by looking at photos mounted on black boards fixed to floor easels or set on side tables. Photos of the life of a man he didn't know. A life of family and friends and travel and accomplishments. A life that ended in freezing darkness in the middle of nowhere with a complete stranger.

The photos spanned decades. Family gatherings. Vacations with friends. Golf, skiing, Europe, Asia. Sailboat snapshots in what looked like the Caribbean or Mexico. The Eiffel Tower. A Chinese junk. As Terry moved from board to board, he sensed more of the man. Beach sunsets and catamarans. Hawaiian shirts. Grass-hut bars serving margaritas. Terry could relate to none of it. He concentrated on the faces. Beaming smiles locked in time. Love and friendship recorded for future use. This was the future use.

As Terry worked his way along the wall of photos, he soon identified the wife.

And the daughters. All three of them.

No sons. Now and then some men appeared with the daughters and family in some pictures. A couple of grandkids, too.

Mrs. DeGraaf, the matriarch, had what Terry thought of as an Irish face. Round with merry features and pale skin. Always in a big hat when in the sun, red-haired and pleasant-looking. Her smile, easy and genuine. In Rome. In London. At ski resorts. Deep-sea fishing. Pheasant hunting. With horses and on boats and at the beach. Always at her husband's side, her arm in his or her hand holding his. Lots of shots of the DeGraafs and friends smiling with raised wine glasses.

The daughters appeared in many photos, too, but seldom did all three daughters appear in one photo. Two were willowy, dark-haired and pretty. In some shots, the older brunette was magazine-cover stunning. The younger brunette resembled her older sister but was gawkier. Shorter. Her ears stuck out somewhat. Mouth a bit wide. The older sister didn't have an awkward bone, curve or eyelash in, or upon, her body.

The third daughter didn't look at all like the other two. She was either the oldest or the middle, Terry couldn't tell. She didn't have the high cheekbones and huge, dark eyes that were so attractive in her sisters. She was more like a younger version of her mother. Short. Ruddy-cheeked. Thick-waisted. Crinkly, reddish hair.

As Terry worked through the photos, it became clear that the youngest daughter was the clown. As a kid, she stuck out her tongue. Crossed her eyes. Wore silly hats and nutty sunglasses. She reminded Terry of Hannah.

A shot of the crinkly-haired, round-faced daughter caught Terry's eye. It showed just her and Michael DeGraaf in front of a Christmas tree too big for a private home. Maybe an office party. It was the only shot he saw of DeGraaf alone with this daughter. Both smiled stiffly. He was in a suit and tie. She wore a white turtleneck. One of her eyes was half closed in the shutter blink. Mike DeGraaf held a glass of red wine. Her hands were out of frame. Among all the photos displayed, Terry saw only one with Mike and all three sisters together as adults. It was also taken at Christmastime in front of a decorated tree. The youngest wore a Santa hat, and she and her father were the only ones smiling. The other two weren't.

Two pretty daughters and one who wasn't. Life wasn't fair. Not when judged by a camera. And these days cameras were everywhere.

As he worked his way toward the exit, looking at photos and avoiding conversation, Terry sidestepped a cluster of sad, chatting people and turned to face two large couches in the center of the crowded room. On one of them was Mrs. DeGraaf.

He recognized her from the photos. Her hair short, curly red and going gray. A round, pale face lined with wrinkles. Powdered, lipsticked, and rouged. She spoke softly and pleasantly to two senior women who stood nodding in front of her, most likely widows themselves. Welcoming a new sister.

Mrs. DeGraaf wore a light gray suit with a pale pink blouse. Terry saw no jewelry at all except her wedding and engagement rings and tasteful pearl earrings. Next to her on the couch was one of the brunette daughters. The older one. More striking and beautiful in person than photos could possibly record. Alpha-class. She was attentive to her mother and held her mother's hand, listening earnestly to the condolences offered by the two senior women. Even in mourning, she was alluring and beautiful. Standing next to her, just past the arm of the sofa, was her husband. Had to be. Average height and looks. Solidly built. Dark suit. Territorial. There was no mistaking.

On the other sofa, facing the mother, was the youngest daughter, solemn and drawn, long dark hair framing her pale face. Sitting next to her was her husband, his arm around her. She was pregnant, maybe midterm. This husband was fair-skinned, simpler and softer-looking than the other husband.

The third daughter was not with them. The one that looked like the mother. Terry scanned the room. His trained editor's eye didn't spot her. Even on his tiptoes, he didn't see her.

A sob pulled Terry's attention back to the group. The pregnant daughter pressed a wad of damp, crumpled Kleenex to her mouth, even though there were fresh boxes all around. Her cheeks glistened with fresh tears. She wiped at them with the sodden tissue. Her husband, head bowed, gently stroked her back over and over. Of all the family, this daughter seemed to be taking it the hardest. Her husband spoke close to her ear, and she nodded. The other husband yawned and crossed his arms, looking around the room. Glancing briefly at, then past, Terry.

"Thank you for coming," said Mrs. DeGraaf, as the pair of murmuring ladies stepped delicately away. Without warning she turned and looked at Terry. She had a gently expectant smile on her round, upturned face. She nodded graciously to him. He was next.

Terry swallowed. He couldn't step back. So he stepped forward. A stranger nobody knew. All their eyes on him. Everyone waiting for him to speak. After a long, awkward moment, Terry extended his big hand to Mrs. DeGraaf, who remained seated. She gently grasped it with her small, dry one without taking her bright blue eyes off his. Her hand had spots.

He bent over and spoke. "Mrs. DeGraaf, I'm very sorry for your loss." She kept her smile locked in place and nodded gently. He released her hand and straightened up and looked around at the family. "I'm sorry for all your losses," said Terry, which didn't sound quite right. They seemed puzzled. "I was, uh," Terry started, "I found Mr. DeGraaf after the, uh … after he went off the road." Terry coughed into his fist. "The other night." Now they understood. The younger daughter released a fresh round of sobs. Her husband, eyes on Terry, continued to gently stroke her back.

Terry felt terrible. Mrs. DeGraaf hadn't altered her expression at all. Her gracious smile was unchanged. He wasn't sure she had understood him. "Mrs. DeGraaf, my name is Terry Holbrook. I was in the car behind your husband when…" He stopped talking.

"You knew Michael?" she asked, her head tilting slightly. Not 100 percent lucid. Terry wondered if she'd taken a pill. Or been given one.

"No, ma'am. But I tried to help."

"Oh," said the standing husband. The solidly built one. Connection made. "You got the check." A humorless smile flicked across his lips. His eyes narrowed.

Mrs. DeGraaf looked at her son-in-law. "What?" she said. The son-in-law pointed at Terry but spoke to her.

"This is the guy dad wrote the check to. Remember? The check? For two million?" He put both hands in his pockets and rocked up on the balls of his feet when he spoke to Terry. "Nice of you to come by."

Asshole, thought Terry.

"Look, I don't care about the check."

"Good, give it back."

"Shut up, Bryce," the beauty spoke, meaning, *This is not the time or place.* Terry caught the tone but didn't see her speak, trapped momentarily in Bryce's withering gaze. When Terry did look, she was looking squarely at him. Fury scarcely suppressed. Rich, dark hair tumbled onto black dress shoulders. Brown eyes miles deep and coldly disdainful.

"Well, you're not going to get it anyway," said Bryce. Terry ignored him and spoke to Mrs. DeGraaf.

"Mrs. DeGraaf, I was with your husband when he died." He saw tears welling in the older lady's eyes, and he tried to smile but failed. "He said to tell you he loves you," Terry lied. But what could it hurt? Terry turned to face all of them. "He said to tell you all that he loves you." Not very convincing.

"Thank you," said the pregnant daughter's husband. He looked up briefly at Terry then back to his wife, whom he continued to hold and comfort. Sandy-haired, balding a little, he let go of his wife to stand and extend his hand. "Thank you," he repeated. They made eye contact, the husband's eyes dewy, nodded, and shook hands. The man sat down and resumed comforting his wife. Terry turned back to Mrs. DeGraaf. "I know this probably doesn't mean much but ... he didn't seem to be in much pain. Considering." He could hear the younger daughter sob again at this. He had to get out of here. "I mean, what I want to tell you is ..." *What did he want to tell them?*

The older sister seemed to stiffen. Husband Bryce looked like he wanted to kill him. Terry looked back to Mrs. DeGraaf.

"What I want to tell you, Mrs. DeGraaf, was that your husband ..." He looked at the daughters. "Your father ..." Back to the mother. "Asked me to pray for him." The youngest daughter looked up immediately and spoke for the first time.

"He did?" She laid her hand on her stomach.

"Yes," Terry nodded. "He asked me to pray for him and I did."

"What? Are you a priest or something?" asked Bryce.

"No."

"Are you Christian?" asked the youngest daughter. For the first time, she seemed fully alert. Big, brown eyes so similar to her big sister's. Her big sister and both of the husbands looked at their shoes or elsewhere.

"Well. Yeah," said Terry. "Presbyterian, I guess." He struggled to hold her imploring, wet-eyed look. Couldn't for long. He glanced away. Looked over at the casket across the crowded room. Again saw the tip of Mike DeGraaf's nose. It looked like a pink gumball. He looked back at the family. "I did the best I could."

"Thank you," said the beautiful older daughter. She stood, tugged her skirt straight, and offered Terry her hand. He shook it. It was warm and tan and dry. Recently in Florida maybe. Must be nice. Long, soft fingers. She wore an expensive-looking black knit dress with long sleeves. High at the throat. "Fran Siehling," she said. "This is my husband, Bryce." Bryce stepped forward, and the two men briefly shook hands. "This is my mother, Millie." Terry and Millie exchanged nods. "And this is Becky and Jim." Terry leaned down to shake hands with Becky and shook hands again with Jim, who nodded back. Fran smoothed her dress behind her, sat, and again took her mother's hand. Bryce resumed his position outside the couch arm.

Then came a very long and extremely awkward pause. Terry shifted heavily from foot to foot. His brown loafers weren't shined. Hadn't been in years.

He wanted to ask about the third daughter.

"Anyway," said Terry, "I just wanted to pay my respects."

"Thank you," Fran repeated. Then, as if on cue, they all completely stopped paying any attention to him.

Poof. He ceased to exist.

Terry got out of there as fast as he could.

11

One eyelid broke its gummy seal. As harsh sunlight painfully broke through, P.J. knew he'd never see his favorite hunting knife again, his black-handled Buck Special hunter, but right now he felt like its long, drop-forged steel blade was pounded right between his eyes. Uncle Bill didn't fuck around when the whisky started flowing. With effort to avoid puking, P.J. levered himself slowly to an upright position on the shabby couch.

The couch was threadbare and stained, and he didn't remember seeing it before. Both armrests were split, showing dirty yellow batting. His snowmobile boots were on but unzipped. The couch couldn't hold all of him. He was sore from sleeping bent. On the filthy plywood floor was his parka. Bright midday sun poured yellowish through grimy windows.

When he moved his head, the knife blade twisted, making neurons flare and spin behind his eyes like angry lightning bugs. Then he threw up.

He cursed and reached for the rank pillow he'd slept on, wiped his mouth with it, then dropped it on the pink splat of vomit on the floor.

He was in some sort of garage loft. Wheel rims and hubcaps stacked everywhere. Struts, axles, and other junk strewn on the floor. A truck transmission lay across cinder blocks. Beyond where the floor edge dropped to the garage below, a chain pulley hung. Now it all came back. He closed his eyes to slow the spinning. He was in Dearborn.

He'd lost the cops easily. Emerging from the woods on a twisting trail, headlights dark, P.J. had shot east to an ex-girlfriend's house outside Port Sanilac, staying off-road as much as possible. After food and a courtesy fuck, he took her car, promising to return soon. She wouldn't turn him in. She loved him and was ugly as sin and gave him money and cigarettes. Plus, she kept the Polaris, which was worth more than her cash and beat-to-shit car combined.

Uncle Bill ran a chop shop from his residence on a desolate, virtually abandoned industrial row on the south edge of Dearborn, just west of Detroit. How he wound up in that treeless, lifeless, cinderblock armpit was anybody's guess, but P.J. figured there was pussy involved. In anything with Uncle Bill, there was always pussy involved. Years ago, for pussy-related reasons unknown, Bill changed his name to Jake Strumm. He wasn't Bill Peet anymore. But he was P.J.'s uncle. And he was afraid of P.J., which helped.

P.J. brought up a nasty lung oyster from too many bong hits and spit it behind the couch. He lit a Marlboro Light, the girl-friend's brand, and looked for something to drink. A metal sink hung from a wall. He stood too fast, a surge of blood pushing behind his eyeballs, and he tried to keep the skull hammers at bay. He walked slowly to the sink, stepping around car parts. The deep metal basin was rust-stained. A long-dead chipmunk lay curled by the drain. No water came out of the taps. He would've sucked the head off the dead chipmunk if he thought there was any moisture in it.

He found a half-full longneck with a cigarette butt in it and drank. Any port in a storm. Swishing as much puke out of his mouth as he could, he spat into the sink onto the dead chipmunk.

Dearborn is a workingman's town. Transformed from pastoral farm community to molten-metalworkers burg by Henry Ford's titanic 20th-century empire, Dearborn became the lodestone of the automotive age. By the 21st century, Dearborn had also become the home of the largest Arab-American Muslim community in the United States. No one knew why.

A knock at the door below.

"Hey! You up?"

"Yeah," croaked P.J.

Uncle Bill brought in a wintry gust and climbed the metal ladder. A plastic grocery bag swung heavily from one hand. He resembled Big Bob in the face but not as old or big or fat. But the sparse ginger hair, bald spot, and russet beard streaked with gray all spoke familiar.

Bill sniffed. "You puke? I smell puke."

"I didn't puke. This shithole just smells like puke."

Bill, a.k.a. Jake Strumm, said, "Lyin' sacka shit," eyeing the pillow. P.J. didn't speak. He sucked on his cigarette. Bill tossed him a can of Pabst from the bag and opened one for himself. P.J. opened his and poured half down his throat fast. Oh god. That helped.

"Last night you said Bobby was in jail."

"Yeah," said P.J., finishing the beer. He flung the can over the edge, where it clattered below against odd lots of sheet metal; car and truck doors, hoods, quarter panels. Bill followed the trajectory with his eyes but said nothing.

"He getting out?"

"No."

P.J. ran through last night in his head. The cops at the single-wide. The run to Port Sanilac. Two hours from there to here in a beat-to-shit car. By the time he got to Uncle Bill's, it was four. Bill's lot fenced and gated. No lights and no dogs and he didn't even know if his uncle still lived there. He'd ditched his phone in the woods to avoid being tracked. Tried sleeping in the car but froze. Climbed the fence and tripped a silent alarm.

Uncle Bill had confronted thieves before. Shotgun cocked, he was out of the tiny house adjacent to the big garage pronto. A little horseplay with P.J.'s hands reaching for the sky soon turned into a boisterous, foul-mouthed family reunion. The two stayed up, drinking and hitting the bong until first light. Uncle Bill was always the party boy.

"I need to know something," P.J. had said at 4:30 in the morning, exhaling a lungful of bong smoke. Bill's homegrown weed was evil harsh going in, but its kick couldn't be denied.

"What?" said Bill in a tattered La-Z-Boy. His eyes drifted to a big, dusty TV where pay-cable tits bobbled. The small living room, a bachelor crap hole, was strewn with ashtrays, beer spills, and old, stained pizza boxes.

"There's a guy I bet chopped a black Ram." That's what P.J. would do. "A pickup. Like a 2013, 2014. Maybe in the last month. Little blond faggot." He pressed a grimy finger beneath his nose. "Little blond faggot mustache."

"Like a real faggot?" Bill limped a wrist.

"How the fuck would I know?" barked P.J. "But skinny. Small. Real blond, like dyed blond. Little fuckin' narc fucked us over. I'm gonna fuckin' kill him." Hate always cleared his head. Sharpened his vision.

Bill torched the bong bowl and sucked deep. Shook his head as he held it. "Nope," he squeaked, lungs bursting. "I ain't seen no black Rams." Meaning through his shop. He exhaled an acrid gray cloud. "Or any blond faggots."

P.J. crushed his cigarette, half-smoked. "I gotta get some fucking sleep."

Bill would have none of it. He stood, got two more beers, and shoved an open can in P.J.'s hand.

"Fuck you," said Uncle Bill.

"Come on, man," said P.J. "I drove all fucking night."

"Fuck you," said Bill, knocking the full can gently against P.J.'s head. "Come on." Bill sucked at his own can.

"Where am I gonna sleep anyway?"

"Over the garage. Come on, you big pussy, drink with your uncle. I got a bottle of Wild Turkey. Been saving it for a special occasion. Most of it, anyway."

P.J. eyed his uncle steady. Pesky little shit. Now was not the time. He took the beer. Bill's face split into a snaggly grin, and he scampered off to get the whisky.

Now, hours later, the Turkey long plucked, P.J. finished his wakeup beer. There was some heat in the loft from a propane burner below. A dirty glare pushed through a pair of filmy windows. Pink insulation stapled to rafters sagged where water came in.

"I need to find who chopped the Ram," said P.J.

"Good morning to you, too." Bill wrinkled his nose. "You puked, man." It was past 1 p.m. on a cold, cloudless day.

P.J. silenced his uncle with a look. Bill looked down, scuffed the floor.

"I need to find who chopped the Ram," repeated P.J., stepping close enough to tower over the smaller man.

"You got a VIN?" Uncle Bill asked finally, glancing up, then down again. Vehicle Identification Number.

"No, I don't got a fuckin' VIN."

"Well, how d'you know it was chopped?"

"It was chopped!" roared P.J., slapping the near-empty beer can out of his uncle's hand.

Blond little shit. Blond fucking John.

Of course, it was chopped. Blond John was a careful little shit. P.J. knew how these things went. He'd spent his entire life in illegal activity.

"I want that little fucker by the balls," said P.J. with Bill carefully nodding along. "Big Bob's in jail. Dougie's in jail. Shitloads of people in jail now 'cause of that little fuck!"

Bill kept his mouth shut, watching P.J. kick two big truck tire rims over the loft edge into the garage below, where they crashed around and broke something. Roaring like an animal, P.J. then heaved a cinderblock, cutting his hands on the rough edges. Then he threw a gearbox, smashing glass and more below. He turned, sucking air, panting at his motionless uncle.

"How many guns you got?"

12

"You got a message." Belinda waved the pink message slip at Terry as he stepped in the door. It was Monday morning.

"I don't get messages. Good morning."

"Good morning. You got this one."

"When?"

"Five minutes ago."

It was 9:15. He plucked the message from her fingers. They were the first two people there. Jeff was at a business breakfast in Detroit.

"Thank you," said Terry.

"You're welcome," said Belinda, then added, "She sounded plastic."

Saturday afternoon, after the funeral visitation, Terry had told Christina about the check. About the promise. About *Save my daughter*.

"You have to give it back," she'd said, like he knew she would. They were in their bedroom, where Hannah couldn't hear, sitting on the bed.

He said he couldn't, that the bank had the check.

"We won't get the money," he said, picturing the snarky husband, Bryce. "There's nothing to give back."

"What about the daughter?" asked Christina after a few moments.

"I don't know," said Terry. He'd told her about the two daughters he'd met, and their husbands. And about the third one who wasn't there.

"Did you ask about her?"

"No," said Terry. "I just wanted to get out of there."

They held hands silently for a while, wordlessly agreeing to let the matter drop. At least for now. Terry still clinging to dreams of hopped up cars and bass boats. Christina thinking about the meaning of promises.

Terry spent the rest of the weekend carrying sore-ankled Hannah wherever she wanted to go, and he relished every moment of it. To the couch. To the kitchen. To her bedroom. Back to the couch. It made him so happy. The softness of her hair on his cheek. Her sweet child smell. Light as a toy and laughing and talking and hugging his neck. They watched TV together, and the family played Jenga and Monopoly on Saturday night. Somehow Hannah always won. Tired but content, Terry and Christina made quiet love after their daughter was asleep. It had been awhile. The last thing he remembered before drifting off was his wife telling him that he was a good man.

Pink message slip in hand, Terry hung up his coat on the back of his office door, powered up the AVID mainframe, turned on all his screens, and only then did he look closely at the message. *Call Tina at McReady Chomsky.* And a number. He didn't recognize any of the names or the number. Pulled out his phone and punched in the digits. Shut the door as an afterthought.

"Hi, this is Terry Holbrook," he said to the woman that answered.

"Good morning, Mr. Holbrook. Thank you for calling back. My name is Tina Kozak with McReady Chomsky. I'm Mr. Cohen's assistant. Mr. Abraham Cohen." She didn't sound like plastic to Terry. More like satin.

"Okay," said Terry.

"Mr. Cohen is Mr. DeGraaf's attorney."

"Oh," said Terry.

Is, not *was.*

"Mr. Cohen would like to meet with you." A brief pause. "Would that be possible, Mr. Holbrook?" She sounded like a college-educated stewardess. On a private jet.

"Sure," said Terry. "I guess so." *How did they know where he worked?*

"Wonderful. When would be a convenient time?"

"Well," said Terry. "Where are you located?"

"Downtown Ann Arbor, sir. Not far from you."

Absurdly, Terry glanced at the ceiling for hidden surveillance cameras.

"Would it be possible to meet at our office?" she asked. "Either tomorrow, Tuesday morning, at eight or ten, or tomorrow afternoon at four. Or Wednesday at ten-thirty. Or Thursday before eleven."

His screens now fully awake and glowing, he stared at a Ford Explorer frozen on a monitor with a compelling lease price in big, bold type next to it.

Terry closed his eyes and rubbed them hard with his free hand, fingers and thumb massaging his tired sockets. "Um, sure. What's this about?"

The check, of course.

"I don't know, sir. I could ask Mr. Cohen. Would you like me to ask? I'd be happy to."

"No, that's okay. How about today?" Get it over with. Get back to Hannah and Christina and watching basketball and cutting Thurgood TV spots.

"Let me ask. His schedule is full, but sometimes he'll move things. I'm going to put you on hold for a moment if that's okay." She waited for a response.

"Sure."

"Very good." She left the line. The hold music was classical. Vivaldi, he was pretty sure. With a few keystrokes, Terry crept the lease price super a few pixels to the left so the Explorer's front tires didn't touch the font.

"He can meet you here today at four," said Tina Kozak brightly, coming back on the line. He envisioned a perfect smile. "Do you know where we are?"

"No."

She gave him the address. He wrote it down. It looked familiar. Main Street. Close to work. That was good. He didn't like to miss work.

"By the way. Tina? Right?"

"Yes, sir, I'm Tina."

"How did you know where I work?"

"I was given this number to call."

"Oh," said Terry. "Okay." He wondered who was doing the giving. "I'll be there at four."

"Thank you, sir. Goodbye."

* * *

No wonder the address seemed familiar. McReady Chomsky was in the same building as the Ann Arbor Third Bank. The bank on the check. Coincidence-I-don't-think-so.

Terry walked through the marble lobby, past the bank's expansive glass wall, to the elevators. He looked into the bank but saw no sign of Ms. Baker. He saw Jade, the friendly, glasses-wearing teller who had helped him last week, but her attention was on her customer. He looked away before she could catch him looking.

At the elevators, Terry perused a discreet tenant registry. McReady Chomsky was on the fifth floor. The top floor. He got in and pressed 5.

Terry stepped out into a rich, cherry-paneled vestibule with a large skylight. The floor was marble, a warm brown. Two large potted plants in built-in marble planters flanked frosted double doors with bronze door pulls. There was no company name sign. The elevator landing was small. The only other visible door had a pictogram next to it indicating stairs.

Terry walked to the frosted glass and pulled a bronze handle. The metal felt surprisingly smooth and warm. Maybe someone had entered moments before.

He stepped into the presence of a beautiful blond woman with an earbud and perfect posture sitting behind a curved pecan reception desk. The wood was beautiful and lustrous. In fact, everything in the waiting room looked perfect. The lighting, warm and indirect. The furniture, artwork, and craft rugs possessed an elegant, understated richness. The two modern paintings on the wall were originals. Fresh flowers brightened a dark quartz coffee table in front of a buttery leather couch the color of espresso latte.

"May I help you?" asked the blond woman with an unapologetically perfect smile. *Must be Tina,* thought Terry. Her dress was not quite robin's egg blue. Her lipstick and nails matched, a pillowy soft red. She wore pearls. Simple rings. Pretty classy for a receptionist.

"Hi, my name is Terry Holbrook. I'm here to see Abraham Cohen. I'm a little early."

"That's perfectly all right, Mr. Holbrook. If you'll please take a seat, I'll see if Mr. Cohen's available. I'm Tina. We spoke earlier. Would you like a water? Or coffee? Or tea?"

"No, I'm fine. Thank you."

"Would you like me to hang up your coat?"

"No, that's okay." Terry took a seat in a large, comfortable armchair that complemented the couch and picked up a magazine from the selection on the coffee table. Every magazine was new. They were arranged in an artful fan so visitors could see the titles. Terry failed to avoid checking out Tina Kozak's posterior as she stood, smoothed, turned, and swayed down the executive hallway behind her. He was only human. He selected *Travel and Leisure.* Beautiful Crete on the cover. He thumbed through breathtaking destinations he would surely never visit.

He was looking at an article about ancient farms in Cork, Ireland, when he heard, "Mr. Holbrook?"

Terry looked up to see a small, dark, exquisitely tailored man of maybe forty or forty-five step toward him. Terry put the magazine down and stood as the shorter man extended his hand and smiled. White teeth against a deep complexion and a relentless four o'clock shadow. His hair was short, black, and neat. Large nose and thick eyebrows. A white pocket square. It looked like silk.

"Abe Cohen."

"Terry Holbrook." They shook. They smiled at each other. Terry had at least 100 pounds on the guy. It made Terry uncomfortable.

"Why don't we go to my office?"

"Sure."

With that, the small attorney did a crisp about-face and strode past the receptionist. Terry followed. Tina Kozak flashed Terry another radiant smile. He smiled back, letting his expression linger longer than normal just to keep hers on him for a few moments more. The extra effort was worth it.

Cohen's office was a corner. High ceilings, large windows, and a perfect view of Ann Arbor's picture-postcard Main Street. Though barely 4 p.m., the sun was February low, a pink-orange orb in a darkening sky. From high up, Main Street's beloved 19th- and early 20th-century red brick storefronts looked like sweet old relatives vying for position amongst a taller, sleeker, younger generation.

Terry's editing eye found nothing out of balance in his surroundings. Cohen's office was a clean, professionally decorated space: modern without being slick. A large desk of reclaimed wood with a wide bookcase behind it. A single artwork occupied an eggshell wall above a low Eames black leather couch. A pin spot in the ceiling lit the framed piece: an Ansel Adams. The face of a mountain, black and white, with a line of undulating pine trees at its base. A spectral crescent moon, haloed, hovered high and to the right in a cloudless sky. Gallery glass. It looked like Adams' signature gelatin silver printing process. Terry was very familiar with Adams' work but had never seen this particular photograph.

"Let's sit by the window," suggested Cohen, ushering Terry toward a pair of contemporary wooden armchairs with matching table near the corner. "We might get a good sunset. Sometimes this time of year it's beautiful. But brief." Cohen directed him to the chair with the best view and took the other for himself. The floor covering was a quiet textile mat on hardwood. "Can I get you anything?" asked Cohen politely.

"No, I'm good. Thanks."

"You can take your coat off if you like."

"I'm good," said Terry. He shifted and his leather sleeves squeaked. Cohen nodded.

"May I call you Terry?"

"That's my name."

"And please call me Abe."

"Okay."

Terry spotted a maize-and-blue U of M football helmet on the desk. A burst of color in the earth-toned office. Bold, thick, metallic gold handwriting on it said, *To Abe, Stay tough. Bo*

Bo Shembechler.

"That's nice," said Terry, pointing to the helmet.

"Thanks," said Cohen.

"U of M law school?" said Terry.

"No. Undergrad." Then Terry saw the Harvard Law School medallion in the bookcase behind the desk.

"I'm from here, though. Ann Arbor. My dad was a chemistry professor. My mom worked for the University."

Terry nodded. Cohen appraised his guest.

"Terry, I wanted to see you because Michael DeGraaf was a friend of mine. A close friend. Yes, I represent him as power of attorney, but I've known him since I was a kid." The eyes of the two men met. Cohen's, brown and sensitive. "I used to mow his lawn, rake his leaves, shovel his snow. Even washed and waxed his car. When he was starting out, I lived a few blocks over. At that time, in that particular neighborhood, no one else would give a Jewish boy a job. Any job."

Terry knew where this was going. He just wondered how long it would take.

"He seemed like a good guy," was all Terry could think of to say.

"He was. He was a good guy."

Terry looked out at the sinking sun. *Probably be done with this and out the door before it even sets.* "I imagine this is about the check," said Terry.

"Yes."

"Where is it, anyway? Cops still have it?"

Cohen sat with his hands steepled on the small table, his eyes on Terry. Then he arose, walked to his desk, opened the pencil drawer, and withdrew the flat plastic bag with the stained check in it. The evidence bag. "No, I have it." Cohen brought it to the table, set it between them, and sat down. Terry hadn't seen it in a while and had trouble keeping his eyes off it. Two million dollars. Made out to him. Signed. And literally sealed. Terry looked at Cohen, who looked at him with concern and, perhaps, sympathy.

"You with the bank?" asked Terry.

"No. But I'm on good terms with the bank."

Terry nodded. *What the hell was that supposed to mean?*

"Okay," said Terry. "This isn't being recorded, is it?"

Cohen blushed, or seemed to. He held up his hands, palms to Terry with fingers widespread, and smiled a sheepish, small smile.

"No," said Cohen. A short laugh. He looked up genially at Terry. "Not my thing." Terry wondered what Abe Cohen's thing was.

"Well, look, Mr. Cohen." Terry's chair creaked.

"Abe."

"Abe," Terry complied, "I'm just going to lay this out because this has been going on for, like, a week now, and frankly, I'm kind of over it." Cohen nodded slowly. Terry continued. "Look, I did what I thought was the right thing. Saw a car go off the road. Bad ice. I tried to help."

"You did help," said Cohen.

"Well," Terry went on, "I did … what anybody would do." He thought of the wine bottle. "You know, he was dying. I said a prayer for him. He asked me to."

"I heard. That was nice. Mike was quite devout."

He heard.

"Okay, then," said Terry. He gulped air. "So then he wrote me the check and … died."

"But not for that," said Cohen, after a bit.

"What?"

"Mike wrote you the check … but not for praying for him. That's not why he wrote you the check, is it?" Cohen was all business now. Corner Office business. No more sheepish smiles or modest manners. Terry went deer in the headlights.

"Hey, like I said, I'm not in this for the money. If you want the check back …"

"I don't," said the lawyer. "Not necessarily." He glanced briefly out the window, then back. "I can tell you, however, that a few people do. More than a few."

"Bryce?" offered Terry. Cohen's easy smile returned.

"You know Bryce?"

"I met him at the funeral home."

"Right." Cohen nodded. He seemed to know about that. "Yes, Bryce would be one. Bryce's wife, Fran, would be another. Becky and Jim. And Mike's wife, Millie. The family. Some bank people." Terry waited for more, but Cohen stopped there.

"What about the third daughter? In the pictures?" said Terry.

Cohen steepled his fingers again.

"Amber," he said. "She's estranged from the family." Cohen glanced out the window. Gray clouds had consumed the sun. No postcard sunset this afternoon.

Terry looked at his own hands, ran his right thumb across his wedding band. "Well, maybe they should take it back." He nodded toward the check, but spoke to his hands. "Maybe we should just rip it up."

Terry glanced up and saw Cohen concentrating, motionless, scarcely blinking, in a way that made Terry feel invisible. For several moments, Cohen appeared to be entirely alone. Then he looked at Terry. "Maybe we should," said the attorney.

Terry nodded. *How dumbass insane is it to tear up a check for two million dollars?*

"What did he ask you to do, Terry?"

Terry shrugged. Attempted to offer a poker face.

"I know Mike DeGraaf," Cohen pressed. "There's more to this than a prayer before dying. He's a business man. What did he want you to do?"

Terry's wedding ring clicked on the chair arm. Gold on wood. He clicked it again a couple more times. Then blew out a noisy stream of air.

What to say.

"Well. Abe." Ring click. Goatee stroke. "He asked me to save his daughter."

Abe Cohen didn't blink. Didn't move.

"What did you say?"

"I said, 'He asked me to save his daughter.'"

Now Cohen smiled.

"No, I heard that. I meant, what did you say in response?"

Terry leaned back in the modern wood chair, his heavy leather coat shifting and squeaking.

"I said I'd do it."

The sun, stolen by clouds, had left behind only a nimbus of bleak orange light. A fading halo in the sky. The street below darkened quickly. Cars blackened behind bright headlights.

"Did he say which daughter?" asked Cohen.

"No," said Terry. "Is it this Amber? The one who wasn't there?"

Cohen stood and stepped to the window, looking out. There was a stoop in his shoulders now that Terry hadn't seen before. A melancholy. "I don't know," said the lawyer. "I don't know which one."

He turned to Terry, but his eyes were looking inward. "I don't know what he was talking about."

Cohen seemed hurt. Left out of something. Something important in his great friend's life.

"Well, like I said, if you want the check back ..."

"Do you want to give it back?" asked Cohen. He retook his chair across from Terry. Leaned slightly toward the bigger man. "Or do you want to keep your word?"

For some reason, Terry thought of merit badges. He'd earned a few as a kid in the Boy Scouts. Could barely remember which ones. Swimming. Computers. Citizenship. He'd wanted to become an

Eagle Scout, but at some point, he dropped out. Got older. Lost interest. It was a regret. A small one, but still it gnawed at him. He could've done it. Should have done it. But he didn't. The pang of regret was still there.

"I want to keep my word," he said.

The attorney smiled.

Abe Cohen walked Terry to the elevator.

"Can I ask you something?" said Terry. He was thinking about those ancient farms in County Cork. About origins.

"Sure," said Cohen.

"Your name. And no offense or anything, but Cohen is a really common...you know..."

"Jewish name?"

"Yeah. And I was wondering where that came from. It must be, like, a really old name."

"Priest," said Cohen.

"What?" said Terry.

"Priest. Cohen, or Ko'en in Hebrew, means *Priest*."

"Oh."

"What does Holbrook mean?"

"I don't know," said Terry. "I haven't been able to find anything. It's Irish. I do know that. Celtic. Probably something about water. Or a river. Like a brook."

"Maybe it means *lucky*," said Cohen, smiling.

"Maybe it means *idiot*."

Cohen laughed. The elevator doors opened. The men shook hands. As Terry rode down, he looked at Cohen's business card cradled in his hand. Crisp. White. Precise black letters.

Before he left the building, Terry went into the bank. Cohen had called ahead. It was after closing time, but a manager unlocked the door and personally assisted him. It wasn't Ms. Baker. Terry presented the check. This time it went through. The account was funded. He was a millionaire.

13

Fran followed the instructions on the white sticker on the back of the playing card. She'd seen what was on the pink thumb drive. Another photo. The worst by far. And the most expensive.

The large white Macy's bag with the red star on it looked much like the bags carried by dozens of other shoppers among the hundreds at the mall. From wealth-bored housewives to cluelessly fortunate teenagers to tight-suited millennial males and their even tighter-clad female counterparts. All races. All ages. All shopping. The only difference between her Macy's bag and the others she saw was that hers carried desperation. Mutual funds cashed. Jewelry sold. All she had. A paper brick wrapped in white tissue. A $50,000 Nu Step shoebox taped shut.

She'd kept all but the first thumb drive. The first she'd smashed to bits months ago with a hammer. Now they all went into a drawer in the basement in a lock box made for a handgun, along with all the envelopes and playing cards. Saved for a retribution she was at a loss to envision.

She entered Macy's from the parking lot with bag in hand, walked through the store's ground floor, and stepped out into the mall proper. The Somerset Collection is an upscale shopping palace in Troy, Michigan, gleaming inside and out and conveniently located between rich Birmingham and wealthy Bloomfield Hills. Four levels of glass, brass, granite, and marble designed to coddle credit card holders, loosen purse strings, and soothe all with its sparkling fountains, lush greenery, and plentiful rest areas for strength-gathering between purchases.

Fran knew the mailings and thumb drives had no fingerprints. She'd had them checked. She'd hired a private detective from Angie's List. She'd paid cash. Used a false name and a disposable phone. Didn't like him. Didn't like the way he smelled or the toothpick he chewed or the grime under his fingernails. Didn't like his look or the way he looked at her. He wanted to look at the thumb drive contents, but she said no. She never called him again.

Wednesday at 2:30, The Collection was crowded but not overcrowded. She pretended to window shop on the ground floor, per the instructions on the playing card. She wore her old glasses with thick brown frames and a subdued scarf over her hair. Her left hand carried the weight of the Macy's bag. Her right, her phone.

After several minutes of gazing unseeing into the windows of Bath & Body Works, then Fossil, then Chico's, her phone vibrated. Once. Just once. She didn't look at it but slowly turned, as she'd been instructed to, until she saw a resting area in the middle of the bustling mall promenade. The phone number of whoever was calling her, she knew, was blocked.

She saw a contoured bench for two, built to look like ergonomic stone. It was the only unoccupied seat in sight. That's where she was supposed to go.

A few feet to the right of it, a large fountain sent arcs of water soaring delightfully from one side to the other. To the left, tots in Izod and Polo scrambled on a swashbuckling play structure boasting turrets, ropes, and bridges cushioned by a soft, green rubber floor.

Fran hurried to the empty bench while trying to appear unhurried, striding swiftly in high boots and sitting down fast before an older, foreign-looking man with a cane could get there first. He muttered harshly in a foreign tongue but she ignored him. As he slowly shuffled away, she kept her eyes on the glossy marble floor.

She slid the Macy's bag under the bench, positioning her boot heels lightly against the bag's stiff paper. She continued to look at the floor per instructions. Her phone held in both hands like a rosary.

After a long minute, the phone vibrated again. Once. Just once. She was looking at the screen when the caller I.D. appeared. It said <unknown>.

She hated the next part. Walking away. Leaving the bag. What if someone else got there first? God, she hated this.

She glanced up, then down. Hundreds of people moving. She dared not look around. She'd been warned.

She took a breath, stood, adjusted her purse strap, and smoothed her jeans behind her. She walked away from the Macy's bag. She didn't look back. Saw the foreign man with the cane give her a dirty look and she almost peed, thinking he was going to hobble over and find the money.

Unless that was him.

"Miss? Ma'am!?" a man's voice behind her said loudly.

She stopped. *Oh, Christ.*

She turned back. The voice was a young man's, a high-school boy. He was holding a baby's red and blue pacifier with a brown rubber nipple. He spoke not to Fran but to a young Hindu mother with a baby in a stroller. "I think she dropped this," said the teen-ager, beaming. He had acne and a bird's nest of unkempt ginger hair. "It was on the floor." He offered the mother the pacifier.

The young mother thanked him, quietly bowing and putting the pacifier in a white mesh basket on the back of the stroller, out of baby's reach. Fran exhaled, not even aware she'd been holding her breath. Then her breath caught again.

The Macy's bag was gone. The man with the cane just sitting down. Beneath the bench she'd just stepped away from was noth-ing. Empty space.

He must have been right there.

Close enough to touch. Or be touched.

It took immense willpower to turn and walk away and not run. To breathe and not scream.

To make it home without a drink.

Driving from the sprawling, northern suburbs southeast to Grosse Pointe took nearly an hour. An hour she couldn't remem-ber afterward. She poured her first glass of pinot grigio with her coat on and drank it quickly, standing up, wearing gloves.

14

C*afé Felix*. Christina's favorite. Candlelight. White table-cloths. French-type waiters with black vests, bow ties, long white aprons, and sleeves neatly rolled to the elbow. Hannah at a friend's house for the night. Him in the zip-front sweater she gave him for Christmas that she loved but he hated.

This should have been a slam dunk.

Instead, the blackness deep inside him had jolted awake. The roil. Aquiver with dissent. Twisting inside him. Feasting on conflict. Starting to getting nasty.

"What do you mean?" Terry set his Pilsner glass down hard on the table. "What are you talking about?"

"I mean we have to give it back," said Christina. "It's not our money. We can't keep it." She looked so beautiful. All dressed up. Did up her hair. Perfume. Pretty make-up. Anniversary earrings dangling. And smiling at him like he was eight.

He'd planned this all week. Ever since Cohen. Now was the big moment.

They were millionaires. The money was in the bank. *How many guys ever get to tell their wife that?*

But he had told her that. And her reaction was not as expected.

She held her glass of chardonnay poised in the air but didn't sip it, keeping her bright eyes on his. "I mean, do you really think they're going to let us keep it? His family? They're not. You know that, don't you?" They'd only just gotten their drinks. The bread hadn't even arrived.

"We don't know that for sure," said Terry. He'd just finished telling her all about Abe Cohen. The corner office. The Ansel Adams. Opening the account at the bank after hours.

"Sweetie." Her eyes were sad but firm. "Think about it. You said one of the husbands was a lawyer."

"I said he looked like a lawyer." Bryce. "That he could be a lawyer."

"But there will *be* lawyers."

"Sure. Probably. Lawyers, whatever. Lawsuits." Tried to bite back the last word but was too late.

"Lawsuits?" She shook her head. "Sweetie, you gotta give it back."

Terry's fists clenched on the white tablecloth. "Honey, I made a promise. To save Mike DeGraff's daughter." He forced his mind away from the money and thought instead about DeGraaf's cold, sticky hand clutched in his own hands.

The promise. Mike's open eyes in death.

"And until someone stops me, I'm going to do whatever it takes to keep my word."

"But you don't know what that even means."

"I know," said Terry. Then sat back. "But I'm going to find out. And Cohen's on my side. On *our* side." He raised his glass to his wife. He drank, wondering when the bread was coming. They had great bread here.

Christina sipped her wine solemnly.

"And you look great," he added.

"You already said that," said Christina over her wine glass.

"Can't say it enough."

"Is everything all right?" Their waiter, Alan, appeared at table-side, slender and smiling at both of them.

"I'm okay," said Terry, displaying his half-full beer glass.

"Of course," said Alan. "And you, ma'am?"

"I'm fine, thank you."

"Maybe some of that bread?" said Terry.

"Of course. It's just coming out of the oven now." Alan slipped quietly away.

"This Cohen was Mr. DeGraaf's lawyer?" asked Christina.

"Is. Still is."

Christina looked perplexed.

"That's what I thought, too," said Terry, "But if you're rich enough, I guess you still have lawyers after you're dead." He drank some beer. "You still get to decide things."

Alan soon appeared with the bread. He asked if they were ready to order. They said they needed a couple more minutes. He smiled and stepped away. Terry offered his wife some bread. She demurred, so he helped himself.

"How are you going to keep your promise?" she asked as he dipped a knife blade into softened butter. She was thinking about the third daughter. About Amber. The one not at the funeral home. They'd discussed her.

Terry looked at his wife's cinnamon bangs above bright, earnest eyes. A few freckles on her pixie nose. The lilac cashmere sweater she wore that was the softest thing she owned. The tiny cross on its slender chain.

Terry set his bread and butter knife down and spread his hands, framing a pronouncement. He was fully prepared for this question. He'd thought this through. "I'm going to hire professionals."

"What?" said Christina.

"I'm going to hire professionals," said Terry. "Like a private eye. Someone who does this for a living. Like *Taken*." He was thinking of Liam Neeson in the movie.

Christina laughed like tiny crystal bells in a forest.

Usually, Terry loved her laugh. Now it sounded mocking. She was mocking him, he felt. The blackness deep inside him told him so. His eyes darkened. Christina reached for her wine, and saw his hurt feelings. She stopped smiling and offered serious consideration.

"I'm sorry," she said. "Who? Who are you going to hire?"

Terry buttered more bread. "I don't know yet. I'll find somebody. There are guys. Black ops guys. I'll get references." He sat up straighter. Addressed his wife. "That's what the money's for." Bit some bread.

"Black ops guys?"

"Well, yeah."

"I think you've seen too many movies."

"Well, whatever it takes. I promised Mike."

"Mike?"

"That's what he asked me to call him. And I gave my word." He washed down more bread with more beer. "And if it all works out…" He swallowed. "We'll be…you know…we'll have some money." With effort, he mentally chased away the boats, cars, and man toys that persistently leapt into his mind.

Christina sipped her wine thoughtfully but said nothing.

"Sweetie." Christina was very quiet now. "Maybe we should think about this."

"I have thought about it."

Her eyes pierced. "I said *we*."

Ouch.

"Alright," he said. "What do *you* want to do? What do you want *us* to do?"

He knew how she thought. This was upsetting for her. Destabilizing. She'd lost people. Both parents. Some friends. Terry and Hannah were all she had.

"What if it's dangerous?" She looked up at him, eyes suddenly moist. "We don't know what trouble this girl is in. This missing daughter."

"Amber," said Terry.

"She could be involved in anything! Drugs. Cults. We have to think about Hannah. We have to protect *our* daughter. Have you thought about her?"

"Yes, as a matter of fact, I have," Terry said. "I've thought about her college. I've thought about her grad school. Maybe even medical school or law school."

Alan came by and refilled their water glasses. "A couple more minutes?" the waiter asked, eyeing their untouched menus.

"Please," said Christina. Alan departed with a smile.

"This is not normal," said Christina after a moment, shaking her head. "I don't like it." Her mind was full of drug dealers, cult leaders, human traffickers. Even terrorists. "How much trouble do you have to be in to need two million dollars to get out of it?"

"Listen, listen," said Terry, working to calm her. "That's why I'm going to hire people. You're right. This isn't normal." He reached for and held both her hands across the small table. "But we can do this. I'll hire people. There are ways to do this." He looked at her. "This could be the best thing that ever happened to us."

"After Hannah," she said quietly. Terry nodded.

"After Hannah. This could be the best thing."

After a long moment, Christina finally exhaled with a shudder so deep it made her shoulders shake. Then took a big sip of wine. More like a gulp.

"Look," she said, looking him in the eye. "If anything … *anything* bad starts to happen, you're out. You give it back. You get out."

"I'm out," agreed Terry, sitting back, hands spread, totally agreeing.

"You walk away."

Terry nodded effusively. He'd won.

"Right," he said. "But nothing will. I promise. I'll hire professionals. They'll find the daughter, get her out of whatever trouble she's in. Rehab. Whatever. Detox. I pay them, I pay for her treatment, and we *still* make a lot. Even if it costs a million dollars that still leaves, like, a half a million for us. After taxes."

"Assuming we get to keep it." She shook her head slowly. "Which we must assume we're not."

Terry rocked his head side to side. "Well. Yeah. Assuming."

They were both thinking the same thing. High-powered family. A lot of money. A S.W.A.T. team of well-paid lawyers.

Christina put her head between her hands and slowly massaged her temples. This was too strange. Merely strange was bearable. Too strange was usually bad.

"Drink some wine," said Terry. "Relax, honey. This is all good." He raised his glass. "We're celebrating." She drank some wine, gazing somberly at him.

"The first bad thing," repeated Christina. "…you stop. Anything even slightly dangerous or weird, or criminal, you stop. You give the money back."

"Deal," said Terry. He held his beer glass toward her. She clinked her glass against his, but her heart wasn't in it.

"You're not James Bond," she said.

"Don't say *that,*" said her big, un-buff husband with a grin. "I just ordered a tux."

Finally, a smile from her. Small. But offered.

It was settled.

His wife lifted her wine glass to her lips, still shaking her head. The girlfriend who married him. The woman who loved him. Terry looked at his menu, still smiling. This was all going to work out.

His eyes kept flitting to the dollar signs printed all over the menu. All those dollar signs. Lots and lots of dollar signs.

Alan arrived to take their order. Once he left they switched to their favorite topic, Hannah. Terry reached for more bread and, for a moment, startled himself.

Inches from his hand, the narrow bread basket on the candlelit table looked just like a little coffin. The remaining bread in it like a wrapped body.

15

"I think I got it," said Uncle Bill.

The sun was high. Daylight lingering longer.

P.J. looked up from cleaning Uncle Bill's Heckler and Koch P7 nine millimeter, a gun as good as the new breed of lightweight compact automatics got. The little asshole didn't know what he had, got it in trade, kept it under his bed in the dust and critter shit. The trigger cocked it. No need to rack a round. Start-to-finish firing with one hand. Brilliant shit. P.J. inhaled the fragrance of gun oil, his blackened fingers shiny with it. This was his now.

Uncle Bill's face appeared at the top of the metal ladder. Under one arm was a scuffed laptop. From his grinning teeth hung a DVD in a grimy paper sleeve. He pulled himself up into the trash-strewn loft.

P.J. sat on the old couch, his bulk hunched over a plywood slab set on truck tire rims. The disassembled P7 was spread out on oil-stained newspaper. The cleaned and reassembled Runt positioned to one side. P.J. stayed indoors mostly. His face was on TV and the internet. He'd shaved off his beard. Uncle Bill's new legal name was a happy accident. No feds had yet connected Jake Strumm to Robert Peet, Jr.

He set down the muzzle brush and wiped his hands with a rag. "Got what?"

"The black Ram," Bill said. "Maybe." His uncle approached, waggling the DVD.

He stepped carefully into P.J.'s space, around pizza boxes, chip bags, beer cans, and bottles. Lots of cigarette butts. P.J. hadn't indicated how long he would be staying. Bill forced himself to smile.

P.J. stood and put the Runt in his belt. Then he carefully lifted the piece of plywood topped with the oily newspapers, HK parts, and the gun cleaning kit and set it on the floor where it wouldn't be disturbed.

"Put it on the wheel rim," said P.J., indicating the laptop.

Bill sat next to his large nephew, whose missing beard exposed a heavy, doglike face, and proceeded to open the laptop on the wheel rim. The couch and his nephew both stunk. P.J. took the disc by its edges. It was silver, unmarked.

"Where'd you get this?"

"Buddy a mine." Uncle Bill accepted the disc back and put it in the laptop's disc drive. The machine started whirring. "Runs a shop by City Airport." Meaning a chop shop in one of Detroit's roughest areas. Renamed the Coleman A. Young International Airport in 2003, the shabby old airstrip on Detroit's east side was still called City Airport by everyone.

"What is it?" said P.J.

"Security camera," said Uncle Bill.

"At a chop shop?"

"Hidden," said Bill. He smiled crookedly. "Never hurts to have a few extra aces, you know what I mean? A little something up your sleeve."

"You have cameras?" asked P.J.

"Shit no," lied Bill.

P.J. ignored him as the screen lit up.

The color image was impressively clear. A still shot. Distorted slightly by a fisheye lens that showed the interior of a big garage, wall to wall. The camera was aimed at a drive-through entry with the garage door raised. Most chop shops did mufflers, shocks, and brakes as cover. Bill's wasn't so high-end. His operation was more like a junkyard.

"Can you make it bigger?" asked P.J. Bill hit a key and the image went full screen. There were no vehicles in view. The camera was up high and angled down. Beyond the open door was an empty driveway, beyond that the street. Looked like morning or dusk.

Bill clicked Play. The image unfroze and video started moving. At the bottom of the frame, digits flickered—time code noting hour, minute, and second. The video began at 8:43 a.m. The date was four weeks ago.

"Have you seen this?" asked P.J.

"Nope," said Bill. "Just got it."

After fifteen seconds a mechanic in a lube jockey's dirty blue shirt and jeans crossed the frame. There was no sound. Vehicles drove by now and then on the street out front. Outside the garage, pyramids of dirty snow heaped by plows looked like burial mounds.

"Fast forward," said P.J.

"Don't you wanna see...?"

"Just fast forward."

Bill clicked, and the footage raced forward.

The video sped through early morning minutes from a month ago. Not much human activity onscreen. Two mechanics raced side to side like puppets. Then a silver minivan pulled in. Bill slowed down the picture.

"Keep it going," said P.J. Bill sped up the picture.

The minivan backed out, left. Time flew by at high speed.

"Stop," said P.J.

Bill froze the footage with the **Pause** button. The still frame showed a vehicle turning in from the street. A black pickup. A skinny workman frozen like a statue, his raised arm waving it in. The time code read just past ten in the morning.

"Okay, play it at regular speed."

Bill clicked the **Play** arrow. The picture sharpened when it moved. Both men watched the black pickup pull into the garage, filling most of the frame.

"Is that the truck?" said Bill.

"Shut up." P.J. leaned closer. The battered couch creaked.

It was a Ram. The big silver ram's head plainly visible, positioned dead center on the chrome grill. The tinted windshield familiar. "Stop there," ordered P.J.

Bill stopped the video. The grill of the black truck was distorted by the wide-angle lens.

"This a chop shop?" said P.J.

"Did I say that?" said Uncle Bill, with a flicker of nicotine smile.

"Well, is it or *isn't* it?" Voice raised. Bill's yellow smile vanished.

"Uh, sure. Sometimes."

"Play the movie."

Bill clicked **Play** and two workmen, one black, one white, both in dirty blue shirts, approached the black Ram. One from each side. The white guy had a stringy ponytail, a scraggly beard, and a bucket of arm ink. He was at the driver's door.

"If they back out like the minivan, that usually means it's not a chop."

"Shut up," said P.J., trying to see through the Ram's tinted glass. That was Blond John's Ram. Or its identical twin. The driver's door opened. No one came out. The skinny white guy talked soundlessly to whoever was inside. Then the driver got out. P.J. leaned close.

The driver wasn't Blond John. It was a dark-haired guy. Not too tall. Thick-chested. Curly hair. Big moustache.

"Freeze it," ordered P.J.

Bill did. The picture blurred in freeze-frame, but they could definitely see the driver's face.

"Is that him?' asked Bill.

"Shut up," said P.J. "Can you blow that up?"

"No," Bill shrank into the couch when P.J. lunged. "I don't know how," he sputtered.

P.J. grabbed the laptop and held it close to his eyes, intent on the curly-haired man. Then he put the computer down again.

"Play more."

Bill followed his nephew's commands. Went forward. Went back. Froze it. Advanced the video, frame by frame. Back and forth. The sequence ended when the swarthy Ram driver shook hands with the skinny white guy, walked out the open garage door, turned left, and disappeared from view. Then the garage door closed with the Ram inside.

"That's a chop," said Uncle Bill.

No money had changed hands. The Ram driver with the dark,

curly hair didn't look or act like a car thief. Didn't carry himself that way.

"Play it again," said P.J.

Bill played it again. Twice. Three times.

"He *looks* Greek," said Bill.

"What?" said P.J.

"He looks Greek. To me, he looks Greek." Bill froze the frame on the driver's face.

"What does that fuckin' have to do with it?" P.J. glared at the smiling, curly-haired man onscreen. "He looks like a little shithole to me."

"My buddy told me. The guy who brought in the Ram was Greek. I got a name."

"What's his fuckin' name?"

"I wrote it down." Uncle Bill dug a scrap of paper out of his jeans and read it out loud. "Larry Onna - sis." He tried again. "Oh-nassis."

"That's a bullshit name," said P.J.

"It's a Greek name."

"It's bullshit." P.J looked at the screen, then at his uncle. "Can you find this guy?"

"Me? Fuck no."

"What about your buddy?"

"Fuck no. He's not Greek. I'm not Greek."

"So?"

"They keep close. You wanna find a Greek, we need a Greek."

"So get me a Greek." P.J. pulled the Runt from the front of his pants and squeezed the fat grips of the ugly little pistol. Its dark metal felt smooth and warm from his body heat.

16

Terry found Amber DeGraaf halfway through a Subway six-inch Steak & Cheese. He'd substituted bottled water for Coke but awarded himself Sun Chips as a consolation, with an apple from home for dessert. Eating lunch at his desk, he'd found her online.

He'd tried Facebook and LinkedIn and Twitter and Snapchat with no luck. But if she was married, it could be a last-name thing.

Then Google found her at an art gallery in Los Angeles. Four years ago. A black-and-white photo showed her looking older than she'd looked in the visitation photos. Still stout. Longer hair, kinky and floating out from her head. The photo showed her with several other people standing by a large, abstract clay sculpture. The clay cut in slabs and roughly assembled and glazed. Not smooth like a pot. Terry didn't think much of the artwork. She was a sculptress, apparently. A featured artist by the look of it. It was a photo of a festive gallery event.

She wore a long, dark dress and was smiling. She looked happy and more attractive than in the family photos. Truly beaming. Others near her in the shot held plastic champagne flutes. White-coated wait staff were visible in the background.

The sculpture seemed amateurish to Terry, but maybe that was because of the black-and-white photography. Maybe color would help. He enlarged the photo, but the sculpture didn't improve. There was no article with the photo but a caption identified Amber DeGraaf as the artist from Silver Lake, CA. The gallery, *Adamo*, was also in Silver Lake. A few keystrokes revealed Silver Lake as a tiny town, of sorts, a couple miles east of Hollywood.

He looked closely at Amber DeGraaf. He saw that she still had freckles. The crinkly hair looked red even in black and white. She looked ecstatically happy. Maybe drunk. The dress looked good on her. The plastic champagne flute she held was empty. He finished his six-inch sub wanting just one more bite. A seven-inch sub would have been perfect. Wiped his hands on a Subway napkin. Bit into the apple. His phone laying on his desk played the opening notes of "Eleanor Rigby."

A Cohen said the ID. Terry hurriedly chewed and swallowed.

His "Hi, Abe!" came out too familiar.

"Hi, Terry. I hope I'm not interrupting lunch." Busy voice. In the middle of something.

"No," said Terry, setting aside the bitten apple.

"Look, I've only got a minute, but I want to recommend someone I believe could help you."

Terry sat back. "What? Like a private eye?"

Cohen laughed briefly at this.

"No. Another attorney."

"Oh. I see. From your office?"

"No, he's independent. Good for this. Some professional distance, you know?" Terry didn't know.

"Uh huh," said Terry.

"You'll want to incorporate. Become an LLC. Limited liability corporation."

"Okay," said Terry. This wasn't what he expected. "Why?"

Cohen seemed distracted. "Protect your assets. In case you get sued. Or whatever."

What's "whatever"? thought Terry

"He's a friend," Cohen continued. "I've known him a long time. He's perfect for this. He knows…" Cohen abruptly stopped talking for a few moments. Interrupted perhaps. Terry heard no other voices. Maybe someone had handed him a note. "He…well, he knows what to do," said Cohen, coming back on the line. "Got a pen?"

"Shoot," said Terry grabbing a pen.

Cohen gave Terry the lawyer's name and phone number. Terry read it back for confirmation.

"Thanks, Abe."

"You're welcome, Terry. And good luck."

"Hey, and Abe?"

"Yup?" Cohen sounding eager to get off the line.

"I just found Amber DeGraaf online."

"Yes, she's in L.A., last I heard."

Terry thought Abe could've mentioned that earlier. But whatever. Terry changed the subject.

"And I, uh, talked to my wife about this, and she's, you know, cool with it."

"Oka-a-a-a-y," said Cohen, drawing out the word strangely. Terry sensed gears turning. "Well," said Cohen. "Then. I would advise you and your wife to not mention this, any of this, to anybody else. Going forward."

Dead air. Cohen didn't fill it.

"She won't talk. She's not a talker," said Terry. She wasn't.

"Good. Don't you be a talker either."

More silence.

"Alright?"

"Okay," said Terry.

"Great. Terry, I really can't talk about this with you anymore, either. You understand."

Terry didn't.

"Okay."

"Call Henry. Will you do that?"

"Yeah. I will."

"Good. You're all set. I gotta go."

"Okay, thanks, Abe. Really, thanks for everything."

"My pleasure, Terry. Good luck. Gotta go, though."

"Okay, bye.

"Bye."

Terry set his phone down on the desk. The editing suite seemed suddenly very quiet. Only the hum of the computers and the silent glow of their tiny LEDs for company. The apple on his desk already browning at the bitten edges.

He looked at what he'd scrawled on the Post-it.

Henry Wallace lwyer

888-982-4766

Terry Googled him and found a simple website. Not much on it. Just one page that looked like a bare bones law office template from Go Daddy or WordPress. It showed an uninspiring stock photo of a gavel laid next to the scales of justice.

3232 Fulbright Street

Ferndale, Michigan

No photo of Wallace. Not remotely at Cohen's level. Terry was depressed. But he called the number.

Henry Wallace's office in Ferndale was two blocks west of Woodward Avenue and a block north of Nine Mile Road, according to Google Maps.

They'd spoken. Wallace sounded African-American on the phone, polite and precise. He seemed unsurprised by Terry's call. They arranged to meet at the attorney's office that afternoon and exchanged contact information while still on the phone.

Like Dearborn and the other suburban satellites, Ferndale was an outgrowth of 20th-century Detroit's ferociously expanding critical mass. Woodward began downtown at the Detroit River and ran north. A notable quirk of waterway geography allows Detroiters to look south over the river into Windsor and Canadians to look north into the U.S.

Google Maps' street view of 3232 Fulbright Street showed an old brick office building that did not fill Terry with confidence.

Driving in from Ann Arbor, he was running a few minutes late and was relieved when the Detroit Zoo water tower appeared. The zoo was maybe a mile, he guessed, from Wallace's office. He hadn't been to the zoo since they'd gone as a family a few years ago. It had been a perfect summer day. All the animals seemed happy that day. Hannah had been thrilled.

He took the exit.

The office building was three floors of sad brown brick from the 50's or even the 40's. It was nestled behind the aggressively stylish boutiques and restaurants that fronted Woodward Avenue. An equally sorry, potholed public parking lot was situated behind the old brown building. Terry put an hour of quarters into the meter. Working in Ann Arbor, he always kept a stash of quarters in the glove compartment. The sun hid behind low, gray clouds. Terry couldn't have found it if he'd tried.

He crossed the alley and walked up the steps. Pulled open a glass door with frayed rubber sealing.

Inside, it was dim and musty and smelled like his old elementary school. He let his eyes adjust. Dead quiet. A flat, plexiglass case on the wall listed the tenants with small, white letters pressed into ribbed black fabric. A *g* had fallen out of a name and lay at the bottom of the case next to two dead bugs. It was so quiet his ears hummed.

Henry Wallace Attorney at Law was in *Ste 303*. There was an ancient elevator, but Terry liked the look of the old stairs. Out in the open with a wooden balustrade worn to a sheen by decades of hands. Stairs that creaked under a threadbare runner. On the third floor, the first door that he saw had an ancient oak frame and said *Dr. Benjamin Boone, DDS* in black, painted letters edged in gold on pebbled glass. No light inside. Wallace's office was at the end of the hallway, his name on a small wooden plaque. Next to suite 303 was a sash window with a slanting iron fire escape visible outside.

Terry knocked. After a moment, footsteps approached. The door opened. A very dark-skinned man with extremely dark eyes, flaring nostrils, white shirt, and dark tie stood perfectly straight and extended his hand. A dark and stormy face.

"Mr. Holbrook?" asked Wallace. A brief flash of white smile.

"Yes," said Terry, shaking the attorney's hand. "Sorry I'm late."

"I'm Henry Wallace. Please come in." Terry came in and Wallace closed the door. The office was warmer than the hallway and stairs. An old-fashioned iron radiator hissed against the wall.

"Can I take your coat?"

"Sure," said Terry. He handed the heavy leather coat to Wallace, who hung it in a small closet. In the closet Terry saw a suit coat and an overcoat. On the top shelf, a wide-brimmed gray fedora. Nothing else.

There was an outer office and an inner office like in old private eye movies. The outer office was small, with a heavy wood desk and swivel chair behind it. Both chair and desk looked old and not in use. The walls were beige. On one wall was a team photo of the 2012 Detroit Tigers and a framed poster for the 2013 Dream Cruise, Woodward Avenue's annual celebration of automobile glory. There was also a small, neatly framed photo of Jackie Robinson. The thing that most caught Terry's eye was a brass umbrella stand by the door that held a furled umbrella, several walking sticks and a knobbed, gnarled shillelagh.

"Cool office."

"Thanks."

Terry followed Henry into the inner office. The door between the two offices was dark wood with an old brass doorknob beneath a large pane of pebbled glass. Wallace left it open.

"Please have a seat."

Wallace gestured to one of two worn wooden chairs with curved backs and wood arms. Probably came with the office. The inner office wasn't much larger than the outer office. But it felt worked in.

Wallace sat in a high-backed chair behind a venerable desk that looked heavy enough to fall though the floor. On it was an open laptop. No phone. A brass torchiere spilled light from one corner.

A motionless ceiling fan hung above. A couple of framed diplomas. A couple photos. One showed Henry Wallace shaking hands with a pre-gray Barack Obama amidst a sea of well-wishers.

"Wow," said Terry, pointing. "That's a keeper."

"That was at Cobo Hall in 2007 when he ran the first time. I'm friends with a woman who worked on the campaign."

A family portrait showed Wallace, his wife, a daughter of about ten, and a son of about seven or eight. All wore red polo shirts, crisp blue jeans, and clean, white sneakers. They looked happy and healthy. And patriotic.

"Nice family," said Terry.

"Thank you," said Wallace. "It's a couple years old." Terry nodded. "Would you like some coffee or a water?" asked the attorney, as Terry spotted a Keurig coffeemaker on a small refrigerator.

"No, thank you," said Terry, turning his attention back to Wallace, who waited with fingers steepled at his desk.

After a beat the attorney said, "How can I help you, Mr. Holbrook?"

"Terry's fine."

Wallace nodded. "How can I help you, Terry?"

Terry selected words. "I have. An unusual situation." Pause. "With tax…ramifications."

"I see," said Henry.

"Did Abe tell you anything?"

"No." Henry shook his head.

"How do you know each other?"

Wallace smiled. Sunshine broke through the dark and stormy face. "We go way back. Our birthdays are actually the same day. We met doing *pro bono* work for Focus: HOPE." Focus: HOPE was a prominent Detroit nonprofit that trained young Detroiters, many of them veterans or high school dropouts, for the emerging job market. A well-known, well-respected organization.

Wallace stopped there. Terry nodded.

"Is this confidential?" asked Terry after a moment. "What we're..." He indicated the two of them. "...this discussion?"

"Absolutely," said Wallace. "Everything we say is confidential the minute you walk in. Whether we agree to a business arrangement or not." He smiled briefly. "That's how it works."

Terry nodded. Thought for a few moments.

Made the decision.

Now or never.

"Okay. I have been given," said Terry, "...or rather, I have been paid...in advance...a large sum of money. To do something."

Wallace nodded seriously.

"The man who paid me," said Terry, "...is now deceased. He paid me two million dollars." Terry watched for a reaction. Not even a blink.

"I see," Wallace said. "To do what?"

"To save his daughter."

"From what?"

"I don't know."

"Did you sign anything?" asked the attorney.

"No."

"How were you paid?"

"By check."

Wallace didn't ask if the check was good or not.

"Is there a verbal contract?"

"Yes," Terry nodded. "There's a verbal contract."

Silence. Everything suddenly serious.

"So," said Terry. "What are, like, the taxes on that?"

Wallace used this cue to sidestep the oddness of Terry's situation and launch into a pat, practiced conversation describing common tax scenarios for small business owners. Was Terry self-employed? Did he have partners? Did he wish to incorporate? Wallace typed Terry's responses into the laptop as he went.

Was the money a gift? Was this a nonprofit venture? Or for profit? What was the money to be used for? Was there an existing business structure? Were there co-owners? Shareholders? Employees? Were there business expenses? Travel? Rent? Office supplies?

Terry answered the questions. Supplied his home address. Work address. Marital status. Salary.

At the end Wallace recommended that Terry establish a Limited Liability Corporation, or LLC, in the State of Michigan. What Cohen had suggested. It would cost Terry a little over hundred dollars plus an hour of Henry's time to register a name and the LLC would protect the Holbrooks' personal assets should any lawsuits occur. The Holbrook home, their cars, their savings, their investments, their life insurance, and Hannah's meager college fund would all be protected.

"You think this is a good idea?" said Terry when Henry stopped talking.

"Absolutely." Wallace smiled professionally. "If you agree, I'll have two documents for you to sign by Friday." It was Wednesday. "And you'll need a name."

"A name?"

"For the corporation. I recommend you not use your name or the name of anyone in your family."

"A name," said Terry. "Okay." He glanced around the room. Looked for inspiration. The ceiling fan. The pebbled glass. The old-time desk and heavy wooden chairs. He got an idea.

"How about Falcon?"

"Falcon?" asked the attorney.

"Like *The Maltese Falcon*. The movie." Terry pictured the fedora he'd seen in the closet. The brass umbrella stand by the door. Very *film noir*. "Falcon LLC." He liked the sound of it.

"I'll check to see if that name is available. If it is, I'll secure it. The sooner you're a corporation, the sooner your personal assets can be protected."

Terry shifted in his chair. "Okay."

"Have you incurred any expenses so far?"

"No," said Terry. "Driving here." He shrugged.

"You should reimburse yourself for that," said Wallace. "All expenses should be paid from the corporate account. Once it's opened."

Terry nodded.

Wallace typed.

Finally, Terry said, "So, like I said, I'm supposed to save this guy's daughter."

Wallace looked up. "Yes?"

Terry fidgeted. "Abe said ... he indicated you could help me."

Henry's gaze was level.

"Do you know what you're up against?"

"No."

"What *do* you know?"

"Not much." Terry shifted in his chair. "This daughter, whoever she is, is in trouble. Maybe lots of trouble. I found her online this morning right before I talked to you."

"What kind of trouble?"

"I don't know," Terry said. "I haven't found that out yet."

"Have you talked to her?"

"No. I just found her picture. That's all."

"Are there other members of the family?"

"Yes."

"Have you talked to them?"

"No." Terry remembered the awkwardness at the funeral home. "Not really."

Wallace dipped his chin twice. Went back to typing.

"Well," said the attorney, "We'll get to that. For now, this is a good start."

Terry nodded more to himself than Wallace. Wallace soon stopped typing. He then clasped his hands in front of him on the desk. After a few empty moments, Terry stood up.

"So, Friday?" said Terry.

Wallace also stood. "Four o'clock?"

"Can we make it three?" Traffic would be bad at four.

"Certainly."

Both men hitched up their pants. Henry got Terry's coat.

"Thank you for coming," said Wallace at the door, as Terry zipped up his heavy leather coat. "I'll call you if Falcon LLC is unavailable."

"Thanks," said Terry, extending his hand. They shook. Henry wished him a safe drive home.

It had gotten dark out. Terry's head was spinning. Amber DeGraaf. Henry Wallace. Humphrey Bogart. He felt like he was in a movie. He rubbed his eyes and started the car. He wished he had a Coke. He put on The Chieftans. Their Celtic merriment always lifted him. Tin whistle, fiddle, and bodhran sang. The Chieftans would get him home. He could always count on them.

As Terry backed out and pulled away, he was watched by a man sitting motionless in a battered Neon. He'd seen Terry arrive and waited until he left. Wallace had called him at Cohen's suggestion. Wallace knew him. Cohen only knew of him. As a shadow. A wraith.

The Sebring's license plate had supplied the watcher with Terry's name, which led to Christina and Hannah's names, to where Terry worked, to where Christina worked, to where Hannah went to school, to what grade she was in, and to who her teacher was. He knew what cars they owned or leased, their street address, their tax status, what investments they had, what they owed on their mortgage, and how much they had in the bank. Not many people could wring this sort of information from a license plate. But he could.

17

Maggot ran. He understood running. Running away. Running so you don't get caught. Running so hard that all you hear are your own pumping gasps, your shoes slapping gravel or grass, and all you feel is *get away.* Survive.

But he'd never understood the sheer power of running before. The exuberance of it. The sweet, weeping pain of it. Like needles jabbing in your lungs. But now he did. Ricky explained it.

Maggot wasn't his real name, but he'd come to realize that it was his true name. He knew that now. Ricky explained that, too.

He should have known it was his name after so many years of hearing it. Year after year, grade after grade, tormentor after tormentor. The name Maggot had been beaten into him. Literally. Kids do that. Bigger kids. Sometimes smaller kids. Always mean kids. Sometimes bunches of them. Bunches of mean kids. With sticks. And rocks. And matches.

Then all those kids grow up and move away. Forget their crimes.

But he never forgot the kids or their crimes. Or his name. He never forgot any of it.

He welcomed the warming weather. It was Thursday. Running

in midwinter made him feel uneasy, too noticeable. But now the snow was melting, and more people braved the outdoors. People different from him. People who didn't know what he knew. People who didn't know Ricky.

The headset he wore was silent. Ricky's idea. The MP3 player on his bicep was turned off. This way he could hear everything in the quiet, old-money neighborhood. He could hear if dogs barked. He could hear his Nikes hit the sidewalk and hear himself panting steady, rhythmic breaths, the moist exhalations streaming from his mouth in white, smoke-like huffs. He could hear cars approach from behind. He was prepared.

Jogging in easy lopes, he couldn't help smiling at the perfect cover. He was hiding in plain sight, just like Ricky said. Grosse Pointe Farms was the most densely populated of The Pointes. Expensively attired joggers and walkers were frequently seen on block after block of grand old homes, the ivy-covered swag of early auto money, trotting or power-walking along the elegant streets and boulevards.

A fly buzzed in his face, the first of the year. He snapped at it, teeth clicking, and grinned. Yes, spring was on its way.

An extra benefit of the jogging was that he was actually getting into better shape. He'd felt soft and flabby when he first put on the tight, black-and-chartreuse running pants and snug shell top, but his wife was thrilled. And why not? He was making an effort. He was feeling the burn. He smiled to himself as he ran. Motivation was all it took. Ricky explained that.

Ricky explained a lot.

When he met Ricky, he'd been unemployed for a month. Fired again. This time, he hadn't told his wife.

Instead, he'd learned to act. He showered and shaved each weekday morning. Left at eight like he always did. After a kiss and a hug, he'd drive off toward the job he no longer had and then just keep driving. For the first few days he drove pretty much all day. To Traverse City and back. To Grand Rapids and back. To Cleveland and back.

The second week, he killed time at some casinos. Losing money that he didn't have. Then whisky at lunch. By the third week, he was in strip clubs. Porno dens. Those who had called him Maggot were right. They'd been right all along.

At home, he deserved the Academy Award.

He met Ricky in the throes of vomiting up a liquor lunch in the parking lot of a Triple-X video store. Bent double behind a dumpster, he looked behind him when he heard the laughing. Ricky's high-pitched, buzzing laugh. A strange, insectoid laugh.

"Life's a bitch, ain't it?" said the skinny young man with the long teeth. The young man wore only a T-shirt, black jeans, and boots. No coat on a cold day.

Ricky stood over the heaving man and watched the streams of steaming puke come surging out of Maggot's mouth and splatter on the pavement. Then Ricky stood him up. Ricky even used his own T-shirt to mop the vomit off Maggot's suit coat, tie, and dripping chin. All the while laughing. Laughing his buzzing laugh. Then Ricky bought him coffee and a few donuts. Sobered him up.

They talked in that donut shop for two hours. Maybe more.

Ricky asked him questions like a father would. But Ricky was young. Maybe mid-twenties. Just a kid. Good-looking. He had medicine, too. Prozac, he said. He offered some. Maggot swallowed the pills.

"It'll calm you down." It did. Almost instantly. Ricky knew things, too. Understood people. Problems.

Power.

"Where you from?" Ricky asked.

Maggot told him. That's when the real conversation started.

Like magic, Ricky laid it all out. In one fell swoop. The whole plan. How it would work. The white envelopes. The playing cards. The thumb drives. The money. It was like he had figured it all out before they'd even met.

It was so obvious. And so easy.

Maggot still couldn't believe how simple it was. How perfect it was.

When Maggot asked what he could offer in return, Ricky just smiled with his long teeth and laughed his high, buzzing laugh.

"I just wanna see you happy, bro," was all he said.

Now, all these months later, Maggot was desperate to see Ricky again. He wanted to talk to Ricky. He wanted to give Ricky some of the money. Share his success. Be with Ricky. But Ricky didn't have a phone.

"If I need you, I'll find you," was all Ricky said, grinning ear to ear.

Maggot had searched the porno stores and strip clubs and casinos but never saw Ricky. He looked everywhere for him. He was dying to thank him but couldn't. He wept sometimes in frustration.

But he dutifully followed the plan. Following the plan would bring Ricky back. Ricky said keep following the plan. That's what Ricky said in the donut shop. Sometimes Ricky even said it in Maggot's dreams.

* * *

Maggot turned south and was glad he was wearing sunglasses. He always wore sunglasses on his runs, but today's low winter sun in a cloudless sky made them essential. The bare trees lining the wide street did little to block the light.

He saw the woman. The jogger. The one he saw a lot. Pounding toward him on the opposite sidewalk while he pounded toward her on his side. An All-Star Titter as Ricky would say. Big, firm ones pushing out tight, pink-and-black spandex. Who cares if they're fake? Like him, she wore sunglasses, her blond-streaked ponytail swinging provocatively beneath her blue fur earmuffs. Her curves tightly sheathed in a shiny, body-hugging running suit. She smiled a small smile at him and waved a small wave. He returned same. They jogged past each other separated by the quiet, moneyed street. After she passed, he swiveled his head to look at her ass like he always did. Most people around here were at work at this hour. That's how the rich stayed rich. Most of them.

This *was* his work. He had to give himself credit for that. He wasn't lazy.

Two more blocks and he'd get to look. He anticipated the excitement.

Felt a stirring in his nethers. A shifting in his balls.

He always approached from the same direction, keeping the house to his right. That way he could pass it quickly in case someone was watching.

As he rounded the corner, he looked for the mail truck. Sometimes he saw it; most times he didn't.

Once last fall he saw the mail carrier, a woman, at the very moment she slid the mail through the brass slot on the door. It almost gave him an erection. If he hadn't been running, he'd have gotten rock hard. Hurtin' hard.

He could be spotted running past, he knew. That was a risk. But it also excited him.

There was the mail truck. On the other side of the street a few houses ahead of him. The mail had already come. He looked for the mail carrier but didn't see her. Then he saw her in the truck, sorting mail as he passed.

He dropped his head, watching his shoes thump along on the sidewalk. He was almost at the house. He knew every step by heart. He anticipated the spot where the sidewalk buckled, split by the roots of the old oak.

Past the crack in the sidewalk, he angled his head slightly toward the houses. The false moustache itched but held. It had taken practice to apply it so that it stayed stuck to his skin. He glanced quickly at the mail slot. Then back to his feet.

He imagined her behind it. He imagined her being fearful. Her regal beauty sapped of power. So beautiful yet so afraid.

He felt his penis swell.

That was the best part. Her fear. Ricky explained it. No one deserved to have it all, Ricky said.

Money. Looks. Power. Why should *she* have everything? She didn't deserve that.

It wasn't right for her to have so much. It wasn't fair. She was selfish. So he would correct her.

It was to up to him to correct her selfishness. That was his job.

That's what Ricky said.

18

"Where is he?"

"He'll be here." Uncle Bill fidgeted, checked the time on his phone, and almost knocked over his beer. Always with the fucking phone. P.J. wanted to ram it down his throat. They were in the back booth of a gloomy New Baltimore bar called the Boatyard Grill that overlooked Anchor Bay, a vast, frozen blister on the north edge of Lake St. Clair. No mansions here. Just the Ojibwe reservation on Walpole Island across the bay and miles of gloomy marsh flats and thousands of wild ducks.

The man they were supposed to meet had picked the place. Some kid named Thano. Bill found him. He was ten minutes late. Nephew and uncle drank wordlessly from longnecks.

"Call him," said P.J. after a minute. He felt out of place in his hooded coat and snowmobile boots. He was a wanted man. There were few diners but a half dozen regulars at the bar. A TV mounted over it played Red Wings hockey. Crappy music came from somewhere. Outside the window, the vast, black bay looked as dark and deep and cold as outer space without stars.

"Here he comes," said Uncle Bill, with relief. P.J. saw a skinny, greasy, olive-skinned kid in his twenties with a wispy high-schooler's beard and dirtstache approach their table, twitching. Junkie? Maybe. Nobody else noticed him.

He squeezed next to Bill but took in P.J. "Hey," he said.

"You're late," said P.J.

"This is Thano," said Bill.

"Sorry, man. Traffic." He reached a bony hand across the table to shake. Reluctantly, P.J. shook it. Thano grinned. One front tooth angled in against the other. Two lower teeth were missing. He smelled like cigarettes and cheap weed. P.J. glared at Bill, then back at the skinny kid.

"You Greek?" asked P.J.

The kid responded with a wide grin and jabber of foreign language. He waved his hands around saying who-knows-what. His black leather motorcycle jacket was worn and torn and had paint on it.

"Don't be an asshole with this guy," Bill instructed Thano, thumbing at his nephew. Uncle Bill made a pistol shape with one hand and indicated P.J., nodding grimly at the kid.

"I'm not a asshole, man." Then, to P.J. "Seriously. I'm not." After a beat, P.J. pulled a printout from inside his snowmobile coat, unfolded it, and slid it over to Thano. It was the best face shot of Onassis they could get from the garage video, blown up and in color. They did it at Office Depot.

"You know this guy?" asked P.J.

"No."

"Can you find him? He's Greek."

"Maybe," said the skinny kid. He had a booger hanging in a

nostril, fused to a hair. "How much you pay?" P.J. gave him the picture. Thano looked at it closely.

"That depends how good you are."

"Five hundred?" Thano looked up, heavy-lidded.

P.J. looked at Bill. Bill knew the local market. He nodded.

"Okay," said P.J. "Five hundred. You got a week to find this guy. It goes down a hundred every week we don't hear from you."

Thano nodded, his Adam's apple bobbing on his skinny neck. "You got it, man. You'll hear from me." Suddenly, he spread both arms so wide so fast P.J.'s hand instinctively went for the Runt.

"'Cause I'm the Transporter, man! I'm the fuckin' Bourne Identity!" Thano's eyes bugged, and he grinned wildly at P.J. Bill pulled Thano back roughly, glancing nervously at P.J.

P.J. stared ice at his uncle. His gun hand reappeared from his pocket, empty. "A week," he repeated.

Thano sat back, smiling and nodding. "What about now?" he said.

P.J. looked at Bill, who looked at Thano. "What do you mean, 'What about now'?" asked Bill.

"I mean, what about something now? You know. Good-faith money."

At the bar, a chorus of groans went up. The hockey game.

"Give him something," said P.J. Bill gave a sour look but glumly dug out his wallet. He wore it on a chain, trucker-style. Pulled out some bills.

"How's sixty?"

"Okay," said Thano. The kid took the money. He was missing half a finger.

"Where you gonna look?" asked P.J. "Greektown?" Greektown

was a tourist destination in Detroit, known for its casino, gyros, and flaming cheese, where everyone yelled 'Opa!'"

"Fuck no, man. No Greeks in Greektown. Greeks are all in St. Clair Shores and Roseville." He smacked the color printout. "That's where you look."

"Just find him."

"You got it, man. I do you a solid." Clutching the photo, the skinny young man stood and extended his hand to P.J. This time P.J. just glared.

"C'mon, man. We got a deal." The hand waited. It was the one with all its fingers. P.J. shook it.

"Time's a-wastin'," he said with a grin. Then to Bill in a lowered voice, "Hey. You got any . . . ?" He left the question unfinished, eyebrows bobbing up and down.

Bill looked at P.J., who gave his uncle a nod. "Let's go outside," said Bill. Bill sold dope. Thano slid out, followed by Uncle Bill. P.J. looked out the window and waited. He drained his beer.

"Can I get you something else, hon?" asked the plump young waitress with a pierce-lipped smile after P.J. had been sitting alone for a minute. A cheer and several hoots of laughter came from the TV-watchers at the bar.

"No," he said without looking at her. He heard her walk away. He was thinking of Blond John bleeding from many wounds. His blood spraying like a hose. Bright red. Like a deer with a severed artery. He'd watched the Ram DVD dozens of times. The blown up still frame sealed the deal. His hunter's instinct didn't lie. He knew Onassis and Blond John were the same man.

19

This was going to be bad. The footage was criminal. A hundred and thirty-three minutes of handheld Flipcam video shot by drunken people at an office party. Terry was supposed to cut it into an inspirational team-building video for Gittleman's Markets. Image Zoo shot and edited their TV spots.

The sprawling mess was shot by wildly partying Gittleman's employees at their holiday party three months ago. The Gittleman family owned a chain of local grocery stores and had rented out a Dave and Buster's for a whole night in December. They'd handed out a couple dozen Flipcams and started filling the beer pitchers. Nobody had looked at the footage until now. It was beyond dreadful. A mouse click froze the inebriated mob on the monitors.

Terry's mind was elsewhere.

He was The Falcon.

Or, put more accurately, he was The Falcon LLC.

Falcon LLC, as it turned out, was already being used as a company name and was unavailable. Henry had suggested adding the word "The" if Terry really liked the name.

The Falcon LLC. Terry liked the new name even more. He'd met with Henry in Ferndale to complete the paperwork.

The papers signed, Terry had then driven directly and fast to the Ann Arbor Third Bank to transfer two million dollars from his personal account into the newly formed The Falcon LLC's corporate account. Done deal. Hand managerially shaken. Checkbook forthcoming.

He'd also zeroed in on Amber DeGraaf. Online, he'd found two Amber DeGraffs in Silver Lake, California. One had a phone number that he was able to track down, the other did not. The *Adamo* art gallery was out of business.

It was past noon. He stared at his monitors. At all those merry Gittleman's partyers. He'd muted the cacophony of the wild Dave and Buster's scene and listened instead to his own music, some John Coltrane. He'd think about the Gittleman's project later. He had been waiting until it was after 9 a.m. in L.A.

Terry shut his door. Called the 818 number. Turned down the smoky jazz. Held his phone to his ear.

A phone started ringing on the west coast.

It went to voicemail. There was no personal message. Instead, a robot voice answered and restated the number before asking him to leave a message. No name was offered.

"Hi," said Terry to a microchip, sounding loud to himself. "My name is Terry Holbrook, and I'm trying to reach Amber DeGraaf. I'm in Michigan." Thinking, *That sounds awkward.* "Amber? Are you in trouble?" *That sounds worse.* He knew he had to stop talking. "Please call me back. It's about your father." Then he left his phone number.

He wished he hadn't said, "Are you in trouble?" He should've planned what to say. He almost called back.

A knock at the editing suite door.

"Come in."

It was Belinda. Widely eye-lined and colorfully garbed with a lot of bright, hanging, fringe-like things. As subtle as a peacock. "Jeff's got Gary Gittleman on the phone. Wants you to join in." The patriarch and CEO of the successful grocery chain, Gary Gittleman also considered himself quite creative and frequently had plenty of advice to offer on his video projects. It was his dime, so Jeff kept him happy. Terry joined Jeff for the call.

After absorbing Mr. Gittleman's many insights, it was all Gittleman's for Terry until quitting time. He focused on his work. Silver Lake slid from his mind.

Late in the afternoon, as he was assembling a reasonably sober-sounding three-minute sequence of upbeat sound bites from Gittleman's team members, his desk phone buzzed. From reception.

His desk phone never buzzed from reception.

"There's a call for you," said Belinda. "A Fran Siehling."

"Oh," said Terry, freezing his screens with a mouse click. He pictured Fran instantly from the funeral home. Dark and somber and beautiful. A face you don't forget.

"Is this a client?" asked Belinda through the phone.

Good question.

20

The day before, Fran had pulled into her otherwise empty garage at 5:30. Ever since September, when the first envelope arrived, she'd made a point of getting home before Bryce. Tonight, Bryce was playing squash after work, so he'd be home even later than usual, probably with a buzz on. After squash and a shower, a couple drinks at the club were *de rigeur*. Her workday had not been easy. She was ready for a glass of pinot grigio herself.

She wasn't worried about the mail. Not after only a week. But it had been a dreadful month. She'd recovered somewhat from the shock of her father's death, the funeral event, helping her mother to the extent that she could, and even the trauma at The Somerset Collection. She'd even absorbed the shame of a secret, pawnshop liquidation of her grandmother's Victorian diamond brooch, given to her years ago by her wrinkled, old Nana. Sold cheap to pay a blackmailer.

She'd called her mother that morning. The visiting nurse was gone. Her mother sounded okay. Millie was a tough old bird.

She'd also spent time with Becky since the funeral, watching her very closely. Trying to peer under her sister's serene, measured

Jesus talk. They talked about their dad. Their mom. About Becky's pregnancy. About little Clark and how excited he was about his soon-to-arrive new little brother or sister. Becky and Jim didn't know which it would be, wanting the surprise.

She'd even left a message with Amber. But had not heard back.

Settled in for a quiet cocktail in the warm, fleece-lined slippers she kept by the kitchen door all winter, Fran carried her wine with her to the front of the house. For the mail.

It lay in small pile on the rug beneath the slot in the front door.

Oh god.

A corner. White. Padded. Sandwiched between catalogs, envelopes, and *TIME* magazine.

This was too soon.

Fran froze. Listened. Only the dim roar of the furnace. The aged grandfather clock. She instinctively turned on more lights. Checked the doors and windows. All locked. She took the wine back to the kitchen. Almost poured it out in the sink. Drank it fast instead.

This was too soon.

Her mind raced ahead of her. Upstairs, she fumbled with the disposable gloves, pulling them onto her shaking hands. She got her tweezers and gold stork scissors. *Too soon, too soon.*

Walking downstairs, she worked to settle her breathing. Already thinking money. Where to get the money.

She squatted next to the mail on the oriental rug, tweezer tips reaching toward the white envelope, when her phone in her hip pocket buzzed, making her jump. Her flash of panic faded when she saw it was Bryce. She put him on speaker, setting her phone on the rug next to her.

"Hi, sweetie, how's it going?" she asked, careful to keep her voice calm as she slid the envelope away from the other mail. Mild bar noise in the background. Men's voices. On the envelope, two Forever flag stamps. Ruler straight.

"Great! How are you, babe?" Fran heard a burst of laughter from wherever Bryce was, followed by someone's off-color remark.

"I'm fine," she said. "Are you at the club?" The Detroit Athletic Club.

"Yeah, we got the courts early." More laughter. She turned the white envelope over. The Avery label addressed to her.

"When are you going to be home?"

"Why you got me on speaker?" His voice had bourbon in it.

"I'm just opening mail." Her gloved fingers felt the thumb drive inside the envelope. "So when *are* you going to be home?"

She heard Ed Smithfield make a rude remark in Bryce's ear, followed by male laughter. "Hey, fuck you!" Bryce retorted, then back to Fran. "I don't know. An hour."

She focused on money. Where to get the money. She didn't have any more jewelry to sell. Nothing that wouldn't be missed.

"Okay, sweetie. I'll wait dinner." Pinching the envelope with the tweezers, she carried it and her phone to the downstairs study. "Don't drive drunk. Uber if you have to." Bryce had Ubered home before.

"Okay, babe." Hoots of male laughter. Someone made obnoxious kissyface noises.

The big clod from the funeral home. That's where the money was.

"Love you," said Fran. She set the envelope on the computer desk. Pushed other papers aside.

"Love you, too. Bye."

"Bye," said Fran and ended the call. Picking up scissors, she carefully cut the top edge of the envelope, making sure not to cut it off completely. This done, she tipped and shook the envelope. A pink thumb drive clattered onto the desktop.

One shake. Two shakes.

The Six of Diamonds.

The tweezers fell from her hands and she slumped in her chair, her eyes squeezing shut.

"Shit, shit, SHIT!"

The pink thumb drive...they were always pink...was poison. That's why she wore the gloves. It wasn't really about fingerprints. It was because she loathed the idea of her skin touching anything he may have touched. It made her sick to picture it.

She rolled the mouse on its pad, and the monitor woke up.

Their desktop background image was a summer family photo showing her and Bryce and their son, Ty, all smiles on the boat. The photo not even a year old, taken just after Ty graduated from Liggett, the Grosse Pointe private prep school. Cornell still a summer away at the time.

Fran had worried that the East Coast would take her only child and never give him back. Her worries were sound. At Christmas, Ty told them he wanted to summer at a friend's whose family had a house on Cape Cod. Home last week for his grandfather's funeral, he'd asked permission again.

She looked at their smiling faces from two years ago. Then at the thumb drive. Everything changes.

She removed the protective cap from the male end of the thumb drive and pushed the pink stick into a USB port. The drive's *whirr* rose in pitch. A window opened onscreen. **View Pictures** it said. She double-clicked it.

Nothing happened for a few seconds. The machine ticked.

Then the photo appeared.

"Oh, my God," she shuddered. This was the worse yet.

Wet, pornographic color. Shiny. Pink and red. Three women naked. One black who looked sixty. One white, fat, and leering, blue eyeshadow and red lipstick smeared on like poster paint. And the third naked woman. Laughing. Young and beautiful. Rutting with a pair of pestilential prostitutes. Fran's hands covered her eyes until she dared look again.

Hands and fingers. Mouths and sweaty pubic hair. Breasts shiny with saliva.

She must be drugged. Nothing else explained it. But where? When? With no memory at all?

How?

Holding in her fury, her disgust, she checked for more photos, but, as always, there was only one. How many remained? A dozen? A hundred? Each worse than the last? A hell without end? But then she realized that's what hell is. Screaming, shrieking torture that never stops. That never ends. Ever.

This went beyond blackmail. This was Evil. She yanked out the thumb drive and hurled it against the wall. It fell to the leather couch. She screamed. She swore. She kicked the wastebasket across the room with a clatter, spilling trash. The computer screen tut-tutted against removing devices before properly closing files.

Her breathing heaved. Loudly. Like an animal in distress. This couldn't continue. But what could she do? She'd been warned that anything less than total cooperation would result in all the photos being released on the internet. A promise from a criminal was the only hope she had.

This was the sixth demand. From nearly two months between the first and the second envelopes to now; scarcely a week apart.

Her tormentor was turning the screws. Each new photo worse than the last.

The Six of Diamonds stared up at her.

Using the tweezers and stork scissors, she flipped over the playing card. To see her instructions. A typed, white sticker centered on a red Bicycle back.

Date. Place. Time.

She had a week to get sixty thousand dollars in cash.

21

The silver Audi pulled up outside Image Zoo at 10 a.m. Downtown Ann Arbor wore a pretty cape of freshly fallen snow. Terry had been waiting downstairs on the ground floor, looking out the window and watching for her. It was the day after she'd called. Terry had cleared his schedule with Jeff. Jeff was very understanding. But Jeff also smelled money. Terry couldn't blame him. Two million dollars made quite a stink. Terry stepped outside when he saw her. He made eye contact, waved briefly, and opened the passenger-side door.

"Hi," said Fran. She'd asked to meet him but didn't say why. He had a pretty good idea why. He'd been waiting for this particular shoe to drop.

She smiled at him as he got in. She wanted him to see her up close when she asked for the money. She knew her effect on men.

"Hi," said Terry. He shut the door. She looked great. Tired, but great. "There's a Starbucks..." he began.

"No," she interrupted. "This isn't going to take long. Is there a place we can just drive to and pull over and talk for a few minutes?"

Terry pointed. "There's neighborhoods that way. Residential. Anywhere in there."

"Perfect," said Fran. "There's a seat warmer if you want it." Terry rocked the switch for the butt warmer. Settled into soft leather. Nice car.

Fran pulled away from downtown toward an old neighborhood of mostly clapboard-and-brick, two-story homes that was on the other side of the railroad tracks. Terry wished he had brought coffee. Fran had a steel travel mug in a cup holder that matched the interior of her car, but she didn't touch it.

"So what's this all about?" asked Terry. They bumped over the tracks.

"Just a minute. Let me find a spot." Fran took a few corners, right and left, as though trying to find a special place. Not many places to park. She pulled into a gap under two naked maples. Cars parked on only one side of the street, with smallish old homes on both sides. Rental properties probably, leased to grad students and transient faculty.

She turned off the engine. She didn't want to look at him, but she forced herself to. She didn't want to smile at him and make direct eye contact, but she did.

On the phone, they'd said little. He'd asked how she found him. She said Abe Cohen.

In the quiet Audi, she smiled as the interior temperature began to cool. The man next to her disgusted her. Fat and low-class. And with their goddamn money. *What was dad thinking?*

Several attorneys representing surviving family members were currently working to establish that Michael DeGraaf was, in fact, *not* thinking—not of sound mind when he wrote the check.

"I need sixty thousand dollars in cash. Right away. Unmarked," said Fran.

Not at all what Terry had expected. Nothing so abrupt.

"Unmarked?" He blinked.

She nodded. Chin high. She didn't have to explain herself to this man.

His first impulse was to ask, *What for?*

Then Mike's plea came into his mind.

The gold pen in the fading dome light. Mike fading to stillness. The dead, open eyes.

I need you to save my daughter.

Terry stroked his goatee. For the last couple of mornings, he hadn't shaved at all. Suddenly he felt embarrassed. He had to stop being such a slob.

Maybe she had a gambling problem. Or maybe her husband did.

And she was Mike's daughter.

"Okay," said Terry.

"How soon can you get it?" said Fran.

A "thank you" would have been nice.

"Can I ask what this is for?" asked Terry.

"No," said Fran. "Frankly, it's none of your business."

Terry flared briefly at the insult. The demeaning glare. Her perfect face. *But was it his business?* Beautiful woman. Nice car. He bet it was gambling. He bet it was Bryce. And if this fixed it, great. Sixty thousand was a lot of money, but it wouldn't break the bank.

So what was the two million for?

"Okay." He drew a deep, noisy breath. "Point taken." He looked at her. She was in trouble. This incredibly beautiful woman.

A damsel in distress.

"I'll get you the money," he said.

"Can we get it now? While I'm here?" Her dark eyes burned into his.

Terry really didn't want her with him at the bank.

"You know," he said, "I don't really know how this unmarked thing works. When do you need it?"

"Now. Right away."

Terry caught a whiff of bullshit.

He let out a long breath. The car was getting cold. The windows steaming up. He missed the butt warmer now that the car was turned off. "I'll tell you what. I'll try to get it today. I'll see about this unmarked thing. I don't know if that's an issue."

Why did it have to be unmarked?

"And if I can get it today, I'll bring it to you. Where do you live?"

"You can bring it to my office. There's a coffee shop downstairs."

"You work?" Terry assumed that women this beautiful didn't work.

"Yes, I work!"

"What do you do?"

"I'm an art buyer—it doesn't matter."

"For who?"

"GM."

"On staff or contract?" Terry was always interested in art-related careers.

"Contractor—look, it doesn't matter! Can you call me when you have the money?" she snapped at him. Her patience spent.

"Okay," said Terry. "I'll call you."

"Thank you," said Fran, showing little gratitude.

She drove him back to Image Zoo. She remembered the way. Neither spoke.

At 2:40, after the lunch hour rush, Terry said, "Hi," to his teller friend, Jade, the stylish young woman with the horn-rimmed glasses.

"Hi," said Jade with a pleasant smile.

He'd called Henry. He'd asked about the unmarked bills. Henry said only the Treasury Department could mark bills. Terry also checked online. Apparently, that was the case.

Terry slid a paper withdrawal slip across to the teller. She picked it up and read it. Eyes widened.

"I'm gonna have to get somebody."

"I figured," said Terry.

Ten minutes later Ms. Baker, prim and bloodless, returned to her office, where, once again, Terry had been invited to sit and wait. She carried a large manila envelope, bulging at the sides, and shut the door.

"Thank you for your patience, Mr. Holbrook. Here you are." She dredged up a perfunctory smile. "All in hundreds."

"Great. Thank you. Unmarked, I assume?" He felt he had to slide that in.

Baker sat at her desk. Her eyes shrank momentarily.

"Yes. Unmarked. Of course."

Terry stood up. He had expected sixty thousand dollars to be bulkier. Like the briefcase of cash in the movies. Not just half a dozen inch-thick bundles.

"I suppose I should count it?" Terry asked.

"Certainly," said Baker, tight-lipped, and turned to busy herself on her computer while Terry counted the money. It was all there.

She walked him out. In the lobby, she shook his hand. "Good luck," she said, quietly.

And at the very moment she spoke, Terry once again felt that strange, shifting, optometrist exam effect he'd felt at the sheriff's office. It startled him greatly. But he definitely felt it. Like a different lens sliding in over reality. An altering. Where everything looked almost the same but not quite.

He looked carefully into Ms. Baker's eyes. *Was she feeling this, too?* She seemed softer somehow. Her smile genuine. Her eyes caring. Even loving.

But when their hands separated, the moment ended. Her smile vanished. Everything went back to normal. Like it had never happened at all.

By four o'clock Terry was on I-94, heading home from downtown Detroit. The wind had picked up fiercely, wildly blowing last night's snow around. Visibility was awful. So was his mood.

The handoff to Fran in Detroit had been unsatisfying. She didn't work in the RenCen, GM's towering headquarters on the river, but in another building a block north. City parking had cost him eight dollars for about eight minutes. She was waiting for him in the designated coffee shop, wearing her coat and sunglasses and carrying a large canvas tote. She said she couldn't talk, couldn't stay, had a meeting to go to, had to leave. The envelope of cash went into her canvas tote. He never even sat down. She rose when arrived, took the money, apologized briefly, thanked him, and left. Terry stood there dumbly, abandoned in the coffee shop. A dozen or so customers,, young and old, black and white, happy to be out of the cold, ignored him. This late in the day, the tall downtown buildings cast dark shadows over everything. He'd driven ninety minutes and parked a block away in blistering cold weather under heavy snowfall for a ten-second handoff. He felt used and stupid.

Terry drove slower than usual on the highway home, seething with anger but cautious in the swirling snow. A big semi roared by on his left, its wind shear shaking the Sebring.

"Eleanor Rigby" went his phone. He felt more than heard the ringtone. Dug it out of his coat and answered.

"Hello?

"Hello?" said an earnest-voiced woman. The road noise made it difficult to hear. "Is this Terry Holbrook?"

"Yes." He spoke loudly. Wind-driven waves of snow pelted the windshield.

"This is Amber DeGraaf." He could barely hear her.

"Really?" said Terry, startled. He raised the phone volume and killed his music, inadvertently juking out of his lane. A Jaguar next to him honked sharply, the driver giving him a dirty look.

"Look," said Terry loudly, over the traffic roar. "Let me pull over!" Terry signaled and pulled onto the right shoulder of the interstate, slowing to a stop. Immediately he felt close cars speeding by, roaring in his ears and vibrating the Sebring. The visibility down to nothing in the windswept blizzard. He turned on his emergency blinkers.

"Are you there?" said Amber DeGraaf, weakly.

"Yes," said Terry, unable to say more as a huge truck roared by three feet from his head. Like it would suck him out the door. "I apologize for the noise," he yelled into his phone.

"Do I know you?," the woman said. From California. Presumably.

"I was...," Terry started, and then he rethought. "You know about your father, don't you?" Another deafening semi went by, closer and faster than the last one. The Sebring rocked violently.

"What about my father? Who are you?" The woman's voice sounded pained and distant.

"You know your father passed away?" Terry shouted to be heard. "About ten days ago? You know about that, don't you?"

He heard nothing from the other end. *Were they still connected?* Another huge truck passed, shaking the Sebring to its rims. "Hello?" said Terry. "Amber? Miss DeGraff?" *Was she crying?* He couldn't hear a damn thing over the traffic noise.

"Yes," said Amber DeGraff, finally, "I know my father's dead." She also spoke loud, to be heard.

Now it was Terry's turn to pause. "Well, uh…I was with your father when he died. I was the last person to see him. And talk with him."

Another truck, another bone-rattling wind shear. He watched his twin emergency light arrows blink on the dash.

The woman spoke. "That really has no meaning for me." Terry could barely hear.

"What?" he hollered.

"I said, that really doesn't mean anything to me!" shouted the woman some 2,000 miles away.

"Look, are you in some kind of trouble?" yelled Terry. This was an impossible place to have a phone call.

"What?" shouted Amber. "What do you mean, trouble?" Then Terry heard someone in the background on Amber's end. Someone yelling. Not pleasant.

"Where are you now?" yelled Terry.

"At home. Look…," said Amber, "I've got to go."

"Call me back," Terry yelled. "Or I'll call you." Terry heard what he thought was more angry yelling at the other end. Something like a shriek. It didn't sound good. Then a hard thump. Or a dropped phone. The connection broke. She'd hung up. Or someone else had hung up. The line was dead.

He tried calling her back. Twice. Nothing.

He didn't know what to make of it. But he'd found Amber DeGraaf.

Save my daughter.

He put the Sebring in Drive. The sky had grown black. Creeping forward along the shoulder, white-knuckled, wind gusts beating at his car, Terry saw a slim gap in the rushing traffic and punched it. With a fishtail and a Hail Mary, he pulled into the treacherous flow.

22

"Yeh, he come in." The old diner manager glanced briefly at the rumpled paper photo printout from Office Depot, then back to his register.

"No shit?" said Thano. "This guy?" Thano rattled the much-creased photocopy in the diner man's face, which perturbed the older man.

"Yeh. Thet guy. Put thet out of my face."

Thano had been up and down St. Clair Shores and through most of Roseville, in and out of at least fifty bars, strip joints, and restaurants. Now, at the Athens Family Restaurant, one of the countless greasy eateries called Athens something, the first hit. It was three in the afternoon. He saw no families in the family restaurant. A couple black guys on stools at the counter. Two hookers. Some old men in the back, talking Greek. Really old men. Canes and shit. Bouzouki music. Pictures on the wall of white temples with columns. The smell of fried onions.

"He still come in?"

"Sure. Sometime." The grizzled man at the register had probably lived in the neighborhood for decades and still hadn't kicked the accent. But Thano was careful of the old Greek's knowing eye.

Thano smiled and put the paper back in his coat. "That's awesome! Because he's my uncle." A disbelieving nod from the owner.

"You going to eat something?"

"Yeah," Thano nodded. "Sure. I'll have..." He glanced at the scrawled board of specials that hadn't changed in years. "...the Gyro Dinner." It was the most expensive item on the board.

"Mm," said the old Greek. He wrote it on an order slip. His hands hard and hairy, not particularly clean.

"Does he come in a lot?"

The old man paused, spread his hands. "I don' know! Sometime. He like my baklava. Best in the world." He turned back to his order pad. "What you to drink?" he asked, not looking up.

"You got beer?"

"No beer."

"How about Coke?"

"Coke yes."

Thano was about to speak when the old guy turned away to yell the order in Greek to the cook at the griddle. The cook yelled back in confirmation.

"I really want to find this guy."

"Your 'uncle'." A crinkle in the manager's eye. Flash of gold tooth.

"Yeah, man, my uncle. When he comes in will you call me? Could you call me?" Thano implored him with a yearning, puppy-dog look that he didn't even know he had.

"I call you?"

"Yeah. Could you do that?"

The old Greek drummed his fingers on the register, gazing at the young criminal. He remembered life on the streets. He hadn't been so different at that age. Smarter, sure, but not so different.

"How much you pay?" he asked.

P.J. came into his uncle's squalid living room with a leather purse. "Hey, where the fuck have you been?" said Bill, barely glancing away from the tit show on TV. It was dark out. Bill was eating cold ribs on the couch. P.J. had left earlier without saying anything. His uncle wasn't necessarily happy that he'd returned. Bill looked away from the TV again as P.J. stepped further into the stuffy, sloppy living room hazy with bong smoke. "And what's with the purse?" said Uncle Bill. "You a fag now?"

P.J. hurled the purse at his diminutive uncle, knocking an ash-tray off the La-Z-Boy armrest into his uncle's reclining lap. Bill jumped up, beating ashes, butts, and roaches off his crotch.

"Hey, what the fuck! What's the matter with you!"

"There's money in there. Credit cards, too. And here." P.J. flung a jangly key ring at his uncle, who caught it with some trouble. Bill sat down, fingering through the keys and shopper discount tags. Chick shit.

"There's an Impala out back," said P.J. He meant the fenced junkyard. "You been bitchin' about money." P.J. jutted his chin toward the keys and the purse. "There's money. Stop bitchin'."

Bill didn't ask any more questions. Then glanced at P.J.

"Thano called." He gave his hulking nephew a slow, loaded nod.

Even sitting twelve feet away, Bill saw P.J.'s pinhole eyes heat up fast across the room, burning through the gray haze of smoke like lasers.

23

This was crazy. But Christina backed him up. Even Jeff backed him up. But Jeff always played the long game.

Terry glanced around the vast, bustling airport terminal. Watched travelers of all kinds stand still while gliding forward on moving walkways. An indoor monorail hummed by overhead. It was all much busier than he remembered.

Amber DeGraaf was in trouble. Terry could tell. He'd called her back for two straight days after that first, abrupt, roadside conversation. He'd left a dozen messages. No response.

She was the daughter Mike was talking about. Terry was sure of it. She was the one in trouble. Maybe big trouble. *But how much trouble do you have to be in to need two million dollars to get out?*

Christina made him promise to come home immediately if there was any hint of trouble. Or danger. He promised her.

Henry's advice was the best. "Look and listen, but don't say much."

"Don't worry," Terry told Christina before he left. "It's just a recce." Pronounced *reckie*. Filmmaker slang for reconnaissance—scouting locations. Then she hugged and kissed him. Then Hannah hugged and kissed him. Then Christina made him repeat his promise again.

Now here he sat at the gate, people-watching. He hadn't flown anywhere in several years.

An elaborately coiffed female flight attendant stepped to the mic at the check-in desk. Her amplified voice turned heads.

"Group 1 may begin boarding Flight 276 to Los Angeles at Gate B9." Group 1. Polite-speak for First Class.

Terry watched the first-class people queue up, roller bags trailing, exchanging smiles with the cheerful Delta staff at the gate. He'd packed a small, red nylon Nike bag with two shirts, two pairs of socks, two pairs of underwear, spare jeans, a Dopp kit, a *TIME* magazine, and a paperback. He sat with the other coach-classers, waiting for his row to be called. He'd only been to L.A. once before, during Spring Break in his sophomore year at college. He wasn't keen on flying then and even less so now. He didn't like the airborne motion. Or the small seats.

After a few minutes, they called his row. He got in line, clutching his wispy paper boarding pass.

He'd told Christina about the brief phone call with Amber DeGraaf, leaving out the part about the roaring semi trucks screaming past in a blizzard, inches from his window. He told her about the person or persons yelling in the background. He didn't mention the hard, thumping sound that ended the call.

"Fly safe," said Terry to the smiling stewardess who greeted him as he stepped aboard the 767. Whether she heard him over the roar of engine sounds and air conditioning, he did not know.

It was only 6 p.m. Michigan time. With the time difference, it would be 7:30 when he landed in L.A., assuming no delays. He'd had a tall beer in the airport plus a McDonald's cheeseburger and fries meal. The beer was sleep insurance.

He had a game plan. He'd found a street address for an Amber DeGraaf in Silver Lake. Whether it was the address of the phone number he'd called, he wasn't sure. He'd printed a map of Silver Lake, and marked her street with a pink highlighter marker.

If it was the right place and she was still there, he knew it was a risk just showing up. But if he left a message and she knew he was coming, she might disappear. Or someone else could hear the message, and then who knows? Maybe something worse would happen.

He didn't know her schedule, obviously. Theoretically, she could be somewhere else when he showed up, at work or traveling or whatever. But he had to start somewhere.

He found his seat, a middle, and crammed his Nike bag in the crowded upper storage compartment. He was glad he packed light. It looked like it was going to be a full flight. The hiss of blowing air and humming electricals tickled his ears.

Wedged into his seat, Terry felt more giddy than uncomfortable. Awaiting takeoff on a cold, dark night. A man alone.

The Falcon.

On a case.

His mouth curled into a small smile. He felt cool and hard-boiled. On a night flight to The City of Angels. He imagined a snap-brim fedora pulled low, leather shoulder holster slung with a .45 automatic.

In a good mood, Terry shared pleasantries with the mercifully tiny older Asian woman who took the aisle seat next to him. She smiled politely but said little. The window seat next to him stayed empty. No one ever showed up. After takeoff, he could spread out a little.

Ten minutes later the big jet roared down the runway and took off. Terry slid to the window. He watched a receding panorama of lit-up buildings shrink away in the Michigan night. Cars and trucks quickly became specks of moving light on a black landscape below.

Terry got drowsy quickly when clouds swallowed the plane, cutting off any view at all. He leaned back in his seat as far as it would go and turned off the overhead light.

Amber DeGraaf, just sit tight.

The Falcon to the rescue.

24

He'd picked Banana Republic because both men and women shopped there, and it was the right kind of bag. He always dictated what bag she must use. Great Lakes Crossing was a giant outlet mall with movie theaters, an aquarium, lots of restaurants, a Lego Land, and a Bass Pro Shops Outdoor World built to look like a giant hunting lodge with a fake trout stream flowing indoors that held real fish.

Great Lakes Crossing also had a big, busy food court. With lots of seating.

This was his job. His profession. He was an entrepreneur now. That's what Ricky said.

Maggot smiled. Everything had led to this.

Ricky said there was a silver lining.

Ricky knew so much. Even how Maggot got his name.

How could he know that? Maggot wondered.

He was eight. September of third grade. Still summer-warm out, all the leaves still on the trees. New school, new grade, new kids. Walking home from the bus with three other boys, they took a meandering route and found the dead dog in a back alley behind some old houses. A big black dog. No collar and its fur scabbed and matted. One eye missing. Just a dry, empty socket. Flies buzzed in the heat. The other eye was open and glassy and stared at them.

It was a hot sun with no clouds and the dead dog stank. It had been there for a day at least. The new boy didn't know it yet, but where they now lived now, dead dogs and cats and rusting shopping carts and abandoned cars did not get removed quickly, if at all.

The stink filled their noses. Like rotten meat but worse. A rank, rancid smell of decomposing flesh and guts. Big flies buzzed around, ravenous, their fat, shiny green bodies winking in the sun. They jittered and landed and took off again, circled and buzzed and landed over and over again on the dead dog's muzzle, nose, and dulled open eye. Landed in its open mouth, walking on the motionless pink tongue between sharp white teeth.

"Turn it over," someone said. The other boys were bigger. Backpacks were dropped, and a stick was found they could turn the dead dog over with. The body was pretty stiff. The legs and the belly showed horrendous carnage when they turned it over, as though the dog had been torn open by claws. The circling flies scattered momentarily.

Originally, they thought the dog was hit by a car, but now they weren't so sure. Its whole underside looked ripped and clawed apart. Drying red flesh rimmed a ragged wound crusted with black hair. It looked like it had been attacked by a larger beast. Bluish and red guts loosened and slid out. Shiny but dry.

The stench doubled from the exposed innards and the boys stepped back, swearing and holding their noses. Whoever had been holding the stick quickly threw it away. A cicada's screeching chirr rose from a faint hum to an unbelievably loud shriek, piercing their ears until they hurt. Then they saw the maggots.

They were in the wound. In the open maw of guts. The only things moving in the dead animal. Squirming, churning, hating the sun, hundreds of them, headless, tailless, faceless wet worms, twisting and burrowing their wet, angry white bodies into putrid dead flesh. Furiously deprived of their cover of darkness.

The other three boys turned away with howls and whoops of disgust. But the new kid squatted down, curious. He and the big, buzzing flies were attentive. He was only a foot away.

Someone shoved him from behind, and his hand had to go into the maggots and dog guts just to keep his balance. He felt wet maggots squirming between his fingers. The other three boys hooted with high-pitched laughter. Mean, buzzing laughter.

Then they shoved him into the squirming maggots again. And again.

They pressed his face into the dead dog's guts, seething maggots moving on his cheek. Someone's shoe on his neck holding him down. Maggots on his lips, squirming against his mouth.

The nickname started right then. From then on, he was Maggot.

It was yelled at him. Screamed at him. For years. Kids hit him with the name like a stick. The teasing. The pushing. The wedgies. Hair pulled. Lunch money stolen. Filthy shoes he was forced to lick.

Ricky knew all about it. Ricky was sympathetic. Ricky was his friend.

Ricky had the best ideas, too. The photos. The playing cards. The money. All Ricky's ideas.

"Just follow the plan," he said with his high, keening laugh.

Ricky said there was a silver lining, and, sure enough, there was.

Maggot saw her from across the food court.

There *she* was.

She was his silver lining.

Holding a Banana Republic bag and looking terrified.

25

Bridget Gunderson got home from the strip club after 3 a.m., sore all over. She tried to forget the things she had done for money that night. Wished her cigarette had a stronger taste. After trudging up four dark flights, the elevator long out of order, she unlocked and opened the door to the tiny apartment. Inside, she flicked the wall switch. Light filled into the room.

Stunned, she thought at first that she must be on the wrong floor. Or in the wrong building. But the key worked. This was 4C. Her apartment. With her things inside. But what her eyes beheld was not the littered pigsty she was used to, the trash-filled rat's nest she called home.

This apartment was clean.

Beyond clean.

Spotlessly clean.

She hadn't cleaned in months. Maybe years. And never like this.

The carpet was vacuumed. She didn't own a vacuum. The stains on it had been Resolved. The small table and mismatched chairs were all dusted. Polished. Arranged just so. She smelled Lemon

Pledge, or something like it. A bowl of fresh fruit sat on the table-top. She saw oranges, apples, and bananas.

She set her keys on the table. "Hello?" she called out tentatively. No answer. She slipped out of her silver fox coat, ready to drop it, as always, in the nearest chair, where it might well slide to the floor. Instead, for once, she hung it carefully over the chairback.

The light was on in the galley kitchen, gleaming off the scrubbed and decluttered '70's Formica countertop. The steel sink basin was scoured; the chrome faucet and handles gleamed. All the dirty dishes and glasses that had been piled in the sink for weeks were cleaned and dried and sorted and stacked in wiped-down cupboards, for which fresh vinyl liner had been cut to size and laid flat. All the garbage was gone. A fresh, white, heavy-duty garbage bag lined a new plastic trash can. The bottles and cans and fast-food bags and soda cups that constantly littered her home were gone. All the ashtrays were emptied and cleaned. She checked under the sink. It was clean down there, too. New bottles of cleaners and soaps and sponges were set neatly in line like soldiers reporting for duty. She ran water over her cigarette and threw it in the trash.

The refrigerator, too, had been cleaned inside and out. It was full for the first time ever. Milk, eggs, fruit juice, yogurt, butter. Ground beef. Some pork chops. Some chicken. She hadn't cooked in weeks. Maybe months. The stove top and oven were cleaned. So were the cooking utensils and silverware. There were fresh paper towels and paper napkins. And the old linoleum floor was scrubbed all the way to the edges and deep into the corners. Several burnt-out lightbulbs had also been replaced.

She explored further. The bedroom and tiny bathroom were

just as clean as the kitchen and living room. New linens were on the bed, along with new pillows and a new blanket and comforter, the bed made up drum-tight with corners tucked. The clothes that had been strewn everywhere when she'd left for the club were now laundered. Folded and stacked or hung in the closet. Her shoes were organized. Her loose jewelry sorted onto a small, decorative tray borrowed from the kitchen. In the corner stood a new vacuum cleaner.

The bathroom was virtually unrecognizable. Toilet, sink, and shower tub scrubbed inside and out. Rust streaks gone. A new shower curtain. The floor behind the toilet was cleaner than she'd ever seen it. The mirror sparkling clean. Her makeup supplies were all wiped clean and organized in a new makeup caddy next to the sink. The eyebrow pencils sharpened.

There were new towels and washcloths. Even a brand-new, white terry cloth robe hanging from a hook on the back of the bathroom door.

"Hello?" she said again, knowing there'd be no answer. Maybe the neighbors knew something, but she didn't know her neighbors. They never spoke to her.

Next to the fruit bowl, she found a note wrapped around a stack of bills, and a small, wooden cross. She read the note with shaking hands.

Give yourself a clean start, Bridget. P.S. I took your liquor.

And a phone number.

She quickly counted the money. Five thousand dollars. She struggled not to scream. When Bridget called the number, a woman who seemed wide awake answered on the first ring.

26

Southern California's morning heat and sunshine thoroughly erased snowy February from Terry's mind, but he was stunned and saddened by the sea of ochre smog that spread in every direction. Neither the smog nor the traffic had been this oppressive 25 years ago, his only other visit to Los Angeles. The sky was the color of weak tea. The buildings mostly scaly beige. Grass was scorched to a sickly tan like rotted straw, and where no grass grew, the caked dirt was baked brown. Streets and sidewalks were flecked everywhere with multicolored fast-food trash thrown from cars.

He'd rented a Ford Fusion at the airport, found the airport Ramada that he'd gotten an online deal at, and slept poorly. His internal clock was a mess. He made up for it with a big buffet breakfast at the hotel. Lots of scrambled eggs and sausage and hash browned potatoes. Silver Lake was three miles east and two miles south of Hollywood. The map he'd been given at the car rental counter didn't show much detail, but the Ramada clerk helped him read it. From home, he'd brought his map printout showing the Silver Lake address: 1210 Raymond Street. It was also on his phone.

Getting there in one piece was another story. He waited until after morning rush hour, but even at 10:30, the raging traffic on the northbound 405 topped any Michigan rush hour. Terry had to floor it on the entry ramp just to sluice into the flow. It was like a carnival ride without the fun. Horns blew frequently. After two or three minutes of bloodcurdling, bumper-to-bumper near panic, Terry unclenched long enough to notice the view.

It was sensational. Heading north on the 405, he saw atop a sunbaked hill the dazzling, futuristic Getty Museum, the richest art museum in the world. To the east more hills displayed rows of slender, twisting cypress and tall, graceful palm trees, rising like exotic giants. Boxlike homes on stilts clung to steep hillsides, overlooking the glittering river of traffic below. Vast porches attached to the boxy houses jutted over tall, dead grass.

After fifteen northbound minutes, Terry curved left in the mad flow of chrome, tire rubber, glass, and flesh swarming east on the Santa Monica freeway toward Hollywood. To the north, brown mountains penned in the San Fernando Valley. To the south, the flat expanse of Los Angeles spread for miles like a vast, quicksilver griddle. Soon, smaller hills appeared on Terry's right. The Hollywood Hills. Then the traffic jammed.

Thirty stop-and-go minutes later, signs forced Terry to choose between left toward Pasadena or right toward San Bernardino. He wanted neither. Fumbling with his map while steering drew instant honks, so he exited at the first opportunity. A sign said *Griffith Observatory*. He remembered seeing it indicated on his Google map from home. Terry knew of the famous landmark from movies like *Rebel Without a Cause* and *La La Land* and loads of 50's sci-fi cheapies. If he remembered correctly from reviewing the map earlier, the observatory was a couple miles north of Silver Lake.

The exit put Terry onto Sepulveda Boulevard with no Griffith Observatory in sight. After a confused couple of minutes, he pulled into a 7-Eleven. It was 11:15 and blazing hot outside. He hadn't thought to bring sunglasses. He kept the A/C blowing and studied the map, wishing he'd brought shorts.

He didn't know where he was. Had to ask at the store. The asphalt felt soft and smelled hot and tarry. A brief discussion with the natty, senior Asian counter man helped. Terry jotted the man's broken English onto the map. He also bought sunglasses and a large Coke.

He drove what he believed to be south. Looked for helpful signs. Didn't see any. If Silver Lake had signs or stores or restaurants, Terry didn't see them. Instead he found himself snaking up and down curving, narrow roads that apexed at the Observatory, then undulated back downhill, unfathomably.

Now he wound past lush foliage and grassy berms upon which sat early Hollywood bungalows. Tiny stuccoed homes of beige, pink, and faded lime. Vines and creepers clung to many of them, stirring silver screen spirits of Bogart and Bacall, Cagney and Hayworth, and Wilder and Welles. He was transported by atmosphere backward in time.

The knobby hills of Silver Lake abruptly swallowed him. He saw a Silver Lake sign. The streets continued winding, and soon the twisting topography disclosed small, terracotta-roofed homes in abundance, many surrounded by green brambles, short palms, and flowering gardenias. Traffic thinned drastically in the residential neighborhood. After three pullovers to reorient, Terry found

Raymond Street and turned left. He looked for 1210 Raymond. The only other cars he saw were parked in driveways and lifeless.

When he saw that the address numbers were going the wrong way, Terry did a three-point turn to reverse course. At high noon Silver Lake was a ghost town. He backtracked. Bend after bend of pint-sized 1920's and 30's houses were set high and back from the street, with sloping grass in front and short, steep driveways. Some had cement steps descending to the sidewalk. He came to a mailbox with 1210 on it. Peeling brown paint. No name.

He slowed but didn't stop, glancing up at the house. Any Bogart fantasies collapsed in his mind. This wasn't a movie.

He parked at the curb two houses away. Peered back at the house. Like most in the neighborhood, it was small, maybe 1,500 square feet. Wood and stucco, not well-kept. The grass a sickly green where a lawn sprinkler sometimes sprinkled and brown where it did not. The sprinkler turned off. A bohemian house in a bohemian neighborhood, sunburnt and shabby. Maybe that's why there were no kids around. Maybe bohemians didn't have kids.

He was stalling.

He cracked the window so the interior wouldn't melt. Opening the door, he was instantly hammered by heat. It had to be over ninety. So this was winter in L.A. A zephyr of hot breeze briefly brushed his cheek. No wonder everyone was inside. Outside, from every direction, Terry heard the throaty whine of air conditioners.

He began sweating, the sun at its zenith.

He walked to the house, paused on the sidewalk, and looked up at the house again. Then he walked up the driveway between the roar of a window air conditioner from Amber's house and the roar of the neighbor's A/C unit on the other side. At the top of the drive, a cracked cement walkway led to the front door. No vehicle in the driveway. He saw a detached wooden, single-car garage in the back with its door down. No lights on anywhere. House drapes shut.

The cement walk was weedy. It led to a wooden porch that creaked when he stepped on it. Shaded by an overhanging roof, a plank porch painted gray long ago was now scuffed to bare wood in a path to the front door. He removed his new sunglasses, breathing hot, old wood smell from the brutally baked eaves overhead. The front door was oak and arched, with cracked varnish, a black knocker, and a peephole. To Terry's left were twin sash windows, curtained. On the porch, a faded red wicker rocker and a vinyl Adirondack chair flanked a tiny white plastic table that held a ceramic ashtray full of ashes, cigarette butts, and two twist-off beer caps.

Terry stood still and listened for any sound inside. Nothing. There was a yellowed plastic button by the door.

He pressed it.

A flat, electric buzzer buzzed inside, the old-fashioned kind that buzzed for as long as you held down the button. He hadn't heard one in years. He gave it another short press just to hear it again.

Inside, a dog barked. Not a yip. Not a woof. Just a bark. Then footsteps.

The footsteps stopped. A shadow at the peephole. After a pause, the inner knob rattled. With a squawk the door swung in, and Terry faced an unreadable gaze from a solid, athletically built African-American woman. She looked maybe in her forties and wore a blue denim work shirt with the sleeves cut off at the shoulders and sweat shorts. She was barefoot. Hair short and nappy.

Thighs thick and strong. Her heavy-lidded brown eyes did not invite.

"Yes?" she finally said.

"Hi," said Terry. "Good morning. Well, actually, good afternoon. Is there an Amber DeGraaf here? I'm here…" He coughed dry. "…to see her. That's…that's why I'm here."

The woman at the door ceded nothing. "Who wants to know?" she asked.

"I'm Terry Holbrook. My name is Terry Holbrook. I talked to…Ms. DeGraaf on the phone. I've come all the way from Michigan. To see her."

The woman at the door appraised him a few moments more. Then said, "Just a minute," and closed and locked the door. Bolted it.

Terry waited. Heard voices inside. Two women. Much crosstalk. Terry heard claws scrabble on glass and looked left to see a boxer or boxer mix on the back of a couch, nosing aside the curtains to look at him from the window. Saw the dog's eye whites as it twisted to see him. He or she barked twice at Terry.

The door half opened, and Terry faced a shorter woman, white, thick around the middle, with wiry, carrot-orange hair and a pale complexion. She looked blankly up at Terry. He wondered how anybody could be so pale in Southern California. It was Amber from the visitation photos. Older. Heavier. Plainer.

"Yes?" she said. She made no move to open the door further.

"I'm Terry Holbrook," said Terry. He offered his hand. She ignored it. "I'm from Michigan. We spoke on the phone. I knew your father." He caught himself. "I mean…I didn't really know him, but, uh, he asked me to help. To help … him."

"He's dead," she said.

"I know."

"What do you mean help?" She showed no sign of remembering the phone call or getting the voicemails. She looked a little out of it. Sleepy.

"Um," said Terry. "It's kind of a long story. Can I come in?" The dog had appeared at the woman's pale legs and eyed him inquisitively. Amber wore a loose, faded yellow sleeveless cotton dress, bare-legged. No bra. Blue rubber flip-flops.

"Sure," she said and stepped back so Terry could enter. The boxer started barking. Through the small, dark house, a dim hallway led to the kitchen in back, where the first woman stood. Kitchen window light silhouetted her. She had her arms crossed, one blocky hip thrust to the side. Terry couldn't see her face.

"That's Gladys," said Amber referring to the dog. "She's very protective." Terry generally got along well with dogs. He stooped down with knuckles held out so the dog could get a good sniff. The dog did so and even favored Terry's hand with a flick of her warm, wet tongue. Terry gave Gladys a generous pat on her head and ears.

"She's a sweetheart," he said, rising. The woman gave him a brief, pinched smile.

"She's still young," she said.

Terry nodded.

"Please," she said, gesturing Terry into the tiny living room. The room with the windows to the porch.

The décor was cluttered, dusty, and disorganized. Colorful but not very good paintings of African-American women decorated the walls, along with charcoal and pencil drawings on the same subject. Women of all ages. All African-American or just African. No straightened hair in any of them. Most in native dress, although some in Western clothes with African designs. To Terry's eye, some of it was passable artwork. Most of it wasn't. He glanced around for sculptures. Something made by Amber. He didn't see anything.

A dusty upright piano, its bench piled with old magazines, stood in a corner. A worn, sagging, bamboo-framed jungle-print sofa faced a wall-mounted flatscreen TV. There wasn't room for a coffee table, but two end tables each held half-full ashtrays. The smell and haze of cigarette smoke hung in the stuffy little room. Amber picked up two used, empty wine glasses. Inside the small fireplace was a many-armed, rusty iron candle holder. It held eight or so squat, dusty, half-melted candles of assorted colors. Skinny black wicks curled like dead rollup bugs.

A rocking chair with a purple afghan on it flanked the couch. The rocker's seat held more magazines. Two built-in bookcases on either side of the fireplace sagged with books, a few photos, more candles, dusty odds and ends.

"Can I get you anything? Tea? A water?"

"A water would be nice," said Terry. "Thank you." He stood in the small room feeling huge and awkward.

"Please," she said, smudged wine glasses in hand. "Have a seat."

"Thank you," said Terry. He sat on the sun-faded cushions of the bamboo sofa, taking up most of it. Gladys jumped up on the sofa, eyeing him as though he was going to give her something to eat. Terry said to it, "I don't know if you're supposed to be up here." The dog blinked at Terry, unconcerned.

Terry heard kitchen-sink clatter from down the hall and low female conversation. All he picked out were the African-American woman's loudest words: "...don't owe him a damn thing!"

After a long minute, Amber returned to the living room carrying a plastic bottle of refrigerated water and a coffee mug of something for herself. She handed the water to Terry, who opened it and drank. He put the cap in his shirt pocket. She cleared the magazines off the seat of the rocker and turned it to face Terry and Gladys on the couch. "I remember our phone call now," she said, sitting down.

"Good," said Terry. "Thanks," he said, raising the bottle slightly toward Amber before taking another swig.

Amber DeGraaf just looked at him.

"So, uh," began Terry. "From our phone call."

"I don't have anything to do with that family anymore," said Amber.

Terry nodded. "Well," he said. "That happens sometimes."

"Because they don't want anything to do with me!" she leaned forward, anger rapidly coloring her voice and face. Terry was taken aback.

"Look, Amber—" said Terry.

"How dare you call me Amber!" She sneered unpleasantly. "'Amber.' Like we're old friends. I don't know you! And you certainly don't know me!" The blood beneath her cheeks blotched her face.

Yikes, thought Terry.

"Look. Miss DeGraaf."

"Mizzz DeGraaf."

"Ms. DeGraaf," Terry corrected. He took a breath. Exhaled.

Looked her straight in the eye.

"I need to know if you're the daughter who needs help, or not."

"What do you mean?"

"Your father asked me..."

"You mean paid you."

Terry paused. "You know about that?"

Amber DeGraaf's eyes went narrow and her lips thinned. "We all know about that."

Terry shifted. Maybe she called Cohen. Or someone called her.

He drank more water. "Okay, then. Your father paid me…hired me, actually…to, and I quote, 'save my daughter' unquote. That's what he said. Those were his exact words. That's all I'm trying to do. Keep my promise."

He couldn't say it any better than that.

"Then why don't you give her the money and go back where you came from?"

Terry glanced to the right. It was the roommate. Housemate. Wife. Whatever. Cigarette in one hand, lighter in the other, looking mean as a snake. Terry kept his mouth shut.

"Rose, this doesn't concern you."

Rose burbled a low, mirthless laugh. "Doesn't concern me? In my house? What anybody say in my house concerns me."

"Rose, please," pleaded Amber.

"Rose, please!" mimicked Rose. She lit her cigarette and crossed her arms in well-practiced defiance. Then, acidly, "I be in de back, Miz DeGraaf. Washin' yo clothes wit' da utha help." A slow turn with dagger eyes. Eased back toward the kitchen. Withdrew from the light.

After a moment, Terry said to Amber, "You alright here?"

"She doesn't wash my clothes."

"You wash hers?"

"She's angry."

He almost said, *Ya think?* but instead said, "At you?"

"At a lot."

"But are you...?" Terry gestured to Amber with both hands. Trying to choose the right word. "...alright?" Abused seemed too forward.

"Absolutely."

"Safe?" asked Terry, after a pause.

Amber nodded mechanically. "Oh, yes," she said. "Safety is in no way a problem."

Terry thought that had a weird sound to it. "Do you need money?" he asked. Amber laughed sharply but didn't look at him.

"Who doesn't?" she snorted.

"How much do you need?"

She looked at him now. Her eyes pale blue. Very pale. Quite pretty, really. Quite peaceful, briefly. "How much have you got?"

Terry thought about the sixty thousand dollars he'd given to Fran. "I've talked to Fran."

"Ah, yes. Franny. Franny, Franny, Franny. Franny and Bryce." She said "Bryce" like snapping a pencil. "The perfect couple. The perfect family. So, *so* perfect."

"She's not perfect," said Terry. "And I haven't talked to Rebecca yet."

Amber pooched her lips at him mockingly. "Little Becky?"

This was getting unpleasant.

"Little baby Becca?" cooed Amber bitterly. "Pretty little Becca? Pooping out babies? All about Jesus? Gentle as a widdle wamb?" Amber mimed vomiting, jabbing a finger down her throat.

Terry drank water, processing.

"When was the last time you saw your dad?"

Amber just glared at him.

"When was the last time you spoke to him?"

"That's none of your business."

"Tell it, girl," said Rose from the hallway. As Terry looked up, she again backed slowly out of sight.

Terry appraised Amber DeGraaf. Tried to. He was beginning to think she was on something. Medicated.

Terry picked his words carefully. "Amber," he began softly. "Ms. DeGraaf." Flicking his eyes toward the dark hallway, he kept his voice low. "Do you need..." He was whispering now. "Do you need..." He tipped a thumb toward the hallway. "...to get out of here?"

Amber DeGraaf widened her eyes. "What?" she said. Then, "How dare you! How *dare* you!" Her hands fluttered to her chest. Covering herself. "Who the hell are you!? Why are you even here?" She stood and backed away from him.

"No!" said Terry, palms up, fingers spread. He stood up. "No! I mean. I don't know. Your dad said, 'Save my daughter.' That was it. That's all I know."

"Then why don't you write me a fucking check and get the fuck out of here!" shouted Amber DeGraaf, pushing her red face at him. He saw white all the way around her blue irises. Gladys started barking.

This couldn't be what Mike DeGraaf had meant. Paying them off.

"Okay," he stalled. "I can do that." He thought quickly. "How does sixty thousand sound?" At this, Amber's eyes settled and her face broke into a big, beaming smile. An Irish smile like her mother's.

"Sixty thousand dollars?" she said. "That sounds fantastic!" Terry was surprised but pleased. The dog stopped barking.

Her smile vaporized. She was mocking him. Her pasty face grew small and hateful. "How about two *million* dollars, you fat, fucking asshole!"

He froze. Not at the insult but at the hair-trigger rage. Fueled by pain he didn't know. Couldn't know.

Eyes blazing, the stocky woman's face vibrated, quivered. Her lower lip shone with spittle. Her eyes flamed hate. Fists clenched.

Terry stood up. "Are you alright?"

Her mouth a twisted grimace. "Am I alright? Who the *fuck* are *you?* Jesus? Jesus *fucking* Christ!?" Terry winced at the curse.

"Don't talk like that," he said, quietly. Now his temper was bubbling. Heating up. A bad feeling. He hadn't lost control in years.

She jerked her head back, mock-stunned. "What? You're the father confessor now? Don't you *dare* judge me! Who the fuck do you think you are? Father Fat Fuck?"

Temper heating fast now.

"Father Fat Fuck diddling little boys in the confessional?!"

That did it.

Terry blew. Red-faced, control lost, on his feet, his index finger jabbing at her eyes.

"You want insults!? Is that what works for you? You…you…fat, stupid, BITCH! Is that what you like?" His arms flailing now. "So *fucked* up in your head you don't even *know* you're being walked on? That you're a *fucking doormat?* Pushed around? *Abused?*" Gladys barking like crazy now.

Outshouted, she cowered, quivering. Her mouth wet, rubbery, eyes welling. But Terry didn't stop. Couldn't stop.

He hadn't lost his temper since before Hannah was born. But here it was. Back in force. His face red, his voice loud, and his eyes bulging. The black roil inside him howled with glee.

He yelled over the dog's repeated barking.

"Is *this* working for you, Amber? Is *this* how you like it? The anger? The screaming? The swearing? Is *this* what works for you?

'Cause I'll tell you…" He breathed hard, gulping air. Took deep breaths. "I'll tell you…" He forced himself to calm down. Lowered his hands to his sides, clenching and unclenching his fists.

"…that…that's a shitty way to live."

He wiped his sweaty forehead with a sleeve. Amber DeGraaf wept into her hands. The roil inside him fled. Raged. And plotted.

"Are we through, white folks?" asked Rose leaning against the archway to the living room. The dog quieted. She inhaled from her cigarette. In her other hand, she held a smartphone with thumb poised and ready. "I just dialed 9 and 1." She eyed Terry. "Want the other 1, asshole?"

Terry heaved out a breath. His shoulders relaxed. He patted down the air with both hands. Shook his head. "No need for that." He closed his eyes for a few moments, rubbing them hard with both hands. "I'm sorry," he said.

Rose didn't blink. Jiggled the phone, thumb raised. "That's assault, what I just saw," she said.

Amber was sobbing now.

"I'm sorry," she blubbered.

"Don't *you* apologize," said Rose through gritted teeth.

"No," Terry swallowed, breathed some more. "She should." He looked at Rose. "She should apologize." Pointing upward, he looked at Amber DeGraaf. "You shouldn't talk about God like that." Amber wiped away tears.

"Ain't no God," Rose proclaimed. "Don't you know that?"

"No? You don't think so?" said Terry, his racing heart slowly returning to normal. "You sure?"

"Couldn't be," said Rose. "World all fucked up. Bombs going off. Babies dyin'." Her final shot aimed right between his eyes. "Men."

Terry blinked first. Looked at his shoes. Amber wiped her nose with a bare forearm.

"I used to think that," said Terry. He glanced down, took a couple more deep breaths, and then looked up at them both. "I changed my mind."

Gladys on the couch watched Terry, muzzle on her paws.

"How?" asked the suddenly calm Amber, her eyes still red from tears.

"I had a kid," he said to them both. "My wife and I. We had a kid."

He remembered the moment he first saw Hannah. And her baby eyes seeing him for the first time. He remembered being jolted, literally jolted in that moment, by a gift. A gift of pure love. A gift from above.

"That's where you see God," said Terry. "Where I see Him, anyway. You have a kid." He spoke to them both. "You watch her grow from ... kind of a blob, really. Less than Gladys here. Into a person. A totally unique person. She's not like you; she's not like your wife. She's a totally *new* person. A new life. A person you love so much. And who needs you so much."

His hands clasped unconsciously. His breathing had calmed. "That's a miracle. A miracle from God. That's the real thing. A real miracle in your own life." Rose had lowered the phone. "You know, I'm not super religious," said Terry. "But when you look at your own child, you see things. Things you can't explain. You see the future. You see the past. You see something *better*. And when you see that, you can't tell me there's not something bigger. Something better out there."

Terry rubbed his eyes, his brain reeling from his uncontrolled outburst, his words as new to him as they were to the women.

"So if that's not God, or what we call God, what is it? 'Cause we're not perfect. Not even close. But something that you see in kids … is. Something in kids *is* perfect. Something we lose as adults. In kids, though, you can see it sometimes. It's there. It's a glimpse of God. I know it. I've seen it."

Gladys hopped off the couch and went to him. Head tilted up, tongue out. Terry stooped down and patted her head. "She's a nice dog," he said.

He stood and moved to the door.

Then he looked at Amber. "Look," he said, "I'll send you a check, okay? Same as I gave Fran." He didn't mention the unmarked bills. "But you gotta call your mom." Amber scowled. Terry held his ground. "No mom, no check. That's the deal. Take it or leave it."

"We'll see," said Amber, "We shall see." He couldn't read her.

Rose glared at him with arms crossed, smoke curling from her cigarette.

Terry looked from Amber to Rose and then back to Amber. "Okay," he said. "Nice to meet you."

He let himself out. Gladys made a lunge for the door, but Amber grabbed her collar. The agitated boxer stayed back, quivering.

Terry left. Heat and glare consumed him. His docksiders slapped the hot driveway walking away from the seedy little bungalow. He felt tired and depressed. Ashamed of losing his temper. He left quickly in the rented car, air conditioning cranked up, roaring in his ears.

He had planned to visit either the Getty or Disneyland or Universal Studios. Instead he checked out of the Ramada the instant he got back to the hotel. Paid for a second night he didn't spend there. Caught an earlier flight.

He missed his family. All he wanted was to get home.

27

Uncle Bill maneuvered the creaking truck around a crater in the two-track that was as big as a kiddie pool. The shocks squeaked, unused to offroad. Mud splattered. March had come in like a lamb for once. Blue sky and warm. A Michigan tease that wouldn't last.

In early afternoon, the dirty pickup followed the track over a hill of tall, dead grass crusted with melting snow.

"Where the hell are we?" said P.J., rocking upright after another axle-scraping dip.

"You said you wanted the middle of nowhere. Well, this is as close as I know."

P.J. looked around the wild-grown field. They hadn't seen a soul for some time. Hadn't seen a farmhouse for miles. "There a town?"

"A ways that a'way." Bill aimed a thumb west. "Buckfield. Almost in Ohio. Nothing around here, though."

"Good for deer?"

"Shit, I don't know. As far as I know, there ain't shit out here." The truck lurched violently. A Pabst bottle rolled out from under P.J.'s seat. P.J. heeled it back under. It hit other cans and bottles.

"You fuck women in this piece of shit?"

His uncle tilted a grizzled grin at him, yellow teeth under snaking nose hairs. "Been known to happen."

P.J. looked out the side window. Off in the distance he saw an old, gray plank barn two-thirds collapsed. No houses or farms anywhere.

They crested a hill and the two-track bent left. Down the back slope and up ahead, out of sight from the main road behind them, where the field ended and forest began, P.J. saw a small wood-and-metal shed, rusted and ravaged. It wasn't much bigger than a one-car garage. It had a garage door on one side and a plain, wooden door on another. The rusty garage door had dull plexi windows yellow with age, and the side door had a window with a cracked glass pane. The roof was corrugated green plastic. Long abandoned, the shed was surrounded by weeds. They stopped. Bill lit a cigarette.

"What's this?" said P.J. "Hunter's cabin?"

"I dunno," said Bill, exhaling. "Maybe. Got it in a swap."

"You on paper with this?"

The older man shot P.J. a look. "Fuck no. Ain't no paper for shit like this." Uncle Bill went back to smoking and looking at the shed.

"Who'd you get it from?"

"He's dead."

P.J. nodded and opened the truck door. There was no wind, but the air was chilly, the day's early sun lost to lowering clouds. Bill stayed in the truck while P.J. stepped through knee-high dead grass toward the small building. The garage door was bolted and padlocked. He went to the door with the broken glass. It too was padlocked. All the metal rusty. Behind him, his uncle took a piss and then joined him.

"I haven't been here in years," said Bill, zipping up.

"Gimme the key."

Bill dug in his jeans and came out with a dull, brass key on a dirty string. He gave it to P.J. P.J. opened the lock and put lock and key in his left coat pocket. Not the Runt pocket.

The door stuck at first. P.J. kicked it open. Inside it stank. The corrugated green plastic roof let in murky light that made everything look underwater. A patchwork of leaves, sticks, and pine needles on the roof blocked light in random furrows. No electricity. No water. Just a shed full of crap.

Animals had been in. Raccoons and smaller things. An old, overstuffed chair had been torn to pieces, cushion stuffing scattered all over the cement floor. It was a good floor. Well-poured. The whole place smelled like bat shit.

Their feet crunched on bits of broken glass, and they left the door open for light and air. The flat roof sloped. There wasn't much room to move around. Mildewed cardboard boxes and plastic milk crates stuffed with crap were piled everywhere. Old chairs and discarded patio furniture. Ladders. Rusty rakes and shovels and a hand scythe hung on pegs. At least two dozen rusty horseshoes were nailed around the walls as some sort of half-assed decoration. Some bigger stuff in the back. Also, a small window.

"You keep looking," said Bill. "There's beer in the truck. I'm going to get us some." Saying no more, he scuttled away.

P.J. began moving boxes. He took his time, careful not to topple the stacks, moving them one by one and setting them to the side in what space was available. All were musty, damp, full of old clothes, toys, stained pillows, ratty blankets. All had animal sign. A few of the boxes split open when he handled them.

P.J. smelled a sudden plume of marijuana smoke.

"Finding anything?" said Bill, joint in one hand, six-pack in the other.

"Not yet." P.J. continued to paw his way toward the back of the shed. He'd seen something he wanted to see more of. "Start taking this shit out to the truck."

"What shit?"

P.J. turned on him fast. "All this shit!" He threw a large, mangy teddy bear at his uncle, who barely dodged it. "We're getting this shit out of here."

"Why?' said his uncle.

"I need room," muttered P.J., continuing to pull old boxes off the stacks. He threw them toward where his uncle stood. Some split when they hit the floor, some didn't.

Bill twisted off a beer cap and threw it hard at the floor. Cursing and smoking and drinking, he began carrying whatever P.J. threw at him out to the truck.

Behind the piles of boxes and milk crates, P.J. found a dead bicycle, spokes rusted. An old metal washtub. A rusted push mower. An ancient post-hole digger. Old fishing rods. A timber saw.

Close to the back he pulled down a box and saw what had caught his eye before. A glint of chrome. A window in the back helped him see it.

A barber chair.

He pushed boxes out of the way, kicked them aside to get to it.

It was antique. Cracked brown leather seat. Headrest. Pitted chrome hydraulic lever. He tried the lever, but it didn't budge. Didn't matter. He rocked the chair on its wide circular base. Heavy. The chair settled back with a soft *whump*. The armrests were marbled red plastic, cracked but intact. It had a footrest. He grabbed both armrests and yanked as hard as he could. They held.

Yanked harder. They held.

He walked around the chair, moving it out from the wall into the small open space he'd cleared, getting ideas. He tried rocking the attached headrest back and forth. It didn't budge until the rust gave, and then it did. It squealed when it moved. Like an animal in pain.

He stood staring at the barber chair.

Thinking of Blond John.

Or Onassis. Or whatever the fuck he called himself.

Tied to the chair with a rag down his throat. Barbed wire around his neck.

His eyes flicked to the rusty saws and hammers on the walls. A hatchet. A sickle.

"What'd you find?" asked Uncle Bill from the door. Outside, the vast field and encroaching forest were silent. No one around for miles.

P.J. gestured absently at the crumpled cardboard boxes and plastic bins around him. He was tall and the roof was low, but there was room enough.

"Get this other shit out of here and dump it," he said not taking his eyes off the barber chair. He'd need rope. Stiff wire. Bleach. Drano. Kerosene.

After a moment, Bill began hauling again. P.J. heard the slide of cardboard on damp cement and the crunch of broken glass. He stepped away from the barber chair. Lifting a rusty hatchet from the nail on the wall where it hung, he turned to face his uncle.

"Leave the tools," said P.J.

28

Fran was shocked to see Bryce's black Chrysler 300 parked in the garage as she sat in her car watching the heavy door rattle up. And she felt ashamed that her first thought wasn't about him, but about the mail. Especially since it hadn't even been a week since Great Lakes Crossing.

The same torture at a different mall. The same fear. The same anonymous commands texted to her cell phone. The same harrowing anxiety of leaving a shopping bag containing sixty thousand dollars in cash under a plastic chair in a thronged food court. Searching wildly for a ladies' room on her way out of the mall, she barely made it into a stall before throwing up.

And now Bryce was home early.

Bryce was never home early. It was only four in the afternoon.

Fran stepped into the kitchen from the garage and set two bags of groceries on the parson's table. "Hon?" she called. Her voice rang through the ground floor. She listened. Nothing. The copper pots that hung on hooks over the range were as motionless as a photograph. She set her keys down. Took off her coat.

All was quiet in the dining room. Drapes drawn, the whole downstairs dim and quiet except for the grandfather clock.

She stepped into the front foyer. No mail on the oriental. It was always here by now. Her heart jumped briefly, but calmed. It was too soon. It hadn't even been a week.

No lights on downstairs. She looked up the curved staircase. "Bryce?" she called. She swept a length of chestnut hair behind her ear to listen.

"Up here." Bryce. From their room. Muted. Fran hurried up the stairs.

Three out of the four bedroom doors were open. Only the master was closed. Fran crept close. Heard nothing. Knocked gently.

"Come in," said Bryce. Fran cracked the door and peeked in. It was dark. The shades were drawn. The bed creaked. And a moist, fetid smell hit her.

"You're sick?" asked Fran, coming in. She could smell it and covered her nose.

"I'm sick," frogged Bryce, and coughed. "A cold." Fran heard misery in his voice. "Pretty bad," he added.

Instinct took over, and Fran went to him, cooing soothing maternal sounds. She sat on the bed and put her palm on his forehead. "Oh, baby," she said. "You're hot."

"I know," chuffed Bryce. "I took my temperature. 101."

"You never get sick."

"Never say never." He didn't get all the words out before succumbing to a mucousy coughing fit. His white T-shirt was damp. In boxers and dark socks, he twisted under the clammy sheets. His hairy belly stuck out where the undershirt rode up. Suit coat, shirt, and tie were thrown on a chair. Pants puddled on the floor. Very unlike Bryce. This was Sick Bryce.

"When did you start feeling bad?" asked Fran.

"Yesterday," coughed Bryce. "I thought I could power through it." His eyes jittered toward her. He looked feverish and sweaty.

"You didn't seem bad last night."

"Tried to power through it," he repeated.

"Well, baby, you take it easy." She stroked his hand. "You take anything?"

"Yeah. I took some Alka-Seltzer cold medicine." He breathed through his mouth and reached for a tissue. Blew his nose and tossed the wet, white wad onto the floor with a dozen others. "You got some mail."

She let go of his hand. Stood up.

"Oh?"

"Yeah. Some letter. Or package. No return address. Over there." He didn't indicate where.

She scanned the shadowy room. On her vanity was a loose pile of mail.

To one side a padded white envelope.

She quickly walked to the mail, picked it up, and straightened it in her hands.

Felt the lump.

"What is it?" croaked Bryce.

"Hm?" said Fran, not looking at him, her mind racing. Her throat tightening.

"The thing for you. The envelope. Felt like there was something in there."

"Oh," said Fran. "It's for work." She was trembling. Felt her husband's eyes on her.

God, she was tired of men's eyes.

"What is it?" repeated her husband.

"Nothing interesting." She set down the mail and went to him. Bent her head close. He smelled awful. She fake smiled and kissed his forehead. "You *are* warm." She slid her hand down his sweaty chest and under the waistband of his boxers. Effectively changing the subject.

"Oh. Hey," said Bryce.

His belly hair and pubic hairs were hot and damp, but she slid her hand past them, around and under. She gently cupped his balls in the palm of her dry, smooth hand.

"Hey," said Bryce. "That's, uh . . . I'm feeling better already." Fran grinned at him. She gently raised and lowered her palm, the jolly weight of his testicles nestled in her soft hand. Her fingers explored more.

Bryce lay back, feeling his beautiful wife's silky fingers stroke and caress his genitals.

"I don't think the cold medicine is going to help me down there," conceded Bryce. Fran made a pouty face and kissed his cheek.

"No?" She stilled her hand but did not withdraw it.

"I don't think so. How about a rain check?"

"Okay, baby," said Fran, sliding her hand out. "Rain check."

She kissed him on the forehead.

"I'm not going to kiss you on the mouth because I don't want to get it."

He coughed. "You don't want it."

"Then you get some sleep, and I'll see if we have some chicken soup downstairs. If we don't have any, I'll get you some."

"Okay," said Bryce. "Thanks, babe." He closed his eyes and rolled over.

Fran kissed his head again, collected the mail, and closed the door behind her as quietly as she could.

She washed her hands. Put away groceries. Put on a pair of the disposable latex gloves and took the padded envelope downstairs to the study. She shut the heavy door and quietly wedged a shaker chair beneath the doorknob. Took no chances.

Hands protected, she picked up the envelope. Last weekend, at Great Lakes Crossing, she swore she heard the sick bastard breathing behind her moments before she paid, stood, and left.

She pushed the repulsive memory away. Controlled her emotions.

Woke up the computer. The curtains were closed. Her stork scissors and tweezers were upstairs in her vanity, but she didn't want to go upstairs again. There were office scissors in the desk. They would suffice.

Snip.

She tipped the opened envelope downward. Objects within loosened, then released. A facedown playing card slid out with a whisper, but the pink thumb drive clattered noisily onto the desktop. She glanced at the barricaded door. Then back to the red-backed card and the thumb drive. The label on the back gave instructions. Lakeside Mall. Three o'clock. A week from today. Her heart clenched.

She turned the card over and her self-control very nearly vanished. She barely suppressed a shriek.

The Ten of Diamonds.

One hundred thousand dollars.

She pressed her knuckles against her teeth to keep herself from screaming, bitterly tasting dry latex rubber.

She had a gun.

The thought came back. The thought she had forced herself never to think came back. She pictured it. Mentally felt the pistol's weight. Smelled the gun oil. Felt the cushiony action of the trigger.

Her father had given it to her years ago. A Browning automatic pistol. Heavy and silver with dark wooden grips. It was locked in a drawer in the basement. She'd looked at it last fall. Took it out and held it.

The thumb drive enraged her.

Always pink. The sick bastard. This couldn't go on. Her life was collapsing around her. Her brain was changing. What she was capable of, mutating.

She pushed the thumb drive into the USB port. The computer whirred. The prompt said **View Pictures.** She viewed.

"Oh, my God," she shuddered, as she always did.

Two men with her this time, erect and being serviced. A third man masturbating, fat, naked, erect. The heads and faces of all the men cut off by the photographer. Only her face showed. Unmistakably her. Eyes wide open. Laughing like a happy child.

It was *impossible*. She must have been drugged. But how? How could she be awake? How could she be *enjoying* it?

"Oh my God, oh my God, oh my God." She repeated the words quietly over and over. Over and over.

This went beyond greed. Beyond merely criminal. This was demonic. This was hell.

There was evil in the world, and she was trapped in it. A few keystrokes typed by a madman could ruin their lives forever. Destroy her family. Her son, shattered. Their friends, lost.

How can anyone recover from that?

She looked at the pornographic nightmare.

Her naked body. Her beautiful face. So innocent. The face she'd grown up with.

Her little sister.

How could Becky be in these?

The good one. The holy one.

"Oh, Becca," Fran sobbed quietly, her voice cracking, her throat tight as tears ran and dripped from her cheeks

"Oh, sweetie. How did this happen to you?"

29

The cartoon pirates on the colorful wrapping paper did not make Fran smile. The bushy beards and swords and pistols did not comfort her. But that was the birthday party theme. Wrapped box in hand, she rang the doorbell. Inside she heard a child's shrill, happy scream.

The door opened, and Becky appeared. Her thin face instantly widened to display a huge grin, and her eyes danced with merriment.

"Well, hello, Aunt Fran!" Becky laughed and opened the door wide. It wasn't very cold out. "Welcome to the madhouse!" As if on cue, shrieking nephew Clark raced by behind his pregnant mother, pursued by two other five-year-olds with plastic hook hands and swords. Becky, in her third trimester, had to pivot adroitly to dodge their onslaught. "Come in, come in!" said Becky, waving Fran in from the porch. Their house, scarcely a mile from Fran's, was newer but much smaller.

"No. Thank you," said Fran. "I just came to drop this off." She gave the gift to her sister, observing Becky closely. She looked intently at her little sister's beaming face. And at her sister's body.

The photo she'd seen two days ago had been the worst by far.

Three men. Naked. Sweaty. Entwined with her like squirming mag-gots. Becky smiling at them. Eyes wide open. Looking as happy as she did right now.

"Come in for a minute! Clarkie would love to see you." Becky made a *puh-leeeze* face.

"Actually, I have a...an appointment," said Fran. More happy screaming came from inside the house. Other kids.

"Oh?" said Becky, eyebrows knitting. She appraised her big sis-ter. "Are you alright?"

"It's nothing," said Fran. She pointed to her mouth with a black-gloved finger. "Dentist," she lied. "Just a tooth cleaning." She then pointed at the wrapped gift in her sister's hands. "It's the Lego thing you told me about. The pirate ship."

"Oh, great!" said Becky, beaming. "He'll love this!"

"Hi, dear," said Millie, as their mother stepped into view and stood next to Becky. "Are you joining us?" Fran was surprised to see her mother, who looked cheery and amiable in a tidy sweater, red turtleneck, and pressed jeans. With jewelry.

"Hi, mom," said Fran. "What are you doing here?" She paused a beat, then stepped up to the open doorway to give her mother a quick peck on the cheek. Becky smiled at them.

"Jim picked me up yesterday. I spent the night." Millie's eyes brightened, and she smiled happily. "Clarkie says I'm the galley slave!" Becky and her mother laughed at this, exchanging amused glances. A month had passed since the car accident that had claimed Michael DeGraaf's life and left their mother a widow. It was good to see her smiling again.

"Hey, what's going on here? A mutiny?" In jeans and a soft plaid shirt, Jim stepped into the small group of adults at the open door.

He was wearing an eye patch and carrying a soft plastic cutlass. He smiled at Fran. "Hi, Frannie." He slid the eyepatch up onto his forehead, beneath a fringe of sandy hair.

"Hi, Jim. You look the part."

"Yo ho ho," he said, then waved her in with the toy sword. "Come on in."

Fran shook her head, pointing at the gift in Becky's hands. "I'm just dropping that off. Have to go to the dentist." She indicated her mouth again.

"Oh, come on," said Jim. "We got six or seven kids in there, all sugared up." Becky and Millie laughed. "Swordfights, stabbings. What's not to like?" Even Fran smiled at this.

"Hello, hello, hello!" said a new voice, coming from behind Fran. She turned to see a peppy young man in a bright blue tuxedo, carrying what looked like a cage under a black cloth and towing a trunk on wheels. The trunk was painted circus red with yellow corners.

"Are you the magician?" squealed Becky, giving the wrapped gift to her husband and opening the door wider. Fran stepped out of the way.

"I'd better be," said the glib young man, who looked of college age. "Or else I'd probably get arrested walking around like this."

"You look great!" bubbled Becky. Fran contributed a tight-lipped smile and stepped aside to make way for the party entertainer to pass.

"Hi," he said to Fran. "I'm Johnny Gerard."

"Hello," said Fran.

He thumped the red trunk up the steps.

"Come on in," said Jim. He leaned between his wife and mother-in-law to assist. "Can I help you with some of that stuff?"

"Is that a rabbit?" asked Becky with glee, eyeing the shrouded cage.

"Now, now," said the magician, eyeing each of them in turn, with a final wink at Fran. "We all have to have our secrets, don't we?"

"Oh my!" added Millie.

A too-loud thump and howl of pain came from the back of the house. Becky looked at Jim. "Honey?"

"I'll check on them. You two help Mr. Magic here. Bye, Fran."

"Bye," said Fran. She watched the tuxedoed man carry in the shrouded cage and roll the red trunk into her sister's house.

"I just need about ten minutes to set up."

"Is the basement all right?"

"The basement is perfect. I live for basements," said the magician, and Becky and Millie laughed on cue. He shot a quick glance back at Fran, who bent her lips into as slight a smile as possible and nodded curtly, once.

Her appointment wasn't with the dentist. Fran had called Terry the same day the Ten of Diamonds arrived and demanded a hundred thousand dollars. She reminded him of his promise to her father. He didn't just give in. He said he'd call her back. When he called back, he had terms. He wanted to set up a meeting. The meeting would be with Terry and Terry's lawyer in Ferndale. After some bickering, Fran agreed.

It was just past two on Saturday when Fran arrived at Henry Wallace's office. Unbeknownst to her, the others had arrived fifteen minutes earlier. Terry plus two men she'd never met.

Terry had not met the third man, either. A friend of Henry's. A George Ginapolis.

"Welcome," said Henry, opening the door to Ste. 303. Fran entered and didn't like anything or anyone she saw. Not Terry or the black man or the other man, who looked foreign and oily. They all looked low-class to her. The Mediterranean-looking man stood when she entered. He was not very tall. Then Terry stood. Hiked up his jeans.

"Hi, Fran," said Terry. "This is Henry Wallace." Henry nodded, and they shook hands. "And this is George...?"

"Ginapolis," said the smaller man, who stepped forward with a smile, his hand out. "I am pleased to meet you." Tentatively, Fran shook hands with him. They were about the same height.

She didn't like any of this. The only one she knew at all was Terry. And she didn't like him.

Henry offered to take her coat. The three men looked at her. She stood there, appearing wealthy, aloof, and untouchable with her high cheekbones, exquisite features, black leather coat, black leather boots, and black leather gloves. Her thin wool scarf was pink and black. Four empty folding chairs were set up facing each other in the outer office. A card game without the table. "I'm not comfortable with this," she said, eyes level and unblinking at Terry.

Terry stepped closer. "Fran. We're trying to help."

"Who are these two?" She pointed at Henry and George without looking at them. Like they were furniture.

"Henry is my attorney." Henry offered a small bow. Wool blazer, Oxford shirt, no tie, shined shoes. Fran looked at him briefly, then back at Terry.

"And George is..." Terry gestured to George, who smiled broadly beneath his thick mustache. "George is like a...sort of like a private detective. A friend of Henry's. Henry recommended him."

Fran appraised George, frowning. "What does this have to do with my..." She stopped. Then, at Terry, "With what I came here for."

The hundred thousand dollars. In cash. Unmarked.

Henry spoke. "Mrs. Siehling, we know you're having challenges. Your father's attorney..."

"Abe Cohen," said Fran.

"Yes, Abe Cohen. Abe Cohen is my friend. He connected Terry to me. As unusual as this situation is, we are prepared to work on your behalf. To respect your father's trust in Terry. To honor his last request, in effect."

"Yeah," said Terry.

"I trust Abe," said Henry. "And I trust George. That's where we stand."

"Why don't we all sit down?" suggested George, then looked at Fran. "Everything will be fine." He wore jeans and a short, brown leather jacket over his thick chest. Fran kept her coat on but removed her scarf and gloves. Henry ushered everyone to the four folding chairs. He had his laptop to keep notes.

"There is coffee and water and soft drinks in the fridge if anyone needs anything," offered Henry. The others sat down.

Fran asked for a water, and Henry got her a bottle. She uncapped it and took a long sip.

"So Terry tells us you're an art buyer. What sort of art do you buy?" asked Henry, sitting. Fran shot a glare at Terry and pressed her lips into a thin red line.

"Look," said Fran. "Let's skip the friendly bullshit, and why don't you just give me the money?" Her next words were directed at Terry. "That's the only reason I'm here."

Terry looked down, mouth shut tight. She'd called Thursday night, asking for money. He'd told her about his trip to L.A. About meeting Amber. She wasn't interested in Amber. She'd just wanted the money.

So Terry called Henry. Told him about Fran asking for the hundred thousand dollars. Henry suggested a meeting. He wanted to meet Fran and wanted Fran and Terry to meet George.

That was the deal that Terry offered Fran.

And now, here she sat, glaring at him.

George watched Fran. Henry spoke. "Mrs. Siehling, no one here is fighting you. We just want you to be aware…" Henry opened both hands. "…that there are resources available. Resources that you can leverage. That can help you."

Fran lowered her chin, arms folded, legs crossed. Her thighs squeezed hard against each other. Her fists dug into her ribs.

Terry shifted, about to speak, but Henry waved him quiet. George didn't take his eyes off her. After a moment, Fran looked at Terry. "The cash. Do you have it, or don't you?"

Terry leaned forward in his chair, his big hands open. "Fran, listen to me. Henry says George here can help."

Her eyes snapped to George. She didn't like the way he was looking at her. Like she was a lab rat. "You don't understand the situation," she said. "None of you do." Her lower lip trembled just once.

"It's not you, is it?" said the Greek.

"What do you mean?" said Fran.

"The blackmail. It's not you. You're protecting somebody. Yes?" The Mediterranean accent was soft.

"How do you know that?" she blurted out.

George made a show of shrugging. "The amounts," he said. "Always escalating. Always round numbers."

Fran turned on Terry. "What did you tell him?"

"Everything," said Terry. "I've told them everything I know."

"George is experienced," said Henry.

"Shouldn't we call the police?" said Terry.

"No police!" yelled Fran. "If there's police, those photos go on the Internet! And...and..." She couldn't go on.

Photos, thought the three men.

Terry saw her pain then. All of it, in a split second. Her anguish. Her helplessness. The three men watched as the picture-perfect shell of this strong, beautiful woman suddenly cracked.

Then collapsed.

Eyes flooding, sobbing in short hard gasps, she gave in to a battle that beauty, position, and privilege could not win. She became like everyone else. A scared child hurt by a hard world.

George immediately went to her. He took a knee and gently placed a folded white handkerchief into her hands. "It's clean," he said, and she used it. "No police," he pledged her, his soft brown eyes calm yet strong.

Fran held the white handkerchief tight to her mouth. Smeared it with lipstick. Looked at George, who did not stand or look away from her tortured eyes. Gently, he nodded. Offering courage without even a hint of judgement. She finally nodded back. The brief motion loosened twin tears. They fell, leaving glistening trails over high cheekbones.

The men waited while Fran composed herself. She dabbed her eyes. Shook back her hair. Kept the handkerchief squeezed in her hands.

"So," she said. Took a sip of water. A deep breath. "So," she addressed George. "If you're so damned smart, what are we going to do?"

Terry and Henry also looked at George.

"When is the drop?" asked George.

"Thursday," said Fran, dabbing her eyes. "Three o'clock at Lakeside Mall." A mall near Utica, another satellite city, north of Detroit.

"You bring the money how?" the Greek asked Fran.

"In a shopping bag. From one of the mall stores. It's always at a mall."

She described the whole procedure to them in detail. Henry asked several questions. Did she suspect anyone? *No.* Did she have any enemies? *Not that I know of.* Did she ever see the same person at more than one mall? *No.*

Fran finished, dabbing her eyes and nose with the handkerchief. George nodded, unsmiling. He said nothing. Looked at no one.

The others watched him think.

A minute passed. All four people sat as still as waxworks. A minute and a half.

Then the man Terry and Fran knew only as George Ginapolis moved.

He smiled. Bright white teeth beneath a bushy mustache.

George sat symmetrically straight in the plain metal folding chair, rubbing his hands together. His dark eyes and bristling eyebrows danced.

"Okay," he said. "An idea."

He stood and spoke, describing what he had in mind. He laid it out step by step. He paced clockwise around the office. And as he spoke, Fran, for the first time in a very long time, began to feel the faint stirrings of an emotion she'd nearly forgotten.

Hope.

30

Uncle Bill and P.J. were watching midday NASCAR and drinking Pabst when Bill's phone rang. He fumbled it off the littered coffee table, scrabbling between snack chip bags, ash trays, jerky wrappers, beer bottles, and the bong.

Bill looked at his phone. "It's Thano."

P.J. muted the TV. The multicolored stock cars raced silently.

"Hey," said Bill into the phone.

"Hey, man, I got him," said Thano.

"What's going on?" said P.J.

"What do you mean you got him?" said Bill, slurry with drink. P.J. grabbed the phone from his uncle.

"Gimme the fuckin' phone."

Bill went back to watching cars and drinking beer.

"What's going on?" P.J. said to the phone.

"I got him, man. Like you wanted."

"Whaddyou mean you got him? You shot him? What the fuck you talking about?"

"No, fuck no, man," said Thano. "I found him. Onassis. The dude you wanted me to find? Remember? I called you. I showed the picture around. Found a asswipe diner he goes to for baklava."

"For what?" said P.J.

"Baklava, man. Baklava! It's Greek. It's sweet. Honey, nuts . . . it's awesome. Paid the owner to call me next time your guy came in. He called me today. I got there just as your guy left, and I followed him. He don't see me at all."

"You at his house?" P.J. turned off the TV, the gush of adrenaline sobering him fast. Bill took a bong hit, still watching the dead screen.

"No, man, I'm in Ferndale. In my car. Parked across from him. He went into a building like an hour ago. Just came out with another guy. A big guy. They're standing there talking now. I'm watching them right now. Your guy and the big guy."

"They see you?" P.J.'s eyes glittered with alcohol and fury.

"No, fuck no, man. I'm way across the parking lot. Your guy drives a Neon, man. A beat-to-shit Neon." Thano watched George and Terry talk outside Henry's building. Fran had arrived alone and left alone, drawing no more attention from Thano than common lechery.

Now, as Thano watched, George laughed briefly. He shook hands with Terry. Terry turned and walked left, toward Woodward.

"Hey, the big guy's walking away."

George watched him go.

"Follow Onassis," said P.J.

George began walking in the opposite direction, but then stopped. Turned. Thano had backed into a space on the far side of the parking lot in order to face the brown office building. Most cars nosed in. George stood motionless, looking in Thano's direction.

"Shit. He sees me." Thano slid down more, and George, after a long moment, turned and resumed walking toward the Neon. "Wait. Maybe not. I don't know. He might've."

"Fuck!" howled P.J. "You fucking asshole!"

A few rows away, Thano saw Terry back the Sebring out of a row of cars.

"The big guy's leaving."

P.J.'s gut spoke. "Follow the big guy."

"What do you mean?" said Thano.

"I mean follow the fucking guy who's fucking leaving, you fucking asshole!"

"But..."

"Just do it! Get the fuck out of there."

"Okay," said Thano and ended the call. He started his engine and pulled out slowly, following the Sebring. He did not look back. He ignored Onassis and hoped Onassis ignored him.

Nearly an hour later, Terry pulled into his street. It was nearly five, but the sky was not dark. A good sign. Spring was coming.

He'd spent most of the drive listening to the 80's. The Cars, The Police, The Specials. What a great decade for music.

And he thought about George. Terry was good at sizing up people. He liked George. How had George known it was blackmail right off the bat? How had he charmed Fran? Terry never saw Fran so polite. And that plan of his. This was all going to work out.

He grinned as he pulled into his driveway with Sting belting out *Invisible Sun* from *Ghost in the Machine*.

He felt good. The Falcon was on the case.

Two hundred yards behind, as Terry pulled into his garage,

a rust-ravaged black Hyundai turned down their street with its headlights off. The driver of the Hyundai saw light pouring from an open garage and heard blaring music coming from the car that he'd seen pull inside.

As Thano slowly drove by, he saw the big guy step from his car to the door connecting the garage to the house. Lights were on in the house. The big guy hit a button on the wall, and the garage door started coming down. There was a minivan in the garage, too.

Thano drove to the end of the street. All he saw in the small subdivision were older ranch homes on modest lots out here in the fucking boonies. He turned left, drove until he found a cul-de-sac, stopped, and dug a pen and scrap of paper out of his crap-filled glove compartment. Then he drove slowly back the way he came. It was dusk, but there was just enough light to see the black metal numbers screwed to a white plank next to the big guy's front door.

31

It was dark when the Neon pulled up to the ornamental security gate that was already whispering open. It shut behind him just as quietly, its hidden motor damped for stealth. The small car sloped down a heated drive and disappeared beneath the vast manor, swallowed from view by a descending metal door. After the meeting in Ferndale, Pearce Butler, in the guise of George Ginapolis, had spent an hour acquiring the supplies he needed.

He parked the car in its vented bay, attached the necessary cables, and ran the vehicle's twice-weekly diagnostic. The exterior of the mud-brown 2005 Dodge Neon SRT hadn't been washed all winter. There was rust. There were dents. It looked like rolling scrap.

Under the hood was a different story; a gearhead's wet dream. Butler had juiced the factory's 2.4-liter engine with a CNNP straight-line exhaust, AEM cold-air intake, Mopar Performance engine computer, Kirk racing header, and a massive, air-gulping throttle body. A performance cam had been installed to bump up the horsepower from 230 to 246 and increase the torque from 250 pound feet to 268 lb-ft. The tires were Hankook Ventus S1's, which wore out fast but jumped like jackrabbits. They were the quickest tires Butler had found, and he'd tried them all. On more than one occasion, he'd outrun bigger, faster cars, thanks to the Neon's disguised combination of stock-car power and balletic maneuverability. The gas tank was armored. The rear bumper sported two bullet holes.

As he climbed the old metal stairs, his footsteps rang and echoed through the vast, open interior space.

Upstairs, Butler stood in front of the mirror in the institutional washroom that overlooked the Detroit River. The residence was silent, the way he liked it. Olive-skinned fingers delicately removed oversized brown contact lenses, revealing pale blue corneas. He blinked, put the hickory-hued lenses in a small case, and put the case on a shelf in an old metal locker. The lockers, a scratched and dented row of twelve, were among the relics that had come with the place.

Still gazing into the mirror, Butler removed from each nostril a soft plastic widener and placed both inserts in a plastic container that also went into a locker. He looked at the backs of his hands, where the swarthy-hued Ben Nye stage makeup feathered into the lighter skin of each palm.

The hands were the hardest part to get right. It was a challenge to blend the artificially darkened skin tone on the backs of the hands into the lighter tone of the palms. He looked in the mirror and saw a blue-eyed Greek.

He removed the human hair wig, custom-woven in New York, which went onto a wig stand in the wig locker. The mustache and eyebrow extensions went into a flat, plastic box.

He hung up George's leather jacket and the subtle torso padding that created a stockier appearance.

With acetone, he removed the dry spirit gum from his upper lip and the hairline of his forehead, temples, and sideburns, where the wig attached. His own short, toffee brown hair was matted down.

He stepped into the industrial shower set on very hot and scrubbed himself clean. Steam clouded the windows, obscuring the mile-wide Detroit River. On the opposite bank, tiny lights from Windsor glowed. Canadian taillights and headlights from distant moving vehicles flickered across the water.

Out of the shower, relaxed and robed, Butler sat in an old wood and leather chair in the loft, gazing at the river. He never tired of looking at it. No matter the season or hour, day or night. A mile to the west, he admired the elegant lines of the Belle Isle bridge. In 1952, it had been renamed the Douglas MacArthur Bridge, but the renaming was subsequently forgotten. Low and graceful, the bridge's nineteen arches stretched half a mile from the mainland to Detroit's glorious garden park island, Belle Isle, larger and more opulent than Manhattan's Central Park.

Upriver, the gleaming skyscrapers of downtown Detroit, reborn and resurgent, sparkled in the night two miles from where Butler sat drinking mineral water in the Boathouse.

He relaxed in a long-forgotten secret. Built on the banks of the Detroit River in 1922 by notorious Purple Gang bootlegger Irving Milberg, the Boathouse, as it was known then to many and now to exceedingly few, was a cavernous warehouse disguised as an opulent mansion. It occupied a large walled lot on the river, tucked out of view three blocks south of Jefferson Avenue. It had taken Butler ten years of relentless third-party bargaining to acquire it.

No one had ever lived there before. It wasn't built to be lived in. It was built to warehouse whisky smuggled by boat from Canada during Prohibition. Butler had renovated the decayed property. He'd restored the surrounding wall and installed an electric gate. He'd repaired and refitted the large garage and private boat channel that opened onto the Detroit River. A screen of overhanging willows on the rear lawn hid a hinged door built into the sheet-iron breakwater. Butler kept a speedboat on slings above the indoor boat slip. In winter, heat from the Boathouse kept the slip from icing over, but the inky black water was formidably cold.

Butler owned other residences. But the Boathouse was home.

On the outside, the Boathouse mimicked the ornate, French-style chateaux that sprang up prolifically in Detroit during the Jazz Age. As an unrivaled manufacturing powerhouse and the fastest-growing city in the world, Detroit had minted "motor millionaires" by the dozens, and from fast money sprang fast mansions, competing to show off more turrets, bigger fountains, and grander ballrooms.

But the Boathouse was different. Behind its wedding-cake façade, it was all business. Three stories of cavernous space supported by bare girders and brick walls. The factory wood-block floor had room enough to maneuver the large trucks that were loaded daily with cases of liquor that were delivered by boat from Windsor at night. To this day the old hideout still breathed the ghostly fumes of the midnight rumrunners: faint traces of gasoline, truck tires, and motorboat oil. Pearce Butler didn't mind the smell one bit. He savored it.

From this ornate, elegant shell of sculpted cement, soaring windows, stone archways, and dummy chimneys, the Purple Gang flooded the Midwest with premium Canadian whisky, gin, and spirits. Constructed by boss Milberg at the peak of his power and arrogance, the Boathouse in the Roaring 20's was no secret to Detroit's amply bribed police force or the society grandees eager to serve premium illegal hooch. But in 1932 Milberg was convicted of first-degree murder, sentenced to life in prison, and the whole operation was mothballed. In 1933, Prohibition was repealed, and the Boathouse receded swiftly from memory.

Butler arose and looked out a tall, mullioned window at the century-old Detroit Yacht Club, gracefully adorning the north-east edge of Belle Isle. Its docks were empty now, but in a month they'd start filling with pleasure boats for Michigan's upcoming freshwater season.

Finishing the mineral water, Butler dressed in comfortable work clothes. In the small kitchen at the far end of the loft, he made and ate a ham and cheese sandwich and drank fresh-squeezed grape-fruit juice. One level down, he went to a large worktable and spread out his supplies. Department store shopping bags. Posterboard of varying thicknesses. Different kinds of tape. Different types of glue. Paint. A brush. String. Cord. Fishing line. A bag of flour. A bag of sugar. Scissors. An X-ACTO knife.

He spent forty minutes making sketches. Then he went to work.

Four hours later he was satisfied with his second effort. He turned the heat down, set the alarms, knelt, prayed, went to bed, and fell asleep under several blankets.

32

Two crows startled and flew in the morning gloom from the bare, black branches of the backyard ash tree.

"Where's my other purple sock?" Hannah's voice rang off close walls in the short hallway as she stomped almost fully dressed from her bedroom to her parents' empty bedroom and finally into the kitchen, where her father was.

"I'm not wearing it," said Terry, dressed and pouring coffee into a large travel mug.

"Where's Mom?" said Hannah, going to the washer and dryer closet near the garage and searching a half-filled plastic hamper for her sock.

"Bathroom, I think," said Terry, adding a little milk to his coffee. He swirled it in the travel mug and appraised his frustrated daughter. Hannah made a face and stormed out.

"Hey!" said Terry sharply, stopping her in her tracks with The Dad Voice. She turned to face him. "It's just a sock," he said. Hannah scowled and spun, stomping back toward the bedrooms.

"This is utterly absurd!" she proclaimed, "Mom!" Terry watched her disappear. He put his coat on.

"What is it?" answered Christina, stepping into the kitchen, fastening her wristwatch. How the hurrying females had somehow missed each other in the short hallway, Terry couldn't imagine. He admired his wife. She looked great. Wearing clean blue scrub pants with a blue-flowered top.

"You look great."

"Thanks." She tiptoed for a quick kiss. Too quick for Terry.

Hannah appeared in the doorway and stuck her bare foot forward. "I can't find my other purple sock." She then reversed position, extending her purple-socked foot to make sure her parents understood the crisis.

"Check your underwear drawer," said Christina. "Sometimes they get lost in there." With a wide-eyed *Eureka!* expression, Hannah dashed out of sight down the hall.

"You taking Hannah?" asked Terry.

"No, she wants to take the bus."

Christina made a sour face.

"What?" said Terry.

"She's got 'friends' on the bus."

"Not your favorite friends?"

She wrinkled her pixie nose. "Not sure. Jury's still out."

"Well, it's not so cold and dark out now. Spring's coming."

"I don't like the bus."

"Of course, you don't," said Terry, hugging his wife close.

"Found it!" yelled Hannah from her bedroom.

"You really look great," said Terry. He appreciated her more since the trip to L.A.

"Thanks. So do you." He held her close for another tiptoe kiss, long enough for Hannah to enter and see them. She rolled her eyes, sighed, and made a gagging noise.

* * *

From outside, the house looked still and quiet, the sky gray but much lighter than it had been an hour ago. It was five after eight. Low clouds. He'd pulled past the house and parked on the opposite side of the street. In the carefully aimed driver's side mirror, P.J. watched a reverse image of the small ranch house with the address he'd gotten from Thano. He slumped low in his seat, chewing a second Egg McMuffin. It was stone cold, but he didn't care. As he swallowed, eyeing the house, he finally saw activity. He slid lower.

The garage door was going up. There was a rolled newspaper in a plastic bag at the end of the driveway. It had been there when P.J. arrived and took up his position. He stopped chewing, a fleck of yellow egg on his lip as he watched a large, bulky man with a goatee walk to the newspaper, pick it up, and go back to the garage. From his angle, P.J. couldn't see into the garage. It was the big guy that Thano had described. Goatee. Brown leather coat. The friend of Onassis. Of Blond John.

The big guy looked soft. Two minutes in the barber chair and he'd spill his guts and crap his pants at the same time.

P.J. stayed low, adjusting the sideview mirror with the little joystick. He'd taken his uncle's car.

A plume of exhaust from the garage. A beige Sebring backed out. It was almost at the mailbox when a small woman in medical clothes ran out, holding a large, dark travel mug in her child-sized hand. Redhead. The Sebring stopped abruptly, and the big guy got half out while his wife gave him the coffee and a quick kiss. Then she trotted back to the garage.

P.J. watched the Sebring back out angling toward him, flash its brake lights, then pull ahead and away from him, heading up the subdivision street toward the main road. It hadn't gone a hundred yards when a small, skinny girl in a brightly colored winter coat tramped down the driveway in plastic boots, a long scarf, mittens, and a colorful hat over long dark hair. On her shoulders was a pink-and-purple backpack. As P.J. watched, the girl stopped walking halfway down the drive and turned, looking back toward the open garage. The girl listened for a few moments. She said something back, waved, and continued toward the street. Once she got to the end of the driveway, she turned in the same direction the Sebring had gone and continued walking. There were no sidewalks.

P.J. weighed this interesting new development.

He stuffed the last bite of McMuffin in his mouth and wiped his hands on his pants. He'd shut off the engine after arriving. When the heat wore off, he'd cracked the passenger-side window a few inches to keep fog off the glass. It was cold but not freezing. He slid his right hand into the pocket of his snowmobile coat. Felt the oiled heft of the Runt.

Another blast of exhaust came from the garage, this time a billowy cloud. An engine that needed a new gasket. As P.J. watched in the rearview mirror, an old Mercury minivan backed out, and the garage door came down. P.J. focused. He bet it was the wife. It was a female for sure. He risked twisting in his seat, turning to look straight at her just as the minivan backed into the street, swinging its rear end toward him. It was the wife. He saw the red hair. He'd seen half her face. He was sure of it.

The minivan pulled forward, catching up to the walking girl. It stopped, brake lights red.

The girl went to the passenger window. The driver and the girl talked briefly, and then the girl, who seemed very small next to the minivan, backed away, waving. The mom drove away slowly.

A quick glance around told P.J. he wasn't being observed. No neighbors visible. No faces at any windows. No vehicles moving. It was a short street.

The van turned left at the end of the street, and P.J. started the engine the moment it was out of sight. Another quick scan showed no movement anywhere. He pulled into the street. Turned around in the nearest driveway, came out pointing toward the walking girl. He was in a nondescript sedan. Stolen plate. Lights off.

As he drove closer, he saw the girl had skinny legs and her pink-and-purple backpack had a cartoon girl on it. Her plastic boots were blue. When he powered down the passenger side window, he could hear her singing a high-pitched little girl song but couldn't make out the words.

He tried to think what to say. Slid the Runt out, fat and heavy in his hand.

To his right was a clatter of aluminum door, and from the next house up, another little girl came galloping down the front steps, through the melting snow, down to the daughter alone on the street. This one was blond and a little taller. When she caught up to the dark-haired daughter, they squealed and made little-girl noises at each other with no awareness of the slowly approaching car. P.J. rolled past them, raising the power window.

When they were behind him, he slowed for a better look in the rearview. He stared at the dark-haired girl giggling with her friend. He imprinted her face, her clothes, her body in his memory. Then he pulled away unhurried as new ideas began to snap and boil inside him.

33

Lakeside Mall was the lodestone that spawned an impressive commercial boom on M-59 near Utica, twenty miles north of Grosse Pointe. The mall's success sired a sprawl of follow-ons: strip malls large and small linked by Chili's, Applebee's, Outback Steakhouse, The Olive Garden, and a throng of lesser eateries. Following a sunny week, Thursday disappointed with low clouds and no sun, but still the shoppers swarmed.

As with past drops, Fran arrived early and parked discreetly. The five thick blocks of cash were in a Lord & Taylor bag.

Inside, shopping bag in left hand, phone in right, she was careful not to hurry. She walked the mall's ground floor from Lord & Taylor to Sears. To Penney's. To Macy's. Back to Lord & Taylor.

The Lord & Taylor bag seemed to swing too much. It was heavy. She tried to slow it down. Slow herself down. She hated carrying so much money. Being watched. She hated whoever was doing this to her.

And today she was also petrified.

She strode past Yankee Candle, her long legs moving fast, and she caught herself again. She tried to slow it down. Tried to slow herself down. Forced herself to stop and look at the candles. An Easter display. She made herself appear calm. She was supposed to be shopping. She wore a scarf, black leather jacket, purse, jeans, little makeup.

Her phone felt dead as a stone. She looked in the window at Bath & Body Works. Moved on to Abercrombie For Kids. Then to Victoria's Secret. Her eyes drifted to a thin plastic mannequin wearing a provocative purple garter belt with matching panties and lacy push up bra. The mannequin had no face. She quickly looked away. She didn't know who was watching her.

Her phone remained silent.

She tried to blend in with the busy lunch crowd. This was not her mall. These were not her stores. When nothing happened on the ground floor, she took the escalator up. That was the system.

On the second level, she passed American Eagle Outfitters and AT&T. She began a loop that would take her past dozens of stores and a large food court. The food court had small tables and six or eight different food counters from Chinese to Mexican to Cinnabon.

She glanced at her phone. It was three o'clock. Fran had arrived on time. Usually it was over by now. The scantily clad Victoria's Secret mannequin returned to her mind unbidden. She thought of Becky.

Drugged somehow. *She must have been.* Posed.

Raped.

With no memory of it.

Was that God's work? Or Satan's? Or both?

She blinked back tears, swiping at them with her phone hand as she walked. The food court was busy.

Her phone vibrated. Once.

Look.

She froze, stopping her tears instantly. Slowly turning toward the food court, she saw a small, littered table with two chairs. Empty. It stood against a half wall that overlooked the lower level. A mother and child were just leaving it. Two middle-aged African-American women sat laughing at the table next to it. The two tables scarcely a yard apart.

Her phone vibrated twice.

Sit.

Fran took long, quick steps toward the empty table and sat. She did not release the shopping bag but set her purse on the table, carefully avoiding a wet spot. People carrying food trays or trash jostled everywhere, inches away. Too close. The din of conversation and eating seemed to engulf her. Her phone vibrated again. Once.

Leave the money and step away.

She set the heavy, white Lord & Taylor bag on the floor between her feet. One hundred thousand dollars didn't fit in a shoebox. She'd wrapped it in paper towels.

Using her heel, she pushed the paper bag backward under her chair. She heard it slide and felt it stop when it touched the half wall.

She did not look around but stood and left.

Purse on shoulder, she wove quickly through the swarm of people and didn't look back. She went to the nearest down escalator. At the bottom, she stepped off and started walking toward Lord & Taylor. Toward the mall's exit.

Only then did she dare steal a glance at her palm. At what

she held. A large metal safety pin painted flat white that she had unclipped from the shopping bag when she set it on the floor.

He'd brushed against her as she walked by. He'd felt her and smelled her. She didn't acknowledge any contact. She kept her eyes aimed rigidly forward, as instructed. He'd felt her round shoulder, tight against the supple black leather of her jacket, brush against his upper arm. It excited him.

The man sat down seconds after she left, the chair still warm—he liked that. Warm from her sweet ass. He had a thick, brown beard and wore a baseball cap, worn khakis, a cheap hooded parka, and tinted aviator glasses. He smiled as he sat, watching her hips and ass sway away in those tight jeans. Sway and disappear into the throng. She didn't look back. He knew she wouldn't. He raised his phone to his ear on an imaginary call. He imagined he was talking to Ricky. Sometimes Ricky even seemed to talk back.

"Uh huh," he said to the phone. He set down a large soda cup, half filled with cola and capped with a plastic lid and straw, to validate his use of the table. He reached down and pulled the Lord & Taylor bag from beneath the chair and slid it between his knees. He glanced down. "Right. Uh huh," he said into nothingness. Saw blocky rectangles wrapped in paper towels. Lots of them. A small smile flickered briefly.

He briefly lifted the bag off the floor. Heavy. He suppressed another smile. "Oh, that's great," he said to his phone. "That's awesome." He scanned the crowd as he continued the fake call. Scratched his upper lip. "Well," he said loudly. "Then I guess we'll have to talk some more about that." As he fake listened, head bent and nodding, he carefully positioned his right calf against the side of the stiff white paper bag.

"Uh huh." Pause. "Yeah." Pause.

With his leg in position, he leaned back awkwardly to slip his right hand into his pants pocket. A slash pocket. He'd tried this with jeans, but getting his hand into a jeans pocket while sitting was difficult. A slash pocket worked much better, and khakis were as forgettable as jeans.

In the pocket, his thumb switched on the bug detector. Four D batteries in a parka pocket powered the metal-detecting wand duct-taped to the inside of his leg.

Ripping it off later was a bitch, but at least it stayed put. He felt a hum and tingle on his leg hairs as it scanned. The chairs and table were plastic. Ricky said always put her in plastic chairs or on cement benches. Never metal.

"Well, I don't think that's a problem," he said as he reached for the bag. "Uh huh. Uh huh. Well, sure, I can see that." He slowly rotated the bag, making sure every inch of the bag's exposed surface brushed against his calf.

No beeps. No tags. No bugs. No metal. His smile widened. So much so that it caused the spirit gum that held the brown beard and mustache in place to loosen slightly on one side. He felt cool air rush into the gap between shaven skin and false hair. He stopped smiling immediately, pressing the flap of hair back onto his face. It didn't stick. Once the seal was broken, spirit gum didn't re-stick. So he held it there.

He put down his phone, turned off the metal detector, and picked up his phone again. "Alright," he said. "Gotta go," and mimicked ending the call. He slid the phone into his parka and, after a final glance around, grabbed the bag's loop handles and stood. He took his hand off the loosened whiskers on his face just long enough to drop the soda cup in a nearby trash can.

Fran had gone left, so he went right. As he walked, the Lord & Taylor bag swung, and from it fell four thin streams of nearly invisible granules, lightly dusting the mall floor. Finer than sand. The granules fell from half-inch slits cut in the bottom of the bag. When Fran removed the safety pin, the simple mechanism had been activated.

As the blackmailer walked, the swinging bag sent pale granules sprinkling to the floor like salt from a shaker.

The Lord & Taylor bag had a false bottom and no metal parts. Butler had anticipated a bug detector.

Ultraviolet detection powder or "spy powder" is virtually invisible except when exposed to ultraviolet light. With the safety pin removed, one tug on the bag's handles pulled four cardboard stoppers from slits on the bag's true bottom via fishing line hidden in the bag's false wall. An inch-deep reservoir beneath the bag's false bottom hid two cups of the lightweight powder.

On the down escalator, the blackmailer who resembled the Unabomber did not notice the slender, young African-American man three people behind him.

The African-American youth had arrived at the food court just as Fran froze, turned, and quickly sat at the small, unoccupied table. When that occurred the young man, who had been discreetly following her from a distance, casually stepped into line for Mexican food, hands in hoodie pockets.

He was still in line when Fran left, leaving the Lord & Taylor bag behind. Then he saw a man with a false beard, wearing a ball cap and talking on his phone, quickly take her empty seat. The bearded man was jumpy. The phone call, clearly fake. His nervous glancing around forced the young man in the Mexican food line to divert his gaze toward the large menu posted above and behind the counter. The phone he'd slipped from his hoodie pocket he held loosely, aimed at the table occupied by the bearded man.

As Brown Beard scanned the Lord & Taylor bag for bugs, the young man pretended to appraise burrito prices.

After a few moments, Brown Beard stood and walked unhurriedly away. The Lord & Taylor bag swung.

"Can I help you?" asked the smiling, light-skinned African-American girl at the counter. She had truly beautiful brown eyes—the real thing.

"Uh, no, thank you," said the youth, with a gentle smile. "Maybe later."

The youth broke from the line, eyes down, black knit cap pulled over his ears. In saggy black jeans, black hoodie, and red-and-white leather Nikes, he looked like a hundred other young black men shopping the mall. That was the idea.

He didn't see Brown Beard. He didn't have to. As he walked in the direction Brown Beard had taken, he slid a tiny penlight from his hoodie pocket. He aimed its ultraviolet beam at the mall floor.

The invisible beam illuminated a trail of glowing violet granules on the tiled floor. They snaked through the crowd like radioactive bread crumbs.

And there was Brown Beard, just ahead. On the down escalator.

The youth kept his head down. If the bag changed hands, he'd follow the money. He glanced up intermittently, but closely watched the tiles. On the ground floor, the trail of glowing granules continued.

The young man picked up his pace.

Eyes on the floor, he saw the glowing violet grains swerve left.

He glanced up. Brown Beard was heading for the exit with the Lord & Taylor bag. Glass doors opened onto a vast parking lot. Brown Beard sped up as he exited the mall.

When the young man stepped outside, he saw cars moving and several people in view. Some shoppers arriving, some departing. But no sign of Brown Beard. He aimed the pointer's beam at the sidewalk. Nothing glowed in front of him. Or to the right. But to the left, a tiny scattering of luminescent grains glowed on the sidewalk. He went left.

Now luck entered the game. Was his vehicle close or far? The young black man added three inches to each stride without appearing to do so.

He followed the grains across the access lane. He walked past parked vehicles. Ultraviolet light worked adequately outdoors, and the gray cloud cover helped. The violet grains turned right at the next row of parked vehicles. But he saw no one. The young man followed the glowing grains, careful not to raise his head. He passed a dirty, white VW bug. As he approached an old gray Sable, he heard, but did not see, the Sable's door shut.

Carefully, the young man slowed his pace. His penlight illuminated no more glowing grains. He heard the Sable start. Heard it back out of its space.

Flip a coin. Would it drive past him from behind? Or turn away from him? Odds were that the car would drive past him, away from the mall. The young black man readied his phone and unzipped his hoodie. Put on sunglasses. He heard the Sable shift into drive, accelerate, draw closer. His phone hung loosely at his side.

As the Sable drove past from behind, the young man activated video cameras on his phone, in his sunglasses, and on his person. He let his hoodie fall open, exposing six tiny lenses hidden in the pattern of a sparkly Pharrell T-shirt. Eight cameras aimed at the Sable as it drove to the end of the parking row, turned right, and sped away.

The license plate had been visible for all of four seconds. Not an easy target while walking, hence the many cameras. The young man had looked at the driver, but learned nothing helpful.

The Sable gone, the young man stopped walking and deactivated the cameras. Took off the sunglasses. Went back to the empty parking space where the Sable had been and aimed the UV penlight at the asphalt. The violet granules stopped there.

In the Neon, Pearce Butler checked all the video he'd captured. Most of it revealed nothing useful. But from the Pharrell T-shirt, a memory chip from one of six half-dollar-sized cameras struck pay dirt.

A Michigan plate on the Sable clear enough to read. He sent the license number to a friend waiting to receive it.

Then he checked the video taken with his phone dangling from his arm while waiting in line at the Mexican food counter. He studied the smartphone's screen. Legs passing. Mall noise. A jostle that jiggled the picture.

Then there he was. Brown Beard sitting at the small table. Somber-faced. Phone at his ear. Reaching down for the Lord & Taylor bag. A sudden, brief smile. Then clutching his cheek.

Then passing mall customers obscured the lens. When the table reappeared, Brown Beard was stepping out of frame.

He sent the video to Fran, Henry, and Terry with the note: Fake beard/mustache. Know him?

A tone from his phone announced the arrival of a text. From his friend checking the license plate. It said **Call me.** The incoming phone number was blocked. Butler knew the number.

The person he spoke to told him the name and address of the plate's owner. The vehicle didn't match the plate. No insurance record. A Clarence Pittman. 111 Beddoe Street. In Delray. A ravaged neighborhood in southwest Detroit. Butler thanked his friend and hung up.

34

He'd been on the road four minutes, heading southwest, when he got a text reply from Fran.

Don't know him.

Within six minutes Henry and Terry also responded. They didn't recognize Brown Beard either.

Delray in Southwest Detroit was a diagonal leap across the entire Metro area from Lakeside Mall. Demographically opposite, as well. The population near Lakeside Mall was predominantly white, younger, and more affluent, while much of Southwest Detroit was aging, of color, and living at or below the poverty level. The robust revival of Midtown and Downtown had not and would not reach rundown Delray for decades, if ever. Instead, on block after block of collapsing wooden houses, a large and largely ignored African-American community of working poor and the non-working destitute survived hand-to-mouth day after day in the shadow of the Ambassador Bridge.

It took Butler fifty minutes to drive the brown Neon twenty-eight miles to 111 Beddoe Street in Delray, the registered residence of Clarence Pittman, age forty-four.

A mile west of Detroit's revitalized Corktown, flush with bustling new restaurants, busy sidewalks, and smiling, mostly white people, Butler entered ravaged, decaying Delray.

Unrevitalized. Unrestored. Overgrown, unlit, and ripped apart by poverty. The scarred, shabby-looking brown Neon fit right in. As he drove slowly forward, Butler saw not a soul on the streets or sidewalks. Old wooden homes built cheap and fast in the 1920's and 30's sagged and buckled all around him. Some had burned, their blackened remains hollow, ghostly. When Beddoe Street appeared, Butler's heart cried out.

Clearly, Beddoe was one of the most fallen streets in one of Detroit's most fallen neighborhoods. He drove slowly, looking for any visible address. Beddoe ran nine blocks north to south from the I-75 bend toward Toledo to its dead end at a jagged pile of cement riprap on the trashed banks of the Detroit River.

The block on which Clarence Pittman lived was devastated. Most houses on it were uninhabited. Smashed windows let in snow, rain, and animals. Weeds engulfed lots, pushing up through dirty snow. Many houses had burned. Others had collapsed into decaying mounds of raw gray boards, broken glass, and ragged patches of torn shingles—the effect of neglect, abandonment, and Great Lakes weather on frail wooden houses. Detroit was getting back on its feet after a sixty-year downturn, but there were still far too many streets like Beddoe. Third-world streets. And not all the ravaged houses were empty.

Butler kept the headlights off in the gray afternoon, driving slow enough to observe but fast enough to avoid curious eyes he could not see. It was past four o'clock. On one block, every single house was burned, collapsed, or abandoned. He played no music. It started snowing.

He saw no one as he steered slowly around a rusting shopping cart in the middle of the street that held a tattered blue blanket. A weary string of cars and trucks, none new or clean, were parked along the curb. A few in driveways. He scanned for the gray Sable.

One car was burned to the chassis, tires melted. He steered around potholes ranging in size from buckets to bathtubs, asphalt chewed away as though rotting from below. Where snow had melted on tiny front lawns, matted grass was sickly and brown. Butler saw a rusty detached fire hydrant scabbed with peeling red paint lying sideways on the street. In an abandoned lot tangled with overgrowth, a dog, or something like a dog, scurried out of sight behind strewn garbage as the Neon rolled by. If mirth came at all to Beddoe Street, it was only the Devil and his demons laughing.

He saw 111 and drove past. A small home with lights on inside. No sign of the Sable. Butler went around the corner and backed the Neon into a driveway between two abandoned, graffiti-smeared homes. The driveway hadn't been shoveled, perhaps in years, but the snow had melted enough. Neither dwelling on either side had glass in any windows. Only one had a roof.

He shut off the engine and watched and listened. Across the street were several abandoned homes and one occupied home with lights on inside. He watched for two minutes. No movement anywhere. Not even a bird or squirrel. He set the Neon's alarm and slipped out the door in his hoodie and saggy jeans, with the knit cap pulled low over his ears. His exposed skin was covered with Ben Nye Matte Foundation RSA-5 Mocha blended with RSA-11 Espresso. Nostril inserts widened his nose, and tinted latex overlays padded his lips. He shut the car door quietly.

Hands in pockets, he walked around the corner toward 111 Beddoe. The cold air didn't mask the ropy stink of wet, rotted wood and dead weeds. Across the street from 111, a vacant lot was strewn with the detritus of poverty: rotting mattress, old kitchen stove, children's clothes, and big plastic toddler's toys. A thin, feral dog appeared from behind the stove, lowering its head to track Butler's movements. Perhaps the same animal he'd seen before. Butler denied it eye contact. He didn't want it to bark.

Shoulders hunched, chin tucked against the falling afternoon snow, the disguise would fool anyone who looked. But nobody did.

As he approached the Pittman residence, Butler glanced quickly up its driveway at the detached one-car garage in back. No snow on the driveway. Someone had shoveled. No car visible. The garage door was shut.

He went up cracked cement steps to the front door. No welcome mat. Above his head a tin awning once painted sunshiny yellow sagged. A metal glider bench, formerly blue, now heavily rusted, skulked sadly on the broken cement front porch. The tiny house was red brick, an anomaly on this wood-framed block, and had lasted better than most.

The front door was metal. Newer. A security door. Thick, black bars with ornamental twists and accents were bolted over every window. Life had not been kind to 111 Beddoe Street.

Butler pressed a cracked plastic doorbell button. Heard no sound within. Tried again, listening. Nothing. Thumped the metal door twice. More thud than knock. He wanted those inside to hear, but no one outside. He returned both hands to his hoodie pockets.

After a few moments, he heard movement in the house. From the back. Coming closer. In no particular hurry.

He saw a shadow flicker in the door's glass peephole then flit away. The rattle of a lock and deadbolt.

With a screech of metal on metal, the door swung in five inches, stopping abruptly when the chain pulled taut. Above the chest-high chain, Butler met the sad eyes of an African-American woman, maybe forty or thirty or fifty, her hair up in pins. She wore a thick cable-knit cardigan, brown and pilly and buttoned to the neck over a maroon velour running suit. She had on gloves, thick socks, and bedroom slippers. A wide headband warmed her ears. Beyond her, in the living room, Butler saw wiry orange filaments glowing from an ancient floor heater. He heard babble from a daytime TV talk show.

"Miz Pittman?" asked Butler.

"Yes?"

"Good afternoon, ma'am."

"Good afternoon." He saw her glance past him to see if he was alone, then back at him.

"Is Mr. Clarence Pittman here, ma'am?"

"Why?" She seemed to talk without moving her mouth. Everything held in check. Kept inside.

"It's about his car."

At this, cautious brown eyes flashed a hint of interest. "You found it?"

"Gray Sable?" said Butler.

"No," she said. She shook her head slowly. "His was a Monte Carlo. Dark red."

"Mm," said Butler. Stolen plates.

She read his eyes. "You din't find it?" She made no move to remove the chain.

"No, ma'am," said Butler. "I'm sorry. Is Mr. Pittman here, ma'am? Clarence?" She shook her head. Her look told him that Clarence was long out of the picture.

"No heat?" asked Butler, raising his chin toward the ancient metal box heater, its bright orange bands glowing. A fire hazard.

Mrs. Pittman shook her head. Pulled her sweater closer around her.

"Kids?" asked Butler.

"One," said Mrs. Pittman. "My boy. He asleep."

"He trouble?" asked Butler. He liked this woman. He respected her. He made himself love her.

It wasn't easy. Loving a stranger. Someone he didn't know.

It didn't come naturally.

But he made himself do it.

"Mostly not," said the boy's mother, thinking of her child. Her baby.

Her eyes fell away.

"But he gettin' there." Even now she was preparing to lose him. Preparing to mourn.

"I got to go," said Butler and took a step back.

"Who are you?"

"Nobody," said Butler. "Thank you." He nodded to Mrs. Pittman and retreated down the steps, his right hand releasing the small pistol held in his pocket. Mrs. Pittman closed the door. She locked and bolted it as another cold night came to Beddoe Street.

As he drove home, Butler made two calls. One to get the heat back on and one to help the boy.

35

Some hours later, he made a third call.

In a small house on the outskirts of Jackson, Michigan, not far from the State Prison, the young woman's phone rang. The ringtone was "Amazing Grace." The volume was set high.

When she got a call at work, she always wanted the prisoners and guards to hear it. She wanted the whole world to hear it.

"Hi," she said in a quiet, silky voice after she saw the caller ID.

"Hi," Pearce replied. "Am I calling too late?"

"Hardly," she laughed. "I'm still working." He didn't need to ask what she was working on. She was a prison chaplain.

"Are you alone?"

"Yes, I'm at home. Just me and Sully." The cat, John L. Sullivan, former heavyweight fighter, now retired, brushed against her leg as she pulled out a secondhand chair and sat at the small kitchen table. She wore loose, flannel drawstring pants, thick white socks, and a gloriously soft, ancient gray sweatshirt. "What's up?" she asked. In her line of work, she was accustomed to calls at any hour.

A long stretch of silence. She was used to that, too, from him.

She pictured him in the Boathouse looking at the river. Or

tinkering with his cars or his boat. Or crunching numbers for his next deal.

"I just wanted to hear your voice."

"How was your day?" she tried.

After a moment he said, "Productive."

Her name was Priscilla Dupin. They'd met under tragic circumstances. A person had died, been murdered, before their eyes. It could've been avoided. Poor decisions were made that terrible night. Human error. Scars remained on them both. Regrets.

She was the only person he'd ever invited to the Boathouse.

"I saw so much poverty today," he said. "I don't know what to do."

"You do a lot."

"Not enough." A pause. "It's not just economics."

"No," she said. "It's not."

"How do we fight evil, Pree?" She went by Pree. "How are we supposed to fight it?"

"I get that question a lot."

"I imagine you do."

"I like to say, 'Constantly. Bravely. And faithfully.'"

"Too glib." She heard the exasperation in his voice. "No jokes, Pree. What I saw today..." He didn't finish. He didn't have to.

"Faith is no joke, my love." She rose and paced to and through the tiny living room, then back to the old kitchen.

"I know," said Butler. "Faith can move mountains. I believe that. But I can't pray a meal into someone's house. Not when they're hungry tonight."

She sat, and Sully brushed against her again, his fur and muscle warm against her faded red plaid flannel pants.

"How do we really *fight* evil, Pree? What do we do?"

"One person at a time, sweetie. That's all I know. *Mano y mano.* We battle for one soul at a time. That's the only way I know of to fight the Evil One and win."

He was uncomfortable when she used that kind of language. The Evil One. Satan. The devil.

Halloween words.

But he couldn't deny their meaning.

There was evil in the world. It was obvious. Evil existed. Take away the storybook horns and pointed tail, and substitute Hitler's mustache. Or Bin Laden's murder-inciting videos. Or the ignorant, giant bully on the playground. Or the rapacious greed on Wall Street.

Evil is not in the womb. Evil overtakes us.

Butler believed in God. And by doing so, came to believe in evil. Not merely random tragedy but a dedicated, sentient enemy. Dedicated to our destruction.

He knew there was a war going on. He felt it in his soul.

He sat in near darkness by the windows overlooking the river while she waited on the phone. Around him were girders and steel. Below him his cars, his boat, the workroom. He was exhausted.

"You still talking to Bridget?" he said, finally. The woman from Keno's condo. Whose apartment he had personally cleaned. As penance, perhaps, for sins past and future.

"Yes. I took her to lunch last week."

"She still a stripper?"

"Yes. But not for long, I don't think." The women had talked and shared together over soups and salads. And wept. And laughed. And prayed.

"She's weakening?" said Butler.

"Strengthening."

For a few seconds neither spoke.

"You're great at what you do, Pree."

"Thanks."

"But why," Butler asked, "...does God allow evil to happen? Why does He do it?"

"I think..." she began with little hesitation, for she was asked this question often, "...that what I truly believe is that we're God's experiment. Perhaps not the only one. And that He loves us and wants us to be joyful in His love. But it's not automatic."

"Free will," said Butler.

"Exactly," said Pree, "We get to make choices. He wants us to make godly choices, but *we* have to choose. And without Satan..."

"There'd be nothing to tempt us. Nothing to fight."

"Exactly."

"Isn't that a little too easy?"

"Is your life easy?"

He did not answer. Then said, "Yet God loves us."

"Yes," she said soberly. "Even with all the pain, God loves us. Every person on earth, every single moment, He loves all of us."

A pause. He thought of Beddoe street.

"I don't understand that kind of love."

"We're not allowed to understand God. That's a line we cannot cross."

"But aren't we made in God's image?"

"Image is what we look like, not what we are."

"You're already my pastor, Pree. Do you want to be my analyst, too?"

"I want to be your wife." There was a smile, he thought, in her voice. A smile he knew well, and that he could clearly hear. She had a wonderful smile.

"I know," said Butler. "I'm working on that."

"Onward, Christian soldier," said Pree. She didn't sing the words, or say them to try to be cute. She simply spoke them. As she often did. To him. To others. To herself in the mirror each morning, each day.

They said their goodbyes and ended the call.

36

It was Sunday. Terry had planned to watch a basketball game. He tried to beg off.

But Henry was quite insistent. "George has something for us."

"Can't I just call in?" said Terry. He paced the kitchen, coffee in hand. Christina and Hannah had just left for church. He was in sweats. Unshowered and unshaven.

"He has something to show us." Henry wanted Terry to come to Ferndale at three. "Enhanced video."

Terry stopped pacing and set his coffee down. "Enhanced video of what?" said Terry.

"I don't know," said Henry.

Terry didn't get to see the game.

The folding chairs in Henry's outer office were arranged foursquare as before. Henry again in jacket, crisp shirt, no tie, shined shoes.

George was there when Terry arrived, working on a laptop. He rose and greeted Terry warmly. The little Greek was always cheerful, Terry had to give him that. Expensive but cheerful. Two thousand dollars a day, charged to The Falcon LLC.

I'd be cheerful, too, thought Terry.

Fran arrived last, five minutes late. Terry had invited her at Henry's suggestion. She seemed pale and withdrawn and she didn't apologize for her tardiness. Once again, Henry offered to hang up her coat, and again she preferred to keep it. She did accept a bottle of water, however. Terry had water, too.

They all sat down.

"How are you?" said George pointedly to Fran. The other men also looked at her, sober-faced but supportive. Fran glanced down at her hands.

"I'm all right, I guess."

"You did perfect yesterday. Perfect." The word sounded like *perfek.*

"Thanks," she said, meeting George's eye for a fleeting moment. She reached into her purse and withdrew a folded tissue. It held something. She unwrapped it and handed the large, white-painted safety pin to George. "This is yours," she said.

"Thank you," said George, with an expansive smile. He dropped the pin in his shirt pocket.

"Did you get more of him on video?" asked Terry. "Is that what this is about?"

"I didn't recognize him," said Fran to George. "Even after I sent you a text, I watched it again. I don't know him."

George settled them with raised palms. "Yes," he said to Fran. "But one thing at a time."

"And what if he'd seen you!" said Fran, rising from her chair.

"He didn't," said George, also rising, mirroring her movements. A calming technique. "He didn't see me, thanks to you. Thanks to your efforts. And your courage." Hands open, palms extended, George soothed Fran back into her chair.

Fran pressed her lips tight. She didn't know about this George. She didn't trust him. He was strange. But she didn't have much choice.

"He took the money?" asked Terry.

George nodded. "Yes." He stood and stepped to his laptop on the desk. "But at great cost." He waved them over. They rose as one and gathered around the desk.

George brought up a full screen view on the laptop, a blurry still frame of mall bustle that showed nothing. When all were focused on the screen, he hit Play.

The image jarred to life. Mall noise and voices. George muted the sound. Silent torsos passed close to the lens. Thighs. A child's head. The view was from the smartphone camera held while standing in line for Mexican food. The camera was held low, as steady as possible.

Then a glimpse of Fran appeared onscreen, sitting at the table with the Lord & Taylor bag.

"You took this?" said Fran.

"Yes," said George.

"I didn't see you."

"No," said George. "You wouldn't have."

After a few seconds, Fran-at-the-mall stood, put her purse on her shoulder and walked out of frame to the right. The white shopping bag she left behind was clearly visible beneath the chair against the low wall. As she stepped away, a throng of people walked by the camera, obscuring the picture.

"Watch," said George.

The people cleared the frame and now the video showed a man sitting in Fran's vacated chair, talking on a cell phone. He had shaggy brown hair over his forehead, a ball cap, tinted aviator glasses, a brown beard and a mustache, and he wore a parka and khakis. George froze the picture.

"Anyone know him?" said George. It was the same clip he'd sent them from the Neon. "Take another look." The others looked closely. Fran looked closest.

"He looks like the Unabomber," said Henry. The others nodded at the reference to Ted Kaczynski, the domestic terrorist who'd planted sixteen homemade bombs in the U.S. before his capture in 1996. The man in the video resembled the well-known pencil sketch of the deranged bomber.

George nodded. He pointed at the image with a pencil. "That's a wig," he said and moved the pencil tip. "That's a false beard and mustache."

"I don't know him," said Fran. George invited Fran to sit closer and get a better view.

"Keep watching," said George. "When he moves. Could be you see something familiar. A gesture. His posture. A certain way of moving." George started the video again, and all four watched the man in the beard listen to the phone while positioning the Lord & Taylor bag against his right leg.

"The phone is a prop," said George. "Not a real call." The bearded man put his right hand into his pants pocket. "Now he's turning on the metal detector."

For a few moments, the bearded man pretended to talk on the phone as he looked carefully around him. Half the time, the view was obscured by passing people. Then the camera jumped and wobbled. "I had to move," said George. "I was waiting in a line and had to step forward."

After a few moments, the camera again found the bearded man from a different angle. Brown Beard smiled briefly, his fingers suddenly went up to his cheek, and he stopped smiling.

"His beard loosened. Right there," said George.

The blackmailer pocketed his phone, stood, dropped his soda cup in the trash can, hoisted the heavy Lord & Taylor bag, and stepped out of frame to the left.

Then the picture went dark. All three men looked at Fran.

"Well?" asked George. Fran's arms and legs remained crossed.

"I don't know him," she said. Terry watched her closely.

"Can we see it again?" asked Terry.

"Yes," said George. He played it again.

And again.

Terry saw something working in Fran. As a video editor, he was accustomed to watching miniscule moments of video over and over. Often a single frame made all the difference.

The man's tinted glasses obscured his eyes and eyebrows. Fran watched the way he arched his body to slide his hand into his pocket. The glimmer of teeth in the brief smile. The fingers rising to the loosened false beard.

George backed it up. Stopped at the man's brief smile. He looked at Fran. "Do you see anything familiar?"

"No," said Fran. "Why would I?" She looked at each of them in turn. Terry shrugged. Henry was expressionless.

"In cases like these," said George, "the victim—you—is often blackmailed by someone she knows."

Fran said nothing at first. Looked at the toe of her boot. "The photos." She pushed the lurid images out of her mind. "I told you before. They're not of me. I'm just..." She managed a bitter smile, wet-eyed. "I'm just paying for them."

There was a moment of silence. Terry kneaded his thick fingers. "That's all I'll say," said Fran.

George nodded. Fran used the tissue in which she'd wrapped the white safety pin to wipe her eyes.

"In that case," said the Greek. "That's very interesting. Can I show you something else?" The freeze frame of the bearded man smiled onscreen.

Fran nodded, not speaking. George worked the mouse. Another photo blossomed onscreen, next to the video still frame. A business portrait, bright and vibrant compared to the drab mall footage.

They all looked at the clean-cut, necktied photo of Jim Ritchie. Becky's husband. Smiling boyishly at the camera.

"Oh, please!" said Fran.

"Look at the smile," said George.

"It's not Jim!" She uncrossed and re-crossed her legs. Even forced a harsh laugh. "Jim's a puppy dog. He's like a twelve-year old." She shook off the idea.

"Who is that?" Henry asked George.

"James Ritchie. Fran's brother-in-law," said George. He looked at Fran. "Her sister Rebecca's husband."

"Where did you get the picture?" said Terry.

"LinkedIn," said George. "Fran. If the photos are not of you, might they be of . . . your sister?"

Fran said nothing, shutting her eyes. Until tears ran.

After several silent seconds, a high, tortured keening came from her throat. The men gave her as much time as she needed.

While her eyes were still closed, George spoke softly, "She was drugged, Fran. That's why it's photos, not video. Video would show her drugged. Listless. Unaware, out of it. Photos—he can isolate a moment. Show open eyes. Make something that's not real…look real."

Without opening her eyes, Fran nodded, mouth in a tight grimace, wadded tissue held to her mouth. When she did open her eyes, Henry offered her a tissue box. She took more.

"Fran." Terry gently laid a hand on her shoulder. "We're going to help you," he said. "Whatever it takes."

He more than half expected her to push away his hand. She didn't. Instead, she reached up. Clasped her hand over his.

"What did he give her?" she finally asked, sniffling.

"You've heard of roofies?" said George.

"A date rape drug," said Henry.

George nodded. "Yes. Flunitrazepam. Sometimes called Narcozep or Rohypnol. The victim is awake but only barely, often very suggestible. Frequently has no memory of the episode. Clinical amnesia. No memory at all. Just a massive headache."

Fran nodded.

After a long minute, she looked at all of them. Then at the screen.

"It can't be Jim." She shook her head forcefully. "Jim wouldn't hurt a fly." And she thought of her smiling sister. Her sweet little Christian sister. Smiling and rutting with whores. Slick, pink, nakedly entwined with evil. She choked back a sob.

It was impossible.

She felt a gentle hand on her arm as George kneeled to look closely into her eyes.

"The photos," he said, "mean nothing." Fran nodded, blinking back tears.

"She was raped, Fran. For money."

Fran released an agonized sob. She thought of little Clark. Of the baby on the way.

George stepped to the screen and enlarged the shot of the bearded man and the LinkedIn photo of Jim Ritchie.

"There," said George pointing to the LinkedIn portrait with the pencil tip. "See? Level with the top of the ear. Toward the eyebrow." He pointed the pencil tip at a faint mole or scar on Jim Ritchie's temple.

"Now look here," said George. He aligned the grainy mall image of Brown Beard next to the LinkedIn portrait.

"I don't see anything," said Fran.

"I'll push the contrast," said George.

The image of the man in the mall went black-and-white. The darks went darker, and lighter tones became pasty white. Gradually, a dark dot, a faint mole or scar, appeared between the top of his ear and eyebrow. Very much like the mole or scar on the LinkedIn photo.

Everyone looked closely. It wasn't conclusive. Finally, Fran said, "So?" Henry and Terry leaned in close to see.

"I don't know, George," said Terry. Henry said nothing.

"You're wrong," said Fran. "It's not Jim."

George shrugged. "Maybe not." He stood and flexed his fingers, tilting his head side to side on his neck, loosening his shoulder muscles. He did a very odd deep knee bend. Then he reached as high as he could, stretching as if to touch the ceiling. A glorious moan escaped him. The others watched, perplexed.

When he turned back to them, his eyes shone merrily. "Let's catch him and find out."

37

P.J. tapped the brakes. He was on the main road, a hundred yards from the turn into the big guy's neighborhood, when he saw the family van lurch into view. He recognized it immediately. It was heading out of the neighborhood. It stopped at the intersection he was quickly approaching, then turned right, away from him, expelling its trademark cloud of exhaust. He didn't see the driver.

He could go to the house or follow the van.

If the guy was driving and he was by himself, that would be good. If it was the wife, even better. It was Sunday afternoon. He followed the van.

Ten minutes later he swore loud. The van had pulled into a grocery store. The wife and the daughter got out. Someplace called Gittleman's. He was about to head back to the house when he got a better look at the wife. She was very small. Pretty.

She was laughing at something the kid said. Her mouth was as small as a kid's mouth.

He watched her shake her hair out, pull her short little coat tight, and walk with her daughter toward the store. They held hands.

P.J. parked a row away. Pulled his ball cap low and got out. It was a busy, modern store. Might have cameras. But he'd shaved recently. The TV story had long died out, and his picture on that was with a beard. The sun was out, but it was cold.

He tracked the wife and daughter at a hunter's distance.

In the cart corral, Christina used a disinfectant wipe to clean the handle of the shopping cart. Then she and Hannah pushed it through the automatic glass doors into the brightly lit, bustling supermarket. "Spaghetti sound good tonight?" she asked her animated daughter. Hannah made a face.

"Didn't we just have it?" said The Product.

"That was ravioli." They'd had it earlier that week. Hannah shrugged, kicking her shiny blue boots against each other. "Well, what sounds good to you?" said Christina, pushing the cart into the spacious produce section.

"Fish sticks!" Hannah jumped up and down with a big grin on her face.

"No, we're not having fish sticks for Sunday dinner." Christina and Terry detested fish sticks, but their daughter could apparently eat them every night. Hannah pouted comically.

"How about a turkey breast?" suggested Christina. "With mashed potatoes? A vegetable. You want to make a salad?" Hannah nodded.

"Yeah-yeah-yeah," she said kid fast.

"Alright, I'll tell you what," said Christina, slowly pushing the cart toward the meat section. "You go get some head lettuce and some leaf lettuce—get the organic stuff—and I'll either be in the meat section or frozen foods." Hannah nodded briskly. "Get a vegetable, too, if you see something good," said Christina. "Green beans or maybe a squash. Acorn squash." Hannah nodded.

P.J. watched the little girl run off to the right and the wife push the cart to the left. He pushed a cart, too. He grabbed something off the first table he saw and threw it in the cart. A bag of bread. He followed the wife. She was small enough to snap in half.

The store was busy, and the wife soon vanished in the crowd. He pushed his cart in the direction she'd disappeared.

Drew a bead on her a few moments later. She was bent way over, looking through different packages of meat. P.J. eyed the black plastic hemispheres flush against the ceiling above the aisles. Maybe cameras, maybe dummies; it didn't matter. He kept his head low. He couldn't make a move. Not yet. Too damn crowded. The noise and harsh fluorescent lights bothered him. All these dumbass people.

His cart was close behind the wife now. He watched her look through the meats. She was still bent over. He could see a nice band of creamy white skin above her ass where her sweater rode up. Her little coat she'd hung on the cart. He watched a freckle on her pale skin dance right over where her crack would be. Her hands were small. Her fingers moved nimbly over the packages of ground beef. Her hair was short and red brown. Like red squirrel but shiny.

He imagined her tied tight to the barber chair. Gagged but eyes open. Better yet, her husband in the chair, gagged and eyes bulging, with the wife doing a little bargaining. P.J. bet she'd bargain a lot. Like that coon bastard and his teenage niece a couple years ago. That worked out great.

He'd rolled close when he heard "Mom!" behind him in the girl's voice and swung his cart too quickly away from the wife. The pivoting cart slammed sideways into the hard-charging ten-year-old with a chrome metal bang. Lettuce and a plastic bag of green beans went flying. The girl fell backward, sprawled onto the floor.

"Oh my God!" said Christina and raced to her daughter, brushing past the big, rough man in the grimy ball cap. P.J. thought fast. He glanced down at the wife, kneeling on the floor next to her fallen daughter. Startled people looking at him.

Running away, no good.

So he bent to the fallen girl, who wasn't crying. He smelled the mom's scent inches from his face. Flowery like shampoo.

Christina stood, lifting Hannah by one arm. P.J. grasped the girl's other arm. They stood her up together. Other shoppers stood and watched.

"Sweetie, are you alright?" said Christina.

"Yeah," said the girl. She glanced up at the man. His coat was dirty.

P.J. released the skinny arm. Like a doe's foreleg. Expressionless, he backed toward his cart. An older woman stooped and gathered the twist-tied bags of lettuce and green beans. After a moment of looking closely into her daughter's eyes, her small hands on the girl's cheeks, Christina looked up at P.J.

"I'm so sorry," she apologized. "She just runs everywhere." P.J. backed another step and slid his hand into his pocket, wrapping his fingers around the knobby grips of the Runt. His eyes flicked over the people looking at him. He forced himself to speak.

"S'long she's okay," he muttered. He looked away from the female eyes. Examined his mudcaked boots.

"Do you still want these?" The woman with the lettuce and beans stepped forward and offered them to Christina.

"Sure, yes, thank you," said Christina quickly, taking them from her.

"You okay, sweetie?" the older woman said to Hannah.

Hannah nodded.

"Hannah, what do you say?" Christina took the lettuce and beans to their cart.

"Thank you," said Hannah to the woman.

"And to the man," said Christina from the cart.

"I'm sorry," said Hannah. He looked down at her with the smallest, blackest eyes she ever saw. He was even bigger than her daddy. He was dirty and stunk, too.

"You shouldn't sneak up on people," said P.J. She had the same creamy skin as her mother.

Hannah made a face. "I wasn't sneaking…" Then Christina was steering her away by the shoulders.

"We're very sorry, sir," she said, looking back and up at P.J. Then she turned to face him, a concerned look on her face. "Are *you* okay?"

He imprinted the wife's face. Like taking a picture. Blue-green eyes. Pink lips. Small mouth. Upturned nose. Red-brown hair. His mind flashed to her hogtied to four bed corners. A hunting knife slicing through thin cotton panties.

He wondered about the red-brown hair.

"Yeah," said P.J. He forced a stiff smile. She didn't smile back. She didn't seem to like his smile. That didn't matter to him.

Without another word, he pushed his cart to the front of the store. He left it next to a steel bin of roasted chickens and walked out, hat low, into the cold.

38

Snowmelt revealed potholes in the tree-lined streets that the Grosse Pointe Farms City Council took great pride in having repaired promptly, as soon as the weather allowed. Before lunch, a jackhammer rang two doors down from Jim and Becky Ritchie's bungalow.

No one answered the first doorbell ring. Butler timed the second ring between bursts of jackhammer activity. He was attired, wigged, and mustached as George. His business card said Larry Stamos. The alias of an alias.

Shortly after the second ring, Becky Ritchie answered the door. She smiled. She'd never seen the Greek-looking man before, and Butler had never seen her, but her resemblance to Fran was unmistakable. He returned Becky's smile with even greater wattage from his own. A glass storm door separated them. "Hello," said Butler.

"Hello," said Becky, one hand on her swelling pregnant belly. The visit was unannounced. He wasn't much taller than she.

"I'm Larry Stamos," said Butler. "For Mike?" Muffled through the glass.

Becky looked confused. Then the jackhammer's din deafened them both. Jim Ritchie joined his wife at the door.

"Is Mike here?" asked the Greek-looking man loudly. Ritchie wore jeans and a comfortable-looking fleece, his fair hair somewhat unkempt. Not unusual for a weekday in today's world of mobile workers. Becky made room for her husband but did not open the storm door. They both looked at the swarthy man on their porch. "Mike?" said the Greek to Jim with a smile. "Mike DeGuarre?" Becky shook her head.

The jackhammer roared.

"I'm Larry Stamos," hollered Butler. "The photographer?" He mimed taking a picture. Then looked over his shoulder at the noisy work truck parked sixty yards away. Becky put her hands over her ears.

"Come in," she yelled. "We can't talk like this." She backed away and let Jim open the storm door. The Greek man smiled and stepped into their home. Jim closed both doors to shut out the roadwork noise. The visitor fished two business cards out of his wallet and handed them to the couple.

"Here you go," he said. He thumbed in the direction of the jackhammer. "Man, you can't have a conversation with that going on." The Ritchies looked at the man's card. It said *Larry Stamos* with a logo of a camera. A photographer's business card.

"They seem early this year, but the roads get so bad," said Becky. The Greek nodded.

"You have a beautiful home. It's a beautiful neighborhood." He held out his hand to Jim. "Mike?" he said. "It's a pleasure to meet you."

Jim shook the hand and said, "My name isn't Mike." The Greek looked confused.

"You're not Mike DeGuarre? Michael DeGuarre?"

"No."

"Oh." The Greek seemed perplexed. "Is he here?"

"No," said Jim. "There's no one here by that name."

"My father's name was Michael DeGraaf," offered Becky. She also shook Butler's proffered hand.

"No, it's DeGuarre," said Butler. He looked closely at Jim Ritchie. Then pulled his phone from his pocket and checked his calendar. "I'm supposed to meet Mike DeGuarre at this address today at eleven o'clock. See?" He showed them both the scheduled appointment. It was the Ritchie's address. The jackhammer had stopped.

"It was for photos of his daughter." Butler looked straight at Jim Ritchie.

Jim looked at the appointment on the phone and then at the stranger in their house. "It must be a mistake," said Ritchie.

"I have not met him," said Butler with a faint Mediterranean accent. "It's a referral." He smiled at Jim. "I was surprised when I saw you, too."

Ritchie shifted on his feet. Butler forced lengthy eye contact.

"Because Deguarre—I got a description." The Greek beamed a smile. From Jim to Becky then back to Jim.

Butler stroked imaginary whiskers. "Deguarre has a brown beard." Then he indicated his eyes. "Glasses." He was watching Ritchie closely.

Ritchie smiled briefly. "Not me," he said. "I don't know who you're looking for, but he's not here."

"Hm," said the Greek.

A small boy in red sweatpants, white socks, and a *Minions* T-shirt scampered into the room and joined his parents. Staring at Butler, he drifted instinctively to his mother. Her pale arm settled naturally on the boy's shoulders as he leaned into her hip.

"I don't think that's him, either," smiled George. The boy was silent. So was the jackhammer. Suddenly, all was quiet.

"Well," said Jim Ritchie.

"I am so sorry to have bothered you. Obviously, a mistake." Butler offered a brief, polite bow.

Becky returned a big grin. "That's okay. I hope you find him."

"Me, too. And if you ever need a photographer..." he pointed at the business cards in their hands. "Go to my website."

Butler as Larry Stamos shook hands with both parents and also with the shy, small boy.

"He has good manners," smiled Butler to the parents.

"Thank you," said Becky. Butler left with a friendly wave. The phone number on the business card went to a dummy voicemail account. The website declared, "Sorry, we're under construction." The street address was bogus. Uncertainty was the goal.

If there was a cage to rattle, Butler had rattled it.

Butler got into a rented Jeep Renegade in front of their house and drove off without looking back. He passed a solitary workman in hardhat and coveralls, standing with a jackhammer by a pickup. The workman was average-sized, white, and clean-shaven. Butler didn't look at him, and he didn't look at Butler. The jackhammer started up again.

One minute after Butler left, the workman turned off the compressor, put the jackhammer and shovel into the back of the truck and picked up the inch-thick steel plate he had been jackhammering to make a suitable racket. Then he too drove away, leaving behind a small patch of new asphalt smoothed over a nonexistent pothole.

39

Life was good at Image Zoo. The animals were happy. The Gittlemans team-building video had been a hit. Terry had found workable footage of people dancing and used the same few sequences over and over: blown up, slo-mo, snap zooms, and even a zany, hippie-style, posterized effect—all combined to create a music-driven leitmotif to hold the piece together. Then he interspersed cutaways of quick, positive sound bites from the employees. Mr. Gittleman had been so pleased, he ordered up a new TV campaign for spring.

It had been one of the warmest days of the new year. Terry and Belinda held down the fort. Jeff and Skip were in Grand Rapids for a furniture store shoot. Terry had taken a walk at lunch just to stretch his legs. Even now, just after five, sunlight angled through the tall stairwell windows as Terry walked down the old, wooden stairs after a satisfying workday.

He thought about Amber DeGraaf. Fran confirmed that she'd called her mother. He'd sent her a check. She'd left him a message, thanking him. She sounded polite. He hadn't called back. Didn't know what to say. He was still ashamed of losing his temper.

When Terry stepped outside, it was colder than he'd expected.

Despite the afternoon sunshine, the temperature had plummeted. He shoved his bare hands into his coat pockets and headed toward the small side parking lot.

As he walked toward his car, a dirty brown sedan lurched from its parking space, blocking his path.

"Hey!" said Terry. The damn thing barely missed him.

Terry leaned down to look through the passenger-side window. He saw the driver. The driver didn't turn his head to look at him but looked straight ahead, motionless. He was a big guy, with a mat of black hair and a week of black beard. It was an older car with an open ashtray stuffed with butts.

"Hey!" repeated Terry. "What do you think you're doing?"

The driver didn't move.

Ann Arbor had its share of crackpots. Terry went closer to the car's window.

"Hey, excuse me? If it's not too much trouble, I'd kinda like to get to my car." *Asshole.*

The guy didn't budge. Didn't look at Terry. The passenger-side window began to power down. The car was full of trash and stank like cigarettes; the guy wore a big, mud-spattered coat.

Once the window was open, Terry leaned closer. "Excuse me, buddy, but you got some kind of problem here?"

Then Terry was looking down the dead black hole of pistol muzzle a foot from his face. A hole as big and dark as a cannon's. Held rock steady. The driver's fierce black eyes staring at him, arm straight, finger tightening on the trigger of the Runt.

"Get in the car or I'll blow your brains out right now. Hear me? I know where you live, motherfucker."

Terry froze. Christina had described the scary man at the grocery store. The description fit.

"Get in the car or I'll kill you now. Then your little redhead wife. Then your fucking daughter. Don't look at me, look at the gun pointed at your face. Now get in the car. Now."

Terry looked at the gun. Began to raise his hands.

"No, use the latch," said P.J. "Get in. Look at the gun, fuckhead."

Terry felt his insides coil like boiling worms, felt he might crap in his pants. He opened the door.

"That's right, get in."

"Look," said Terry.

"Shut up," said P.J. "Don't talk. Shut up." Terry got in. "Close the door, buckle your seat belt and sit on your hands," said the gunman. Terry did as he was ordered while P.J. pulled out of the parking lot with one hand on the wheel and the other aiming the gun at Terry's head. He drove away from Main Street, into the residential area. P.J. took his hand off the steering wheel for a moment and threw Terry a plastic zip tie. "Put this around your wrists," said P.J., pressing the Runt hard against Terry's ear. The barrel against his skin made Terry wince and tears come.

Silently blinking back the tears, Terry put the narrow plastic loop around one wrist then put his other wrist through. A slender plastic tongue on one end poked through a molded ratchet block on the other.

"How do I...?" started Terry.

"Use your teeth. Pull it tight."

Terry got the plastic tongue in his mouth and pulled the zip tie tight.

"Tighter," said P.J. "Bite it. Pull it."

Terry bit and pulled harder. The plastic strip tightened a few more clicks, biting into his wrists. The car drove away from town, staying within speed limits and stopping at stop signs. Traffic thinned.

"Don't hurt my family," said Terry looking down. In response, the pistol barrel jabbed his head painfully.

"Don't talk."

In minutes, they were a world away from downtown Ann Arbor's art galleries, bookstores, and coffee shops, driving north past wintering cornfields and beanfields. Where Ann Arbor stopped, farmland instantly took over.

After a while, P.J. turned down a muddy cut that crossed a dormant field and followed the cut for a few hundred yards before pulling behind a small stand of trees. The trees hid the car from the road. He shut off the car. The instant quiet made Terry's ears pop. He was too scared to think. The gun barrel pulled away from his ear, but he dared not look at the man. He looked at his bound hands.

He heard paper unfolding next to him. Terry didn't dare move a muscle.

"Hey," said the driver. "Hey." Terry moved his eyes only. The gun was still aimed at his head, mere inches from his skull. There was a piece of paper on the seat. A printout of a photo. "Pick that up." Terry picked up the paper. "You know him?" said the driver. Terry glanced briefly at his kidnapper. Black eyes glittered beneath shaggy black hair. Then Terry looked at the photo printout.

It was George.

Terry nodded. "Yes," he said. The photo was grainy, pulled from a video. Blown up. Bad color. But it was George.

"Onassis?" said the driver. Terry shook his head.

"His name's Onassis, right? Short little fucker?"

Terry shook his head. Looked at his kidnapper. "No," he said.

"No?" said P.J. He pressed the muzzle of the Runt hard between Terry's eyes. Terry jerked back, but with nowhere to go, his head smacked against the window.

"What's his name?" The muzzle kept pressing Terry's head back against the cold glass.

"George," said Terry, his eyes closed. "George Ginapolis."

"Where does he live?"

"I don't know," said Terry. The muzzle jabbed his forehead painfully. "Honest!" said Terry, "I don't know! I don't know where he lives. I don't even have his number."

P.J. believed him. This guy was soft. If he knew, he'd tell. The guy was shaking, crying, practically pissing his pants. And Blond John was a tricky bastard.

"Okay, look at me," said P.J. "Don't piss your pants; look at me." He shoved Terry's head again with the gun barrel. Terry looked at him. "Don't piss your pants in my car or I'll blow your fucking dick off, you hear me?" Terry nodded, the gun pointing at his face. He suddenly needed oxygen.

"And don't you faint on me, I swear. I'll choke you and leave you here dead. Hey. Hey!" P.J. smacked Terry's cheek lightly with the barrel of the Runt. Terry's eyes went wide.

The driver reached into his coat pocket with his free hand and pulled out a pack of matches. He took the photo printout from Terry's bound hands and substituted the matchbook. "Look at it," the driver said.

Terry looked. On the matchbook was the name of a bar.

"That's in Wayne. You know Wayne?"

Terry nodded. "Yeah." Wayne was a raw, tough, blue-collar town anchored by two big Ford plants west of Detroit.

P.J. pointed the gun at the matchbook and then at Terry. "You bring him to that bar tomorrow night, ten o'clock, and I don't kill you and your family. Deal?"

"I don't…"

"Shut up."

"I don't have his number," said Terry. "I don't know how to reach him."

Henry.

P.J. thumbed back the Runt hammer inches from Terry's face. "I know where you live. I know what your wife looks like. I know what your daughter looks like." P.J. leered. "Long, dark hair. Purple backpack. She's pretty." Terry felt sick.

Before Terry saw where it came from, the driver had a knife out, a big one, silver blade shining. "Hold up your wrists," said the driver. Terry did so. With a flick, the driver cut the zip tie, the knife's sharp point nicking Terry's inner wrist. A drop of blood oozed out.

"Get out," said P.J. "Go home. Bring him tomorrow. Ten o'clock. I smell a cop, your family's dead, understand? And you're dead." Terry nodded, blood on his shirt cuff.

"You understand?" barked P.J.

"Yes," said Terry, looking up.

"Get out."

With mud and gravel spraying, the dirty sedan sped away, leaving Terry nearly fainting on all fours, his knees soaked in puddles and his palms pressed in mud. He bit the cold air in hard gasps. As shadows stretched and the sky grew dark, he vomited behind the desolate stand of dark trees deep in a farm field north of Ann Arbor.

40

Terry sent Christina and Hannah away. He had to. He'd called his wife from the lonely farm field, covered in cold mud. His phone GPS guided her to him. Before she showed up, he called Henry to make sure Christina could access the account. She could. He didn't call the police. He couldn't. He couldn't put Christina and Hannah at risk. Henry asked what was going on, and Terry told him. He told him the man had a gun and wanted George. Had called him by another name, a Greek name Terry couldn't remember. Henry said he would try to reach George.

In the car, he told his wife everything. Christina was terrified. When Hannah's name came up, she started crying.

She'd wanted him out at the first sign of trouble. They'd agreed to it. He'd promised her. But now the first sign of trouble was already too late. Terry insisted she and Hannah get out of the house. Take a leave of absence from her job. Pull Hannah out of school. The gunman knew who they were and where they lived. There was nothing else Terry could do.

"For how long?" asked Christina, wiping tears as she drove.

"I don't know," said Terry.

Both of them felt it could be forever.

He assured her she'd have plenty of money. Saying that made her sob harder.

She drove him to his car at Image Zoo. Driving home, he called Henry again. Henry had called George. He'd left a message. He apologized for being unable to do more.

The Holbrook family went to a hotel. They told Hannah they had to get the house checked for radon, and she didn't question it. They stopped at an ATM so they could pay cash for the hotel. They spoke little before Hannah went to bed.

Terry gave Henry's number to Christina and gave her number to Henry. He kept telling her it would be all right. He tried to believe it himself.

The next day Terry spent quietly at work. Christina cried when he left. She didn't want Hannah to see, so Terry had to keep hugging her for as long as it took for her to settle down. More than a minute. Christina let the school know Hannah wouldn't be in.

Jeff and Skip were still gone, and Belinda took a long lunch. She asked him if he wasn't feeling well, and he said he was fighting a bug. He kept his eye out for the dirty sedan but didn't see it in the lot or on the street. He called Christina frequently.

Late in the afternoon he finally got a call from George. Terry wanted to call the police. George said no. They spoke for twenty minutes.

Now, hours later, Terry felt stiff and scared in the bar in Wayne. He'd eaten dinner alone at The Olive Garden, in case he was being followed. He'd called his wife and daughter from the table. He let Hannah do most of the talking. He didn't have any wine. Now he sat alone in a dark bar called The Hideout at 9:55, in a worn, sticky booth, scared shitless, with his fingers around a cold Budweiser. With his coat on. He was going to have a Coke but thought it would draw attention. After one sip, he was glad it was beer.

The place was a cinderblock dive for customers who couldn't care less. Windowless. Lit-up plastic beer logos. Mirrors with more beer logos. A flat screen TV with the Red Wings playing Montreal. A few regulars. Country music on. No women on either side of the bar. No apparent food.

He tried to sit up taller but felt stiff and uncomfortable. Drank more beer.

He was in the back, facing the front door, when a shadow fell on his head from behind. He looked back and saw the large shape of the man from the car. Bigger than Terry remembered. Bigger than Terry. Both hands buried in deep coat pockets.

P.J. glanced down at Terry dead-eyed, then toward the front door, then toward the back, where he'd come in. He pointed with his chin. "Switch places," he said. P.J. stepped back, eyeing the room. Nobody looked at him. Terry slid out and around to the other side of the booth. P.J. sat where Terry had been. The plywood booth seat creaked under a torn vinyl cushion.

"Where is he?" said P.J.

"I contacted him," said Terry. "He'll be here." The bigger man's narrow eyes made Terry feel like a small game animal.

"Get me a Bud Light. Bottle."

Terry got him a Bud Light from the bar.

"You talk to him?" asked P.J.

"I left a message. I...I don't have his number." Terry drank nervously. P.J. took a long pull at the longneck.

"Then how'd you leave a message?"

Terry glanced up from his hands to P.J.'s heavy-lidded face, which was as cold as a slab of cement. "Like I said, I don't know him. We have a mutual…acquaintance. That's how…that's the only way I can get in touch."

"Who's the mutual acquaintance?"

Terry shifted uncomfortably. When he did, his leather coat caught the table edge. He was sweating. "He's my, uh…he's my lawyer."

"What's his name?"

"Look," said Terry. "If we just wait…"

P.J.'s face darkened. He leaned toward Terry and thumped something hard against the underside of the table. Hard and metallic. "Do you know what this is?"

P.J. seemed very close, his eyes sharp. The stink of beer and cigarettes blew hot and rank in Terry's face.

Terry breathed heavily. "Yes."

"It's your fucking wife and daughter *dead*, you fucking dumbass!" hissed P.J.

"Look," said Terry, hands clasped to keep them from shaking. "He's going to be here." He nodded at a clock behind the bar. It had Clydesdales on it. "It's only five after."

P.J. scowled at him. Didn't look at the clock. Then said, "I don't think so."

Terry looked at him. P.J. kept staring, then sat back with both hands back in his coat pockets. Terry reached for his beer.

"Come on," said P.J. "Let's go."

Terry's hand stopped in mid-reach. P.J. slid out and stood up. Shook his shoulders back. He moved with startling swiftness for a big man. "Come on," said P.J., jerking his head toward the back. "We're going."

"What do you mean?"

"I mean come on. Let's go."

"What if I stay here?"

P.J. leaned close over the table. "Then you stay here *dead*," he hissed, jutting his right coat pocket. There was no mistaking the shape within.

Without another word, Terry slid out of the booth and stood, the gunman's fast left hand shoving Terry in front of him. Nobody at the bar took notice. Their eyes were on the hockey.

With P.J. inches behind, Terry walked past the end of the bar to the grimy back hall where the bathrooms were. Poorly lit by a dirty bulb screwed into a lone ceiling socket. The damp cinderblock walls smelled musty and urinal. At the far end was a scuffed metal door with an *Exit* sign above it. The *Exit* sign unlit.

Terry opened the door and stepped outside. Behind him P.J. had the Runt out, twitching and jumpy in his right hand. The night air was cold, their breath exhaled in clouds. A pair of yellow bulbs on wood posts barely lit the small parking lot, shared by the bar and a closed-for-the-night lube shop. Most snow had melted, except for the remains of dirty mounds piled by snowplows for three months.

"At the end," said P.J. indicating the row of cars. Terry saw the dirty brown sedan. Backed in, pointed out. P.J. was close behind him, right arm loose, the steel gun barrel prodding the base of Terry's spine, nudging him toward the sedan.

"Halloo!" came from behind them. P.J. and Terry both turned, P.J. palming the compact pistol flat against his leg, to see a smiling George emerge from the shadows of the bar's dumpster. He stepped toward them, rubbing his hands together for warmth. "I'm sorry I'm late," he said, grinning. P.J.'s eyes narrowed. Terry stopped breathing.

And saw P.J.'s hand curl around on the pistol's grip.

Then, "Hi, P.J. Long time, no see," said a different voice. From the left, Terry and P.J. both saw a very blond man with a white-blond mustache step from between two trucks.

"P.J.!" called a third voice, from the far right, and Terry and P.J. spun to see another compact, blond-haired, blond-mustached man emerge from shadows into the yellow light. A twin of the first blond man. Both waved at P.J. Terry's eyes were popping.

The distraction was good but not good enough.

P.J.'s gun arm straightened, and he turned to face George with a two-hand combat grip.

"You!" he growled. When Terry saw P.J.'s trigger finger tighten, he lunged at P.J.'s arm. The pistol shot exploded, deafening, sharply ringing off cars and trucks. Butler, as George, leapt forward as the shot went wide.

Terry saw P.J.'s small, hard eyes flare and burn as the short pistol swung toward him. The pistol's barrel aimed directly at Terry's face.

Deep inside, he felt the twisted black roil shriek with glee. Terry saw fangs. Insanity. Twin yellow slivers of swelling reptile eyes. He fought the horror with love for Hannah. With love for Christina. With the glimpse of God he knew was real. Then he saw the muzzle flash.

Through a slightly different lens. Everything the same but not quite.

Terry heard the air roar from the handgun and felt his chest explode. He flew off his feet. Fell heavily onto his back.

An instant later, Butler and the two blond decoys tackled the outlaw. Before P.J. could fire again, one blond man collapsed P.J.'s legs with a side hammer kick to the big man's knees. The other pounced on P.J.'s right arm, and Butler took away the Runt with a thumb dig at a pressure point on the back of P.J.'s hand. P.J. screamed in agony as Butler and the two blond men flipped him facedown, a heel in his neck and a knee in his spine. All within seconds of the first shot.

The back door of the bar flew open and two men in faded jeans ran out, guns drawn, badges out. Without a word, they descended on Robert Peet, Jr. and cuffed him as Butler sped to Terry, who lay motionless on his back.

Kneeling, Butler pressed two fingers against the carotid artery in Terry's neck. While P.J. shrieked and swore on the ground behind them, George pushed aside the flap of Terry's coat, revealing a sweatshirt with a small hole in it, next to the heart.

George dug his fingers into the fabric, ripping it wide. A glimmer of silver. The bullet distorted. Flattened against the Kevlar vest.

"Terry! Terry!" said Butler, maintaining the faint Greek accent of George, his breath clouding in huffs. Gently, he slapped Terry's face. "Get him water!"

Without a word, one of the blond men ran inside, past the stunned bar owner and a pair of slack-jawed regulars at the open back door.

"Terry!" said Butler. He snapped his fingers rapidly next to both ears. With a gasp and a choke, Terry's eyes flew open, his mouth gulping for air. George laughed—Butler swiftly back in character.

"Terry, my friend! Wake up!" The blond man appeared with a

beer mug of water. George took it and raised Terry's head slightly to get a sip into him. Terry drank greedily. "Not so fast," said George quietly. The blond man slipped off his coat and bunched it on the pavement to cushion Terry's head, then disappeared. An electronic whoop signaled the arrival of two lit-up police cruisers followed by a black SUV, quickly crowding the small lot.

"I'm shot," said Terry. He saw the gun in his face. Firing.

"Yes," smiled the man Terry knew only as George. "But not dead." Terry tried to sit up, but the Greek gently pushed him back. "Don't," said Butler. "You've got broken ribs, I'm sure of it. Lie back. Help is coming."

"Christina," said Terry, voice strained. All wind knocked out of him.

"I'll call her."

Another siren whoop, and EMS arrived, red and white lights rotating. Butler held Terry's hands until the medics took over.

"Thank you, Terry," said Butler, and stood, looking the big man in the eye. Unable to speak and with an oxygen mask suddenly on his face, Terry nodded once and squeezed the hand of the man he knew only as George.

Butler's eyes swam. "This wasn't supposed to happen," said Pearce Butler, blinking back tears. No accent now. "I'm so sorry, Terry. I'm so sorry. I miscalculated." Terry just stared, breathing oxygen. Bewildered.

Terry had seen the muzzle flash. In his face. Aimed at his face. *I should be dead.*

But he wasn't. Something had changed. Something had changed in the moment of the flash.

An altering.

That no one else on earth had seen.

Shouting threats and obscenities, P.J. was quickly manacled hand and foot. Terry was placed on a stretcher and slid into the ambulance. Butler went to the one blond man remaining, who gingerly pulled off the straw-colored mustache Butler had supplied.

"Where's Deleano?" Butler asked, looking around for the other blond-wigged accomplice.

"He left when the cops took over," said Butler's ally. His name was Nate. "You know Deleano." Butler nodded.

One of the uniforms stepped to Butler and Nate, displaying the Runt zipped in a clear plastic bag along with two shell casings. "Here's what packed such a wallop," he said, holding up the bag. "Ugly thing."

Butler and the fake Blond John appraised the small pistol. "Thank you for your help," said the smiling Greek, resuming his Mediterranean persona.

"You're welcome. Your friend okay?" asked the officer as they watched the EMS truck pull out, lights spinning. A brief electronic whoop.

"He will be," said Butler. The policeman nodded and rejoined his fellow officers, who were reading Robert Peet, Jr. his rights.

"It sort of worked," said the blond man. A friend of Butler's. The man who'd operated the jackhammer.

"It worked," said Butler.

"You weren't supposed to draw the shot."

Butler thumped his padded chest. Kevlar. "It still worked. Just enough misdirection. We didn't want a head shot."

The blond man nodded. "He made you, though."

Butler nodded. "Yes," he said. "My posture. Something."

"Sometimes they just sniff you out. Glad your friend's okay."

"He insisted on coming." Butler recalled the phone call. The humility in Terry's voice. "He felt he had to." There had been tears, but also enormous bravery. There was no talking him out of it.

"Probably didn't think he was going to get shot," said Nate.

As they watched the uniforms forcefully cage P.J. in the backseat of a cruiser, another man, thin, almost bald, with a narrow face and a long overcoat, split off from the group of law officers and approached Butler and Nate.

"Bye," said Nate, quickly. He and the law were not on good terms.

"Bye," said Butler, and the blond man disappeared into shadows. As the cruiser and its captive pulled away, Butler did not blink or look away from P.J.'s monstrous glare.

"Your man down okay?" asked the lean, balding man in the long coat.

"Yes, thank you. One or two broken ribs."

The lean man nodded. "Where're your friends?" he asked. The blond twins.

"They had to go."

The lean man pursed his lips. "Well," he managed. "Thanks for the heads-up. Although we're not exactly used to … freelancers."

Butler turned to the plainclothes man and flashed his biggest George Ginapolis smile. "Nothing succeeds like success, yes?" He offered his hand. After a moment, the lean man permitted himself a tight smile and shook it.

"If you say so," he said. "Have a good night." He returned to his black SUV.

Butler called Christina. He told her that her husband was fine. That Terry was a hero. That he had a couple of broken ribs, but would be okay. That she and Hannah could go home. The criminal was caught. The danger was over.

He listened while she wept. While she rambled, sobbing and overcome and thanking God. He spoke only soothing words. He didn't mention guns. When she asked about the broken ribs, he told her that there'd been a fight but Terry was fine. He said that Terry had saved his life.

He meant it.

Long minutes after all the others had left, Pearce Butler paced slowly clockwise, then counterclockwise, alone in the cold, dirty parking lot, listening to Christina as hard as he could.

Listening to a brave wife and mother talk and cry for as long as she needed to. He listened closely. Because in her tumble of words and tears, she revealed what he sought most.

She revealed light. And love.

In the cold, dirty parking lot, he stopped his pacing simply to bask in what she said. The raw, wet humanity of it. The hurting and the bleeding and the weeping and the healing.

The very miracle of it.

41

For nearly thirty years, the Detroit Pistons played home games forty minutes north of Detroit in The Palace of Auburn Hills. Only in 2017 did the Pistons return to a gleaming new arena downtown, further evidence of the Motor City's dazzling comeback. Five miles northeast of The Palace are three patches of connected wilderness, owned by the state, that make up the Bald Mountain Recreation Area.

Interspersed within the state land are a dozen small, grandfathered farms and half as many similarly sanctioned private residences. The wilderness areas offer scenic outlooks, mountain biking, hiking, a shooting range, dog runs, and several small fishing lakes.

Because of its residential population, the recreation area requires no state park permit to enter. Its maze of dirt roads winding through deep forest is accessible through eight ungated, unmanned entry points.

Bald Mountain Recreation Area achieved brief notoriety when its state-owned cabin on Lake Tamarack, available for rental, made global headlines as the rustic laboratory of Dr. Jack Kevorkian— "Dr. Death" to the media. Kevorkian performed two assisted suicides in the cabin in 1991, was convicted of second-degree murder in 1999, and was sentenced to ten to twenty-five years in prison. Paroled in 2007, Kevorkian died of natural causes in 2011. He lived to be eighty-three. He also composed music.

In late March, neither watercraft nor ice shanties were on Graham Lake, a small lake deep within the recreation area, out of sight from any roads. Even the hardiest kayakers and rowboat fishermen were unlikely to appear for at least another week.

Fran drove to the Graham Lake boat launch per the instructions. The package was in the trunk.

The rules had changed.

The location was different.

And the demand was greater. $500,000 in cash. But then it was over. That's what the last note said. No more padded envelopes. No more playing cards. No more games. Pay up, and it was over.

Fran believed him. This felt different. This felt like the end.

She hadn't even looked at the thumb drive. She didn't want to see what was on it. She didn't need to. It didn't matter. All that mattered was that it was over.

She'd asked Terry to set up another meeting. At Henry's office, she'd told the others about the new demands. Terry, stiff with his chest wrapped tight and clearly uncomfortable, had objected to the sum at first but ultimately complied. George listened closely but said little until Fran finished.

Jim Ritchie's name was not spoken.

It was 11:30 on Saturday when she exited I-75 at The Palace and headed north on Lapeer Road. She steered left-handed, her cell phone in her right. Traffic was light. The weather, chilly. The low sky was an endless gray cloud. An infinity of nothing.

She'd left hard pavement a mile back, rumbling slowly along a winding mud and dirt road. Some washboard-like stretches rattled her car so much she had to brake almost completely, barely creeping along the rustic road.

Rattled. That's what George said the blackmailer was. That's why, he maintained, the pattern had changed.

"Greed is a cowardly evil," said George.

No one was around. Fran hadn't seen another vehicle for some time as she steered around and through vast brown puddles. The road crews wouldn't grade the road's pocked surface until all the snow and slush was gone, and that was still several weeks away.

She turned left on what the website map called Predmore Trail. There was no posted sign. An eighth of a mile in, she saw a brown wooden sign with yellow letters carved in: Graham Lake Boat Launch. Permit required beyond this point. She turned in on a seldom-used two-track that curved away from Predmore Trail, sloping down through a tunnel of trees. Even without leaves, the dense, black branches blocked what gloomy light there was. After a hundred yards or so, it opened up, and she saw gray sky as she approached the small, marshy lake.

To her right was a crude boat launch, no more than a pebbled ramp dug out of a dirt bank. Next to it, weathered aluminum posts marched out from the shore. Fran imagined that a dock went there in season. Ringed with pale, dead reeds, the lake was small and still and inky black. No sunlight to reflect.

She felt desolate. As if lost in the Yukon.

Ahead was an empty parking area big enough for maybe five vehicles hauling boat trailers. Log posts prevented visitors from pulling too far into the brush. An empty blue plastic trash bin was

chained to a tree, and a faded fiberglass sign read, Graham Lake
Nature Walk. Dogs must be kept on leash. The path beyond the sign
was choked with overhanging branches. Fran pulled into the spot
that gave her the best view of the barely discernable nature trail.
In her rearview mirror, she saw nothing coming behind her. She
cracked a window. After a moment, she turned off the engine.

Silence.

No birds. No sound. She held her phone, feeling its warm plastic. Turned her body so she could keep an eye on both the path
and the two-track.

She waited. The stillness was unsettling. No wind. Not a cattail
moved. She pulled her coat tighter. Her doors were locked, but she
hit the button to lock them again. Looked at her phone. 11:58. She
watched the digits become 11:59.

She looked up when she heard the faint rumble from the direction of the two-track. The rumble paused. She could almost sense
the unseen vehicle breathing. Waiting. Watching. Then its engine
revved again. The vehicle approached.

A dirty black work van, muddy and decrepit, lumbered into
view with shocks squealing, rocking over the rough ground. It
stopped near the boat launch. Then it reversed, turned, and rattled
backward into a parking spot. The space closest to the lake. Four
spaces from Fran.

No windows in back and all the cab windows tinted. The engine
kept running. Through darkened glass, Fran saw the dim silhou-
ette of the driver, a man, who glanced briefly at her. She sensed
a dark knit cap pulled over the ears. Glasses. A beard. The man
from the mall. She watched him put something to his ear. Fran's
phone buzzed once. She looked at the ID as it buzzed a second
time. <Unknown>

Three times. Four times. She answered and put it to her ear. "Yes?"

"Look at the path, not me." After a moment's hesitation, she did as instructed. She didn't know the voice. "Trunk or backseat?" he said.

"Trunk," said Fran. The money.

"Pop it."

Fran obeyed, popping the trunk lock with the button. "Now walk away." The voice. He was altering its natural sound. Speaking from low in his throat.

"What did you say?" said Fran. He was hard to understand. The words garbled.

"Walk away. Take the path. Leave your phone and keys on the hood. Take the path, keep walking. Don't look back." He hung up. Fran looked at her dead phone.

She opened her door. She was wearing a large, loose barn coat with big pockets.

She got out and shut the door, her phone and keys in her left hand. As ordered, she did not look at the van. She walked to the front of the car, set her phone and the keys on the hood, then continued toward the path. In her coat pocket, her right hand tightly held the grips of the Browning Hi-Power 9mm automatic her father had given her. Newly cleaned and oiled by the man at the range. From whom she'd taken a lesson yesterday. He said it was a fine weapon. Heavy, he said, but a classic.

The barn coat was out of fashion, but its wide pockets were perfect for drawing a pistol. She'd practiced. Now her thumb was on the hammer and the safety was off.

She stepped toward the nature path's entrance then abruptly

changed course, taking long strides straight to the van's passenger-side window.

She looked at the driver, her face close to the tinted window. Her eyes burned at him. The man in the van did not expect this. His mouth gaped as he fumbled with the door lock switch, clicking it locked. Fran lowered her head, glaring at him through faintly tinted glass. He refused to look at her. Faced front. Pulled his knit cap lower.

"I know it's you, Jim!" Fran yelled. "I know it's you!" He didn't move. She didn't leave. She looked at his profile, penetrating the wig, the phony beard and mustache. She stood staring, breathing hard on the cold, dark glass as ten long seconds ticked by. Slid the Browning out, thumb on the hammer. A round already chambered.

She pounded her other fist on the passenger window. "I know it's you, Jim! You fucker!" She pounded the window again, then kneed the passenger door loudly. "I'm going to cut your fucking balls off!" She backed a step and kicked the door hard with her heel.

Then she turned and walked quickly to the pathway entrance. She ducked under scraggly branches and in moments was gone.

The driver exhaled, shuddering. His gloved hands trembled on the steering wheel. He clutched it over and over. Squeezing and releasing.

Ricky said there'd be moments like this. Confrontations. Ricky said to stay in control.

The van smelled like rotten meat. He'd rented it for cash in a bad neighborhood. No names. Two hundred bucks a day.

He slid over to the passenger seat and looked down the path. No sign of Fran. That bitch. She'd pay for this. He had her by the short hairs, and she knew it. He breathed again. Slid back across the bench seat to the driver's side over stained, torn vinyl fabric. Malt liquor empties and fast-food trash littered the van's floor.

That would cost her. This wasn't over. Not by a long shot. That was uncalled for. She'd pay for that. They'd all pay.

The driver stepped out, leaving the door open and the engine running. He walked around the van and slid open the side panel door closest to the Lexus. It let out a rusty screech and a faint, rancid meat smell.

Five hundred thousand in cash. A duffel bag full of options. Maybe two duffel bags.

He smiled and his mustache loosened, but he didn't care.

James Ritchie studied the nature trail before stepping toward the sedan. He saw nothing. He heard nothing. Took off the tinted aviator sunglasses. No sign of her. He didn't worry about a second phone. She'd play ball for Becky's sake. For Clarkie. For the baby. It was all good. This worked for everybody.

Just like Ricky said.

He stepped to Fran's unlocked trunk, scanning all around him.

Ritchie had done his research. The path went roughly a mile around the lake. No cops for miles and miles. He'd spent all last Saturday right here with his Kindle. Five straight hours. A ranger drove her truck in at 9:30 a.m. and then again at 2, same ranger. He'd left his car and hidden in the woods each of the two times he'd heard a vehicle approaching. Both times it was the ranger, just a girl, who leaned out her window to look at the State Park permit on his car but didn't get out. No other cars all day.

He lifted Fran's popped trunk and two Taser darts pierced his skin, a steel needle in each thigh. He heard the airgun discharge.

With a high yelp and a violent, electrified body spasm, Jim Ritchie fell unconscious to the ground. His face glanced off the bumper. A front tooth broke. His inert left forearm was the last to hit the dirt, rubbery against the rear of the sedan. Twin coils of thin wire disappeared into the trunk.

Pearce Butler rose from prone position in the guise of George. He'd lain flat on a foam pad for an hour. He looked down at the blackmailer, crumpled and silent in the cold dirt and decayed leaves.

Setting aside the Taser unit, for which he had no permit, Butler climbed out of the trunk. He confirmed a pulse in the neck of bearded blackmailer. Then he stood up straight, stretched his arms, and did several deep knee bends to flex the stiffness from his body. He pulled the darts from the blackmailer's thighs, each puncture leaving a dime-sized blood spot on the fabric. The thighs had been the target. Level with Butler's sight line, wide and fleshy, with fabric pulled tight to the skin. The electrified darts easily penetrated.

He put the Taser, darts, and wires into the van. He blew a silver police whistle, shrill and sharp. Loud across the water. Then he dragged the unconscious man to the van and lifted him through the open side door into the dirty, rancid cargo compartment. He pulled off the man's knit cap, wig, false beard, mustache, and glasses. Shreds of dry, yellow spirit gum still clung to the unconscious man's face. The van was still idling. He shut off the engine and took the keys. Then slid the side panel door shut with a dry screech. Fran emerged from the tangles of the walking path.

"Success?' asked Fran.

In the character of George, Butler nodded. "He's out. You should go."

"It's Jim, isn't it?"

Sadly, the Greek nodded once more. Fran looked at the ground. Her lower lip trembled.

"What are we going to do?"

"I'll call you," he said. "I have an idea."

Fran nodded and stepped to her car. She reached for the open trunk lid.

Butler stepped close to her. "You did great," he said. Fran managed a tight smile. "Distracted him perfect," said George. Pronouncing it *perfek*.

"Did you know it was Jim?"

"I guessed."

"What if it had been someone else?"

George Ginapolis smiled, his eyebrows rising, his smile wide beneath the thick, completely deceptive false moustache. "It still would have worked."

Fran nodded and opened her car door.

"Fran." It came out *Frahn*.

She stopped, looked at him. Her face pale. She seemed suddenly quite lost.

"Don't give up," he said. "On him."

Fran said nothing. She looked away, then collected her keys and phone off the hood of her car. When she looked back, he was picking up something small and white from the ground, examining it. He straightened and smiled at her.

"Oh, and Fran," he said. "Make sure the safety's on." Her eyes flared momentarily as she felt the pistol's weight in her pocket and put her hand over it. She'd told no one about the gun.

At that, George laughed. A short, raspy bark of a laugh. Then he gave her a quick wave, got into the van, and drove away. Its shocks creaked as it swayed side to side, disappearing up the sloping, desolate two-track.

Fran watched him go. Such a strange, strange man. She sensed something familiar about him, but couldn't put her finger on it.

She took the Browning automatic from her coat pocket and put the safety back on. She removed the magazine and then ejected the chambered round. The unfired brass cartridge spun to the ground. She picked up the unspent round and put it into her coat pocket. She put the magazine in one pocket and the pistol in another. Then took off the coat and shut it in the trunk.

She shivered in the cold, wrapping her arms around herself for warmth.

For half a minute, Fran looked at the lake and let the quiet outdoor stillness calm her. Not a breath of wind or breeze disturbed the small, glassy lake. No rustling in the mostly bare, spidery branches all around her. Only a few had tiny green buds on their tips. She listened for birds but heard none. Spring not quite here yet. She was suddenly very tired and hungry.

She saw no sign of George or the van or her brother-in-law as she made her way home.

42

"She's beautiful," said Pearce Butler, peering at the phone screen. And she was. A bright-eyed, round-faced baby, cheeks as plump and pink as a cherub, with a pure, joyful smile. A wisp of chestnut hair, her mother's hair, peeked from beneath a pink-and-white headband that had a pink bow on it.

"Thank you, Mr. Butler," said Jim Ritchie, taking back the phone.

"Please, call me Pearce."

They sat by the window at Sinbad's, the venerable boater's saloon and business lunch restaurant on the Detroit River across from Belle Isle. It was a sunny day, the warmest of the year. The wide river had a breezy chop, and glinting sparkles on blue-green waves promised short sleeves before long.

"Excuse me?"

Butler and Ritchie looked up to see a stocky, graying business-man who had approached their table. Brown-suited with a ruddy face, he fidgeted from foot to foot.

"Mr. Butler? I'm Al Barron, and I couldn't help noticing you across the room."

Butler immediately stood, smiled, and extended his hand. "Well, thank you for coming over, Al. It's nice to meet you." They shook hands. Barron beamed. Pearce gestured to Ritchie. "This is my friend, Jim Ritchie." Ritchie abruptly stood, jostling a water glass. Barron and Ritchie shook hands. Butler alone wore no tie, his light brown hair and boyish look relaxed and composed in a navy blazer, gray slacks, and open-collar dress shirt.

"Sir," said Barron to Butler, "I don't mean to intrude but I just...I just saw you, and I...I just wanted to thank you for all you're doing to help business and the local economy and for all you've done to help this town get back on its feet again."

"Thank you very much for saying so," said Butler.

"I saw you on TV last night!" the stocky businessman burst out.

Butler laughed. "Well, I'm glad someone did." Butler had spoken at a press conference on a new proposed rail tunnel to Canada. The deal was coming along. "Al, do you have cards for us?" He turned to Ritchie. "Jim, do you have a business card for Mr. Barron?" The three men exchanged business cards. Al beamed at Pearce Butler's card, holding the crisp, clean rectangle like fine crystal between his thick fingers.

"Wow," he said. "Pearce Butler." Butler's company was Empower.

"And you're with Larson Webb," said Butler, looking from Barron's card to Barron. "Conveyors? Warehouse robotics? In Farmington." Barron was elated. Pearce Butler knew their company.

"That's right!"

Butler shook Barron's hand again. "It's a pleasure to meet you, Al. Please call me, will you? That's my cell on the card. I'd like to learn more about your business."

Pearce flashed the famous smile. The brilliant businessman's trademark smile had been on the cover of *Forbes, Bloomberg Businessweek,* and *TIME* and had appeared twice in the engraved-style, front-page, pointillist portraits famously employed by *The Wall Street Journal.*

"Sure!" said Barron, "Absolutely!" He pumped Butler's hand and also Ritchie's but scarcely took his eyes off Butler. "Thank you, sir. Thank you very much!" And to Ritchie. "Nice to meet you, too."

The burly businessman headed back to his table. As Butler and Ritchie took their seats, a chorus of attaboys rose from Al Barron's table of lunch companions. Butler and Ritchie saw Barron holding Butler's business card aloft like the Stanley Cup. One man stood to give his beefy friend a high five.

"Wow," said Ritchie. "Does that happen a lot?"

"Pretty often. It's a great way to make contacts. And he seems like a good guy." Butler gestured to Ritchie. "But we were talking about your family. How's mom doing?"

Ritchie's head seemed to tighten on his neck. "Hm?" he asked.

"Your wife." Butler pointed at Ritchie's wedding ring. "How's she doing?"

Ritchie managed a smile. "Oh, she's great. She's doing great. She's a great mom. Healthy. Doesn't complain."

"Really?" said Pearce. He took a sip of ice water. Straightened his fork on the folded paper napkin.

"Nope. She's . . . she's good."

"You're lucky." Butler returned his water glass precisely to its wet ring on the table.

Jim nodded vigorously. At Pearce Butler. Two feet away. The most important businessman he'd ever met, or probably ever would meet. "I am lucky," he said.

312 | MARK BEYER

Their food came. Butler thanked the waiter by name. The sun shone on the sparkling river and the American flag snapped colorfully at the marina next door, more than half its boat slips already filled with cruisers, speedboats, and sailboats. A few pleasure boats were moving on the river, but most wouldn't show for a couple more weeks.

As Butler's guest, Jim had ordered modestly: a burger, fries, and coleslaw. Butler chose broiled perch, a side salad, and iced tea. They were meeting to discuss opportunities that Butler had articulated as the keynote speaker at a recent business event. Ritchie had attended the event and had gotten his nerve up to approach Mr. Butler at the wine-and-cheese networking session after the presentation. But he scarcely had to approach him at all. In the throng of conversing business people, the legendary Pearce Butler essentially bumped into Jim Ritchie by accident. They'd shaken hands, introduced themselves, and exchanged business cards.

Ritchie practically peed his pants when Butler called to invite him to lunch. He couldn't believe his luck.

"So, tell me more about Histonix," said Butler. Ritchie beamed at the mention of Histonix, the company he'd pitched at the business event over cheap wine and cheese, and his new employer. Butler saw a faint horizontal seam in Ritchie's left front tooth. An effective cosmetic repair.

Ritchie launched into his elevator speech. "Histonix is, no lie, ready for takeoff," said Ritchie, who'd been there a month.

It was, he continued, a tissue sample archive serving a global health services market. Histonix acquired, labeled, and cryogenically stored diseased human cell samples preserved on microscopy slides. The cell samples can be shipped virtually anywhere in the world overnight packed in dry ice, to be studied by researchers, teaching physicians, or clinical physicians. Then, like library books, the samples are returned intact to Histonix, packed in dry ice and shipped overnight.

"It's taking off, Pearce. It's gonna. Seriously. It's second stage."

"How many employees?"

"About twenty." *More like ten.* "But we're, uh, expanding. Looking to expand."

Butler nodded and ate. He squeezed lemon juice from a yellow wedge onto a piece of perch. Speared it and ate it.

"That's great," said Butler. "This is through Wayne State?"

Ritchie nodded. "Yes. They're a partner." WSU was downtown Detroit's powerhouse university, with the largest School of Medicine in the country.

"Jim," said Butler thoughtfully, setting down his fork, "I don't want to make a mistake."

Ritchie shook his head in *No, sir* total agreement.

Butler leaned in. "I'm actually here today because of you. Not because of Histonix."

"Thank you, Pearce," said Ritchie sincerely.

"I want you to succeed," said Butler quietly. "I want you to succeed for yourself. And I want you to succeed for me."

"And I want to," agreed Ritchie. "I want to succeed for you."

"Have you made mistakes, Jim?"

Ritchie's mouth hung open before he shut it. "Uh. Well, some," he said. "Sure."

"I've made mistakes, too, Jim. Some big ones."

Ritchie nodded. This was getting good. Getting personal.

"I don't want to make one now," said Butler.

"Me, neither." Nervously, Ritchie took a bite from his hamburger and a sip from his Coke.

"Tell me one of your mistakes, Jim," said Butler. "Tell me your biggest mistake."

Ritchie stopped chewing. He swallowed. "What do you mean?" A sesame seed clung to his upper lip. It fell of its own accord.

"Just what I said," said Butler. "Tell me your biggest mistake. We learn from our mistakes. I want to know what you've learned."

Ritchie nodded earnestly. "Okay," he said, after a moment. "Fair question." He dutifully frowned, doing his best to appear thoughtful and reflective.

"I guess my biggest mistake," said Ritchie, "was quitting my first job. 'Cause that company went platinum." He grinned at Butler. "So, dumb me, I left before it took off. To join a startup that—" He gave a thumbs down. "—didn't go anywhere. Nada. Belly up."

Butler nodded.

"That was your biggest mistake?" Butler asked. Leaning back, he steepled his fingers.

"Well." Ritchie shifted in his seat. "I mean. When I was young, I did a lot of stupid things."

"When you were young?"

"Well, sure. Didn't you?" Ritchie caught himself. "I mean, respectfully. Didn't you?"

"Yes, I did." Butler didn't blink as he spoke. "What about when you weren't so young?"

Their waiter appeared. "Can I get you anything else, Mr. Butler?" He smiled at both men. Butler smiled back.

"I'm fine, Pete, thank you," said Butler. "Anything for you, Jim?" Again, the famous smile.

"I'm good," Jim managed, neither smiling nor meeting the waiter's eye.

The waiter departed. Butler looked at Ritchie and waited.

"We were talking about mistakes," said Butler.

Ritchie smiled weakly and shrugged. "I really can't think of anything. Nothing major."

Pearce Butler leaned close and spoke in a low voice.

"Jim. You drugged your wife. You posed her in sex acts with prostitutes. You took pornographic photos of your *wife*. Of Becky. The mother of your children. Then you used the photos to blackmail her family for money." Butler leaned back without releasing Ritchie's ever-widening eyes. "That was a mistake."

Ritchie paled with each successive word. Blood vanished from his cheeks. His fingertips went cold. He couldn't move. The ice in his drink glass shifted audibly.

The restaurant had gotten busy. Butler continued in low voice.

"You remember the lake? Fran's car? The five hundred thousand?" Butler casually stabbed, chewed, and swallowed another piece of perch. "I'm sure you remember that. Then, I imagine you remember waking up. In your own bed. At home. In clean clothes. The spirit gum off your face. With a terrible headache."

Butler indicated his own front tooth with a fork tine. "I imagine you were surprised to see half your front tooth in a pill bottle next to your bed." He ate a bite of salad. "They did a good job, by the way."

Ritchie sat frozen, motionless in his chair. No deer ever saw brighter headlights.

Butler continued, again leaning close. "The only reason you're not in prison is because your wife, a devout Christian woman, has forgiven you. Becky has forgiven you. She knows exactly what you've done, and she's forgiven you." Butler ate a bite of salad, reflecting. "I don't think I could do that. After what you've done. What about you?" he asked Ritchie. "If someone did that to you, Jim, could you forgive them? If they drugged you? Then raped you? Then blackmailed you? Could you forgive that?"

Ritchie didn't speak, didn't move. Didn't appear to breathe.

"She took you back," continued Butler. He dabbed his mouth with a napkin. "She took you back to be the good husband and the good father that she believes you can be. The husband she deserves. The father your children need you to be." Butler narrowed his eyes. "Are you with me, Jim? Stay with me."

"Yes," said Ritchie, lips barely moving. He could no longer sense his body. He was in free fall. He glanced down.

"Don't look away, Jim. Stay with me," instructed Butler. "Becky forgave you." Butler speared a cherry tomato from the small salad. "You want to believe in miracles, Jim? Start there." He ate the bite-sized tomato. "The rest of the family? Well. They'd like to see you at the bottom of a deep, deep hole. And then they'd like to fill it in."

Ritchie nodded murkily, as if underwater, while the famous man, his host, chewed and swallowed and had a sip of iced tea. The glass replaced just so on the moist circle on the table. "I want to forgive you, too, Jim. But it's not easy for me. To forgive your trespasses."

"How do you know this?" asked Ritchie. It never went public. And this was Pearce Butler. A total stranger.

Butler reached into the side pocket of his navy blazer and withdrew a closed fist.

"I know a lot," he said.

He set a light blue plastic thumb drive next to Ritchie's plate.

Ritchie wrinkled his nose. "What's that?"

"Photos," said Butler, smiling. "Like the color?"

Ritchie looked at the baby blue thumb drive. Then at Butler. Butler was smiling. Not the famous smile. A different one.

Truth began to gnaw at the edges.

"After the Taser at the lake," said Butler, glancing at his watch. "You were fed roofies. You know what roofies are, don't you?"

Ritchie swallowed.

"Don't you?" Butler repeated.

"Yeah," said Ritchie, scarcely audible.

"Then you were taken to a warehouse and photographed with prostitutes. Many photos. With many partners. Doing many things. Maybe some of the same men and women you used. Video, too. Quite a bit of it." Butler raised an eyebrow. "You don't remember?"

Ritchie shook his head. More of a frightened quiver.

"We had to hose you down afterward. And brush your teeth. Have your ever tried to brush somebody else's teeth?"

Ritchie nearly spilled his Coke groping for it. Some dribbled down his shirt as he drank with shaking hands. He tried inadequately to clean himself with a napkin. Butler kept his eyes on Ritchie until the younger man settled down.

Ritchie stared at the baby blue thumb drive by his plate.

"It's eight gigs," said Butler.

Ritchie looked up at Butler, horrified. His host's face cold and expressionless.

"The river's right there," said Butler, pointing out the window at the sun-dappled waves where, a quarter mile out, a small, red sailboat dipped and rose on the crisp breeze. "If I were you, I'd take that—" He nodded at the thumb drive. "—and throw it as far as I could."

Butler steepled his fingers and leaned back, eyeing the shaking, sweating, speechless younger man. Then glanced at his watch.

"Time to go," said Butler.

"Are there copies?" asked Ritchie.

"Time to go," repeated Butler. He stood and left fifty dollars on the table. He waited until Ritchie stood. Then waited until Ritchie picked up the blue thumb drive.

Outside in the sunshine, a stretch limo was waiting by the door to Sinbad's.

Butler walked to it. He waited by it. It was not the car he'd arrived in.

"What's this?" said Ritchie.

Butler opened the rear door, and Fran Siehling stepped out, dark-haired and dark-eyed. She stepped away from the vehicle and stood without uttering a word. Behind her came Millie DeGraaf, grim-faced. Both women glared at Jim Ritchie. They were followed by a third woman Butler had never met. He stepped to her and offered his hand.

"Hello, I'm Pearce Butler." He smiled. "It's nice to meet you." She managed a small smile back and accepted his hand.

"I'm Amber," she said. "Amber DeGraaf." The three women stood together outside the limo, the breeze fluttering their hair. All glared at Jim Ritchie.

One more woman stepped from the car.

"Hello, Jim," said Becky. She looked thin and pale. She extended an arm to her sisters and mother and got hugs and handholds in return.

After he blacked out at Graham Lake, the next thing Ritchie remembered was waking up in the guestroom of his own house.

Becky knew everything. They'd subsequently met with her pastor. They were in counseling. Forgiveness was a process. A bridge built slowly of small, fragile pieces. He still slept in the guestroom. Becky and the baby shared the master. It had been six weeks.

Tears were streaming down Ritchie's face. Quietly sobbing, he wiped his nose with the back of his hand. Butler gave him a clean handkerchief.

"Give me your car keys," said Butler.

"What?" sniffled Ritchie.

"Your car will be delivered to your house. You're going to ride with your family. Give me your keys."

Awkwardly, his actions wooden, Ritchie placed his keys in Butler's outstretched hand. Butler walked to Fran and the other women.

"Ladies," Butler said, "thank you."

"Can I say something?" said Millie. Butler responded with a brief and courteous bow. Millie left her daughters and walked up and into Jim Ritchie's face.

"This isn't over, you little shit," she said, her hard eyes burning into his.

Ritchie looked down, shoulders quaking. He wiped his eyes and nose with the handkerchief.

"And be a man for once." She shoved his chest hard with her wrinkled hand. "Before you forget how." She rejoined her three daughters.

Butler took Ritchie by the arm and walked him to the limo. Becky got in first, followed by her mother and her sisters. Butler paused with Ritchie by the open door.

"Jim," said Butler. "In the warehouse during the photo and video session... you talked. While you were drugged." Butler spoke mat-ter-of-factly. "You asked for someone." He held Ritchie's shattered stare. "Who's Ricky?" asked Butler.

Ritchie, red-eyed, snot shiny under his nose, stared at Butler. "My friend," he finally said.

"No," said Butler. "He's not. Where can I find him?"

Richie shook his head. "You can't," he said, weakly. "I can't."

"No phone number? No last name?"

Ritchie shook his head.

"How did you pay him?"

"I didn't. He wouldn't take any money."

Butler reset.

Calculations whirred inside.

"Has he been in touch with you since the lake?"

"No."

Then he looked at Ritchie's clenched fist. "Do you want me to throw that in the river?" He held out his hand. "Believe me, you don't want to see what's on it."

Ritchie gave him the baby blue thumb drive.

"No copies?" he asked.

Butler smiled darkly. "That's up to you," he said.

Ritchie got into the back of the limo with his wife, Fran, Millie, and Amber. Butler shut the door and walked to the front of the limo as the driver's door opened and the driver stepped out, with some difficulty. A big man.

"Thank you for taking time off to do this," said Butler.

"Thank you for asking," said Terry Holbrook. "And it's nice to meet you, sir." They shook hands. Terry indicated the limo. "I appreciate you thinking of me for this."

"George and Henry thought it was only right," said Butler.

"Does George work for you?"

Butler shook his head. "No. He works..." Butler glanced up at the warm, pleasing sun, then back to Terry. "He works here and there."

Terry nodded and lowered himself carefully back into the driver's seat, still feeling the ache in his ribs.

"Drive wherever you want. Take your time. The more you drive, the more they'll talk," said Butler.

"Okay," said Terry.

The limo pulled away.

Pearce Butler walked alone in no hurry to the marina next door. He walked the length of the longest dock, to the very end. Beyond the tips of his shoes, the Detroit River lapped and churned in merry fury. He inhaled the fresh, clean air and closed his eyes, tipping his head toward a bright, warming sun in a cloudless sky. The lively breeze rippled his clothes.

He looked from the wide, sparkling river to the small thumb drive in his hand. There was nothing to throw away. It was empty. There hadn't been a photo shoot. The only images were the ones he'd put in Ritchie's head.

43

"Thank you, Mary." Abe Cohen smiled at the bonnie young barmaid as she set twin beers down on the bar in front of them, glistening and frosty in their tall, Pilsner glasses. They'd chosen Conor O'Neill's Irish pub on Main Street in downtown Ann Arbor.

"Thanks for coming," said Abe, raising his glass.

"Thanks for the referral," said Henry, raising his own and clicking it lightly against his friend's. Both sipped. Both wore suits. Neither had overcoats. Theirs were the only neckties in the place. It was 4:30 on Thursday. They hadn't seen each other since before the events at Graham Lake.

"How are Melanie and the kids?" asked Cohen.

"Doing great, thanks," said Henry. "How are Ruth and the girls?"

"All well. Thank you."

"Say 'Hi' to them for me."

"I will," said Abe. "And me, too. To yours." Henry nodded. Both men sipped again.

"So, you do okay?" asked Abe, casual and comfortable in the way of old friends.

"Very okay," said Henry. "No problems. It helps when they have a checkbook."

Cohen nodded. "Indeed, it does." It was good beer. A summer brew crafted in Petoskey, Michigan. Crisp and bright with a smile of citrus. "You think you're going to see Terry Holbrook again?"

"About the DeGraafs?" said Henry. "I doubt it. Maybe about something else, if he needs something. But not about this."

Cohen raised his glass again. "To Terry. To the man who kept his promise."

"To Terry," said Henry. *Who got shot and survived by God's grace and Kevlar.* They clinked glasses and drank. "I really do appreciate the referral. Thank you."

Cohen waved it off. "You were the right man for the job. I wasn't doing you any favors."

"Thanks."

Cohen directed a level gaze at Henry. "And I thought about, you know—your friend." George Ginapolis.

"Yes," said Henry. Cohen had met "George" once. Through Henry. It involved a bizarre kidnapping that ended well and stayed out of the news. At several business gatherings, Cohen had also met and spoken with Pearce Butler. He never imagined they were the same man.

Henry, however, knew the truth. He'd met Butler one night in a house fire. Years ago, in the midst of a hellish inferno, they'd managed to improvise a daring, multiple rescue and avert a horrific tragedy. A bond formed that night. Together, they'd averted other tragedies since.

"He's interesting," said Cohen, sipping beer.

"Yes," said Henry. "He is."

Cohen turned meaningfully to his friend. "Are you ever going to tell me?" he asked. He knew there was more to the story.

"No," said Henry, shaking his head. "I'm sorry. I can't." Cohen nodded.

"He seems very capable."

"Yes," said Henry and changed the subject. "You want to order something?" He pulled an appetizer menu from a metal stand on the bar and looked at it closely.

"Not for me. But if you want something, go ahead, my treat."

Henry shook his head and set the menu down. Abe sipped his beer. Henry sipped his. Then he said to Cohen, "Terry's going to give most of the money back."

"I know," said the Ann Arbor attorney, and thought about Terry. The big man who didn't take his coat off. Who kept Mike DeGraaf from dying alone.

"He's a good guy," said Cohen. He thought about Terry's wife, too, and their little girl. He'd done his homework. "Nice family."

"Christina," said Henry. "And Hannah."

"Yes. Christina and Hannah."

"All they want is enough for their daughter's college and a kitchen makeover. And he got a new car."

Cohen smiled. "What did he get?"

"A Volt."

Cohen laughed. "Not a Tesla?" Henry shook his head, smiling.

"No. A Volt. He loves it. Took me for a drive in it. It's nice."

"Good for him," said Cohen. "Help stop global warming." He smiled at his beer. "Mike would like that." The Holbrooks wouldn't have to worry about money. Millie had spoken to Cohen about that.

When he looked up, Henry's deep brown eyes were on him.

"I'm glad Mike met Terry," said Abe.

"Me, too," said Henry. He wanted to ask Cohen more questions about the DeGraaf daughters. About Michael DeGraaf's last request. But he didn't ask. It was none of his business.

Theirs was a profession of maintaining confidences.

After a few silent seconds, Henry asked, "How's the husband?" Jim Ritchie.

Cohen's shoulders dropped slightly as he looked at his glass. Then looked at Henry. Then back to his glass.

"He seems okay," said Cohen. "He's the luckiest guy in the world, if you ask me."

"His wife loves him." Henry knew she had taken him back.

"Yes." Cohen sipped his beer. "She loves him."

Both men tried to imagine a love that strong.

A love that brave.

"Let's hope it's contagious," said Henry Wallace.

"Yes," said Cohen. "Let's hope that it is."

They raised their glasses together and thoughtfully sipped good Michigan beer on a sunny afternoon in the growing chatter of the steadily filling pub.

44

The ultramodern house on the wide, deep, heavily wooded lot had no windows that could be seen from the street, and the dense trees within the walled grounds effectively shielded both sides as well as the back of the building. The small camera drone Butler had piloted over the residence weeks ago had mysteriously lost power moments after video transmission had begun and had plummeted irretrievably inside the property.

Now Butler studied the house with night-vision binoculars from a cluster of evergreens on the front lawn of the nearest neighboring house a hundred yards down the street. The broad lawn on which he trespassed belonged to a wealthy, retired couple presently in Naples, Florida. They weren't scheduled to return to Michigan for another two weeks. Butler didn't know them but had, with a few keystrokes, accessed their travel itinerary.

Coming out of unconsciousness after the Taser at the lake, Jim Ritchie had pleaded for Ricky over and over. He'd cried out to Ricky. He'd begged Ricky for help.

Ricky who orchestrated insidious blackmail. Ricky who

accepted no money. Ricky with no last name. And Ricky who had abandoned Jim Ritchie.

Jim Ritchie couldn't find Ricky.

But Ritchie wasn't Pearce Butler.

It had taken many weeks of digging. Probing. Hacking. Bribing. To lead Butler to this street on this night.

Well-hidden, Butler had observed the house for hours on end over several nights but had yet to see any signs of life. Lights went on and off on a precise schedule, with timers. He knew the expensive home was owned outright with no mortgage. By someone named or who called himself Richard Lucien.

The rumors were difficult to sift through. Drugs. Prostitution. Petty crime. But also politics. An international presence. Weapons. Terrorism. Human trafficking.

Thermal imaging provided nothing. The cement walls of the odd, flat-roofed, virtually windowless home were either too thick to penetrate or shielded in some way that blocked Butler's many attempts to electronically peer within.

Butler was able to put together a physical description of Ricky from conversations with Ritchie. He was apparently quite young. And yet, other intel Butler had procured indicated that Richard Lucien was born in either 1954 or 1966.

He'd managed to locate one unconfirmed photo. It showed a smiling, handsome, angular-jawed man at a crowded outdoor rally. Baring oversized teeth at the camera. His crinkly dark hair was cut short, pelt-like, and he wore a *Make America Great Again* T-shirt, standing amidst a cheering throng. The dark eyes, queerly wideset, seemed to stare directly at Butler. The disproportionate, long-toothed smile was strangely alluring. Neither of the alleged birthdates for Richard Lucien fit the man in the recent photo. The man in the photo was clearly much younger.

There were no lights visible on the property presently, inside the brick wall or out. Butler watched. No moon showed in the midnight sky.

The gate protecting the low, black residence began to slowly grind open.

Butler had purchased a tip. Tonight, he'd been told, Lucien was on the move. Where to, Butler's source didn't know.

Butler set down the binoculars. He crouched three inches lower in the thatch of spruce branches. And held his breath.

A black SUV, its lights out, rolled out from the darkened driveway. The gate behind it began to close. The SUV turned left. Butler was prepared for either direction.

Eighty feet from the driveway entrance, the SUV approached a scrap of scuffed plywood that lay flat in the street, no bigger than a Kindle. As the SUV rolled over it, Butler pressed a button on a remote. A compression spring built into the hollow wood scrap lofted a padded pouch upward. The small, black felt pouch contained a neodymium magnet and was calibrated to reach a height of ten inches. As the vehicle passed over, the powerful airborne magnet did the rest, soundlessly adhering to the chassis of the moving vehicle.

Six seconds later, Butler watched the SUV's headlights flick on as it paused at a stop sign, preparing to exit the silent, wealthy neighborhood. It then turned left toward the main road.

Butler checked the tracking signal on his phone. It blinked as it moved, heading east on a digital street map. If undiscovered, the beacon would operate for thirty hours.

As if a switch had been thrown in his soul, Butler felt the unmistakable energy flow into him. He retrieved his equipment from the street and sprinted to his car, a black Chrysler, feeling the energy surge into his fingertips, shoot into his toes.

There were no cosmetic dents or rust on tonight's vehicle, but it was juiced even more than the Neon.

He slipped inside, shut the door, and glanced at the pulsing red beacon on his phone.

He thought of Pree. He said a prayer.

He turned the key and drove.

Marching as to war.

ACKNOWLEDGEMENTS

It's with humility and love that I thank the dozens of people who actively supported the creation of this book. Some inspirations go as far back as my 4th grade teacher, Mrs. Gibson, who supported early literary efforts. Thank you to my friends Jim Croce, fellow-writer Paul Skalny, Mike Sullivan, Don Hart, James Pinard, Terry Oprea, Jim Gorman, Jack Frakes, Chris Lozen, Craig Van Sickle, Steve Mitchell, Bill Evashwick, Nat Bernstein, Bart Cleary, Chris Rizik, Robert Buckler, Terry Brennan, Jeff Carter, Todd Skipski, Danielle Saigeon, Melissa McCrosky, Randy Stephenson, Mort and Brigitte Harris, Janet and John Mooney, Janita Gaulzetti, Catharine Hansford, Rob Hendrickson, Mike and Mary DiStefano, and David Peterson. My inspirations include Daphne DuMaurier, Elmore Leonard, Jonathan Kellerman, Steve Hamilton, Stephen King, Clive Cussler, and H. P. Lovecraft, among many, many other great authors. Thank you to all of my Organic, Inc. friends, particularly Freddy Orlando, Daniel Smith, Paul Piziks, Dwayne Raupp, Lori Bender, Matt Tait, Stephen Timblin, Lori Jo Vest, Alex Altman, Deleano Acevedo and Nate Rogers. Special thanks to my brilliant teacher and lifelong friend, Neal Gabler. Thanks also to

Craig and Kathy Nash and all my Kensington Church friends, and Pastors Joe Casiglia, Paul Arndt, and Clint Dupin. Thank you to my parents, my Great Aunt Evelyn, my steadfast brothers Jim and Dan and to my extended family. Thank you to the great team at Thomson-Shore in Dexter, Michigan who guided this story to completion and through production. And, of course, thank you to my beautiful and wise wife Linda and our two relentlessly wonderful sons, Sean and Michael. No husband or father has ever been shown more support and love. Lastly, and mostly, thank you, God. This book is for You.

Did you enjoy *Hired Man*? If so, I would be very grateful if you left a positive review on Amazon or Goodreads or both.

Thank you, and happy reading!

—Mark Beyer

Mark is always thrilled to hear from readers.
Contact him at beyerbooks.com or at 248.330.4196.